WAITING FOR
THE REVOLUTION

WAITING FOR
THE REVOLUTION

Sally Clark

Cormorant Books

Canada Council   Conseil des Arts
for the Arts   du Canada

ONTARIO ARTS COUNCIL
CONSEIL DES ARTS DE L'ONTARIO

The publisher gratefully acknowledges the support of the
Canada Council for the Arts and the Ontario Arts Council
for its publishing program. We acknowledge the financial support
of the Government of Canada through the Book Publishing
Industry Development Program (BPIDP) for our publishing activities.

Printed and bound in Canada

NATIONAL AND ARCHIVES CANADA CATALOGUING IN PUBLICATION

Clark, Sally, 1953–
Waiting for the revolution / Sally Clark.

ISBN 978-1-897151-41-9

I. Title.

PS8555.L37197W33 2010   C813'.54   C2009-907171-1

Editor: Marc Côté
Cover photograph and design: Angel Guerra/Archetype
Interior text design: Tannice Goddard, Soul Oasis Networking
Printer: Friesens

This book is printed on 100% post-consumer waste recycled paper.

Mixed Sources
Cert no. SW-COC-001271
© 1996 FSC
FSC

CORMORANT BOOKS INC.
215 SPADINA AVENUE, STUDIO 230, TORONTO, ONTARIO, CANADA M5T 2C7
www.cormorantbooks.com

To Mo

chapter one

GIRL'S OWN ANNUAL
1974

AT THAT TIME, there was much talk of the Revolution amongst Jay's peers. The Revolution would arrive and you were either a part of it and would be embraced or you were not part of it and would be gunned down. Jay had a morbid fear that the Call to Revolution would occur when she was having dinner with her godfather in one of the expensive steakhouses that he frequented. One minute the waiter would be gaily tossing the Caesar salad; the next minute they would all be lined up against the wall for execution. Jay would try and explain that her godfather had taken her to this restaurant, but that would imply that he should be lined up and shot first and that wasn't altogether fair — though he *was* a capitalist. He drove a big huge car that he referred to as his "bucket of bolts." He said "positive" and "negative" instead of "yes" and "no." He said "zero seven hundred hours" instead of "seven o'clock." He lived in a penthouse apartment and made investments. He was very happy to be a capitalist. Jay was not. She was a Revolutionary-in-Training. She wondered if the handsome young man with the cold eyes and the machine gun would realize that she was on his side. She thought not. Revolutions seemed to bring out the worst in people.

Jay had an unrequited passion for Nicholas Woodbridge that was festering quite nicely until Nicholas became a Revolutionary. He had been a shy, diffident young man, brilliant and prone to bouts of melancholy. Jay tried to manipulate Nicholas into becoming her boyfriend, but he never obliged. They remained, elusively, friends.

When Nicholas moved to Toronto to attend university, Jay followed him. She convinced herself that it was a pleasant coincidence that the university he chose was ideally suited to her needs as well. Victoria was a cultural backwater. Jay needed to go to Toronto where the real artists lived. Jay actually believed that the real artists lived in New York.

Nicholas left a few weeks before Jay. He had not arranged to keep in touch — an unpleasant fact Jay might have taken to heart, but instead ignored. Jay was convinced that being away from the comforts of home would invoke a need for human company in Nicholas. He would finally be primed for love and she, Jay, would be nicely in his line of vision.

When Jay first arrived on campus, she searched for Nicholas, but didn't see any sign of him. Having travelled across Canada to be near her object of desire and finding herself within one hundred yards of it, Jay was suddenly stricken by a shy pride that prevented her from pursuing Nicholas any further. She became absorbed in her life in the student residency, her classes, the ebb and flow of new people, and a month or so later, it was Nicholas who discovered Jay.

In that short time, Nicholas had undergone a complete metamorphosis. He had become a Revolutionary. The passion that Jay felt should have been hers by right, Nicholas now funnelled into an unholy devotion for a Cuban revolutionary named Che Guevara. Nicholas dressed in military fatigue wear, sported a black beret and grew a beard and moustache, presumably to look like his hero, but succeeding only in looking more like Fidel Castro than Che.

Nicholas frequently began sentences with the phrase, "When the Revolution comes...." Jay's biggest frustration was that she was never given a clear answer on what the Revolution was. It was vaguely tied in with Movements. Movements were different from Revolutions in that a movement was heading towards Revolution but was not as drastic as a Revolution, though the net result could be far worse. Jay found it all quite confusing because she thought the Revolution had come.

In Russia. In 1917. And what a mistake that was. Nicholas disagreed — it wasn't a mistake. He told Jay that her history professor was a pawn of the Establishment and that the history books were lies written by power mongers.

"But what about Stalin's purges? That's history," Jay protested.

"An exaggerated version of history."

"He killed people who disagreed with him. I don't think you can make up things like that."

"Sure you can. Print it up in textbooks. Make children read them as part of their school curriculum and it becomes fact. Where do you think you got your knowledge of Stalin?"

"So you think Stalin was good?!"

"Good, bad, it's so definitive. I don't think he was as bad as the West makes him out to be. Anyway, it's not like that in Russia now."

"How do you know? The people who've defected didn't seem to like it."

"Bunch of sissy-assed athletes and ballerinas. They're always going to complain. Anyway, the Revolution wasn't supposed to happen in Russia. Wrong environment. It's supposed to happen in a highly evolved capitalistic society. The real Revolution still has to happen. Here!" Nicholas's eyes gleamed with a supple ardour.

Jay sighed, then registered what he said. "Here?! In Canada?!"

"Or the States."

"Definitely not here."

"Why not?"

"Nothing happens in Canada."

"Lots of things happen here. We just don't hear about them. It's all capitalist propaganda. A massive brainwashing campaign to turn everyone into mindless consumers. Like the nuclear family!"

"What about it?" asked Jay, fearing she would get a lengthy reply, yet wanting to know his views on the subject. Jay still entertained the hope that Nicholas would fall in love with her and the two of them would get married.

"This bullshit about a man and a woman needing their own separate little house away from other people. People never lived like that before."

"They didn't?!"

"No — they lived communally."

"Like in hippie communes?" Nicholas had somehow made the jump from no sex to communal sex. Monogamous sex, i.e., romantic love, had been sadly bypassed.

"Well, not entirely. It wasn't uncommon, say in England in the nineteenth century, to live with your grandmother, aunts, great aunts, uncles. Many people sharing one home. Much better for a person psychologically."

"Why?"

"Well, say your parents are assholes ..."

Are your parents assholes? Jay desperately wanted to ask. Nicholas didn't talk about his home life.

"Then you're stuck with them. You've got to spend the next twenty years in one house with these morons. They control your life. Or maybe they're okay — maybe you're the asshole; then, they're stuck with you. Whereas in an extended family, if your parents are driving you crazy, you can go talk to your uncle or your aunt. You have options."

"I guess that depends on how you feel about your aunt," Jay said.

"No point going into specifics."

"But what if your aunt or uncle is a horrible person and you're stuck with them?"

"You would accept the situation. The way kids accept their parents."

"But most kids I know hate their parents."

"Look, the point is, as a society, we once lived communally. The capitalist regime is dividing us up into smaller units so we'll buy more. They don't care about the nuclear family. They'd be quite happy if the couple split up and everyone lived on their own because then we'd all have to buy more stuff. Look at apartment buildings — all those people living in their little boxes, all needing their living room couch, their TV, their bedroom set. You break down the social structure so people can't rely on each other anymore. People will forget how to co-operate. The social mechanisms will no longer be in place. Take our generation. The baby boomers. Well, we are one huge target for these mindfuckers ..."

Somehow, salty language was a necessary part of a revolutionary's vocabulary. Before Nicholas underwent his metamorphosis, he was very polite and soft-spoken. When Nicholas went off on one of his tirades, Jay was not even certain that he was aware of who he was talking to. He spoke to her as though she were some young, ignorant neophyte. Their conversations followed the form of a Socratic dialogue, with Jay doing Plato's lines: "Yes, Socrates. That's very true, Socrates. What do you think, Socrates?"

"... We're all encouraged to be independent. That's part of the plot. 'Cause if we all co-operated together, we could defeat the military-industrial complex. But we won't. We'll all grab what we can. And when we're old, we'll be up shit creek, 'cause there won't be any system in place to look after us. We'll have to buy our way out of our problems. And if you don't have money, honey, you're sunk. 'Cause that's what capitalism is all about: money."

Jay always felt very guilty when revolutionaries talked about the evils of money. She came from a wealthy family. She liked to think of herself as upper middle class but she knew that, compared to a poor person, she was rich. Nicholas's parents were also rich, but

Nicholas was able to throw off the shackles of his moneyed past with more conviction.

Jay didn't join Nicholas's cell because it seemed patently obvious to her that she couldn't be a revolutionary. She wore the wrong clothes. All the revolutionary women wore either blue jeans or baggy, dirty-green military fatigue gear. Jay didn't look good in jeans, which seemed to be designed for women with big waists. The ideal figure at that time was a big waist, narrow hips and large, but not drooping, breasts. Height was another beauty asset. Jay was short. She had small breasts that appeared even smaller in the imperative tight T-shirt. Her narrow waist made her hips seem larger, giving her an old-fashioned hour-glass figure, except the hours on top were smaller than the hours below.

Seeing female revolutionaries with their long, lanky bodies, clad in jeans and tight-fitting tops, Jay felt a pang of envy. Didn't they feel silly, all of them dressed alike? Apparently not. The women all wore heavy boots. The men wore sneakers. Jay supposed that the differing footwear was somehow related to their social duties. The women were expected to stay and man the camp, have babies — basically, do things that required heavy, pragmatic shoes — whereas the men were free to ramble, roam, run as fast as the wind would carry them.

Jay wished she could throw herself into the revolutionary game: be Natural, not bathe for weeks at a time, wear her hair in long dirty strands, parted in the middle, plastered on either side of her face. Jay knew what she had to do to fit in, but it was as though she had a little old woman in her brain, saying "You're not going to be this age forever. This is the only time in your life that you'll be attractive. Make the most of it. Wear pretty clothes while you can." Jay always had this sense of her body as some foreign article that was on loan to her so she mustn't mess it up because, sooner or later, the original owner was going to want it back.

Nicholas sighed with satisfaction, as he always did after a long rant. He smiled at Jay. Nicholas's smile was a shaft of light after a thunderstorm: brilliant, warm and full of promise. "Guess you'll be heading back to Victoria when the term's out."

Jay had told Nicholas several times what her plans were but he never remembered. "No. I'm staying here for the summer. I'm going to art school."

"Oh, right. Art school. You know, I never think of you as an artist."

"You don't?"

"No. You're, ah, too ...." Nicholas lingered to find the word. Jay was about to suggest *intelligent*.

"Tidy."

"Tidy?!"

"Yes. I always think of artists as crazy and messy. Well, you know — inspired."

"And I don't strike you as inspired?"

"Um, I guess you're looking for a place to stay," said Nicholas, quickly changing the subject. "There might still be a room at Mamma Sunshine's. I'll ask for you."

Jay did not want to live in Mamma Sunshine's house. Mamma Sunshine was a large, belligerent woman in charge of a commune in the student annex. Most of these homes had a big fat woman running things. Hippie communes favoured matriarchal rule. Nicholas was always urging Jay to move into a commune, though never the ones where he was staying. Jay had once feigned interest which, unfortunately, led straight to an interview with Mamma Sunshine.

To Jay's surprise, Mamma Sunshine's commune was very clean and well-organized. Jay was reconsidering her views on communes when Mamma Sunshine informed Jay that Saturday would be her day. Jay thought that sounded rather nice till she discovered it meant that she was responsible for cooking all the meals every Saturday. She tried to politely extricate herself from the interview but Mamma Sunshine insisted that she stay for lunch and "get a feel for the place."

Lunch was a revolting affair: vile-tasting, hard, black and orange lumps imbedded in a sandy, grey bean mash — looking and tasting like cigarettes in an ashtray. Jay pretended to eat the mash by shifting it from side to side on her plate.

A thin, scrawny man, accompanied by a young girl, scurried past the dining room in a futile attempt to escape upstairs, unnoticed. Mamma Sunshine stopped him cold.

"You're late!" she barked.

"Sorry, Sunny, but I, ah, had to —"

"If you're not coming for lunch, I need to know."

"Yeah, well, things came up." He looked nervously at the girl.

"Will you be home for dinner?"

"Ah." Whatever romance that had been blossoming between the couple rapidly wilted under Mamma Sunshine's intrusive glare.

"Is she staying for dinner?" asked Mamma Sunshine, driving the point home.

"Um ..."

If the food wasn't bad enough, that little interchange put Jay completely off. Living with her own mother in Victoria would be a piece of cake compared to the surrogate scrutiny of Mamma Sunshine. Jay wondered how Nicholas, who claimed to be such a free spirit, could tolerate such conditions.

"Thanks anyway, Nicholas, but I think I've found a place."

"Not the student residence!"

"No, it's full. Somewhere else."

"A rooming house?" Nicholas asked excitedly.

Jay was ashamed to tell Nicholas that she was thinking of renting a room in a sorority house.

At that time, sororities were extremely unfashionable. Smart young women of the time did not want to ally themselves with a fascist, cliquish, retrograde organization such as a sorority house. Sorority houses were considered sexist as well, because they only housed women. *Unisex* was the catchword of the times. What sort of woman would not relish sharing her morning ablutions with a lot of strange men in a unisex toilet? The "new" woman embraced this liberated vision, shedding those antiquated notions of separate sex, separate species. Men and women were the same. They should dress the same. They should be the same. As a true test of mettle, many women learned how to pee standing up.

Jay's aunt had been a member of the Kappa Alpha Theta (KAT) sorority. She insisted that Jay apply for a room there. Jay paid a grudging visit to the house. It was fitting that the Kappa Alpha Theta sorority was in a beautiful old Victorian house; built to last, despite the ravages of modern thought. Like attracts like. Girls who weren't sure about the merits of joining a sorority fell in love with the house. It had a serene, gentle energy. Jay fell under its spell.

The sorority sister who showed Jay the room seemed very nice, not at all 'snobby,' as the current wisdom would dictate. The room was lovely: pretty and spacious. A green Tiffany lamp hung from the ceiling; the room bathed in a soothing verdant glow. Jay put down a small deposit to hold the room while she made up her mind.

Nicholas hated sorority girls, with a blind passion that only a revolutionary can possess. For some arcane reason, he dismissed them as "bourgeois pigs." Nicholas never elaborated and Jay didn't dare ask. She felt that, in his regard, she was perilously close to becoming a bourgeois pig herself.

If Jay were a true student of the Revolution, she would have lived in a rooming house run by drug addicts and thieves. That would have been the honourable choice. Jay could entertain the idea but it was the small day-to-day realities that defeated her. Given the choice between sharing a bathroom with a heroin addict or a sorority sister, Jay preferred the security of middle-class women. She knew what to expect.

"Yes. A rooming house," said Jay. "What have you got against the student residence? I lived there all year and you never said anything against it."

"It's so bourgeois. I was waiting for you to outgrow it."

"Pardon?"

"That puerile stage. Being with a bunch of pampered children. My God, you didn't even go co-ed. You stayed on the girls' floor. Too uptight to face a guy in the morning."

A deep blush rose up from Jay's neck and emblazoned her cheeks.

A smug, knowing smile crept across Nicholas's face. "You're still a virgin, aren't you?"

So far Jay had managed to ignore the sexual aspect of the Revolution. When she first arrived at the university, a grubby individual thrust two cumbersome, newsprinted booklets at her: one on birth control and another on venereal disease. Jay saw that the booklets were full of information that might be useful to her at some later date, but she didn't want to carry them around in full view from class to class. Unfortunately, they were an awkward size, large and floppy. They didn't roll easily and they didn't fold, either. They perched in Jay's clear vinyl book bag for all the world to see. Jay pushed the booklets between two binders and worried about their visibility all day.

When she got home, she leafed through them. Both showed pictures of happy, hairy people making love. The women in these pamphlets did not shave their leg or underarm hair. The men had long hair and scruffy beards. These couples looked just like Nicholas's friends. The pamphlet-makers made it appear as though every person between the ages of sixteen and twenty-six was a hippie. There were no pictures of clean-cut, well-groomed young men or women. Presumably, these people did not exist or if they did, were certainly not having sex. Sex was the domain of the hippies or the "love generation." All of the people portrayed had beatific smiles that contrasted oddly with the accompanying paragraphs on genital herpes and venereal warts.

Venereal disease was now an outmoded annoyance. A foul-smelling pus issuing from one's loins no longer ruined one's life. A person simply took the appropriate antibiotic and the offending discharge disappeared. Jay found the pamphlets repulsive, yet compelling. Sex was a lot of work: so much research and equipment

involved in its practice; so many precautions needed to avoid venereal disease and pregnancy. (These two being equal in the minds of
the pamphlet-makers.)

The birth control pill was blazing new trails in sexual relations.
By mimicking pregnancy, the Pill fooled a woman's body into thinking it was pregnant, thus preventing conception. Constant headaches,
nausea, a possible stroke, the abrupt appearance of hair on the
upper lip were minor inconveniences to the huge advantage of
being sexually available at all times. Feminist literature of the time
lauded the Pill for liberating women from their biological imperative. Women were no longer doomed to suffer the ignominy of
an unwanted pregnancy. Tragedy, ruin and retribution were alien
concepts to Jay's generation. And why should they feel any other
way? It was a brave, new world and they were its eager pioneers.

Many of the girls in Jay's dormitory were on the Pill. They liked
it because it made their breasts bigger. There was still a social
stigma attached to being sexually promiscuous. Very few girls would
admit that they were on the Pill so they could have unlimited
sexual intercourse. The Pill's safest and greatest endorsement for
young womankind was that it regulated their periods. One was on
the Pill for health reasons.

Jay felt she must have been a throwback to some other century
because she worried about things. She instinctively knew that there
was a price to be paid. If something came too easily, well then, there
was a hitch, a hidden flaw that would bring the flimsily constructed
edifice tumbling down. Jay called it common sense, but "common"
implied that this was a view shared by others, and Jay felt quite alone
in her beliefs.

She could see why the Pill was so popular. It was easy; take a pill
every day and that was that. The problem for Jay was that you had
to take the Pill every day, regardless of whether you were going to
have sex. Jay hated waste. She felt she should get her money's worth.
None of the dorm girls who were on the Pill seemed to be having sex.
They spent more time arguing with their boyfriends than making

love. Granted, Jay didn't know the girls in her dormitory well and they might have been weird and cranky before but it seemed someone was always on some crying jag or other. The dorm was a wailing wall of weeping women. Weeping for what? Jay could never get a coherent word out of them. They were restless, plumped up with estrogen; big mamma bears lumbering around the halls, alert to nurture offspring that weren't going to be born.

"You should have sex." Nicholas eyed Jay thoughtfully.

Jay sighed. So, this was how it was to be with Nicholas. Years of patient expectation and finally, the big declaration: *You should have sex*. Scientific, analytic, wholesome, as though sex were good for you. Like eating bean sprouts. Not very appealing, but maybe that was how shy boys hid their real feelings: offer to render a biological service rather than declare themselves. "Okay, Nicholas, you're on! Let's have sex," Jay replied in a vain attempt to be nonchalant.

"Oh, well, I didn't mean me."

"What?!"

"I suppose I *should* have sex with you because after all, it doesn't mean anything. Sex is simply a means of communicating. It's like a body shorthand."

"Huh?"

"But I think sex only works if you're attracted to the other person. I could try it with you, but I just don't think it would work."

"Forget it."

"I've offended you."

"You're so goddamned self-involved and rude! Rude! That's what you are! Rude!" Jay stormed out and that was the end of the Revolution for her — for a while, anyway.

chapter two

KAT HOUSE

"FEEL FREE TO use the house! Mi casa es su casa!" Eve's shrill voice rang out with a hearty yet utterly false joviality.

"Thank you, that would be great. Is there a room where I can paint?" asked a soft-spoken but determined voice.

"Pardon?"

"The basement, perhaps? Could I paint there?"

"Um ..."

"It didn't look like anyone was using it for anything."

"Sure ... I guess so."

"Su casa es mi casa. Thanks!"

Few people got the better of Eve. Lily opened her door a crack to get a look at this person. She watched a seemingly frail girl haul her enormous suitcase up the stairs with quiet dispatch. An older woman led the charge, exclaiming at intervals — "My, what a lovely house! We never had a house like this. We were in the basement of the Greek Orthodox Church. Oh! It's so lovely!" Two sullen boys followed. They carried an old-fashioned steamer trunk, which, judging from their grunted teeterings, was very heavy. Lily could feel the reverberation of its thud as it was deposited in the room. The boarder darted back downstairs and returned with an artist's easel. She carried it, in triumph, as if she were bearing a coat of arms.

"Now that you're so nicely settled, let's all have lunch!" the older woman announced and the entourage trooped back down the stairs and out the door. Lily was intrigued. Few boarders arrived with such fanfare. Most slipped into the house after dinner, unpacked their meagre belongings and rarely ventured forth from their rooms.

The sorority sisters usually ignored the boarders. They were tolerated because they brought in the necessary income to maintain the house, but they were not thought of as suitable companions. Their very presence was an affront. The rooms should have been filled with eager young Kappa Alpha Thetans. But sororities had suffered a mysterious decline in popularity. The girls of KAT House struggled unsuccessfully to attract new members. Lily had joined because it was a family tradition. Her mother and sister regaled Lily with tales of riotous adventures in the sisterhood. Days long past.

Fashion is capricious. Its invisible spirit alights on an object and imbues it with an ineffable grace. All who look on the object are mesmerized in a collective spell. They flock to it, until Fashion's spirit moves elsewhere. The grand cosmic joke of Fashion is that it can land anywhere. When Fashion's spirit is present, even a chess player can look sartorial. And of course, when Fashion departs, the gilded coach turns back into a pumpkin.

Lily felt its loss. There was something obscurely depressing about living in a place that was spurned by Fashion. In Rose's day, the sorority was robust with the clashing of the different personalities who joined simply because it was "the thing to do." Now, KAT House attracted sedate, unadventurous young women who wanted to live in the past. They were the cream of Toronto's society and received all of its attendant honours, the "Coming Out" parties leading up to the thoroughly antiquated, "Debutante Ball."

Lily was ashamed to admit it, but she, too, had been a debutante. Lily's mother didn't like the boy Lily was seeing, so she arranged for Lily to have a military escort for the ball. And of course, Lily couldn't be accompanied by a stranger, even if he was endorsed by the Canadian Army. She had to go out with her Escort on a series of strategically-planned dates: the Get-Acquainted Tea, the slightly more intimate Picnic in the Park (Lily had to prepare the picnic), a Movie Date (he chose the movie), and finally, the Debutante Ball. Lily agreed to this farce because she was initially intrigued by the notion of a military escort. She imagined him to be tall and handsome, charmingly chivalrous. Lily's grandfather had a military escort for his funeral but in his case, it referred to the long procession of cars that stopped traffic. So, what would a one-man military escort look like?

Not like Roger Wilkinson, Lily was certain of that. Lily was democratic in her taste in men. One might say that she was easily pleased. And Roger Wilkinson was not, strictly speaking, bad-looking, but there was a willowy formlessness about his body that made Lily shudder. He was tall and gangly, his face moonlike in its white, pasty sheen. Lily's stomach turned every time she got near him. Their pre-ball dates reminded Lily of the time her parents tried to breed their female corgi. During the inauspicious picnic, as Roger waxed rhapsodic about his gun, Lily watched a piece of spinach that had become lodged in his front tooth bob up and down, in rhythm to his speech, and noted to herself that the corgi had a choice of studs, whereas she was stuck with one.

Lily was now twenty-three. The horrors of debutante balls were well behind her. When the new girls who joined the sorority talked about their wonderful "Coming Out" parties, Lily wondered if these girls were living in some other universe than the one she was occupying. Didn't they realize that being a debutante was shamefully old-fashioned? Lily, who once relished the girl-talks in the KAT House kitchen, now found herself bored beyond measure by their juvenile chit-chat. She was still friends with Kathleen, the oldest sister in the house. A few years before, she and Kathleen planned to move out and share an apartment together but Lily failed her courses and had to repeat the year. Kathleen graduated and got a well-paying job with the government. The two stayed on in the house, with the proviso that, should sororities become popular again, they would leave to make room for the new members. Lily appeared far younger than her years, so most of the girls forgot that she was as old as twenty-three.

Lily knew she was living on borrowed time. She couldn't expect to live at KAT House forever. She wanted to have some direction in life. She thought of arbitrarily choosing one — north — and living her life in a northerly fashion. South seemed a direction more temperamentally suited to her, however. That was her dilemma. Each time, Lily picked a direction, another one appeared to be equally attractive. South, though, was Lily's compass point. She loved hot weather. The stifling humidity of the Toronto summers was balm to her soul. Her parents had a house in one of the leafy suburbs just outside the city. They had a swimming pool put in so they could always take solace from the heat. They were proud of having defeated the weather. Lily was a heat-seeking, pleasure-loving sensualist born in a northern climate that advocated temperance.

ᴗᴗ

"PLEASE FLUSH THE toilet." A small drawing of a happy face punctuated this unnecessary announcement. "Who wouldn't flush the toilet?" Jay wondered, then realized that these helpful missives were directed at her. "Please scrub the bathtub when you're finished!! (Happy face) The cleanser (happy face) and cloth (happy face) are behind the sink! (happy face)." Jay decided that Eve was probably the author of these annoying notes, which pursued her from one communal area to another.

In the kitchen, other hands joined the frenzy of communication, all with varying views on the running of the house. The refrigerator door was a battleground upon which warring happy faces engaged in combat. And inside the fridge: nine separate half-pint milk cartons, all carefully designated by owner; an uncooked pork chop named "Kathleen," many small blocks of mild cheddar cheese distinguished only by the names attached. The girls were away at their summer jobs. Jay skimmed a small amount of milk from each carton. She needed some milk for her tea and she didn't feel like going to the store. She could almost hear the squeals of indignation as she looted the supplies.

Jay liked being alone in the house. She could pretend it was her house as she took on the proprietary task of collecting the mail. Mail received when one is twenty is very different from mail received when one is thirty. In one's middle years, the mail is more plentiful but it's usually of an unpleasant nature: bills, bank statements, solicitations from charities and environmental groups. At twenty, one is still a mail novice, an unknown entity to the consumer mailing lists. The mail one receives is personal and sporadic. Jay wrote irregularly to her friends back home, and they responded in kind. The letters that arrived for Jay betrayed the personality of the sender. Barbara liked to draw penguins on her envelopes. Sheila liked to write Jay's name in Latin — "Wrightus, J." Jay scanned the mail quickly. None of her friends had written to her.

She gazed at the pink parchment envelope addressed to "Miss Susan Lipton." Susan Lipton received mail every single day — lavender-scented envelopes that fluttered daintily through the slot. Receiving mail on a daily basis was not so unusual for someone living in the nineteenth century, but in the twentieth century, with the advent of the telephone and rude and spontaneous discourse, letter writing seemed, at best, an arcane activity. And receiving letters on a daily basis was nothing short of miraculous.

"Miss Susan Lipton," addressed in different hands, but all ascribing to the H.B. MacLean Method of Writing, a system of handwriting learned by all Canadian schoolchildren at the age of seven: large, round, perfectly formed, forward-slanting letters. Jay found it very indicative of a person's mental and emotional development to see how far one deviated from Mr. MacLean. In Jay's opinion, it was a mark of character to have handwriting that was illegible. The handwriting on the letters addressed to Susan Lipton showed a frightening lack of character. Susan's mail didn't resemble real mail so much as an exact facsimile of mail: single, perfect, Hallmark-card-sized envelopes arriving every single day.

Who could all these people be? Susan was a mousy young woman. It was unlikely that she had a devoted letter-writing public at large. Jay pondered this slight mystery before turning her attention to more urgent matters. Art school commenced in two weeks. Jay had to get her paintings started before she became unduly influenced by the classes and did bad work. There were no windows in the basement so she had to work under the green and purple glare of cheap fluorescent lights that some enterprising soul had strung up. She would have preferred to work in the parlour, a small room off from the kitchen, but there were limits to the liberties a mere boarder could take.

⌒

MOST SOCIETIES HAVE a hierarchy and the sorority was no different. Eve was the queen bee around whom the virginal drones buzzed. Eve had lost her virginity and was now a woman of experience. Twenty years earlier in the 1950s, her inordinate sexual appetite would have disqualified her from occupying a position of power. Eve would have been regarded as a slut. But now, women were supposed to aspire to sexual liberation. Eve gained authority over the others because she had not only lost her virginity, but more importantly, had mastered the art of multiple orgasms. She was clever enough to recognize that at any moment, the virgins in the sorority could band together and depose her, so she was careful to stress that she was engaged and it was her fiancé who was helping her achieve these orgasms.

Unlike their liberated counterparts who never talked about sex, but simply did it, the sorority girls were obsessed with sex — more specifically, their virginity. Late one night, shortly after she arrived,

Jay overheard them indulging in war stories of a near-miss nature. Kathleen's stories were the most harrowing. At age twenty-five, Kathleen hardly qualified for girlhood but she was hanging on to it by the skin of her still-intact hymeneal membrane.

"Yeah, we were parked in the woods —"

"The Old Mill Ravine?"

"Yeah, and —"

"The cops come by quite often now."

"Do they? Oh. Well, anyway, we were necking and I had nothing on —"

"Was he naked too?"

"Of course not! Anyway, we must have been necking for an hour or so —"

"Just necking?"

"Well, maybe I let him get to first base. Anyway, we were necking and doing a bit of heavy petting —"

"That's second base."

"All right, second base."

Jay was never entirely clear on what the terms were. She knew that "necking" meant kissing and "petting" meant touching, but that "heavy petting" meant something much more sinister than "petting." She deduced that "first base" meant the boy could kiss you. "Second base" and "third base" were sources of confusion. "Fourth base," or "the home run," was self-evident but these girls never got to that spot. They spent a lot of time discussing second and third base.

"But just second base. That's all. We must have been there for an hour or so and suddenly, he starts to take his clothes off!"

"No!" A chorus of disapproval.

"Yes. So I said, 'Just what do you think you are doing?!' And he said, 'Well, aren't we going to?' And I said, 'Of course not. What do you take me for?'" Murmurs of agreement. "Well, he got really mad and said I was leading him on. I said to him, 'I told you my virginity was important to me.' And he said, 'Well, for Christ's sake, we've done everything else!' So I said, 'That may be, but I have to draw the line somewhere.' Then, I put my clothes back on and he drove me home. He was really mad. I thought for a second he was going to push me out of the car and take off. It would have been hard getting home, without any clothes on. But you know, he might have been mad but he respects me." The girls breathed a solemn sigh of assent.

No one asked Kathleen if the boy in question respected her enough to ask her out again. Jay thought not. Jay hoped that when she was Kathleen's age she would not be prancing around naked in cars, defending her virginity. If you postponed the event indefinitely, the time would come when you couldn't give it away. Your body would be an overripe fruit, a mushy banana that no one wants to peel. Jay suspected that Kathleen was approaching that time. Her body was white and fleshy. Her face had long white hairs sprouting out around the mouth and chin.

Jay hated being a virgin. Most of her life was well-organized, everything in its place at its appointed hour. She never gave her virginity a second thought until, suddenly, it was upon her, an embarrassing stigma, one of the few things in her life that had somehow got away from her — or rather, wouldn't leave.

The girls usually waited until Eve was safely out of the building before discussing their sexual escapades. Eve could spoil a salacious discussion faster than anyone. If someone was describing a "hot" moment, Eve would raise her eyebrows and smile smugly to herself, perhaps murmuring "ah children, children." Inevitably, Eve drew the conversation to herself.

"Judd says I'm sexually precocious. I come at the drop of a hat." Giggles. "I mean, really. Sometimes Judd just looks at me and I come. Come? Oh that means orgasm. I have about twelve a night. Judd has three. It's this fabulous gushy feeling — of course, you don't know about it. Well, you might, Kathleen. You've come awfully close — Oooh! Forgive the pun — a couple of times."

"You don't have to have penetration to have an orgasm," Kathleen replied tersely.

"Oh, but it's the best way. 'Cause then your whole body's into it. And it's just like this big ocean wave. Beating on the shores. Badoom. Badoom. Badoom." Eve proceeded to give a lively demonstration of her orgasm, then added nastily, "Of course, Kathleen, I guess you have to make do with what you've got."

Kathleen represented the old social mores and Eve, the new. Most of the girls detested Eve but they grudgingly acknowledged her ascendance. The taint of spinsterhood was starting to descend upon Kathleen. The girls could smell her failure and were quietly withdrawing their friendship, lest they inherit the jinx.

Sexual liberation had not infiltrated the sororial ranks to the point where the women believed they should be financially, as well as emotionally, independent. Procuring a husband was still the name of the game. Most of the sorority sisters viewed their university years as a good time to hunt for prospective husbands, on the principle that free-range animals are livelier than the imprisoned species that one later encounters in the workplace

Lily had no particular status in the house. She was a wild card. There was no telling what she would do next.

JAY COULD SEE ghosts. She wasn't sure whether she should call them ghosts. She didn't always see them. Sometimes, she heard them and other times, she simply received information. It came to her, unbidden. It wasn't a talent she was proud of, or even one she was trying to cultivate. Ghosts had things to tell her and she was willing to listen.

When Jay first started painting in the basement, she heard people arguing in the house. It sounded like it came from the main staircase. She ran upstairs to see who had come in, but no one was there. She went back to her work and, after an hour, the shouts started up again. She ignored the noise and continued painting. A curious inertia had overtaken her. As if in a trance, Jay remained painting while ghostly arguments raged about her.

The next day when Jay was in the basement, she heard men and women laughing together, as if planning to go out somewhere: sounds of women's feet scampering up the main staircase, and lilting voices calling merrily down to the men. Jay assumed it was the KAT House girls and their boyfriends. She went upstairs to see who had arrived and found no one.

Puzzled, Jay returned to the basement and resumed her work. Some time passed, then the ghostly laughter started up again. This time, it was a man and a woman. There was still a sense of gaiety but there was a secretive cast to the laughter. These voices were different. Jay went up to the kitchen. No one was on the main floor. Jay heard giggles coming from one of the upstairs rooms. She crept up the stairs. The voices came from Eve's room. Eve had probably slipped her boyfriend into the house, thinking no one was home.

Watching other people engage in sex was far more terrifying to Jay than a couple of ghosts. The trouble with the Sexual Revolution was that, like any new religion, the people engaging in it felt obliged to procure converts. It wasn't enough that people were making "free" love, but they felt that everyone else should hear about it and see it. At one of the summer arts camps she attended, Jay shared a room with a girl who had a boyfriend. There were two narrow single beds in the room, with a two-foot space in between the beds. Jay was expected to lie in bed and pretend to be asleep while the girl and her boyfriend went at it. They stayed out late and slipped into the room at one or two in the morning.

A short time ago, it would have been unthinkable for two people to have sex while a virtual stranger lay beside them, yet now, the onus was on Jay to mind her own business and keep her trap shut. The first night it occurred, Jay was so shocked she did just that. The boyfriend left the room early in the morning and the girl made herself scarce as well, thinking that if Jay didn't find her, they didn't need to discuss it. Jay grabbed the girl as she was in line for lunch and hissed in her ear, "Don't you ever do that again!" The girl shrugged. Jay was a nervous wreck all that day, wondering what was going to happen. She didn't see the girl until two a.m. when she and her boyfriend slipped into the room and went at it again.

What was Jay to do? Should she snap on the light and demand that they stop? She didn't know the boyfriend. It was hard to tell what a person was like by the pleasure grunts he made in coitus. He might be very embarrassed and apologetic, though Jay figured that, if he were willing to copulate next to a total stranger, this was unlikely. He'd probably be like the girl, utterly shameless. The two of them might think it great fun to embarrass Jay further by leaving the lights on, stripping the sheets off the bed and giving her a full show. Jay lay immobile, working out these various scenarios as the couple sweated and grunted their way to bliss.

By the time morning came, Jay was exhausted by their mutual enterprise. She saw that she was not going to win this battle so she asked to move to another room. She stuck to some degree of truth when she said she was allergic to the girl's musk oil. She knew the authorities at the school would expel the girl if she told them what had occurred but she also knew that she would then be shunned by the other students, for the social code had shifted sufficiently that sympathies would be with the sex-crazed roommate and not with Jay. Jay would be viewed as an uptight prig, a spoiler, a bad sport in a world where sex was the only sport going.

As she was about to knock on Eve's door, memories of that night, of lying rigidly in her bed listening to barely suppressed moans, groans and giggles, filled Jay with shame. She turned tail and fled downstairs to the sanctuary of the basement. The sounds of enthusiastic lovemaking filtered down through the walls, through the pipes, straight into Jay's ears as she, grim-jawed, set about her work. The lovemaking continued for about two hours. Jay was annoyed at being held captive in the basement, but under the circumstances, she didn't want to venture upstairs again.

Later that evening, Jay let Eve know that her trysts were not entirely private. "It's great to have a studio in the house. It's very nice of you girls to let me paint here during the day."

"Oh?" asked Eve, a little puzzled by this sudden declaration.

"Yes, I'm downstairs working in the basement. But occasionally, I go upstairs." Jay gave Eve a pointed look.

"I don't know how you can stand being here by yourself."

"Pardon?" asked Jay.

"It's creepy. Don't you think it's creepy?"

Jay had to clarify matters. "Excuse me, Eve, but when I was down in the basement, today, I could have sworn I heard you come in."

"Wasn't me. I'm at work."

"So, you weren't here," Jay hesitated, then added, "this afternoon?"

"No, why?"

"Oh, I thought I heard people going up and down the stairs."

"That's what I mean. Creepy. People say this place is haunted."

"Oh," said Jay. She weighed up the advantages of a private place to paint versus the occasional inconvenience of amorous ghosts and decided to continue painting in the basement. Over the next week, the couple's moans of passion turned into murmured conversation, and then the low treble of another man's voice entered the soundscape.

There were shouts and arguments between the two men. Jay heard footsteps running up and down the main stairs. The footsteps were so loud that Jay got up. She was starting up the basement stairs when she heard the door at the top of the stairs open. She looked up. There was no one there and the door was shut, but the two men's voices boomed down the stairs. Jay leaped back in fright and quickly hid behind one of the house's foundation posts.

The men were arguing over the woman. Although their voices were loud, they sounded as if they were coming from the bottom of the ocean, words upon words in a reverberant echo. Jay peeped out cautiously to see something, anything.

Suddenly, she heard the sound of a shovel scraped across the ground and then a thwack as it hit its target. There was a groan of surprise and the dull, hollow thud of a body landing at the bottom of the stairs. After a moment of silence, she heard the sound of feet running quickly up the stairs and the click of the lock at the top. Jay was about to leave her hiding place when, right at her feet, she heard the echoing heaves of the dying man gasping out his last breaths in rasping, wheezing agony.

Jay stood there, willing it to end, and just as she thought she would be pinned to the spot forever, the gasps ceased. The room was silent for a moment. Then the sounds of the twentieth century resumed their insistent hum: the slight buzz of the fluorescent lights, the quiet electrical thrum of Jay's clock radio, the cranking sound of air sifting through the idle furnace. Jay ran up the stairs, tore open the door, which was unlocked, and headed for the kitchen — a bright, sunny room streaming with broad, comforting daylight.

Jay sat and considered the matter for a long time. She'd experienced the worst of it. She was sure of that. Jay reasoned, quite sensibly, that the ghosts, having told their story, would not need to tell it again. However, ghosts are repetitive creatures and are unable to do anything but tell their story over and over again. When Jay next stationed herself in the basement, she heard the ghostly laughter of people planning an outing. The cycle continued as before. Jay was careful to absent herself just as she felt it was building up to the murder. She let a couple of days pass, just to be on the safe side. However, as soon as she set up her paints, the two men resumed their argument on the stairs and the man again died his grisly death. Ghosts prefer an audience. This time, Jay ignored the "kerfuffle," as she described it to herself as a means of keeping the horror at bay, and continued painting. Over the summer, she grew accustomed to the ghostly saga and found its repetitive re-enactments strangely comforting.

chapter three

RITES OF SPRING

THE KAT HOUSE girls invited Jay to their Spring Barbeque. Jay didn't want to go but saw that it would be difficult to continue living in the house if she refused.

She often found herself caught between the Radicals and the Straights. Nicholas's friends were Radicals. They were dirty, unkempt and rude. Life to them was one big experiment. Most of them were stoned on some drug or other. Nicholas was unusual in that he could be high as a kite and you could still get a good conversation out of him. His "comrades" would slump, lined up against a wall, their eyes glazed, nodding their heads in silent agreement, like old men in a nursing home. Then there were the Straights; people who didn't drink or do drugs, people who supposedly lived ordinary and routine lives.

By definition, Jay was Straight. She didn't like Straights, however. And she didn't find them to be all that Straight, either. Underneath their bland conforming exteriors lurked the most demented people you could meet. The sorority house was a prime example of just how crazy Straight people could be.

Susan Lipton was a prime example. She seemed to have modelled her life after the Barbie doll. She wore clothes that were direct copies of Barbie's. Jay knew this for a fact because she used to play with Barbie dolls and remembered the clothes from the catalogue. Barbie was consumer culture in miniature. Jay made a mental note to bring up Barbie when she had one of her discussions with Nicholas.

On the night of the barbeque, Susan wore Barbie's Barbeque Outfit. The other girls wore similar clothes, uniforms of cashmere sweater sets and pleated skirts. Unbeknownst to Jay, there existed in Toronto small, expensive dress stores that specialized in clothing this particular class of women. Fashions would change, the proprietors acknowledged, but cashmere, pearls and a fine wool skirt would never go awry for a woman of substance. The girls of KAT House wore youthful versions of their mothers' clothes and saw no shame in it.

"Scary, isn't it?" a voice at Jay's shoulder muttered. Jay turned to see a girl with wild red hair grinning at her. "They stop wearing cashmere after the Victoria Day weekend. Then they bring out the white shoes. We haven't met — I'm Lily MacFarlane."

"Jay Wright. Are you a boarder as well?"

"Nope. I'm one of *them*. Full-fledged member. Cleverly disguised." Lily wore a short pink sundress with a plunging neckline. "The rent's cheap and the house has style."

"The house is beautiful."

"And the girls are nice, basically. Just a little uptight. Like Barbie over there." Lily flicked her head in Susan's direction.

Jay was astonished. "You think of her as Barbie, too?"

"What else? See the guy with her?" A well-groomed young man with small, even features stood next to Susan. He looked ill-at-ease. "The Ken doll. The ultimate accessory."

Jay and Lily burst into laughter. The Ken doll in question turned his face in their direction and smiled at them. Jay saw that he was extremely handsome and remembered that she'd met him before.

"She'll have him wrapped up by the end of the summer," Lily observed.

"Do you know her well?" Jay was looking for a tactful way to discuss Susan without appearing like a gossip.

"Does anyone? She's exactly what she appears to be."

"Which is?"

Lily leaned in conspiratorially. "She's not human."

"What?"

"She's from some other planet. At some point in time, she took over Susan's body."

"When Susan was seven, when she got her first Barbie doll."

"Of course! The aliens live in Barbie dolls, incubi waiting for their chance. Susan Lipton opens her Barbie doll present for Christmas and SCHLURP! The incubi's inside her in a second."

"I used to play with Barbie dolls," said Jay, enjoying the game but working out the ramifications.

"So did I. We were probably deficient hosts. Anyway, maybe it's not Barbie. But at some time, she got replaced. She mimics what she thinks is human behaviour."

"What's their mission?"

"What it always is: to destroy the human race."

"How do you do that as Susan Lipton? She seems pretty innocuous."

"That's exactly how. You bore the living shit out of people. Eventually, it kills them. She'll marry Ken. And she'll be the perfect wife. She'll do everything right. She'll never say anything nasty about his parents or brothers and sisters. She'll appear to get along with them and they'll appear to get along with her. But something will be missing. Ken will find that he doesn't want to listen to her when she talks and he won't know why. He'll think, 'Oh well, this is the way life's supposed to be when you're married. Dull.' And he'll remember when he was a child. And how much fun he had. And actually, how much fun he had as a teenager. And he won't quite be able to arrive at the logical conclusion that he stopped having fun when he met her. 'Cause just as he's about to figure it out, she'll get pregnant. So, he's got to be happy about that. It'll be a pod baby.

She'll have another, and then a couple more till he's outnumbered. Four of them to one human being. He'll be so confused about his natural instincts versus what's going on in his home that he won't care anymore. He'll surrender."

"What would go on in his home?"

"They would all let their hair down, be their pod selves."

"They'd be having fun, then."

"Not in the way that we understand it. Their aim is to extinguish all signs of life. Abolish spontaneous behaviour. Good question, though. Keep a close watch on Ms. Lipton and report. It'd be interesting to know what she does when she thinks no one's looking."

"What if Ken's an alien?"

"Not a chance. Susan wouldn't be after him, then. Their mission is to conquer through assimilation. Plus, he's got too much life in his eyes to be one of them."

"Hey, she's left him alone. He's staring at us."

"I should go save him," said Lily. She ran her fingers back through her hair in a seductive gesture, met "Ken's" gaze and walked boldly over to him.

"Do I know you?" asked "Ken," perplexed by Lily's audacity.

"Do you want to?"

"Sure."

"I'm Lily."

"Brad."

"Well, Brad, it's time to get trucking."

"Pardon?"

"Let's get out of here."

"Well, I ... ah ... can't. I ... ah ... I'm here with Susan."

Lily leaned over and whispered in Brad's ear. "She's an alien. Ditch her."

Brad laughed, "Well, that's —"

Lily whispered in Brad's other ear. "Not a human being. Get rid of her."

"And what are you offering in exchange?"

"That's a little mercenary of you, Brad. What do you want?"

"You."

"Too much. How 'bout an unchaste kiss?"

"What?"

"Chaste is what you get from Susan. I'll give you unchaste."

"How much unchaste?"

"Not as much as you want; more than Susan. You game?"

"Yeah."

"Let's go."

This negotiation was conducted in under two minutes, the time it took for Susan to refill her glass of Sprite from the makeshift bar in the far corner of the patio. Susan's antennae must have alerted her to the takeover because she suddenly trembled in a rage, her face a study of impotent fury, a fleeting impression of a predator deprived of its kill. What Jay found vaguely chilling was that Susan was angry before she actually turned to see that Brad had gone.

It was surprising how much evidence could support Lily's theory. If Susan were an alien, then her bizarrely perfect mail could be from alien counterparts relating their progress at assimilation, conveying helpful tips on how to appear human. The concept of pen pals was probably an invention of aliens. Jay had once casually remarked to Susan that she got a lot of letters. Susan blushed crimson and said defensively, "Do I?" and in the following week, the letters dropped off somewhat.

None of the other girls in the sorority seemed to like Susan. Neither did they actively dislike her, which was odd because they usually had very strong opinions one way or the other. Susan was her own no-man's land. One never had interesting conversations with Susan. She wasn't stupid, just profoundly dull. She lacked any sense of spontaneity.

She conducted a series of rigid little dates with Brad, always on Friday and Saturday nights. Brad would arrive at 7:30. He would have to wait in the communal living room because Susan would not be ready until ten minutes to eight. Once, Jay found herself trapped into making small talk with Brad while he waited. Jay wondered why Lily chose to go after Brad at the barbeque when there were ample opportunities in the seven-thirty to ten-to-eight slot. She then remembered that Lily was the same girl who had come tearing around the corner wearing only a scanty towel. She pretended to be looking for something, glanced up at Brad, allowed the towel to slip strategically before gasping in a breathy Marilyn Monroe voice, "Oh! I didn't know anyone was here!" Then she dashed out again. Yes, Lily had had her eye on Brad for some time. And the barbeque was a sufficiently dramatic event to pull off her coup d'état.

Jay was disappointed that Lily had left. She had enjoyed finding an ally. She couldn't think of any suitable friends to bring to this event. Nicholas would have done something rude. Watching the girls idly flirt with their boyfriends, Jay felt some vital part of the human mating ritual was lost to her. They were good-looking young men, well-exercised. They exuded a bland, genial energy but they held no attraction for her.

Jay was searching for a specific soulmate, a thin tortured artist with haunted eyes and wild hair. Even Nicholas did not fit those requirements. Nicholas was bathed in a golden aura of summer boyhood. There was something permanently childlike about him. He had pale blue-green eyes that appeared to be open slightly more than was necessary, a constant state of surprise. His eyelids were covered in freckles, so even though he could be making some adult statement about overthrowing the government, Jay kept thinking she was high up in a treehouse with one of her male cousins.

"Where is she?" Susan's brittle voice interrupted Jay's reverie.

"Who?"

"Lily. Where is she?" Jay looked at Susan's flat blue eyes: eyes with a mission, eyes untroubled by human pain, eyes that simply wanted the piece marked "Brad" put back in its proper place.

"I don't know."

"You know where she is. Tell me."

"I don't. I just met her a few minutes ago." It occurred to Jay that she had a tendency to attract charismatic individuals who would perform outrageous acts, then abruptly depart, leaving Jay to account for their transgressions. "Why? What's the problem?" Jay replied, knowing full well what the problem was.

"She's got Brad."

"So?"

"I'm worried about her."

"You are?"

"Yes. We're all worried about her."

"We?"

"The sorority. She's a concern."

"How so?"

"She's a nymphomaniac. Among other things."

"Oh, so you're afraid that she's going to —"

"It's compulsive with her. We have to protect her."

"And Brad."

"That's not funny."

"Well, I don't know where she is." Jay started to move away.

"She lies."

"Lies?"

"Yes — compulsively. Everything she does is compulsive."

"Why don't you kick her out?"

"That wouldn't be right. She's our responsibility."

"What about Brad?"

"What about him?"

"It's a pretty rotten thing for him to do to you."

"Boys have their urges."

"You're taking it very well."

"I don't believe in sex before marriage. Brad respects me for this, but he has his needs." Susan pronounced "needs" as though they were some appalling infirmity. "A girl like Lily throws herself at him. What's he to do?"

"Refuse?"

"This is really none of your business. Brad is my fiancé. We have our life worked out. I have my values." There was a slight pause as Susan considered them. "Besides, a man's not going to buy the loaf, if he can have one slice at a time." Susan left Jay to ponder the sheer ruthlessness of that last statement.

Susan roamed the party for about half an hour, valiantly pretending that Brad had simply gone out to get cigarettes. She could hear the other girls whispering in and around her, no one daring to address her directly. When it became patently clear that Brad was not coming back and Susan suspected that the girls were not, in fact, silent in sympathy, but quietly relishing her humiliation, she stormed upstairs and slammed the door to her bedroom. The sound reverberated through the house, its Victorian walls cringing in disbelief and outrage that Susan Lipton, one of its sisterhood, should have been so cruelly mistreated.

Jay now found herself the hub of the party as the girls were anxious to know the details of Brad's desertion and Jay was the only reliable source. By dint of being an important witness to a scandalous event, Jay was now privy to their confidences. Sympathies seemed to be with Lily. Lily had been a member of the sorority for years, whereas Susan had only joined the year before. No one mentioned Lily's nymphomania. Most of the young men at the party were from the fraternity house down the street, brought in to liven things up. Susan and Eve were the only ones who had steady boyfriends.

"I'd like to see Lily try and steal Judd away from Eve," said Kathleen.

"I guess we should go check on Susan," remarked one of the girls solicitously.

"Yeah, we should."

No one moved. The girls cautiously sipped their drinks and glanced around guiltily, upholding the requisite moment of silence to commemorate the event. Eve gave her fiancé a meaningful look, indicating that unbridled passion would not be on the agenda tonight. He kissed her on the cheek and took his leave. The remaining male guests, completely unnerved by the silent female conspiracy afoot, also withdrew. When the last man left, the girls breathed a sigh of relief and the gossip flowed freely.

"Where do you think they went?"

"To his room, of course."

"That's sort of yicky. A grungy Sigma Chi room full of dirty underwear."

"You talk like you've been there lots of times."

"My brother lives there, remember?"

"Yeah, right."

"Anyway, Lily's got more class than that. She'd go to the Park Plaza," said Eve.

"Is that where you and Steve went?" Kathleen inquired politely, her voice dripping with malice. Steve was the boy Eve dated before she met Judd. Eve always swore that she kept her virginity until she became engaged.

One of the girls deflected the attack. "She may have class but neither of them has money."

"Brad's got money."

"Not really."

"Oh? He dresses like he has money."

"Yeah, well, that's how you get it. People will always give money to someone who doesn't look like they need it."

"I don't think Lily's sleeping with Brad."

"Sure she is."

"She doesn't even know him."

"Has that ever stopped her before?"

"She's done this before?"

"Well, no —"

"So, they might have just gone somewhere to talk."

"Yeah, right," smirked Eve.

"Well, Eve, you may assume that Lily's sleeping with Brad, but not everyone operates on your level. Lily's not like that. She's not a slut." Kathleen pronounced the last word with a certain relish.

"Are you calling me a slut?!" shouted Eve. The lines of combat were drawn and the girls knew they were in for a long catfight. Since Lily's whereabouts could not be predicted with any accuracy, the wise girls went to bed, leaving Eve and Kathleen to their quarrel.

LILY AND BRAD had gone to the beach. Brad assumed that Lily would follow him to his room in Sigma Chi, but Lily craved adventure, not sex. Brad was like most young men of that time in that he would willingly hang off a cliff for hours if there was some faint promise of sex as a reward. He reluctantly drove them to the beach.

As soon as they arrived, Lily made a mad dash for the sand. She danced and cavorted on it as if her life depended on it. Brad stood on the boardwalk and watched in bemusement.

"So, how 'bout that unchaste kiss?"

"Later."

"What are you doing?"

"God, I love it here!" Lily whirled around dramatically, her arms outstretched.

"Why? It's ugly."

"It's not ugly!"

"Yeah. It is. There are dead fish all over the place where you're jumping."

"Dancing. And they're just smelts. They always die on the beach this time of year."

"That makes it better?"

"Come on! Dance with me! Dance on some dead fish!"

"You're crazy."

"Come on!" Lily hauled Brad off the boardwalk.

"I hate sand. It gets in your shoes."

"Take 'em off."

"Take yours off."

"All right." Lily reached under her skirt and deftly pulled off her pantyhose, tucking them into her shoes. His hopes raised, Brad quickly took off his shoes and socks. He danced reluctantly at first, then fell into her play.

"So, what's your name, anyway?"

"Lily. I told you."

"I mean your last name."

"MacFarlane."

"MacFarlane? Hey, that's kinda interesting. My best friend's last name is MacFarlane."

"Yes, I know."

"Well, you know everything, don't you?" Brad said jovially.

"I have spies." Lily smiled up at Brad. He looked at her with cold grey eyes. Something in his look frightened Lily so she quickly relinquished an explanation. "Paul's my brother. We're twins."

"You're what?! Shit. You're kidding." There was an awkward silence as Brad contemplated the ramifications of this piece of information. His jaw made odd little motions, as though he were chewing on a piece of gristly meat. "He never mentioned you."

"No, he wouldn't."

"You two don't get along?"

"I wouldn't go that far."

"Did you do that kid sister stuff like hiding in closets and spying on him?"

"I'm not his kid sister. I'm his twin."

"Why'd you come on to me?"

"Is there a law against talking to my brother's friends?"

"You weren't planning to talk."

"How do you know? We're talking now, aren't we?"

Brad looked at Lily more carefully. She didn't look like her brother. Paul had small, well-defined features. Lily's were blobby: a wide-bridge nose, lips that were full and broad, a face that was a mass of freckles, and extravagantly red hair. Red hair usually signified a bad temper. And a passionate disposition.

"Shit. Paul's sister."

"Why does that have anything to do with it?"

"You don't mess with a guy's sister."

"You were planning to mess with me?"

"Well, you know." Brad regarded Lily as a bull contemplates a poisonous, yet tantalizing, grassy weed.

"You mean, like this?" Lily drew Brad to her and kissed him.

"You're a good kisser."

"Thanks," said Lily, kissing Brad again.

Brad broke away. "I'm sorry. It's just too weird."

Lily laughed. "Okay to screw around on your girlfriend but not on my brother?"

"Brothers get mad if you — oh, you're kidding; we were gonna screw?"

"No."

"Yeah. I figured you for a tease."

"Why'd you leave with me?"

Brad gazed out at the flat lake water. "I'm glad we came here," he said and took Lily's hand.

They walked in silence, their feet sinking into the crackling bodies of the smelt. Finally, they arrived at a stony embankment so they turned and headed back to the car.

Lily's mind was madly racing, desperate to pin Brad down to some sort of verbal declaration, but silence was the name of the game so she said nothing. As they approached KAT House, Brad glanced up anxiously to Susan's room, which was on the top floor, overlooking the street. The car's motor idled softly. Lily was about to leave when Brad shut the motor off, reached across to her and said, "Stay." His eyes were urgent and pleading, like those of a small child. He took her shoes and purse from her hand and laid them on the floor in front, his hand gently brushing her leg as he did so. He stroked her thigh, signalling a range of goose pimples that went up and down Lily's body.

Brad slowly unzipped Lily's dress and pulled it down. He fondled her breasts, slowly and deliberately, taking them out of the bra, gently unhooking it, so that it, too, fell.

Lily felt chilled and somewhat foolish — exposed to any passersby. "I, ah —"

"I just want to look at you for a while," Brad said in dreamy distant tones.

"Someone might —"

Brad leaned in and kissed her, a long, slow, sensual kiss — the kiss of a man who had all the time in the world. Lily flung herself into Brad's arms to create some sense of urgency. Urgency did arrive and Lily was then sorry that she had precipitated it.

It seemed a little late for Lily to tell Brad she was not as experienced as he thought and his thrusts were hurting her. "I'm not on the Pill," she gasped, which stopped him in his tracks. He snapped out of his trance and became more gentle with her. He looked at her tenderly and solicitously put some of her clothes back on, "in case the police should come by." They resumed their lovemaking until both were thoroughly sated. Brad heaped kisses on Lily as she tumbled in disarray out of the car.

Lily slipped into the sorority house and crept up to her third floor bedroom. She paused at Susan's door, hoping that she would come out of her room. Susan remained inside. She had chosen to play possum. She would exploit what remaining advantage she had by pretending that none of the traumatic events of the evening had occurred. Women are good at ignoring unpleasant realities, particularly if they don't fit into their game plan. None of the other girls were up, either. Lily would have sworn they'd be gossiping about it till the early hours. She checked for a light under Jay's door, but found none. Lily glanced at the clock. Four a.m. She had to get up for work at six. Lily threw herself into bed and slept fitfully, anxious to make the two hours she had left count for something. She finally fell into a deep sleep at 5:30 and was cruelly awakened by the six o'clock alarm buzzing, signalling another inglorious day at Hydro.

chapter four

LILY

WHEN SHE WAS sixteen, Lily started working at the offices of Toronto Hydro Power Authority during the summers. It was a good way to earn money so she could go to university because, as her father flatly declared, "he wasn't going to pay a whole lot of money to educate a girl who had no brains." While Lily was offended by the comment, she couldn't help but acknowledge that, on some level, it was true. Her brains took a vacation when the evil spectre of school reared its ugly head.

As a child, Lily couldn't understand why she was supposed to learn all this useless information. It was clear to her that the adult world bore no resemblance to what she was taught at school. Social studies was a subject that was particularly baffling to her. The teacher would choose some hot-climate country and they'd have to memorize a series of facts about it: population, rainfall per year, national product, national bird, national flower. The textbooks featured pictures of smiling, dark-skinned people carrying bundles through a marketplace. Some countries stood out because the people had quaint customs or they wore odd clothes.

Mexicans wore sombreros and went to sleep in the middle of the afternoon. Lily found it hard to imagine an entire population of Mexicans taking a nap, their bodies slumped over their desks like her classmates during "rest-time." Lily learned that the men of India wore diapers and the women wrapped long silk bandages around their bodies. When someone died in India, they threw the body into the river. The other children in Lily's grade school class memorized this information and dutifully regurgitated it back to their teacher. Lily could not see the sense in it. If she lived in a foreign country or were planning to visit one, then there'd be some reason to learn about it. But to memorize hundreds of dubious facts about every country in the world simply because it was part of the course and they had to cover the world by Christmas, well, it just seemed too stupid for words. Lily did not hide her contempt from the teacher.

She held similar views about mathematics. She didn't see any point in solving theoretical problems. (How many men in how long a space of time could fill a hole? To Lily's mind, if you need to fill a hole, you get whoever's around to help you and you do it till it's done. Lily didn't think she'd need to fill any holes anyway, so who cared. Not Lily.)

Thus, Lily was branded, early on, as a poor student. She liked her position as class rebel. In her backroom realm, Lily was the undisputed queen. High school was a lost cause but Lily felt that, in university, she might finally be able to learn about subjects that interested her, which, in turn, would lead her to some fantastically exciting career. Lily didn't know what she wanted to do, exactly. Perhaps she should go in for journalism. She saw herself striding through seamy streets of Toronto, notebook in hand, alert for Her Big Story. The naysaying voice in Lily's head informed her that she would have to get better marks in English if she planned to pursue journalism. Besides, it went on, she probably shouldn't even think of going to university. She wasn't bright enough. University was too expensive for someone who didn't have a hope in hell of winning a scholarship.

Lily couldn't pinpoint when exactly she started hearing this Voice. It wasn't like the voices Joan of Arc heard. It never made heroic suggestions like "The Prime Minister's in trouble. Go save Canada." Lily was fairly certain that it wasn't the sort of voice crazy people heard. It didn't tell her to go kill anyone. This voice was irritating, sniggering, the voice of a persistent know-it-all who had somehow taken up residence in Lily's mind. The Voice wasn't audible. It was more like having an interior dialogue with a very pessimistic person. Whenever Lily tried to improve her life, this admonishing voice would burst into her thoughts and outline all the problems in painstaking detail, giving cogent reasons why she could never achieve her goals. The Voice was so logical that Lily inevitably succumbed to its authority. For all the advice it gave, none of it was helpful. It was always discouraging. Frustrated, Lily would suddenly lash out and commit some furious, desperate act. She needed to do something. Anything. Get drunk. Fail the exam. Break a leg. On these occasions, the Voice was silent.

⌒

SPIRIT INVASION IS a radical concept for the people of the twentieth century. The people in medieval times recognized evil spirits and they tried to exorcise them. In the twentieth century, we pretend they don't exist. Denial becomes a cogent means of dealing with life's displeasures. Exorcisms are still conducted in this century, mainly by Catholic priests. Accounts of successful exorcisms always state that the demon was rousted by the host crying out, "I love Jesus!" several times. The name, "Jesus," is apparently extremely offensive to demons and will send them scurrying out of a human host immediately. However, the human host has to really love Jesus, in order for the exorcism to work. He can't simply mouth the words. And as most human beings in the twentieth century are doubting heathens, they would be more likely inclined to query the chant with cynical apprehension: "I don't know Jesus. I've never met Jesus. How can I love Jesus when I don't know him?" So, the rationalists of this century get their demons and keep them, and perhaps that's all for the best.

How does one contract a demon? In many accounts, the demon was first encountered on a pleasant walk in the woods. "I suddenly looked around and I saw the beauty of the landscape. The wind was whistling in the trees and the grass was swaying. And everything was moving in unison and I was filled with joy and I felt myself at one with Nature." Now, one would think that this would be a spiritually uplifting experience, but according to the ex-possessed, this was the moment when the Demon entered their bodies. After this initial contact, the possessed would make many more trips to the woods: hiking excursions, rock-climbing expeditions and the like.

While this is disappointing news to those of us who love the great outdoors, there is no immediate cause for alarm. The woods have always been regarded as the dwelling place of pagan spirits. And pagan spirits, by virtue of their non-affiliation with a specific religion, must therefore be evil. Pagan spirits are, in fact, non-partisan. They go where the spirit moves them.

It seems unjust to vilify the woods for harbouring evil spirits. Nature herself is under attack, struggling to maintain herself against the onslaught of mock-pastoral housing complexes, suburban malls and other crass artifacts of civilization. It seems more likely that demons, like the rest of the world, joined the Industrial Revolution and went to the cities for their human prey. Demons are fond of boxes. They probably now reside in television sets and computers, patiently waiting for unwitting Pandoras to let them loose.

More specifically, how did Lily contract her demon? One has viruses inside one's body that can remain dormant for years and suddenly a haphazard series of cell mutations, can activate it. The virus springs into action, lethal, hell-bent for leather.

Lily never had a clear sense of herself. She shared her mother's womb with her twin brother, Paul, so she was used to accommodating others. Though her mind was rebellious and contrary, her soul was pliable. She was too willing to believe that other people knew best. Secretly, she resented their interference but she would always follow their lead. It was a confusing soul makeup because, to others, Lily appeared to be strong-minded and opinionated, a natural leader. However, her talent lay in rebellion, leading the revolt against a system that someone else had set up. She was, by nature, someone who could not create, only react. Lily's soul flowered when she was around other people. Through reacting to them, she came alive. It was a mutable happiness, depending so much on the nature of the interchange.

Lily had a calm, placid childhood. Her parents had their ambitions pinned on Paul. They did not expect much of Lily and so did not urge her to be more independent and strong-willed. They loved their cheerful, laughing, daughter. She was always amusing, always getting into some scrape or other. Lily's oldest sister, Rose, was the serious one in the family. Rose was going to be a nurse.

Adolescence is the best time for spirits to invade a human host. The body's endocrine system is working at full-tilt. Hormones are being shifted and rearranged. The body is in a state of chaos. The old lore recounts instances of incubi preying on young novitiates while they slept. This is how the Demon entered Lily.

One night, Lily had a particularly vivid dream. She dreamt that a young man approached her. He was wearing a dark, hooded cape. She drew nearer to look at his face. He had the most mesmerizing eyes — green and glistening like a cat. He caressed her, then drew in to kiss her. Lily allowed him to kiss her. She remembered thinking, "This is odd. In real life, I would never kiss a total stranger, but this is just a dream." The most unsettling aspect was that Lily did not enjoy the kiss. It wasn't like the time she kissed Peter Lawson in the hall closet. No, this was a vaguely repellent kiss. She drew away but the strange man tightened his hold on her. She was now almost awake, aware that she was lying down on her bed, aware that an entity of some sort was pressing down on her, suffocating her. She knew that it was very important that she wake up. She had to struggle with all her might to attain consciousness, because if she didn't, this man, creature, would engulf her.

Now, here is where a strong sense of personal self becomes useful. Other girls have had this dream and other girls have woken up. But Lily heard the man say, "I'm not going to hurt you. This isn't a rape. This is just a dream. Why are you being so silly? It's silly to be afraid. Why do you think you won't wake up? Of course, you'll wake up. People always wake up. You can always change the dream if you don't like it." In her gut, Lily knew that, however she changed the dream, it was still going to involve this man with his horrible, gleaming cat eyes. But she allowed herself to be swayed by his reason.

She relented a little and felt the man press further into her. "Now, that wasn't so bad, was it?" Lily could breathe again. She didn't have that strange constriction at her neck, the feeling of cotton wool being jammed in a ball and rammed down her throat. No, the cotton wool was gone. It had dispersed. Instead of a localized pressure, all of Lily's body felt slightly heavy, as if it had gained an interior weight. Lily fell into a deep sleep and had a very erotic dream involving the hooded man. They were floating in a carpet. Sometimes, he *was* the carpet. He was on top of her and he was underneath her and he was weightless, now.

When Lily woke up, she had no memory of the dream, but her body had uncovered a vague, restless yearning the Elizabethans would have called lust. Overnight, Lily's mind acquired a cynical, astute precociousness that would have frightened her parents had they sat down and had a conversation with her. Lily now saw, all too clearly, the baser aspects of the human heart. It was as though a filter had been put in front of her eyes. It enabled her to see with the distance and clarity of a hawk, but the filter was tinged with grey, so even though Lily saw more, nothing was as clear and beautiful as it was before.

To Lily's parents, the day passed uneventfully. It was a Saturday. Lily crashed in and out of the house, flinging doors open, always in a hurry, off to meet some friend or other. Lily had a lot of friends. Her best friend at the time, was a girl named Sonya Morris. Sonya was a gentle girl who liked Lily because she was so rambunctious. Lily was a tomboy. They were always going off on walks together, to find the perfect park to play in. On this particular day, Lily surprised Sonya by saying, "Let's get Jimmy Kerr to come with us."

Jimmy was an aggressive little boy who at some point during the long school day, inevitably did some awful thing to some unwitting little boy or girl: threw his tartan lunchbox at Sondra Lipchuk, its sharp metal corner narrowly missing her temple; threw two large rocks at Alden Turner, one cracking Alden sharply on the knee, the other hitting him smack in the solar plexus. Alden spent ten minutes, doubled over, gasping for air, certain he was going to die. Jimmy had a good aim. He was remorseless in his random antagonism. He had no grudge against Sondra or Alden. He just liked to practise his shots.

Like most sensible children, Sonya was terrified of Jimmy Kerr. She put an immediate veto on that plan and could not get over her astonishment that Lily had suggested it. Lily then said she knew of a wonderful park that was off the track from their usual route. They headed out. As they walked, Sonya had the horrible misgiving that their destination lay suspiciously in the vicinity of Jimmy Kerr's house. Lily assured Sonya that the park was nowhere near Jimmy Kerr's house, but lo and behold, who should they find in the park but the notorious Jimmy Kerr, himself. Jimmy's favourite day was Saturday because by then, he had the patina of a full week's dirt on his body. The challenge of getting Jimmy into a bath more than once a week (Sunday nights) was too much for Jimmy's mother, so she and the unsuspecting public were held ransom to Jimmy's stench. On the weekends, Jimmy could be smelled from twelve yards away. It was hard to ascertain what skin colour Jimmy had. He was dusty brown all over: an accumulation of years of summer tans that were never washed away; layers upon layers of epidermal bedrock, scabs, encrustations that were never disinfected, forming alternate layers of dermal substrata.

"Lily White! Lily White!" Jimmy planted himself in their path.

"Run!" Sonya whispered to Lily.

"It's all right," Lily replied, coolly.

Why should it be all right? Sonya's heart leaped to her throat and pounded there for a few minutes. To be alone in the park with Jimmy Kerr. No teacher to protect you. No principal to threaten him with the strap. Sonya glanced quickly around the park. There were no adults in sight. No one. Just them and Jimmy Kerr. Why in God's name should that be all right? Sonya did not say any of these things to Lily. She remained beside Lily as they continued walking towards Jimmy Kerr.

"Hey Lily, ya wanna fuck?"

Sonya knew that was a really bad word. She didn't know what it meant but she knew it was bad.

"Hey Jimmy, you know what 'fuck' means?" said Lily. Sonya thought that was an incredibly clever thing for Lily to say. Now it was Jimmy Kerr's turn to look embarrassed. "Tell me what it means, Jimmy." Lily boldly walked right up to Jimmy and stared him down.

"Um ...," Jimmy ignored Lily and lunged instead at Sonya. "Now or never!" This was an oft-used taunt, vaguely threatening and totally meaningless.

"Now!" said Lily. "How bout *now*, Jimmy Kerr."

Jimmy was entirely nonplussed by this strange turn of events. Girls always cried "Never!" and ran away when he delivered his ultimatum. Lily gave Jimmy a "come on" flip of her chin, spun around and walked slowly and deliberately to a low-slung weeping willow tree. The tree was very unusual in that it had bent in on itself so that the top of the tree was only six or seven feet off the ground, the long branches and leaves trailing along the ground, forming a tent-like canopy.

"It would make a perfect fort," Sonya marvelled to herself. It was a shame that Jimmy Kerr was here, spoiling their discovery.

Lily disappeared inside the tree. Jimmy followed as though in a trance, then stopped a few feet away from the tree.

"Are ya chicken, Jimmy?"

Lily was being very bold today, mused Sonya. What if Jimmy calls her bluff? Just as the thought crossed her mind, Jimmy walked resolutely into Lily's bower. Sonya knew she had to save her friend. She ventured tentatively to the tree. She heard the sounds of giggling, but it couldn't be Lily. It was a woman's throaty laugh.

"Lily?"

The giggling continued.

"Lily, are you okay?" Sonya tried to peer in. There was a sudden flurry of activity and Lily was gently pushing Sonya away.

"Go home, Sonya." Lily was flushed red all over her throat and across her cheeks. She was panting. Her lips were bright red and her eyes seemed small and glittery. "It's time you went home."

At school on Monday, Sonya was cool to Lily, but Lily neither noticed nor cared. It was as though there had never been a friendship between them. Sonya was simply no longer part of Lily's frame of reference. Jimmy Kerr had undergone a significant metamorphosis. In the first place, he was clean. Jimmy was not so smelly on Mondays because he had his bath on Sunday nights, but usually Jimmy's baths consisted of adding water to the dirt so that on Monday, his skin had the appearance and texture of caked mud that had been left to dry. But last night, Jimmy had actually washed with soap. Jimmy seemed uncomfortable with his new look. He was very nervous. He kept glancing at Lily, trying to catch her eye. At recess, he crossed into the girls' yard and grabbed her. The other girls and boys wisely kept their distance. For a moment, Jimmy regained his cheeky composure. He leered up at Lily. She was a good four inches taller than him.

"I'm gonna tell everyone! You're a whore!"

"Go ahead, Jimmy. Little Jimmy. Only little boys tell. Big boys keep their mouths shut."

"Why should I keep my mouth shut?"

Lily leaned in conspiratorially and whispered in Jimmy's ear, "'Cause, if you're lucky, maybe it'll happen again."

Jimmy did not say another word.

The Demon had its foothold in Lily but that didn't mean she was condemned to do its bidding. It was only a small demon and at present, could only make small suggestions. Lily had free will. She could choose to follow or reject the Demon's proposals. She did not become the school slut, although engaging in a sexual activity with Jimmy Kerr would seem to be a fast route to the position. The Demon liked dirty little boys. Lily did not. There was the initial daring thrill of going into the willow bower with a boy, but Lily had to contend with the fact that the boy was Jimmy Kerr. The air in the bower was close and Jimmy's rank odour overpowering. After fifteen minutes of unrestrained groping, Lily had to say, "Jimmy, you stink," and she hiked her underpants back up and left. The encounter with Jimmy in the schoolyard on Monday confirmed for Lily that she had to cultivate a secret life. She must keep these strange new urges separate from school.

AT THAT TIME, there was a new fad on the telephone system called a "hotline." One would dial a particular number. It would ring and no one would answer. While it was ringing, one could hear the ghostly voices of teenagers trying to get dates, shouting their hellos and phone numbers across the gentle whooshing sounds that accompanied the sound of a telephone ringing in the void. Lily's latest obsession was to dial the number and listen to the voices. It was eerie. It made her think this was the way dead people in a cemetery would communicate: bodiless entities whispering between the graves. At nights, the hotline was a busy crush of voices. Lily liked to call during the day. There weren't so many people trying to get through. One day, she heard a man calling out, "Anyone there?" and she answered. She called out her phone number to him, then hung up, trembling. The phone rang a few seconds later. She let it ring twice before she picked it up. She didn't want to appear over-eager, but if she waited too long, her mother might answer it.

"Hello."

"Hi," the man's voice was clear now. Often boys would call the hotline pretending to be men, but this was no boy. "What's your name?"

"Lily."

"Nice name."

"Thanks. What's yours?"

"Steve."

"Oh." There was an uncomfortable pause.

"Well, Lily, shall we get down to brass tacks? How old are you?"

"Oh, um ...." Lily was twelve. She busily calculated how old she could appear to be. "Sixteen."

"You sound a little younger than that, Lily, but I like younger girls."

"You do?"

"A lot. So much I won't even ask you what your measurements are."

Measurements? What did he mean by that? Lily suddenly remembered. "36-24-36," she said.

Steve laughed, "That's cute. Well, Lily, how 'bout a date?"

"Um ...." Lily's heart was racing. Was she out of her mind? How was she going to go out on a date?

As if reading her mind, Steve said, "I guess it wouldn't be a good idea if I came to your house. Why don't we go to a movie on Thursday afternoon? How 'bout *The Sound of Music* at the Uptown? I'll meet you there at one o'clock."

"Okay," said Lily.

"How will I know you?"

"I have red hair," Lily blurted out, then quietly cursed herself for making it impossible for her to spy on him before revealing her identity. "How will I know you?" she asked, too late.

"I'll be the good-looking guy looking for the redhead."

"No. What do you look like?"

"Told you. Good-looking."

"Brown hair? Black hair?"

"Brown."

"How old are you?"

"Eighteen. Tell you what, Lily. I'll wear my Varsity sweater. How's that? Think you'll be able to find me then?"

"Okay."

The Demon was hoping for a lurid sexual encounter, but Lily simply wanted an adventure. She called her new friend, Suzy Budgins, who lived several blocks away and did not attend Lily's school, told her all about the hotline and Steve and suggested that Suzy Budgins come with her to spy on him.

"He won't be looking for two girls. I'll put a scarf over my head to hide my hair and if we like him, we'll tell him who we are."

"Ooooh!" squealed Suzy Budgins with delight. Suzy would have made a far more conducive host for the Demon than Lily. Suzy, truly, was sex-crazed. Her body had exploded into a voluptuous woman's figure overnight. Her breasts bounced up and down with abandon every time she moved. They could not and would not be contained in the stern bras her mother bought her. While Suzy's body was a feast to contemplate, her face left a lot to be desired. Suzy had large buck teeth covered in a maze of flashing, silver-wire braces, small rabbit eyes that appeared even smaller behind her thick, pointy-framed glasses and two enormous ears that came out at right angles to her head. Suzy's frizzy hair, thankfully, concealed the ears.

The major impediment to the rendezvous was Steve's choice of film. *The Sound of Music* seemed, to Lily, a curious choice for a movie for a first date. It was a romantic musical about nuns and Nazis and was extremely popular with most twelve-year-old girls, Suzy Budgins being the exception.

"*The Sound of Music*?! That sucks! He must be a perv."

"Why do you think he's a perv?"

"He chose a kiddie film to keep you happy while he does stuff."

"Does stuff?"

"Yeah, you know — feels you up."

"Say Steve isn't a perv. Say he's only a year or two older than us. You're saying he'd pick another movie."

"Yeah. He'd pick one he'd want to see."

"And he wouldn't try and feel me up."

"Well, he might."

"So, the only difference between a perv doing something to you and some jerk-off boy our own age is that with the perv, it's a film we like."

"You might like it. I hate *The Sound of Music*."

"Ya gotta come with me, Suzy. You're my cover."

"I don't know ..."

"We'll get to skip school."

"Okay."

On Thursday morning, Lily and Suzy went to their respective schools. At lunch, they pretended to have stomach flu, thus establishing an excellent alibi for the afternoon. Lily ran over to Suzy's house to prepare for the date. Suzy's mother worked in an office during the day. Usually, Suzy resented her absence but there were times when it came in handy.

Lily's main obstacle to looking sixteen was her unformed twelve-year-old body. She decided she would go for the sophisticated waif look that was popular at the time. In the waif look, the main difference between a twelve-year-old and a sixteen-year-old was the amount of makeup one applied. Lily dusted her face with white powder, put a rim of black eyeliner all around her eyes, making little downward branches on the lower lid. The black twig-like lines around the eyes coupled with Lily's flaming red hair made her look like a live Raggedy Ann doll. Lily was not entirely happy with the effect. Suzy offered Lily her mother's high heels to appease her.

Suzy had no trouble looking older than her years. She opted for a French look. She owned the requisite navy-blue and white striped

jersey. She added a short navy-blue skirt, red shoes and net stockings (net stockings were very French) and inadvertently followed a
more traditional line of French apparel, that of the French whore.
Lily and Suzy studied themselves in the mirror and practised the
gestures with which they would enthrall Steve. Just as they were
about to leave, Lily experienced a surge of panic and insisted that
they put trench coats on so they could disappear into the crowd,
which would have been a clever thing to do had there been a crowd
at the Thursday afternoon screening of *The Sound of Music*.

Steve was glaringly apparent, being the only man present under
the age of sixty-five and wearing a bright red Varsity sweater. Suzy
and Lily spied on him from a safe distance while he paced up and
down waiting for his date. It was hard for the girls to ascertain
Steve's age and possible intentions. While it was patently obvious
that he wasn't a teenager, he didn't seem old enough, in the girl's
eyes, to qualify as a pervert. As they had dressed to make themselves
appear older, Steve had decked himself out in the clothes of his youth:
his sweater, saddle shoes and checked pants. The clothes had likely
been lying in a rumpled moth-eaten pile at the bottom of a closet
for some time. Whereas they might have fit Steve the boy, they no
longer fit Steve the man. Their air of brash innocence was completely at odds with the predatory guile of the man he had become.
Steve paced impatiently in front of the theatre. He stopped and
scanned the surrounding area.

"He's seen us," squealed Suzy.

"Don't move."

Steve did a small pantomime of giving up the wait and going
elsewhere. He headed down the street towards Suzy and Lily, but
as he was looking in the far distance, apparently preoccupied, Suzy
and Lily remained where they were. Steve walked past them, then
stopped, fumbled in his pockets and pulled out a package of
cigarettes and a lighter. He was having some trouble lighting his cigarette so he pulled into the shelter of the wall, which happened to

be exactly where Lily and Suzy huddled. Steve took a long pull on his cigarette, then said to Suzy, "Well, Lily, are we going to see this movie or not?"

"I'm ... not ... Lily," Suzy stammered.

"I'll even take your friend. What's your name?" Steve leaned over and smiled at Lily. Steve had gleaming white teeth and familiar eyes. Lily didn't like his eyes.

"Her name's Suzy," Suzy volunteered, relishing the opportunity for confusion.

"So, are ya coming? The movie's starting."

"You're not eighteen," Lily observed.

"You girls aren't sixteen. So we make up a few stories on the phone."

"How old are you?"

"Not that old."

"How old?"

"Twenty-one." The girls scrutinized Steve. "Ya coming or not? I'm paying."

"Okay," said Suzy as she allowed herself to be led to the theatre.

"Okay," said Lily as she hurried to catch up. The balcony was closed. Steve was disappointed. He liked to sit in the balcony. He bought them both popcorn and candy and pop and guided them to an area off to one side and at the back. Suzy wanted to sit in the middle, close to the front. Steve grudgingly obliged but insisted that he sit between them.

The movie had already started. Julie Andrews was singing and running around on the mountain peak. Suzy Budgins noisily chomped on her popcorn. Steve didn't buy any for himself. He said they would share. Steve kept dropping pieces of his popcorn into Lily's lap. He'd then retrieve them and apologize. Once, he took a very long time in finding the popcorn piece, till Lily finally found it and handed it to him. Steve then helped himself to Suzy's popcorn. In the middle of the scene between the young girl and her Nazi boyfriend, Steve lost something. It fell underneath Suzy's chair.

Lily glanced over at Steve crawling on the ground. It was hard to relax and enjoy a film in the company of a sexual pervert, wondering at any moment if you might be molested. She was bored with the film and annoyed by Steve's antics. Time to go. Suzy kicked Steve in the face and the two of them leapt up and ran out of the theatre. They'd eaten the popcorn, drunk the pop and wisely put their candy in a safe place.

Though the dull and rather sordid incident with Steve deterred Lily from making further dates through the hotline, it did not stop her from listening to other people calling their phone numbers over the phantom line. A longing rose in Lily as she listened. She assumed that these teenagers were meeting attractive counterparts; that it was Lily's bad luck to wind up with shabby, dismal Steve. Lily started to see the world as a place where other people succeeded and she failed. Instead of maintaining a healthy skepticism about what was on offer, Lily felt she had been deprived of a natural right to happiness.

IT WAS THE Demon's idea to work at Hydro. Lily had originally planned to try for a summer job with a newspaper. "You think you'll just be able to walk in there and get a job. Everyone wants to work for newspapers," cautioned the Demon.

Lily had the specious privilege of being born when a lot of other babies were born, forever consigned to a demographic bubble known as the Baby Boom. Nothing was available to her because there was always harsh competition from the other members of the bubble. Her Darwinian counterparts were swift of hand and fleet of foot. While Lily was scratching her head, idly speculating about interesting summer jobs, these devious, forward-thinking individuals had submitted their applications years ago.

"You need to find a job that nobody else wants. Those are the jobs that pay. Your dad's got connections at Hydro. Go there."

The Demon was correct, in one respect. The position of girl Friday at Toronto Hydro Power Authority was a job that nobody in their right mind would want. However, contrary to the Demon's assurances, it did not pay well. Having drawn upon her father's business acquaintances to procure this undesirable job, Lily was now morally bound to remain there. It was tedious but it served a purpose. Eventually, she would try and break into journalism.

Each year there was a stampede for summer work and each year the prestigious jobs went to the bright students who showed promise. Lily's promises were bankrupt but in her last year of high school, she set about to change the patterns of a lifetime. She found that, through unremitting diligence and hard work, she could scrape together a grade average that enabled her to apply for university.

Lily was so excited about going to university that she didn't give much thought as to what she was going to study once she was there. Her father suggested that she apply for a degree in business. It seemed as good a choice as any.

Having sorted out her profession, Lily's parents debated over where she should live. Her mother suggested that Lily live in KAT House. What Lily lacked in intellectual prowess, she made up for in social graces. People liked Lily and Lily liked people — that was her downfall. Many of the young men in her business classes belonged to a fraternity so Lily's life at university was one glorious social whirl after another, her classes providing a pleasant backdrop for all this activity.

Lily garnered the reputation of being a sexual tease, which stood her in good stead with the sorority sisters but kept the eligible young men at bay. Lily would not curtail her cherished freedom by tying herself down to one man. Life was still a game to her and Lily was, by nature, playful. In some ways, Lily would have been wise to have taken a cue from the socially regressive members of her sorority: recognize her academic deficiencies and set her sights on marrying one of the more ambitious of these young men; find herself a good provider.

Lily failed her first year business courses so she switched to a Bachelor of Arts degree. Her father remarked that a BA was useless but to Lily, any degree would do as long as she could continue to live the student's life. She vowed to do better in her second year but once again found the extracurricular activities irresistible. In an attempt to defuse her parents' ongoing disapproval, Lily signed up for courses on subjects that they knew nothing about, thus rendering them impotent to comment on her status.

Though it was a conversational icebreaker to say you studied anthropology, the subject itself bored her silly. Who could remember the names of all those tribes? It seemed to her that anthropology books were always omitting the most salient details. She read an entire book on one tribe and didn't discover till the last chapter that they were cannibals and they ate their own shit. Deep-fried and wrapped in banana leaves. Tribes, as a whole, were either warlike and unbelievably bad-tempered or peaceful and well-adjusted. Individuals didn't seem to be taken into account. Perhaps they changed tribes. If Lily were a bad-tempered member of a peaceful tribe, her tribe might tell her to join that nasty tribe down the river. Perhaps, in anthropological terms, that was the tribal equivalent of being told to work at Toronto Hydro Power Authority for the rest of your life.

All told, Lily spent seven summers at Toronto Hydro and three years at university and acquired mere passing grades in a smattering of unrelated courses. Her father pulled the plug on Lily's university education and she returned that summer to Hydro to work there permanently until she could sort herself out.

Lily loathed her job at Hydro. It represented everything she was trying to avoid: hard, dull work, miserable, discontented people (herself and her co-workers), monotony and routine. A boxed-up life for boxed-in people. Lily was suspended in mid-air, her ultimate fate; the slow but inevitable journey to lifetime secretarial work, the spider of nine to five, waiting in the centre of the web as Lily kept putting one sticky foot in front of the other.

chapter five

ENTRE-ACTE

HOW DID PEOPLE get lives? Jay often wondered. It seemed to Jay that life was something that fell upon you suddenly. One moment, you had so much spare time, you bored yourself silly. A mere three years later, you could find yourself married, with a child and another one on the way. Jay was at the free-agent stage. She knew it wouldn't take much to alter her life forever. Falling in love seemed to be the main route to taking on life's responsibilities.

Jay got a bit of a shock when she first looked around the room at her fellow art students. It was a very small class, only seven students. They weren't like the eager, young, confident people in her art classes at university. And they certainly weren't like the 'girls' in KAT House. No, these people were old. They'd been around life's blocks several times. It was pretty obvious they didn't sit around, wondering what life had in store for them. They were thrust into it, head-first and screaming.

These people had secrets. Each of them nursed some hidden pain.

Jay was keenly aware that she had no secrets, painful or otherwise. She was intimidated by their sadness.

The school offered the summer session as an experiment. Only fifteen students enrolled. Eight of those students were returning for their second year. Although they were financially accounted for, they never appeared. Like Jay, these students were from upper-middle-class families. The parents viewed the two years at art school as a fob to satisfy their sons' and daughters' cravings for adventure before settling down to their rightful destiny: entering a profession and raising a family in a nice upper-middle-class neighbourhood. They hoped that by witnessing, first-hand, the day-to-day squalor of life as an artist, their children would realize that being an artist was, indeed, a singularly stupid and worthless endeavour.

What the parents had not counted on was that the artist-instructors were not, in fact, poor, but quite well-off, and in addition, possessed a zest for living that was intoxicating. The parents had not reckoned on the lurid appeal of the artists' life and were most distressed when their sons and daughters embraced La Vie Boheme and became drug addicts and alcoholics in the process.

The second-year students were too preoccupied with their new lives as budding geniuses to attend classes. Their absence annoyed the artist-instructors who preferred their worshipping disciples to be present. Where was the fun in promoting La Vie Boheme if there was no one around to inflict it on? They vented their frustration on the students who remained. They were not impressed by their sad, secret lives and bluntly referred to them as "that bunch of losers."

After the first week of school, Jay resigned herself to the fact that she would not embark upon a torrid romance that summer. Jonathan was the most likely candidate in that he was tall and resoundingly male, but Jay found his blatant masculinity unnerving. He walked with his legs turned out and slightly apart, as though there was no room for all his manhood to be gracefully accommodated. Jonathan's friend, Susannah, had signed up for classes as well. She had no ambitions, whatsoever, to succeed in the art world. She was there because Jonathan was there. Susannah was very voluptuous, only a few years older than Jay, but decades older in sensibility. Jay took an immediate dislike to her and, as often happens with people one dislikes, wound up spending an inordinate amount of time with her because she and Jonathan were the only students in the class who were friendly.

Consuela was from Spain and had some grim secret that she kept to herself. Jay had tried to make friends with her but it was difficult, for they had nothing in common. Consuela was thirty-five years old and had a small child. She could neither paint nor draw and didn't care if she learned. She told Jay that she'd gone to art school to take her mind off "tings." She pronounced "tings" in such a dark manner that Jay was nervous about enquiring further.

Brian and Sheila formed a tight little unit that brooked no interference. They pretended to be friendly but Sheila didn't like it if anyone talked to Brian, and as Sheila didn't want to talk to anyone other than Brian, few people spoke to them for long.

In sensibility, Michael was the most likely match for Jay. He had the haunted eyes and eccentric manner of a possible romantic candidate but he was only seventeen years old. He had attended a series of boys' private schools before winding up at the art school. He wore his tattered navy-blue school blazer to demonstrate his disdain for the moneyed Establishment, at the same time alerting everyone to the fact that he had once been a member, however disenchanted he was now. In many ways, Michael reminded Jay of Nicholas. However, she could not seriously entertain a romantic liaison with a school boy.

The second-year students were mysteriously absent from classes but Jay retained some hope that her future lover lay in those ranks.

⌒

LILY RELIVED THE events of the last night, turning them over in her mind, examining them from every angle. There was something exquisitely luxurious about the way Brad undressed her, as if he were unwrapping an expensive, perishable present; the way he gazed at her, his eyes dark and luminous. One of her bosses, Mrs. Hinckley, handed her a stack of cards to file. These contained the names, addresses and pertinent information of every citizen in the province, all devoted consumers of Hydro Power. Every month or so, Lily took out the old card and replaced it with a new card. She pondered on the sheer stupidity of the task. She wondered whether her job would make more sense if she worked in a smaller office — say a real-estate company. The paperwork would at least be connected to something tangible. Whereas, Hydro, what was Hydro? It was a monolithic organization devoted to power: water power, electric power, the buying, selling and leasing of power. And who was she? Some little minion hauling stones to put another slab in the pyramid. Except at Hydro, there was no pyramid. You worked and your labour counted for nothing.

Lily had several bosses. It was impossible to keep track of them all. Lily didn't respect her bosses since it was painfully obvious that their working life was just as miserable as hers. There were no advantages to being a boss. The bosses didn't have offices. They had cubicles. Status was determined by the height and breadth of the grey slabs of carpeted foam surrounding one's desk. Mrs. Hinckley had been promoted, so her slabs were raised six inches. She was also given an extra foot of space around the desk. Lily couldn't get over how easily people were fobbed off with small rewards. Mrs. Hinckley was so busy organizing the details of her newly acquired space that she did not notice Lily taking small catnaps at the reception desk. Lily daydreamed about what Brad was likely to do next. She presumed he would break up with Susan Lipton.

And here, we have one of the many differences between the sexes. For Lily, the events of last night had changed her life irrevocably. For Brad, they'd hardly made a dent. He would continue dating Susan Lipton. Assuming that she had, in fact, gone to bed and not been witness to his extravagant act of rebellion, he would crawl on his knees in abject misery, beg forgiveness and carry out a series of meaningless penances to win himself back in her favour. If she had seen him, then the game was over. There would be no forgiveness. There was the pleasing possibility that Susan would not tell him if she had seen him, in which case, they would both pretend it never happened, though he would still have to stage an excessive apologia for skipping out on her at the party. For Brad, the difficulties in maintaining a relationship for which he had no true interest substituted for passion.

Brad conducted his life the way most young men of his social class did. He was fairly intelligent. He knew that he would eventually get a good job that would pay him a great deal of money. He needed a helpmate in these matters and he'd found one in Susan. He hadn't needed to think or feel deeply about anything in his life to date. Why should he suddenly start? Brad believed that men and women were a different species. Men wanted wealth and careers. Women wanted babies so a healthy compromise was reached through marriage. Certainly, there were women who wanted money but they were fairly easy to spot and Brad was secure enough in his good looks not to be flattered into taking one of them on.

Though he was quite willing to proclaim that he felt no love for her, Brad would never admit that Susan Lipton bored him senseless. He began the long, slow, arduous process of winning her back. First, he needed to establish how much Susan knew. He should call Lily and suss things out. Where did she work? She mentioned something about a job. He could either call KAT House or Paul to get the number. Caught between a rock and a hard place, he called Paul. Things were still awkward between them. He made some small talk, promised to drop by sometime next week, casually adding that Lily had offered to type up one of this term papers and he needed her work number. Paul didn't buy the excuse but he didn't ask any questions. Brad steeled himself to call Lily. As he waited for the operator to transfer him, he reminded himself that it wasn't a personal call. However, as soon as she answered, his heart leaped into his throat.

"Hello. Lily MacFarlane here."

"Hi. It's me."

"Oh!"

"Surprised to hear from me?"

"Well, yes."

"Just had to talk to you. How're you doing?"

"Oh, fine. I'm at work." Lily instantly regretted saying that.

"Oh, okay. I guess I better go."

"No! No. It's quiet right now." All the lights on the switchboard suddenly flashed for her attention. "Oh, back in a sec." Lily quickly put the other lines on hold so they could talk undisturbed. She clicked back onto Brad's line.

"Everything okay?"

"Yeah."

"No trouble?"

"No."

"I felt bad leaving you to face her alone."

"She wasn't awake."

"Oh." Brad tried not to let the massive wave of relief alter his voice. Time to bow out gracefully. "We were both pretty drunk last night."

"I wasn't drunk," Lily said firmly.

"God, you weren't? You're always like that?!"

"Always."

"Wow. Well, let's get together again, sometime."

"Yes, let's." When? Lily was dying to ask. Boys were always vague on this salient point.

"I'll call you."

But you're calling me, now! Lily wanted to protest. Mrs. Hinckley strode up to the reception desk and glared at Lily. Instead, Lily said "I'm afraid she's not in right now. Can I take a message?"

"Boss?"

"Yes."

"Write this down: I'd like to fuck you senseless."

"Yes, yes, I'll tell her." Lily suppressed a giggle and hung up.

"No personal calls at the office, Miss MacFarlane."

"But —"

Mrs. Hinckley leaned over, untied the lines and stomped away. The switchboard flashed incessantly, its electric libido unplugged. Lily's body went through the motions of answering lines and transferring calls, while her mind busily dissected the substance of Brad's call. She wondered why Brad didn't make a definite date. He sounded as if he couldn't get enough of her, yet Lily had this vague, unsettled feeling that something was not quite right. Lily decided to avoid the sorority house for a few days. She had lost her nerve to duke it out with Susan Lipton. She would let Brad break up with Susan and she would stay away till it was done. Lily hated it when she had to do all the planning, but men were hopeless at scheming. They had no knack for it.

~

JONATHAN HAD SET up a large canvas in the corner of the studio. Susannah lay curled up on a mattress on the floor. Jay was surprised at their audacity. They occupied the studio as if it were their private loft.

"You're painting here?"

"There aren't many of us. I can always move next door when that room's free."

"Oh," said Jay. "I paint at home. Don't you find it hard to paint in public?"

"Public? What do you mean?"

"Everyone walking in, looking at your work, commenting on it, all that stuff. Doesn't it put you off?"

"No. I like it. It's feedback."

"I don't mind feedback when I've finished something. But when I'm still figuring it out, it drives me crazy."

"Oh well, we're different."

Susannah glanced lazily at Jonathan to make sure he wasn't flirting with Jay.

"Do you have any feedback for me?" Jonathan asked Jay.

"You've put the charcoal on way too thick. It'll be hard to take it out."

"Take it out?"

"Yes. When you do the line painting over top."

"I'm not going to take it out."

"It'll wreck your painting."

"Ah, you're one of those people who can't stand change. The charcoal is integral to the piece. I can't understand why more artists don't incorporate charcoal into the finished painting."

"They have their reasons."

"Like what?"

"Well, the obvious one. The charcoal's going to ruin your colour."

"Yes, well, I knew about that," Jonathan replied huffily. "Any other problems?"

The charcoal would react with the oil paint and would, in time, destroy the painting. "None that need concern you," Jay replied.

"Do you paint?" asked Susannah, as she roused herself from her stupor.

"Yes," said Jay. "I do."

"Could you show me sometime?" Jonathan swung around from his painting in surprise. "Jonathan's too busy," Susannah added.

"Sure," said Jay.

"Thanks." Susannah lifted her head and smiled up at Jay. She had heavy-lidded eyes and her mouth hung open, slightly in a daze, giving the impression that she had just tumbled out of bed.

"Susannah wants to learn how to paint realistically. You strike me as a realist."

"Yes, I am."

"Realism's dead, you know."

"Yes, that's what they tell me."

"You disagree?"

"I don't have an opinion," Jay lied. At university, the teachers always began by announcing that Realism was dead.

"You have a tone, you know," said Jonathan.

"A tone."

"Yeah, you say one thing but it feels like you mean something else."

"I'm very polite. It's a fault these days."

"Sarcasm. You're sarcastic, aren't you?"

"Sure, why not? I'm a sarcastic Realist. Are you happy now that you've pigeonholed me?"

"You can strike back. What would you say I am?"

"Ambitious."

Jonathan bobbed his head in agreement. "Yeah, that's right. I am ambitious. I'm going to turn this town inside out." Susannah gazed up at him in admiration. She had heard this speech many times and never tired of it.

Jay burst out laughing. "I can't believe you said that."

"You have to believe in yourself."

"I guess so, but do you think it's wise to tell everyone?"

"Tell everyone what?" inquired Sheila, pertly, as she and Brian hurried in to set up their places.

"Nothing," said Jonathan.

Susannah dragged herself up and adjusted her dress, smoothing it out over her body. Susannah claimed to be a hippie. She wore the granny glasses and the loose flowing dresses but there was a rampant sexuality to Susannah that hippie girls, in general, did not possess. Hippie girls engaged in sex frequently and, probably because of this, they were curiously asexual in their dealings with others. Sex was reduced to a function; no more mysterious or forbidding than eating a meal. Hippie girls tended not to be flirtatious. Susannah prided herself on her sexual allure. Her flimsy cotton hippie frocks had plunging necklines and her ample breasts serendipitously fell out, from time to time. Susannah stretched and yawned. The men watched her breasts rise and fall with the motion. "God, is this IT?!" she proclaimed. "Is this IT for our class? Isn't anyone else gonna show up?"

"There's Consuela and Michael," said Jay.

"No — I mean, there's no one here. It's so small. What happened to the others?"

"They're in second year. I guess they don't bother coming."

"I wish they would. It's too small."

Michael stumbled into the room, his clothes in wild disarray. "Christ! I almost got robbed! I walk up Spadina every day and I see this old bum. And he asks me for a quarter and I always say I don't have one. And I don't know, I figure everything's fine between us. I see him today and he grabs me by my lapels, pulls out a knife and screams, 'GIMMEE A QUARTER!'"

"He only asked for a quarter?" remarked Jay.

"Yeah, pretty weird, eh? He's got the knife and everything. He could have asked for a lot more."

"So did you give it to him?"

"Didn't have one."

"You didn't have a quarter?!"

"No. I'm flat broke. The guy went through my pockets, turned them inside out. Then, he sat down on the pavement and cried. I said, 'Sorry, buddy.' I felt bad for him." The others agreed. Jay made a mental note not to walk alone down Spadina.

"I wonder if the teacher's gonna show up today," said Sheila. "He's a half hour late already."

"They're always late," grumbled Brian.

"Who is it today?"

Jay pulled out a schedule from her bag. "Dennis Sherman," she read aloud.

"Oh no, not Dennis Sherman!" cried Jonathan in alarm.

"He never stopped talking last time."

"I had to leave at four. He went on?" asked Jay.

"On? For hours! We didn't get out till seven."

"I had to crack his back," added Jonathan. "I had to lift him up in the air and shove my knee into him."

"Then he lay on his stomach and we had to walk on top of him," said Susannah.

"And he still kept on talking."

"Shit! We better get out of here before he shows up," said Brian, decisively.

"Oops, I'm sorry. I read last week by mistake. Today it's abstract expressionism painting with Harold Bowen."

"Every class is abstract expressionism," Sheila complained.

"Better than conceptual art. At least, you get to draw from a model," said Jay.

"She's late, too," Brian observed.

Meana the Model shuffled into the room and gave everyone an evil look. Jay was thoroughly intimidated by Meana. The models at Jay's university art classes were pleasant, young, female students, earning a little spending money on the side. The models at the Artists School were, for the most part, derelicts. Meana stripped as soon as she arrived; a habit Jay found distasteful. Most models waited until the instructor officially started the class. Meana belonged to some arcane religious cult that advocated nudity. She was skinny and belligerent, adept at using her nakedness to unnerve people. She had taken a vow of silence but wore bells all over her body. She thrust her emaciated wrist into Michael's face and rang her bracelet bells at him.

"Oh God, what now?" Michael moaned.

"I think she wants you to get the model mattress for her," observed Susannah, who had just been lying on it. Meana shook her head up and down vigorously — her earrings and necklace bells jingling furiously. Michael hauled the mattress over while Meana hopped up and down in delight.

A short, plump older man appeared in the doorway. He clutched a styrofoam coffee cup. His face fell when he saw Meana. Meana danced gaily over to him, bobbing up and down, as if saying a thousand Hosannas.

"Yeah, hi, Meana. Great to see you, too." The man pulled a small silver flask out of his pocket, unscrewed it and poured its contents into the coffee cup. "Morning everyone. I'm Harold Bowen." He wandered into the room. "There's a record player around here some-where, isn't there?" Jonathan pointed it out. Harold Bowen handed him a record. "Put that on for me, will you?" He glanced at the students and gave a long sigh. "We're playing it loose today." Latin American jazz rhythms filled the air. The students looked at each other in puzzlement. Meana took her usual sitting-Buddha pose. Harold Bowen grimaced. "You're gonna have to move today, Meana. Slowly dance to the beat. Yeah. Ring those bells. But don't spoil the music." Meana grinned and started to dance. Harold Bowen motioned for the students to begin. He ambled over to a chair at the back of the room, sat down and took a large swig from his coffee cup.

⌒

LILY'S MOTHER WAS not pleased to see her. "Oh. You've come home. For how long?"

"Just for a couple of days."

"What have you done?"

"Nothing. Why do you always assume that I've done something wrong?"

"I'm sorry, dear. I wish you'd given me some warning. I've just got dinner ready and there isn't enough. Paul's home, too."

"Oh. Right. I forgot."

"He stays here when it's hot. He likes to swim." As if on cue, Paul strode past in his bathing suit. He grunted something to Lily — or was it to their mother? "Would you be a dear and just buy another chop for yourself? And another vegetable, broccoli. Oh, no, Paul hates broccoli."

"I don't like it, either," said Lily.

"Corn — yes — a package of corn."

"Yes, yes." Lily was exhausted and wanted nothing more than to fall asleep in her old bed, but she drove out to the huge subur-ban supermarket to buy herself a dinner that she'd be too tired to eat.

Lily didn't know why Paul disliked her. It had been like that since they started school. She'd assumed it was one of those phases that boys go through but as they grew older, Paul remained as distant and unfriendly as ever. Paul never told people he had a twin sister. He acted as if her presence were a constant rebuke to him. She remembered so clearly the days when they were each other's best and only friend. When they were very little and shared a bedroom, they'd wake up in the morning and find they'd had the same dream. Paul would begin the dream and Lily would tell him what happened next. Paul would be astonished and go on with the next section, as if to test her out. But Lily knew. Lily always knew what was going to happen next.

Paul was the more feminine of the two. He was beautifully formed. His face had a doll-like quality: bright, blue eyes, long, black lashes, small rosebud lips and a white, creamy complexion. He was small and trim, whereas Lily was tall and ungainly. In their games of house and dress-up, Lily always played the man. Paul didn't mind. He liked wearing his mother's clothes and pretending he was a girl. When they first attended grade school, Lily made the mistake of telling the other children that Paul liked to play dress-up. She meant no harm by it. The words simply fell out of her mouth. Jimmy Kerr, who'd taken great offence to Paul's childish beauty, seized upon it and teased Paul unmercifully.

"Hey, pretty boy. Isn't he pretty? He's just like a girl. How come, eh? How come? How come he's so pretty and his twin sister's so ugly? How come?"

That day, Paul walked home all by himself, leaving Lily at the mercy of Jimmy Kerr and his gang. He demanded that he be sent to another school, a private school. Tuition for a boys' private school was costly. Mr. MacFarlane balked at the idea. Paul threw a series of temper tantrums until his father relented and agreed to send him to one of the less expensive boys' schools.

Where Lily had no memory for slights, Paul could hold a grudge for years. From that day hence, he turned his back on his twin and pretended she didn't exist. When he did deign to refer to their kinship, it was only to point out Lily's flaws.

"You know, there are two eggs growing in the mummy's tummy. That's what twins are."

"I know that," said Lily, who didn't know but hated to appear stupid in front of her brother.

"Sometimes one egg splits in two. Then we would have been exactly the same. We would have both looked like me. Or like you. But I think we would have looked like me. But we're two separate eggs. And we had to share the tummy. Right?"

"Right. You and I were sharing Mummy's tummy," Lily smiled at Paul, hoping that this was leading up to a reconciliation.

"And it's a small space, right?"

"Right."

"So, things get divided up."

"Yeah?"

"So, like, you're bigger than me, right?"

"Yeah."

"Well, you got the size but I got the brains."

"Why can't things be even?"

"'Cause they're not. You're bigger. Look at yourself."

"Then why couldn't I have gotten the brains, too?"

"'Cause it doesn't work that way. I'm the small one. You're the big one. I'm the smart one. You're the dumb one."

"I don't think I'm dumb."

"Well, no. That's the point. Dumb people never know they're dumb."

Over the years, Lily grew accustomed to being mistreated by her brother. So she was most surprised, on her return from the supermarket, when he motioned airily for her to come out and join him at the pool.

"I want to talk to you."

"Great. How've you been? It's been years." Lily knew that perhaps this was not the right moment for sarcasm, but it slipped out
before she could stop it.

"What are you doing with Brad?"

"Pardon?"

"What are you doing with Brad?"

"Um, nothing. Why?"

"He asked me for your office number."

"Oh. I wondered how he got it."

"You're up to something."

"Everyone's so suspicious of me. Anyway, what if I am? What's
it to you?"

"He's my best friend."

"So?"

"So, stay out of my life."

"I'm not allowed to talk to your friends?!"

"Just back off."

"What is it with you? Everything's always 'Mine, mine, stay
away.'"

"I don't want you messing around in my life. Let him find someone else to type up his term papers."

"To what?"

"Type up his term papers."

"That's what he told you?"

"Christ! I knew it. You're sleeping with him."

"Well, I don't type!"

"Christ, do you have to screw every single guy in my frat house?"

"I am not screwing every —"

"Dinner's ready!" Mrs. MacFarlane's voice chimed out to the
pool. Looking at the twins, rapt in conversation, she thought how
nice it was to see the two of them getting along for a change.

JAY LIKED MR. BOWEN'S class — at least it was lively. She didn't particularly like abstract expressionist paintings but she could see they were a lot of fun to paint. You got drunk, listened to loud music and painted your head off. It didn't have much form or content, but there was lots of passion.

Jay distrusted passion. Nicholas liked to talk about passion and Dionysus and how he was a Dionysian, albeit, a recent convert.

"Nietzsche. It's all in Nietzsche. He saw it coming. He predicted it."

"Didn't Nietzsche go crazy?" Jay tried to ask politely. More and more often, Nicholas allied himself with lunatics.

"So what if he did?"

"Well, I would think that would mean that we shouldn't take anything he said too seriously. And wasn't he a Nazi, too?"

"No. He was NOT a Nazi."

"Well, didn't Hitler use his theory about the Superman to —"

"Why are you taking all those history classes? You should study philosophy."

"I'm not interested in philosophy."

"You should be. You should broaden your mind."

"Are you taking courses you don't like?"

"No. But I have a wide variety of interests."

"Just because I don't know much about Nietzsche doesn't mean —"

"You don't know zip about Nietzsche. If you did, you'd realize that our culture is changing from an Apollonian one to a Dionysian one."

"Well, big deal. Who cares?"

"*You* should. You're an Apollonian. You're going to be obsolete in twenty years."

"Well, if you keep doing all those drugs, you're going to be dead, so who's winning that race?" Jay replied, smugly.

"That's a typically Apollonian thing to say. Look around you.

It's all about emotional surrender. Giving in to the moment. Losing yourself."

"Drinking yourself into a stupor."

"Well, yeah. That's part of it. That's essential to the Dionysian culture. He was the god of wine."

"Wait a minute. Is that where everyone gets really drunk and they have an orgy and kill the king?"

"That's a simple-minded way of putting it."

"They chop him up into little pieces."

"Dismemberment. So the king's life-force will dissolve and be distributed through the community."

"That's what we're all going to become? Cannibals?"

"They weren't cannibals. Who told you that?"

"Theatre history. Chopping someone up and distributing him sounds like —"

"Theatre history," scoffed Nicholas. "No wonder you're confused." He rummaged through his bookshelves, grabbed some books, and thrust them into Jay's arms. Most of them were by Nietzsche, though he included a few science fiction novels to brighten up the workload. Jay didn't like science fiction. However, she always read the books Nicholas gave her. They provided some sort of access into his mind, though they didn't tell her much. Jay knew by Nicholas's tone that being an Apollonian was not good, so now she could read and find out why.

To her surprise, she liked the Apollonians. They seemed to be clear-headed, sensible souls who lived their lives in a pleasant, moderate fashion. If she was a lone Apollonian living in a Dionysian culture, so be it. Why not be moderate? Why not have one glass of wine? Why the compulsive need to get drunk? Life was hard enough — though Jay secretly acknowledged that her life was pretty easy — why complicate it with the vagaries of excess? Jay's parents were Apollonian and when Jay thought about it, most of her friends in Victoria were Apollonian. It was only the people she was meeting in Toronto who were Dionysian. Now that she was away from the protective custody of her parents, she had to reckon with this group of sensualists.

Jay learned from Nicholas that, in addition to the Revolution, there existed an amorphous organization known as the "counter-culture," consisting of like-minded Dionysians. Although Jay's generation claimed to be the authors of the "counter-culture," Jay could see that the seeds for the movement were sown by older people like Mr. Bowen. The counter-culture's rallying cry was "sex and drugs and rock and roll." And that was more or less the sum of it. One descended into a downward Dionysian spiral. The rock and roll segment was fun. It involved dancing oneself into an orgiastic frenzy, which, of course, led to uninhibited sex, which led to drugs to enhance the sex, causing one to go back up the spiral for more dancing, then more sex, then, more drugs. After a while, the drugs started to interfere with the dancing, which, in turn, put a halt to the sex so the participant was usually left with the drugs, the only things that still worked. None of these activities made any sense to Jay.

It was odd seeing Nicholas change from being a sweet, shy intellectual into an overbearing, opinionated sensualist. Sometimes he forgot his new religion and reverted to his old self. On the rare occasions when that happened, Jay fell in love with Nicholas all over again.

Jay hadn't seen Nicholas since she started art school. He had never asked for her new phone number. He wasn't even curious to know where she was living. He simply assumed that she would find him when she wanted him. Granted, he was easy enough to track down. Although he appeared to be a laid-back wanderer, he kept to a very strict schedule. Jay could predict, to the day and the hour, where Nicholas would likely be. However, she was tired of always being the one to seek him out. He'd been very dismissive of her lately. Though she was desperate to find him and ask him more about passion and Dionysus, her pride forbade her.

chapter six

THE REVOLUTIONARIES

The Revolutionary's Handbook
Tenet One: Revolutionary Love

NICHOLAS HAD NEVER met a girl like Irina Nemirovitch-Dantchenko before. All the other girls he'd known were like Jay, simply girls, but Irina was a woman. His woman. He even called her that — "my woman" — and got a secret thrill out of doing so. Irina took it all in stride. She'd been with a lot of men and they had all adored her.

Irina had one personal mannerism that should have put men off. She scowled. And not a fleeting look of disappointment, but a long, upside-down horseshoe. It was a full, deep, scowl and she meant it. Men saw her scowl as a personal challenge to try and make her happy. When she was in a scowl, a darkness lay over her but if something pleased her, her entire face lit up. The striking contrast between these two states of being — quiet gloom and frenetic excitement — was the key to her beauty. Men liked to watch the light go on and off and it was particularly pleasurable to be the one flicking the switch. Few men managed that sort of mastery over Irina for long, but it was what drew them to her and it was why they wouldn't leave.

For now, Irina was content to have Nicholas in her thrall. Her previous men were fairly rough. Nicholas was a boy in that respect. He was only pretending to be a rough and tumble dirty kind of guy. Irina liked the contradictions in Nicholas — his desperate longing to be one of the proletariat when it was fairly obvious that he'd been brought up to be a perfect little gentleman. She could picture him as a little boy, trudging dutifully off to private school in his grey flannel pants and his polished black oxfords. Sometimes she imagined him in grey flannel shorts. Irina knew it was dangerous to see the boy in a man: it was the first step to falling in love and that was something Irina would not do. She was a heartbreaker. She had to keep her distance.

Irina didn't deliberately plan to attract men. It was simply her nature. As a fox will raid a chicken coop, Irina plundered the hearts of men. She was both needy and aloof. She had no independent means of support. She relied on men to take care of her. But instead of being grateful for the support, she was disdainful and men loved that. They loved the fact that they could attend to her every whim, bust their butts trying to keep her in a grand manner and at a moment's notice, she would take off with some guy she met in a bar. That was how Nicholas met Irina.

He was at the Pilot in the late afternoon. A couple at the next table were having an argument. At first, he paid no attention. It was a typical bar room squabble. The man was complaining that the barbeque sauce on the hot beef sandwich didn't taste the same.

"Oh, you're always complaining," the woman replied. She had a low, husky voice. Nicholas wasn't facing the table so he couldn't turn around and take a look, but her voice intrigued him. He listened and tried to imagine the face and body that went with such a voice. Often, he was disappointed. Usually, the low sexy voices belonged to scrawny forty-year-old women with dyed red hair who wore leopard prints and smoked a lot.

"No, this is different. Taste it."

"Honestly," she drawled.

"Taste it and tell me it's the same. I dare you."

A quiet moment ensued.

"It's the same."

"Bitch."

"It's just a fucking sandwich." The woman pronounced "fucking" with a venomous precision that raised the hairs on Nicholas's neck. "Is it that important?"

The man raised his voice, "HEY YOU! BUDDY! YEAH YOU!" A timid busboy approached the table nervously. "This is not the same sauce."

"Pardon, sir?"

"It's not the same sauce. You say it's your special barbeque sauce but it's not."

"I think it is, sir."

"It's not, goddammit! I demand to see the chef!"

"The chef?"

"Who made the sandwich, fuckface!"

The busboy blushed and could not speak for several moments. Finally, he stammered out that a Mrs. Sinclair made the sandwiches.

"Bring her out!"

"Pardon?"

"You heard me!" The busboy reluctantly walked back to the kitchen.

"You are ridiculous," the woman hissed. Nicholas immediately felt ashamed for the man, but the man didn't seem to mind. He took her contempt as a matter of course.

"You'll see," he said, with certitude.

"As if I give a fuck," she retorted.

Nicholas decided that he had to get a good look at this woman. He stood up on the pretext of going to the men's room. When he turned around to catch a casual glimpse of her, he saw that she was staring at him, as if she fully expected that he would want to see her face. She locked eyes with him and would not let him go. Nicholas was surprised to see that she was young. She was slim and elegant. She had long, dark hair and impenetrable brown eyes. She could have been pleasantly pretty but there was a ferocity in her countenance that rendered her beautiful. Her eyes said, "See what a fool I'm encumbered with. Only you understand. Only you can save me."

When Nicholas came out of the men's room, the man was engaged in an animated discussion with Mrs. Sinclair. The woman turned her head to watch Nicholas walk to his chair. He blushed under her scrutiny, but she smiled seductively at him, so he knew she liked what she saw. Before he sat down, Nicholas arranged his chair so that he could catch her eye, if he chose.

"But you haven't always made this sauce, have you, Mrs. Sinclair?"

"Well, no, but it's the recipe we always use."

"It's NOT the recipe. There's ketchup in this!"

"It's a barbeque sauce. It's supposed to have ketchup."

"The old sauce didn't. I asked!"

"ALL RIGHT ALL RIGHT, HE DIED! EMILE DIED LAST NIGHT! I thought I knew how he made the sauce. Apparently, I don't." She spoke with complete impenitence and added, with a small sob, "There are more important things in life than the sauce on your sandwich." Mrs. Sinclair held her head high and the tears streamed down her face as she walked back to the kitchen.

"See?!" The man crowed in delight. "I knew it! I knew the sauce wasn't the same! I was right!" The sheer fact of being right brought such a state of exhilaration to the man that he immediately felt the need to relieve himself of it. "I gotta piss," he said and hurried off.

The husky voice suddenly whispered in Nicholas's ear, "Take me away from this moron." Nicholas turned to find the woman's face close to his. "Now!" He took her hand, rose quickly from his chair and the two of them scampered away like two children on a dare. Irina fell about laughing as soon as they were out of the bar but she didn't slacken her pace. She didn't want the man to catch her. They ran for several blocks down Yorkville Avenue, weaving deliriously in and out between the astonished passersby, for very few people run and laugh in Toronto. It was a deliciously shared joke.

"There are more important things in life than your sandwich," Irina gasped in hysteria, doing an impeccable impersonation of Mrs. Sinclair.

"I think she was in love with Emile."

"That's obvious. But Emile wasn't in love with her."

"How do you figure that?" Nicholas was intrigued by Irina's sudden knowledge of people she appeared to have no interest in when she was in the bar.

"He would have given her his secret sauce," she replied with a throaty giggle and the possibility of an evening of sexual extravagance hit Nicholas full in the face.

"Well, you can't give your sauce to just anyone."

"No, you can't," she said and kissed Nicholas. Nicholas was transported. No girl had ever kissed him like that before. It was a bossy kiss, the kiss of a woman who knew what she wanted and how to get it. And Nicholas was entirely willing to submit. He would go to the ends of the earth for this woman. "Where do you live?" she whispered in his ear.

"I'll take you there."

There was a casual bluntness in the manner in which Nicholas and Irina got together and yet, there was a mutual understanding that this cursory encounter would lead to a romantic liaison. Women like Irina were very good at performing this emotional sleight-of-hand. They could be as crude and vulgar as they pleased, yet men would always attribute an aura of romance to their actions. Jay could make no romantic inroads with Nicholas at all. She insinuated herself into his life to the point where by rights, he shouldn't have been able to live without her and yet, Irina captured his heart in a second.

What is that mysterious catalyst that transforms some women in men's eyes into divine beings? Perhaps there is no catalyst. Perhaps, the magical elixir comes from the woman's talents of discernment. Irina knew her men and she could pick them to suit her needs. The roast beef sandwich man was certainly no romantic, but Irina didn't want romance at that time. She needed a man with money, more specifically, a man who was free with his money. At first glance, the roast beef sandwich man did not look like a man of property. He didn't wear a suit and a tie. He wore dirty blue jeans and plaid shirts. Most women might be easily misled by his commonplace appearance, but not Irina. She could sniff out money as a dowser finds water. The roast beef sandwich man was an electrician and he earned a very good living. He worked hard for his money, but more importantly, he liked to spend it. And he liked to spend it on women. So, Irina applied for the position in his heart and filled it for a time, until she got fed up.

Sex wasn't a problem for Irina. She could easily spot the men who would make meagre demands of her. They were the ones who talked a lot. The less a man spoke, the larger his appetite. That was Irina's rule of thumb. Occasionally, it backfired and she would have to leap out with no place to land. Irina hated those dry spells between men. It was always easier to meet the new man when you were with the old one.

Irina felt ancient stirrings of lust when she saw Nicholas. She'd been putting the roast beef sandwich man off for some time. A conciliatory sexual act was imminent. She could tell by the way he obsessed about the sandwich that he was due for a quick fix. Irina appraised his sagging belly — cinched in by the large leather belt but rolling out, uncontained, over the top of it — his thick, blunt, hairy hands, the black tufts of hair growing out of his ears and nose and thought, "Do I need this?" And that's when she noticed Nicholas. She could only see his back but it was a nice, straight, youthful back. His hair was a beautiful shade of golden brown that flowed in a long mane to his waist. Truth be known, at first she thought he was a woman and since women did not feature in Irina's world, she thought no more about it. But when Nicholas rose, she saw that he was not a beautiful young woman but a beautiful young man and he would suit her purposes to a T.

During her sojourn with the roast beef sandwich man, Irina had saved a large sum of money and put it aside in her private bank account. She could afford to take a vacation and please herself for a bit. And when the account drew low, as it would, she'd find a dentist and hook up with him. The beautiful young man didn't look like a wage earner, but people can surprise one, though Irina was rarely surprised. She could not articulate what she wanted from people. She was guided by her intuition, which led her from one watering hole to another. Irina's intuition told her that she should get laid by this handsome young buck before she lost interest in sex altogether and that seemed as good an idea as any, so Irina put the whammy out and Nicholas walked right into it.

Nicholas was all set to take Irina back to his place but Irina had other plans. Irina knew that terms had to be set at the beginning of any contract. These terms were disguised as pleasurable hoops for Nicholas to jump through. Nicholas thought it was a great lark but Irina knew it was very important that he jump, just the same. Between the Parliament Buildings and Chinatown lay a nondescript and slightly seedy section of Spadina Avenue. Irina knew by matching Nicholas's clothes with the location and the slight bounce he acquired to an ever-hastening pace, that they were nearing his home.

"Oysters!" Irina exclaimed, as if God had just spoken to her.

"What?" Nicholas did not think he had heard correctly.

"I could really use some oysters," Irina said in her sexiest voice.

This statement seemed patently absurd to Nicholas as he couldn't conceive of any possible use for oysters, edible or otherwise, but he played along. "You'd like to eat oysters."

Irina nodded mutely, fixing him with her little-girl-in-need look.

"Well, I don't usually eat oysters. Some of the Chinese restaurants have dishes with oyster sauce so they must serve oysters, I guess." Nicholas hesitated, before leading them in the direction of Chinatown, inwardly praying that Irina would change her mind. The fastest way to kill sexual desire was to take a girl to a Chinese restaurant. They were always brightly lit by long, fluorescent lights, so one felt as though one were back in school again. Some people thought the restaurants were lit so brightly because Chinese people liked to look at their food. Nicholas thought the fluorescent lights remained through attrition, the restaurant having once been a derelict real estate office or some other fly-by-night operation. It was too much trouble to take them out, so they stayed. The tables in Chinese restaurants were never small and intimate. They were large and round, suitable for hungry families of ten and covered in layers of thin white plastic. One ate the meal and at the end, the waiter came along, grabbed the outside edges of the plastic tablecloth, flipped it over the contents of the table — knives, forks, plates, serving platters, glasses, teapots, beer bottles, ashtrays — bundled it all together and hauled it off the table like the great huge sack of garbage it was. After witnessing such a despotic end to the meal, most people wanted to flee the premises. Needless to say, it rarely put a girl in the mood. Nicholas frequently took Jay out for Chinese food.

"No, not a Chinese restaurant," Irina said quickly for she, too, knew the perils of such places. "Kensington Market's around here. Let's get some oysters!" Nicholas inferred that his bed was still on the list of possible places to disembark so he was most anxious to please. Oysters, it was.

The fish store in Kensington had some. Though it was the last day in April, the month still had an "r" in it, so the oysters were safe to eat, the man assured them. Irina selected what appeared to Nicholas to be a dozen or so barnacle-covered rocks. The man wrapped them up in newspaper and Nicholas once again attempted to lead Irina to his grotto.

"Champagne!" she said brightly.

"Champagne?"

"It goes with the oysters. Let's get champagne!" Women like Irina often used words like "get" instead of "buy," as if all the nice, expensive things in the world were just sitting in a tree, waiting for someone to pluck them down. Money is never an issue when you are "getting" something.

Usually, Nicholas had no ready cash on him so there would have been no question of indulging in such an extravagance, but earlier that day, he had been to the bank and had taken out money to pay his rent. Nicholas also had a large sum of money in his bank account, for in throwing himself into the role of student revolutionary, he had no need of superfluous material goods and so, rarely spent it. Who needs money when you are Che Guevara running through the jungle? In Nicholas's case, it was the urban jungle and though his shabby rooms put a small dent in his savings, the balance remained intact. Many students scrimp and save and thoroughly enjoy being misers. Nicholas was on the verge of becoming one of these avaricious bores. Whatever may be said about Irina, she saved him from this pitfall.

She could see him hesitate. This hoop was more challenging. She'd held it a little high but she needed to know: Did he have money? And was he generous with it? She could have made the trick a little easier by suggesting a half-bottle of champagne or a bottle of cheap bubbly, but she didn't. This was the moment of truth. If Nicholas refused, she'd be left high and dry. She couldn't return to the roast beef sandwich man but there was no way on earth that she'd sleep with a cheapskate and it was better to find these things out at the beginning. It wasn't evening yet — she still had plenty of time to find someone else. She might pick someone bigger. Irina worried about getting her stuff back. Nicholas had a slight build. He'd be no match for the roast beef sandwich man if he happened to be home when they went to retrieve her things. That was the trouble with electricians. They kept odd hours. He'd probably thrown her clothes all over the street by now.

She had one last resort if Nicholas didn't pan out. She could always go to her so-called parents. They owned a small apartment building in the neighbourhood. She'd been back for a couple of months and she still hadn't seen them. They were nice enough people, she supposed. They would look after her and feed her and do all the things that parents were supposed to do. The only thing linking her to those two primitive life forms was genetic inheritance and since Irina decided, early on, that she'd been adopted, it wasn't a worry. She'd reclaimed their original family name, however. It was a long, complicated, beautiful Russian name, not like Spinoza, that silly name her foster father had picked out of a hat.

Irina knew she had no means of finding her real parents. She liked to think they were Russian dissidents, brilliant intellectuals who'd been locked away in a gulag. There are the facts and then, there are the stories one builds around the facts. Irina was somewhere between one and three years old when the Spinozas left the U.S.S.R. She could never get a definite answer, which would have indicated that they were altogether too preoccupied at the time or, as Irina decided, they were lying. The Spinozas remembered how old her brother, Mickey, was. He had just turned three. When Irina first asked her mother how old she was, Mrs. Spinoza replied without hesitation that she was two. Irina's birthday was in March and if the Spinozas left the U.S.S.R. around Mickey's birthday, which was in September, that would mean that Irina was two, plus the months intervening, which would make her two and a half, which caused no concern to Irina when she was small and knew nothing about biology, but when she was old enough to understand the process of human procreation, it gave her pause. When Irina accosted her "mother" with the irrefutable facts, Mrs. Spinoza clapped her hand to her mouth, made a big grin and said, "Oops, I make a mistake. You were one and a half. Just seem like you were older." This suspicious response sowed the seeds for Irina's future daydreams.

Irina had concocted several tales of her abduction, but her favourite was this: Irina's real mother was a beautiful Russian ballerina who was secretly descended from Russian aristocracy. Or royalty. Although Irina liked the idea of being related to the Czars, the fact of the entire royal family being allegedly executed put a crimp on the daydream. As a baby, Irina's real mother had been hidden away to be raised by peasants, but her aristocratic bearing eventually won out. She was such a beautiful, graceful child that people couldn't help but notice her. It seemed natural that she would train at the ballet academy. In Irina's fantasy, the Soviet Union was kind to artists. She rose to great heights in the Bolshoi Ballet, played all the glamorous parts: Sleeping Beauty, the Princess Swan, the Firebird. Irina's father saw her dance and went backstage to pay tribute. They fell madly in love, got married and had a brief but stimulating life together. They lived in a grand house, suitable for a prima ballerina and her husband. Irina's fantasies about her real father were not so clear. She knew he was a genius but whether he worked at a university or wrote great books or worked as a research scientist or was a high-ranking government official — she couldn't decide. All those occupations were up for grabs. The crucial fact was that he had said or done something to offend Stalin around the time Irina was born.

Irina could picture it. Tears of remonstration from her passionate mother — "How could you do it? How could you do this to us?" Her father begging for forgiveness, but there was no time — the men were at the gate. "I will face them, my darling. You and the child must escape," says Irina's father. Her mother is in a state of hysteria but she obeys her husband and runs upstairs to the nursery to grab her newborn baby girl, Irina. The laundress, a slovenly woman named Sophia Grushminsky, is collecting the dirty sheets to take away and wash. Irina's mother hears the horrible commotion downstairs and knows it is too late for her to escape. She thrusts Irina into Sophia's arms. "Please, take her. I have done nothing wrong. They will let me go. I will come back for her. Please! She will die, otherwise." Sophia mumbles something about not having breast milk for a newborn, but Irina's mother remembers that Sophia had a baby a short time ago, so she persists. "I know you have milk. You must help me. Please!" There isn't a moment to lose. She leaves the baby with Sophia and runs out of the room. Sophia Grushminsky bundles the baby up with the laundry just as the men arrest Irina's mother. The men are in a hurry and not interested in the ballet. They don't know that the prima ballerina has just given birth to a beautiful baby girl. They don't even search the rest of the house. They were told to arrest the husband and his ballerina wife and that is enough for them. Looking at the broad-faced, flat-footed Sophia Grushminsky and looking at Irina's mother, they have no doubt as to who the ballerina is. Sophia is allowed to trudge off into the sunset.

So, Irina wasn't abducted, per se. Sophia Grushminsky and Gregor Nemirovitch-Dantchenko look after the baby while the parents go to the gulag. Under the circumstances, it is hard to keep in touch. Joseph Stalin dies a year later. Sophia and Gregor emigrate the following year. In that interval, they could try to return Irina to her rightful parents but they don't, and Irina never forgives them for it.

Before the fantasy took complete hold of Irina, she made some preliminary accusations in her youth.

It was Sunday. Mrs. Spinoza was making dumplings. She hadn't made dumplings for some time. She liked making them. It put her in a nostalgic frame of mind. Irina was about eleven at the time. She observed her mother carefully and saw that, as she handled the dough, she became visibly more relaxed. Her body seemed to breath a big sigh of relief, taking in the air, allowing it to fill every pore and push the flesh out in a big comfortable balloon of contentment. Irina waited for the balloon to fully expand before she stuck the knife in.

"Why didn't you try and find them?" Irina asked, quite out of the blue. When there is a sudden hole in an inflated balloon, it will burst with a loud smacking explosion. Irina was hoping Mrs. Spinoza would burst forth with a sudden confession. She did not. Her behaviour followed the other deflation process in which one blows the balloon up, keeping one's finger on the end. One releases the finger and the balloon will scutter around the room, making frantic farting sounds. Mrs. Spinoza did not scutter but her thoughts flew about in all directions and her contentment was certainly dispelled.

"Who?" she replied with great agitation, "Who you talking about?"

"My parents. You knew if you left Russia I'd never see them again." Irina scrutinized Mrs. Spinoza's eyes for a quick glimmer of guilt, but saw nothing but bewilderment.

"What are you talking about? I'm your parents."

"You know you're not."

Mrs. Spinoza laughed. "Sometimes, Irina, sometimes I think how'd I get such a beautiful daughter? How this possible?"

"I'm not your daughter."

"Doan joke about such tings. Never joke. We very lucky to get such a beautiful girl."

"You don't even know my age!"

"That was little mistake, Irina. Things very busy in Russia. We gotta lot going on, then. I remember Mickey 'cause it was his birthday. You big girl for your age. Learn to walk early. It was such a help for the trip. You such a smart girl." Mrs. Spinoza hugged Irina in a big Momma Bear hug, smooshing Irina's face in between her big warm breasts, but Irina was not to be mollified by such abject flattery. Her fantasies were much more exciting than this bald truth. If she chose to believe Mrs. Spinoza, then she'd be forever consigned as the lumpen child of two lumpen parents. Irina liked her fantasies and wanted to live in them — permanently.

"I don't even know your name." Nicholas decided that if he was going to spring for an expensive bottle of champagne, he should at least know the mystery woman's name.

"Irina Nemirovitch-Dantchenko."

"Wow! You're Russian! Did you defect?" he asked excitedly.

For a split second, Irina thought about reinventing herself as a recent defector but the young man looked as though he'd ask a lot of difficult questions. Irina had her other scenarios worked out. She didn't like to venture into unknown territory. But it was a good angle. She'd have to read up on it, sometime. "No," she replied. "My foster parents fled Russia in the early fifties. They took me with them."

"Oh?" Nicholas hesitated. He could see that the subject was painful for her. "Your foster parents?"

"Yes. It's a long story. My real parents are — well — I don't know where they are —"

"I'm sorry," Nicholas said.

"It's all right. I should be used to it by now." Irina smiled wanly. "I've been an orphan almost since I was born. Sometime, I'll tell you about it. But not now. What's your name?"

"Nicholas Woodbridge."

"Nicholas." The name struck a chord in Irina's soul, a password to her inner life. She thought of the tragic Czar Nicholas and thought how it must be significant that she should meet this modern name-sake. He could have changed the name to "Nick" or "Nicky" but no, he was Nicholas. She had intended that this young man be nothing more than a diversion, but she found herself irresistibly drawn to him. "I've always liked that name," she admitted.

"Nicholas and Irina. We sound good together," he said and fixed Irina with such a passionate gaze that she actually blushed for the first time since she was a little girl. Nicholas bought the champagne without too much hesitation but by this time, Irina was too spell-bound to care. All the hoops that she'd carefully set up threatened to spoil the magic between them. Nicholas had a terrible time with the oysters, as Irina knew he would. He didn't have an oyster knife. No man ever did until he'd spent an "oyster night" with Irina. Then the man would rush out and buy one, in case another occasion like that arose. It never did.

Nicholas kept stabbing himself in the soft fleshy part of his palm as he tried to pry the oyster open, but he kept his temper. Watching a man try and open an oyster was an excellent way of reading his character. How patient was he? How smart was he? Would he figure out the proper entrance or would he just keep hammering away at the wrong crack? Some men did bring out a hammer. Irina never stayed on those occasions. Nicholas had trouble with the first few. Then, he suddenly got on to it, held them in the palm of his hand, placed the knife in exactly the right spot, inserted it, and the oysters seemed to give a little gasp as they opened. Nicholas moved with extraordinary grace when he was absorbed in a task.

While he was occupied with the oysters, Irina prowled around Nicholas's place — a small flat above a novelty supply store. It wasn't as she'd pictured it, and was like no place she'd ever seen before. Most of the men Irina had been with were older. They either lived in the cast-off home of their last marriage, so the furnishings conformed to the ex-wife's taste, with blank spots to commemorate the furniture or pictures she'd taken when she left; or, as in the cases of the confirmed bachelors or the men who'd been without a regular woman for a very long time, they lived in homes curiously devoid of personality; blank, dark slates waiting for someone to inhabit them. The same could not be said for Nicholas's home. One room seemed to be a shrine. It had huge posters of a very handsome man. Irina had seen his face before. She knew he was vaguely political. The posters covered all the walls and showed this man from his early youth to around his mid-thirties. The bed was in this room but Irina was loathe to call it a bedroom.

Nicholas's kitchen and main room were one, the demarcation being a strip of linoleum tacked onto the wood, indicating the kitchen portion of the room. There were no kitchen appliances. At least, Irina didn't recognize them as such. When Nicholas took a lemon out of what looked to be an upright child-sized coffin, Irina realized it must be the refrigerator.

"That's your fridge?" she asked incredulously.

"Yeah."

"It's kind of strange looking."

Nicholas shrugged. "It's just old. Got it at Crippled Civilians. Fifteen bucks. Still works. I got this flat in a hurry so I didn't notice there was no fridge or stove."

"There's still no stove."

"Hotplate." Nicholas pointed to it. "First time I've had my own place. I've always lived in communes."

"You're a hippie."

"It's not such a bad thing to be," Nicholas smiled, "but I wouldn't call myself a hippie. They're sort of passé, anyway." Nicholas wondered if he might be relegated to the hippie ranks, despite his best intentions. He wasn't used to entertaining a woman in his own place. It felt strange to him. In the commune, sexual relations were pretty easy. There were always people in the main room, sitting around, smoking joints, chatting and occasionally slipping upstairs for a quickie. Nicholas could check out a girl for some time before he made the moves. He found that the girls in the commune were sort of possessive. They pretended to be easy and casual about sex, but the minute you did the deed, the entire commune knew about it and you were labelled a couple. Some men had no trouble slithering in and out of their traces but Nicholas had a hard time of it. Once the girls caught him, they were loathe to let go. There'd been a nasty altercation between Morning Dawn and Starhawk over who got to keep him. All the while, Nicholas nurtured a budding passion for Bliss but she was hooked up with Big Bob (who wasn't that big, but was bigger than Little Bob). Big Bob was a large, inert man who lay in a semi-stupor most of the time. Bliss ministered to his needs, which were few. She rolled his joints and fetched his beer and seemed to be happy with the arrangement.

Nicholas was asleep in his room early one morning when Bliss suddenly walked in, put a chair against the door (there were no locks), took all her clothes off and slipped into bed beside him. "Hi," she said. Hippie girls were known for their understatement. Nicholas took her behaviour as a sign that she and Big Bob had gotten tired of each other and she wanted a change. In his naivety, Nicholas made his first big mistake. While it was true that Bliss was tired of Big Bob, it was by no means true that Big Bob was tired of Bliss. Nicholas should have been more cautious but it was first thing in the morning and he hadn't really woken up yet and it seemed like a good idea at the time. Bliss had been reading the Kama Sutra. There were a number of positions she wanted to try and Big Bob was not very flexible so she and Nicholas spent the morning in the ardent enterprise of interpreting the book. Several hours later, Bliss left to take a shower. Her solitary ablution should also have tipped Nicholas off. Commune couples always took showers together. It was one of the not so subtle means of communicating their recent coupling.

While Bliss was taking her shower, the door to Nicholas's room was needlessly kicked in and there stood Big Bob in a murderous rage. His bloodshot eyes were even redder than usual. His face was flushed, his nostrils flared. He looked like a bull priming itself for the charge and Nicholas had to admit that standing, fully erect, in this rare instance, Big Bob was big.

"Where is she!" he roared.

"Having a shower," replied Nicholas in a friendly, helpful manner. He was always willing to overlook problematic personality traits. Perhaps Big Bob was a bad-tempered person when he stood up. Jealous rages were such an anachronism in the commune that, and this was his third big mistake, it never occurred to Nicholas that Big Bob could be jealous.

"You've had her! Haven't you, ya little fag!" Big Bob saw Bliss's Indian cotton clothes strewn about the floor and he grabbed Nicholas by the hair. Nicholas was doubly insulted, first for being called a fag and second for having his hair used as a means of securement. It was humiliating, but Big Bob could hardly grab on to his shirt because Nicholas wasn't wearing one. He yanked Nicholas close to him, spun him around, pulled Nicholas's arm behind his back and was in the process of breaking it when Bliss appeared, freshly scrubbed and glistening, in the doorway.

"Bob, honey, I missed you," she said and walked over to the bed and lay on it. She patted the place beside her. "I wanna show you something." In his surprise, Big Bob released his grip for a split second. Nicholas darted away, blushing as he did so, for he had never run away from a man in his life. While Big Bob gaped at Bliss, Nicholas collected as many personal possessions as he could and fled the premises.

He had gotten fed up with communal living but there were many useful aspects to it that he had previously taken for granted: readily available sex, regular meals and a continuing supply of drugs. He never had to worry about buying dope when he was at the House. Someone was always selling something. The living room was a regular marketplace on the weekends. Nicholas had been without dope for the last week. It was odd being straight. He felt ragged, edgy. It was like getting used to cutting meat with a dull knife and suddenly being given a sharp one. First time out, you almost slice your finger off. In some ways, he liked being so alert but it made him uncomfortable. He had this desperate urge to please Irina and he knew he wouldn't have felt that way if he were stoned.

In fact, if he were still living at the House, he would never have got her upstairs. She would have been set upon the moment she walked in the door. Not in a bad way, Nicholas assured himself. The people in the House were simply very friendly. They wanted to know about people. Jay said they were a bunch of nosy parkers but that was because Jay didn't get on with them. Jay was too straight. She looked rigid and unapproachable, whereas Irina looked mysterious and exotic. The men in the House would have clustered around Irina and that would have been the last Nicholas would have seen of her. Normally, Nicholas wasn't possessive and was quite happy to engage in the house policy of lease-lend. He felt differently about Irina. He was glad now that he had his own secret place to take her to.

Nicholas took the platter of oysters to the "living" section of the room and placed it carefully beside the "couch," which was a foam mattress. Nicholas had propped pillows against the wall to make it look less like a bed. He motioned for Irina to sit down, while he brought the champagne and the plastic cups. The surroundings were so incongruous with champagne and oysters that Irina barely suppressed a laugh. Nicholas also seemed out of place with this sparsely furnished room. There was an aura of money around him. This Spartan life was a game to him. The question was, how long was he going to play it?

"To new beginnings!" Nicholas said, and they clumped their plastic glasses together in a toast.

"Who's that guy in the other room?"

"Guy?" Nicholas looked slightly alarmed, as if one of the people from the commune had somehow materialized in his room.

"On the walls."

"Oh, that's Che. I'm going to take those down. I needed them when I lived in the commune."

"Needed them?"

"Yeah. They defined my space. I guess I tried to be communal but I could never get past that male territorial bullshit. My space. My room. My girl." At this point, any other man would have put the moves on Irina. She was fully expecting the awkward segue but instead, Nicholas smiled, looked her straight in the eyes and took another sip of champagne. He seemed to be in no hurry to bed her. She could not place Nicholas in her catalogue of men. This Che person might provide a clue. "Why all those pictures of that guy, though?" she asked, "Why not other pictures?"

"I was kind of obsessed with him."

"Are you ... ah ... you know ...?"

Nicholas looked at Irina blankly.

"Well, I don't know," she stammered. "He's a very pretty man."

"Do you think I'm into men?"

"Well ... ah ... I didn't mean that exactly, but —"

"It's Che Guevara," Nicholas stated simply, as though that should explain everything.

"Whatever his name is. He's very —"

"No, no. His name's important. He's important. He's one of the major figures of the twentieth century."

"I've never heard of him."

"You will."

"He looks, ah, artistic."

"He was. He wrote poetry."

"So, he's a poet."

"You're making an assumption."

"But you just said he wrote poetry."

"You're assuming he's a pansy 'cause he's good-looking and wrote poetry." Irina nodded mutely in agreement. Nicholas leaned in and said ferociously, "He would have slit your throat for even suggesting such a thing."

"Oh."

"That's the trouble with our society. We pigeonhole men and women." Nicholas eyed Irina thoughtfully. "Actually, he wouldn't slit your throat. He'd fuck you silly, instead. He liked women. A lot."

"Oh," said Irina.

"He was a doctor as well. At least, that's what he trained for. Didn't get the certificate. But he practised. Illegally, and only if there was no doctor around. But really, he wasn't a doctor or a poet. He was a revolutionary. These oysters are great, by the way. I've never eaten them before. West Coast oysters are big and flabby."

"These are East Coast oysters," said Irina.

"I like East Coast oysters," Nicholas said and leaned in to kiss her. It was a long intense kiss. When it was over, he resumed talking as though nothing had happened. Irina found his take-it-or-leave-it attitude very erotic. He spoke about the life of a revolutionary and how it was a calling. "You must be ready. You live your life as you normally would live it, but you must always be ready for the Call."

When Nicholas told Irina that he, too, was a revolutionary, she didn't understand. "But there's no revolution here."

"There will be. In Quebec."

Suddenly, it was as though someone had set a bomb off in her. Nicholas was finally on a topic that Irina felt passionate about. "That's what I thought, too! But it didn't happen."

"Too?" thought Nicholas, a little disturbed that Irina was climbing onto his bandwagon. "It will happen," he replied with authority.

"I don't think so," stated Irina flatly.

Nicholas was not used to being contradicted, particularly by a woman. "Why would you say that?" he asked.

"It should have happened during the FLQ crisis."

"It could still happen."

"Possibly. If someone assassinated Trudeau and the new prime minister was —"

"Assassinate?" Nicholas was appalled. "We don't assassinate leaders in Canada." Though he purported to being a revolutionary, he was not radical.

"It's an American thing?"

"Yeah."

"So is civil war, so I guess it's not going to happen. What happened to Che? Is he still alive?"

Nicholas was still reeling at the speedy way in which Irina dismissed the argument. "Ah, no. He's dead."

"Did Castro kill him?"

"Why do you say that?" asked Nicholas, getting more confused. Irina plunged from one appalling assumption to another.

"That's the way things are. Two people in power. One person left in charge. Who else would kill him?"

"They were comrades!"

"Pheh!" scoffed Irina, in a manner very similar to Mrs. Spinoza. Nicholas was somewhat put out that Irina was now voicing opinions on subjects very dear to him.

"You don't know anything about that," he stated flatly.

"You're right. I don't." Irina immediately capitulated. She didn't want to spoil a romantic evening by arguing with Nicholas. Arguments could come later. She was puzzled by Nicholas's naivety. He seemed to be very intelligent, yet he didn't seem to know much about how the world worked. "Have you lived in Montreal?" she asked demurely, assuming that he had, hoping to return to a safe topic.

"I haven't been there much. I've just read about it," Nicholas said with some embarrassment.

"Oh," said Irina.

"Have you been there?"

"I've spent the last few years there. I was at McGill." Irina laughed harshly. "Not for long."

"Why? Didn't you like it?"

Irina hesitated. "I loved it."

"What happened?"

Irina's scowl returned in full-force and the light disappeared from her face. "I can't talk about it."

Nicholas dropped his posturing in an instant. "I'm sorry," he said and drew her close to him.

Irina collapsed into his arms. "Just hold me, okay? I just need to be held."

Nicholas rocked her gently. He felt uneasy. It was as if a large hand had reached out from Irina's insides and grabbed him and held him fast. He wanted to get away, but he couldn't. Nicholas usually hid behind his intellectual facade but this woman had blindsided him. The girls at the House made no emotional demands on him. They were big on hugging and cuddling, and that often led to sex, but the sex felt like some officially sanctioned activity. Apart from Big Bob's aberrant fit of jealousy, making out with one of the House girls was never dangerous. It was a pleasant way to pass the time. Nicholas felt in his gut that Irina was dangerous. His days as a free-spirited revolutionary were numbered.

chapter seven

THE BOURGEOISIE

Tenet One: No Handbook

BRAD DIDN'T CALL Lily at work the next day, nor the days after that. Though it was written in the newspapers that women were liberated and could have sex without fear of reprisal, the prevailing view of Lily's social set was that a girl who had sex on the first date was a slut. The fact that Brad and Lily weren't even on a date and that the sex took place in a car was even more damning. It offended Lily that Brad should have the upper hand in this respect.

She spent the week at her parents' house. The weekend was a particular agony for her. She pictured Brad and Susan blithely resuming their Saturday night ritual date: Susan malevolently clad in powder pink, Brad in blue; younger, mocking versions of their parents.

To Lily, marriage and family life were a farce. The images that instantly sprang to her mind were not ones of her own life, but rather, ingratiating scenes from television shows: sanctimonious fathers having serious talks with their children, everybody learning something. In these shows, Lily observed caricatured reflections of her own life. Lily's family lived in one of those suburban ranch-style homes that were prominently featured in the shows. Lily's mother wore nice clothes and high-heeled shoes, just like Mrs. Cleaver. Her father dressed in a suit and a tie during the week and wore sweaters on the weekends. Like the television fathers, he, too, came home from work at six p.m. every day. Mr. MacFarlane was somewhat louder than the television dads but he still fit the routine. Lily desperately wanted to be unique but everywhere she looked, she saw she was just like thousands of other North American children growing up in the suburbs. The surface similarities gave credence to the lie. In her mind's eye, she would have to take on the role of loving wife, and it came complete with costumes and mannerisms. Television provided the illustrated guide.

Images from the shows intruded into her own memories. Lily would have a sudden vision of her kindergarten teacher's huge face looming down at her and then realize that it wasn't her kindergarten teacher. It was Beaver Cleaver's teacher. Or it was the librarian at his school. Her face was so close and so familiar. Lily suspected that, for Brad, too, the worlds blurred together. When he spoke of marrying Susan, he probably envisioned a life similar to one of these shows. He was already subtly adjusting his appearance for his metamorphosis from wild youth to settled family man. Lily could see that she, too, was expected to tone down and become someone's wife. However, not Brad's wife.

Lily saw that it was pointless to remain at her parents' house, like some woebegone child. She would return to KAT House and adopt Brad and Susan's attitude; nothing had happened.

Lily's mother expressed mild disappointment. "Must you leave so soon, dear?"

"I better. No sense wasting my rent."

"That's too bad. Paul's having his friend for dinner tomorrow."

"His friend?"

"Yes. A charming boy. Brad. You'd like him."

"Okay. I'll stay. But do me a favour, Ma. Don't tell Paul I'm staying."

"He's touchy, your brother."

"Yes, he is."

⌒

LILY PLANNED HER next assault on Brad very carefully. She hurried home from work and slipped into the house very quietly so neither her mother nor Paul knew she was home. She then waited in her room. After about a half hour, her mother called, "Paul, your friend's here." Paul was, as usual, stretched out on an inflatable mattress in the pool, "getting some rays." Lily eavesdropped on Brad's polite chit-chat with her mother, then headed down the stairs. Brad looked up in surprise.

"Uh, hi."

"Hi. When are you going to give me that paper of yours?"

"Oh yeah," Brad laughed tensely.

"Well, aren't you going for a swim before dinner," suggested Mrs. MacFarlane.

"Great idea," Lily beamed at Brad.

"Brad doesn't want to swim, do you, Brad?" Paul hurried in to claim his friend.

"Um —"

"Well, you're in your suit and he brought his." Lily indicated Brad's rolled towel. "I think I'll swim, too. The changing rooms are out here. We'll just be a minute, Paul." Lily commandeered Brad to the cabana.

"Your changing room. My changing room."

The changing rooms were separated by a flimsy partition that left a foot of space at the bottom and a foot of space at the top. Brad gave Lily a searching look.

"I meant to call you ..."

"Better get changed."

She withdrew into the girls' room and closed the door firmly. The air was charged, every sound amplified. Brad could hear Lily's quiet breath, the unsnapping of her bra, a slight sigh as she took her skirt off and lay it over the chair. Her underpants fell just within his line of vision from the gap between the floor and the partition. Lacy and pink. Lily gave Brad a glimpse of her foot stepping into her bikini bottom. She pulled it up and gave it a little snap as it arrived in place. It was the smallest bikini she owned. She adjusted her breasts so that they gently rode over the surface of the top. Lily had a voluptuous body. It was her main sexual weapon and she employed it to the fullest.

Brad walked out of his changing room, cursing himself for having worn bikini briefs, which revealed, with overt clarity, the wayward moods of his errant penis. Lily gave Brad an appraising look and went outside. Brad couldn't help comparing the two girls. When he and Susan Lipton went swimming, which was a rare event in itself, Susan kept her gaze fixed firmly above his chest, smiling glassily, her head bobbing up and down like some marionette on a string, stealing an occasional furtive glance down, quickly, before the puppeteer jerked her head back up. Brad wondered: What on earth was he doing with Susan Lipton? Why not Lily? Why not?

Lily made certain that Brad got a good look at what he was missing. She clambered out of the pool so that her prominent cleavage was displayed to advantage, floated on her back indolently, executed swan dives, then came up gasping breathlessly, "Oh, almost lost my suit," laughed, giggled in all manners sultry. Brad couldn't take his eyes off her, mesmerized as a small mouse waiting for the snake to devour it.

If Lily's antics seem childish beyond measure, bear in mind that upper-middle-class youth of the mid twentieth century were encouraged to linger in adolescence. Many Baby Boomers retained their precarious youth and childish attitudes till the age of forty, whereon their bodies either fell apart or ran to fat — a brutish and abrupt ending to this artificially prolonged youth. Were Lily born in other times, her life would have been decided for her in pretty short order. However, in this particular passage of history, Lily had the means and leisure to pursue many options before making a choice.

Paul was not amused by Lily's frolics. "So, when's the big date?" he asked Brad.

"Huh?"

"The big date. When are you and Susan going to tie the knot?"

"Yes, when *are* you going to tie the knot?" Lily was in the shallow end now, languorously weaving up and down, her breasts gently bobbing to the motion.

"Um ... um ... I don't know. Think I'll do some lengths." Brad broke into a furious Australian crawl.

"Guess he didn't like your question, Paul."

"What the hell have you done to him?"

"What's your problem? Why couldn't we go out? Why does he have to stay with Susan Lipton?"

"Isn't it enough that your own life's a fuck-up? Do you have to mess everyone else's life as well?"

"How am I messing with Brad's life?"

"Okay, do you want to marry Brad?"

"I hardly know the guy."

"You've always said you weren't going to get married."

"Yeah, so?"

"So, he wants to get married. He's met the right girl. You don't know what you want so you should just stay away."

"Since when did you become Brad's dad?"

"Just don't ruin his life, too."

"Why do you hate me so much?"

"I don't hate you, Lily. I know you." Paul took a deep breath and swam underwater the entire length of the pool.

Brad noticed a strange sadness in Lily's walk as she headed for the changing room. He hurried out to join her. The air in the changing room was now damp and clammy. Brad stood outside Lily's cubicle and listened to the wet smacking sound of her bathing suit peeling away from her body, working its way down her thighs, her knees, culminating in a blip sound as it landed in a little pile at her feet; then, the soft scrubbing sound of her towel brushing against her skin.

He waited for her to say something provocative, but she was curiously silent.

"Uh, Lily?"

"Yes."

"I'm sorry about not calling you. Can I see you sometime?"

"Mmmmm. I guess so. When?"

"Tomorrow. After your work. When do you get off?"

"Five. But I'd like to freshen up. Why don't you pick me up at KAT House?"

Brad shifted uncomfortably. "Can we meet somewhere, instead?"

"Why don't you pick me up?"

"You know why."

"Well then, there's no reason to meet, is there?"

"Look, I really want to talk to you. Couldn't you meet me for dinner say, at the Blue Cellar Room?

"Well."

"Please."

"All right. Six. I'll meet you there at six."

⌒

THE BLUE CELLAR Room was a dank chamber situated at the end of a long corridor at the back of a modest Hungarian restaurant called The Europe. The Blue Cellar Room was not actually underground, though the demeanour of its patrons was certainly furtive. In contrast, The Europe was a bright, cheerful place with big picture windows, framed by white homey curtains. The food was more expensive at The Europe, but more fortifying. One ate large full-course meals, drank big bottles of wine and belched surreptitiously while listening to the gypsy violinist. Bud vases containing a single long-stemmed red rose adorned the crisp, white, linen-clad tables. Just before one arrived at the Europe, there was a cleft in the building as though it gasped slightly, forming a small shallow alley, leading to a blue door. There was no sign on the door. A first-time visitor would open it and hope for the best. One then walked down the narrow corridor, lit only by a single bare blue light bulb, to arrive at a curtain of jingling, blue, glass beads.

One parted the curtain and lo and behold, there lay the Blue Cellar Room in all its dark and dangerous glory. The aging, red-checked tablecloths and sturdy dark wooden furniture evoked operatic tales of star-crossed lovers and Student Princes. For the politically inspired, the Blue Cellar Room conjured up back alley taverns where Russian dissidents met before they were arrested. Dostoevsky would have been in a place like this, consorting with his colleagues, signing his name to the infamous petition, moments before a harsh clattering of beads, announced the arrival of the Czar's finest.

All in all, it was the perfect place to kindle an affair. Its subservient relationship to The Europe proclaimed its clandestine purpose. One took one's wife to the Europe with its big, broad tables and bright, yellow light. One took one's lover to the Blue Cellar. While there was a menu at the Blue Cellar Room, its clients were not there to eat. The most favoured dish was the Theatre Special, consisting of an array of cold cuts left over from previous meals served at The Europe. One never knew what was going to be in the Theatre Special, an ideal repast to share with the woman who would not be wife. There was no steady clientele at the Blue Cellar Room but it maintained itself nicely, due to the plethora of people beginning or ending ill-fated romances.

Lily arrived fifteen minutes late. She felt it was good to make Brad wait. He was seated in a small alcove at the back. The room had its usual atmosphere of hushed concentration as the various diners were meeting their lovers for the first or possibly last time. The early evening hours in the Blue Cellar were more jovial. It didn't settle into its clandestine gloom till the late evening. Brad spoke quickly, as though he had important business looming.

"Look, I'm sorry about what happened."

"You're sorry."

"Yeah, I ... ah ... I don't know what got into me."

"Yeah, me, too. I felt so stupid the next day. I mean, really, what was I doing with you?"

"Pardon?"

"I understand, Brad. I felt exactly the same way. I must have had a lot to drink to get THAT crazy."

"Well, I don't know that —"

"Anyway, you're here to tell me that you're committed to Susan."

"Um ...." Brad hated it when women took words out of his mouth.

"And that's good. That's a sensible decision, Brad." Lily undressed Brad with her eyes while she was making these declarations. Brad couldn't put his finger on what was happening but for some mysterious reason, he found himself sexually aroused. Lily let her hand rest on the table close to his hand. His fingers started to weave themselves around her fingers.

"And well — I've known Susan for years and I know we're right for each other. And I don't know you at all."

"No. You don't." Lily toyed with her necklace, drawing Brad's attention to her breasts, rising and swelling with her every breath. Her bare leg accidentally grazed against his, thus completing the electrical field. "So, Brad, let's just have a nice dinner and get to know each other. But as friends, of course." Brad, by this time, was beside himself with desire.

They ordered a light meal, finger food. Whenever Brad had dinner with Susan, she put her face to the plate and ate, concentrating fiercely on the business at hand, cutting her food up with precise, delicate motions. With Lily, food was insignificant, a mere prop. She kept her gleaming yellow eyes on Brad and chewed slowly and seductively, as if to say, "I'm eating you up, every little bit. Brad found this thrilling and slightly threatening. Towards dessert and after they'd consumed a large amount of wine, Brad took Lily's foot out of her sandal and placed it in his lap. He ran his hand up and down her bare leg.

"I'm very attracted to you."

"Really?" said Lily.

"But I'm committed."

"You are, indeed." Lily withdrew her leg.

"I really like you."

"I like you, too."

"Well, that's great. So, we'll be friends."

"Of course."

Quiet sobbing could be heard at the other tables as lovers, ending their affairs, announced their intentions. Lily and Brad left before the sobs erupted into raging arguments.

The summer heat enveloped them in warm, moist gusts. Lily gave a luxuriant, "ooooh," her body embracing the heat, softening out and becoming supple. They slowly drifted towards their houses, neither wanting the evening to end. Brad took Lily's hand. Lily swayed when she walked, her hips gently undulating to some exquisite internal rhythm. They arrived at Sigma Chi first. KAT House was further down the street.

It was still early. They were engrossed in conversation so Brad suggested Lily come to his room for a bit. She agreed, everything now being above-board and non-sexual. She prowled around his room and oohed and aahed over his "conversation pieces," fetish objects that he'd bought for precisely such an occasion. He poured them each a glass of Scotch and they saluted their friendship.

Lily stretched out on the floor at the foot of his bed. Brad lay down beside her. It was so natural, so comfortable, so unlike being with Susan who perched nervously at the threshold of his room and peered in anxiously as he ran in to get something. She would never enter the premises. That would be unthinkable. Brad had never seen Susan's room but he imagined it: pink and spare, a stuffed animal on the pillow. He found Lily easy to be with and even easier to talk to. Normally, Brad was reticent with women but he confided things to Lily that he'd never voiced to anyone.

"I used to want to be an architect. When I was little, I built houses — drew up little designs. Worked out rooms. I loved the

Roman houses with their inner garden. I'd never seen anything like that before."

"Me, too. I always wanted to live in a house like that."

"Really?" Brad looked at Lily in amazement. "Anyway, I was really bad in all my drawing classes and my dad wanted me to go into law. Be part of the firm. So, I told him I'd try it for a couple of years. I could still switch to architecture if I wanted."

"Yes, sure you could."

Brad felt such a wave of pure unmitigated joy at finding a kindred spirit in such a lovely girl that he could contain it no further and he just had to kiss Lily. The embrace lasted a very long time. Lily murmured, "We shouldn't be doing this." Brad agreed as he gently slipped his hand inside Lily's top and cupped her breasts. Lily's breathless whispers of "we should stop" and "this isn't right" acted as an aphrodisiac to Brad and spurred him to the next level of love-making. By the time Lily had outlined all the reasons why they should cease and desist, she was laid out, stark naked, with Brad busily employing all his powers of persuasion to argue for a continuance.

They made love all night. Lily staggered out of his bed the next morning and tried to make herself presentable for work. She tried to tone down her "it's just a friendly dinner" outfit; an ensemble that had succeeded spectacularly in its ulterior purpose last night but might get her fired this morning. Lily didn't feel like braving KAT House to change into something more appropriate. She had stupidly left things up in the air with Brad. Most young women negotiate some sort of treaty vis-à-vis the man's intentions before capitulating to sexual ecstasy. Lily had simply surrendered. She was feeling reck-less. She went to Hydro in her sleazy temptress attire, daring them to fire her and be done with it.

⸺

BRAD WAS FIRMLY resolved to break up with Susan. However, he couldn't do it over the phone. He waited till their Friday date. He employed what he thought was a tried and true technique. He began by saying that he wasn't sure if he loved her. Most girls usually got mad when he said this and broke up with him, which saved him a lot of trouble. Susan didn't appear overly upset by his bald statement of fact and said, "You'll learn to love me."

"Well, now, that's just it, Susan. I don't think you can learn to love someone. I think it just happens."

Most girls would, at this juncture, have asked, "Have you met someone else?" which would have given him a good lead-in to talk about Lily, though running off with her should have provided an obvious clue as to who it was exactly whom he'd met. Susan simply repeated her mantra, "You'll learn to love me." This annoyed Brad, who thought, "I should just really give it to her." So, he did.

"No. I can't learn to love you, Susan. I don't love you. I never will ... Oh my God, are you crying?"

Small tears, diamond-like in their clarity trickled down Susan Lipton's porcelain cheeks. "Remember when we first met, Brad? How magical it all was?"

Was it? He didn't remember any magic but now she was crying in her restrained Geisha manner — tiny little sobs, nothing too vulgar. He was powerless in the face of these tiny tears. Susan was only nineteen. They'd been dating for three years. Although she was very mature in practical matters, she was still a girl. He had always felt like the older man with her. Initially, he found her innocence captivating. He'd presumed that somewhere along the line, she would metamorphose into a woman who, like Lily, would have gloriously uninhibited sex with him. However, Susan remained resolutely girlish, clinging to her virginity as a drowning man to a lifebuoy.

On one occasion, Brad had almost broken the hymen barrier. Susan was so upset by her perilous journey into uncontrolled love-making that she allowed no further concessions. If he so much as touched her breast, she froze and looked reproachfully at him. Brad tried to remember that night of the near bull's eye, to ascertain whether Susan was really frigid or simply pretending to be so. It didn't sit clearly in his memory. He assumed it would be the beginning of a long series of nights of mutual pleasure. He didn't anticipate that the curtain would come crashing down and he'd be locked out on the other side, into the chilly intimacy of a Cold War.

Brad no longer had any intention of interfering with Susan's virginity. It was the only thing that saved him from the immediate obligation of marrying her. She was still an unopened gift for some other dutiful bridegroom, should a better prospect than Brad come along.

"You know when I left you at that party, Susan —"

"We don't need to discuss this any further, Bradley."

"I took her to the beach and —"

"Please, Brad. I know you have needs and when we're married, I'll satisfy them." Susan lowered her head demurely but her eyes flashed up at him. "And trust me, Brad. You'll be satisfied." Brad felt a chill go up and down his spine, which he mistook for lust.

"I'm glad we've sorted this out."

"Huh?"

"Come on, we'll be late for the party at Steve and Cindy's." Susan clasped Brad's hand and he was dragged to an engagement party before he could say Jack Robinson.

⌒

IF THE GIRLS at KAT House had been anticipating a showdown of sorts between Lily and Susan Lipton, they were sadly disappointed. The summer heat of Toronto built to its slow, humid boil. Jay was heading to the air-conditioned bookstore when Lily appeared, seemingly out of nowhere, but in actuality, out of the Sigma Chi Fraternity House.

"Hi."

"Hi? Where have you been? We've been worried about you."

"Worried? I told Kathleen I was at my parents."

"No one told me."

"Oh, well, sorry. Where're you going?"

"Bookstore."

Lily walked alongside Jay. "Anything to report?"

"I should be asking you that, shouldn't I?"

"Are you mad?"

"No."

"We fooled around a bit. That's all. Is that what you wanted to know?"

"No, of course not." Jay blushed furiously. "Fooled around" was another euphemism the girls of KAT House used. It could involve second and third bases, and depending on the speaker's sense of understatement, could even indicate the rarely discussed "home run."

"How's Susan?"

"The same. She and Brad are still going out."

"I know."

"I guess you couldn't save him."

"Um ... I'm sort of seeing him."

"You are?"

"Well, they aren't dates, per se."

"What are they?"

"I mean, it's pretty casual. He calls me up and I see him."

"Do you think that's a good idea?"

"I don't give a shit about Susan. All that feminist solidarity bullshit."

"I meant for you."

"Yeah. For me it's fine. I'm not girlfriend material."

"You're not?"

"No. I'm the other. How old are you? Nineteen? You haven't really entered the scene, have you? Do you want to get some ice cream?"

"Huh? Oh, sure. Let's go to the bookshops first, though. Just a couple. The air-conditioned ones."

"Sounds great," Lily lied, as they glided into one of the numerous small bookshops that lined the street.

"Oh my God! The Classics! Three for ninety-nine cents!" Jay dove into a bin and grabbed as many as she could carry. She rushed up to

Lily, cheeks flushed. "Look at that! *Moby Dick*, *Pilgrim's Progress*, *Pride and Prejudice*! Don't you want some?!"

Lily fingered one of the books gingerly. "The paper's thin."

"Oh look! *Jude the Obscure*!" Jay shouted and grabbed another.

After Jay had satisfied her book lust, they went to Lily's favourite haunt, the ice cream parlour. Lily glanced around at the young couples who dominated the room. "It's too crowded here. Let's buy a cone and walk back," she announced. Jay had her hands full with the books, but she agreed.

Chocolate ice cream dribbled onto the cover of *Pride and Prejudice*. Jay licked it off. The paper left a nasty taste in her mouth.

"Tasting it to see if it's worth reading?"

"It's a great book," replied Jay, somewhat sternly. "One of my favourites."

"You've read it?"

"Yes."

"Well, why would you buy it if you've already read it?" Lily circled her tongue carefully around her ice cream.

"So I can refer to it."

Lily stopped in mid-lick. "Why would you do that?"

"I don't know," mused Jay. "Sometimes I like to read them again."

To Lily, reading a book once was tedious but to read the same book twice bordered on insanity. She could see that Jay was about to elaborate so she hastily changed the subject. "Have you ever had a boyfriend?"

Jay grudgingly replied, "Well, sort of."

"What's his name?"

"Nicholas."

"Nice name. Is he a good kisser?"

Jay laughed. "We've never kissed."

"Not after a date?"

Jay laughed again. "We don't go on dates."

"Well, what do you do?"

"I don't know. I used to go to his cell meetings."

"He's a convict?!"

"No, he's a revolutionary. He has these meetings. Well, they're more like parties. Afterwards, I mean. After they've done all their meeting stuff."

"Is that his job? Being a revolutionary?"

"Well, no. He's a student. The meetings are just for fun."

"You need to go out more."

"I guess I do." Jay suddenly felt ashamed; a fool out on her fool's errands, following Nicholas around to his sundry meetings — what was the point of all that? A hopeless crush.

"Here's how it works. You have these choices. You can be The Girlfriend. Basically, it's like a pre-wife. Susan Lipton is a really nauseating example. But take Eve. Well, she's pretty nauseating, too. Think of someone you know who's nice and who has a boyfriend."

Jay pictured her friends, Denise and Roy.

"And think of all the things she does — figures out what movies they're going to see, whose parties they're going to go to. Basically, she plans their lives. Now the guy has some say in it. And it's all very nice, isn't it? When you think of your friend and her boyfriend, they seem like a married couple, right? They get horny, sure, but there's no Grand Passion."

"Grand Passion?" Jay asked, finding the concept incongruous to apply to Denise and Roy.

"Exactly. No grand passion. Just happy homemaker. Well, I want more out of life."

"And you think you'll find that with Brad?"

"Brad's just a fling. It's all in how guys see you. Some women are The Wife. Some women are the Other. I'm the Other. You might be the Other, too. You could be a wife, though. Could go either way."

Jay wasn't entirely sure that she wanted to be the Other. It sounded vaguely sinister. But she did want a Grand Passion and she was pretty sure that Grand Passions were not to be found in movie dates and burgers at Fran's Diner.

Lily's pace slowed as they approached KAT House.

"So, are you coming back?" Jay looked at Lily.

Lily stood and contemplated the house. "Of course." A male voice from the Sigma Chi House shouted something. Jay couldn't make out what he said, but Lily heard. She turned and smiled and ran back down the street.

"See ya!" she called out to Jay as she slipped up the fire escape of the Sigma Chi house.

⌒

BRAD'S ROOM WAS a warm cave. Lily lost all sense of time while she was with him. Part of her wanted to succumb and get lost forever, but her practical side demanded that the affair be made public. "Do you want to see a movie tonight?"

"A movie? We're in a movie right now. It's called — oh, great tits!"

Lily pushed him away. "I'm serious. I'd like to go out."

"Do you think I'm oversexed?"

"Don't change the subject."

"I mean it. I want to make love to you all the time. I can't get enough of you."

"Why won't you take me out?"

"A date," Brad replied, barely concealing his disdain. "We're much more than that, Lily. We've gone way past that boy-girl stuff. We're lovers. You're my lover."

"Oh," said Lily as Brad kissed her breasts. "Do you love me?"

"You bet," said Brad.

After they made love, Brad lit a joint and they smoked that for a while, chatting aimlessly. They got wildly hungry and ordered a pizza. Lily wanted to go out but Brad didn't feel like standing up. Lily got mad and said he never took her out anywhere. Brad dialled the pizza number while she ranted. Lily tried to stop him from phoning but she was hungry, too — naked and stoned and craving pepperoni. She straddled Brad, bearing down on him, shouting, "When are you going to take me out?! WHEN! WHEN!"

Brad, shushing her — women weren't supposed to be in the house — and laughing at the sheer hilarity of it all, gasped out, "Sunday! Sunday! We'll have our date on Sunday."

Lily smiled, raised herself up a quarter of an inch and tweaked him. "And what'll we DO! DO! DO!"

"We'll ... we'll —"

"It's gotta be good, Brad. It's gotta be outside."

"Oh, it's outside, all right."

"Out of this room. You get my drift." Brad moaned. Lily had a diabolical manoeuvre that she employed when she was on top.

"We're gonna go ... SKYDIVING."

Suddenly, there was a pounding on the door. A series of images flashed into Lily's mind, like sped-up film. Lily could not make them out clearly. Brad gaily tossed Lily off him and ran to answer the door. "Pizza's here!" They fell upon it, like hyenas on a carcass.

"So, you game?" asked Brad.

"I was thinking more along the lines of a date."

"What is it with you and dates? This is a date. A date with destiny."

"Don't say that!"

"What?"

"Don't say ... forget it. I feel very weird."

"You ate too fast."

"Yeah. I don't know, Brad. Skydiving's a little —"

"Dangerous?"

"Well, yeah."

"What happened to my Wild Thing?"

Lily loved it when Brad called her that. He shoved her teasingly and started to sing, "Wild Thing, you make my heart sing! Boom Boom Boom ...." He pulled her up and they danced.

"It's not dangerous, Lil."

"It's not?"

"No. You take this course. They're very careful. It's not like you go freefall."

"Freefall?"

"Yeah. Without a parachute." Brad caught the look on Lily's face and hastily added, "Just kidding. You don't jump till you've had a few classes and even when you start jumping, your parachute's attached by a line to the plane. It gets pulled automatically. You just float down through the sky. It's great!"

"You've done it?!"

"Well, no, but my friend did it. The course starts this Sunday and there's a couple of prep classes during the week. Then, on every Sunday after that, we jump! It's a blast. Come on. Just come to the first class."

"Well ..."

"What's the matter? You chicken?"

"Well ..."

"Come on, Lil. We don't jump immediately. You have a whole week to think about it. Just try the class. It won't be any fun without you there."

Lily smiled to herself. She was fun. And maybe, if Brad saw enough of her and had enough fun with her, he might fall in love with her.

"Okay, I'll do it."

"That's my girl." *My girl.* The phrase sang in Lily's heart. "Meet me here at nine o'clock Sunday morning."

"Nine?"

"Once we start jumping, we'll start even earlier. So, gorgeous, you better get home and get some beauty sleep."

"It's not till Sunday."

"You should go." Brad helped Lily on with her clothes, gave her a long, lingering kiss and sent her on her way.

Lily strode down to KAT House, high as a kite and happy as hell. She liked being the other woman, the fun one. She was priding herself on her friendship with Jay. Normally, it would have been unthinkable for a sorority member to befriend a summer boarder. But Lily liked Jay. Jay looked up to her. Jay needed her. She'd teach Jay about life. Yes, that's what she'd do because Jay needed to know.

Lily was idly working out how to spread the wealth of her new-found knowledge when the Voice boomed into her ear. Boomed.

"Fraud."

"Must be the dope," Lily giggled to herself. "My Id's talking to my Ego. Or my Super Id's talking to my Id."

"Fraud!"

Lily froze in her tracks. This was scary and unpleasant. As if sensing her fear, the Voice reverted to its quiet wheedling, "Do you actually believe all that bullshit you spew out? The Other. Waiting for my Grand Passion. Make do with Brad in the meantime. You're pathetic. Brad doesn't care about you. He's simply using you."

"That's not true," Lily blurted. She knew it was a mistake to talk back to the Voice, but the words were out before she could stop them.

"Oh, that's right. I forgot. You're using him. 'Brad's just a fling,'" The Voice imitated her tone exactly, before launching into its next diatribe. "You would love to be his girlfriend. You'd give your eye teeth to be someone's pre-wife, ex-wife, any wife. Just to have a shot at it. To be in the running. But you're out before the race is even on."

Lily tried to figure out what caused the Voice to suddenly burst into her mind. Sometimes it was dope. But not always. Usually, it happened when she was uncertain about something, trying to work it out. Then, the Voice would offer advice. It had never come before when she was happy. This was new. And it seemed stronger, more aggressive, more sure of itself.

"Men don't desire you. Be honest. Realize that. They don't want you. They don't think about you. They take what you offer. Precisely for those reasons. Because it's on offer. And now, you think you've made a friend."

"She likes me."

"A CON-FI-DANTE," the Voice laughed. "What a pile of crap. Why would she like you?"

"I don't know why, but she does."

"Have you told her what your job is?"

"She knows I work downtown."

"Does she know you're an office drone?"

"Why should it matter?"

"A grey sludge job for a grey sludge person."

"Stop it!"

"Fetch and carry. You can't even type."

"If you learn to type, you get slotted. You spend the rest of your life being a secretary."

"Well, you don't have to worry about that."

"No. I don't plan to be a secretary."

"I meant the rest of your life."

Then abruptly, the Voice stopped. Lily never knew when it was going to start up again. Its unpredictability made it all the more powerful.

⌐

"ENTERING A NEW host is like embarking on a love affair," sighed the Demon, with satisfaction, though he'd never actually experienced love. In some ways, the Demon, whose name was Little Beelzebub, Bubula to his cohorts (demons don't have friends), wished he'd entered a more interesting specimen. "However, there is definitely a thrill to it all. A new person, completely different from myself and over the years, I mould her to my caprices till we are one."

That was the object of the exercise and yet, when the union was consummated, Bubula found it startlingly unsatisfying. It happened every time. The host would behave more and more like the Demon, until finally, he was indistinguishable from the Demon. In a successful possession, the host would commit all sorts of heinous crimes. It took a stronger demon than Bubula to inspire a host to murder. Bubula had to content himself with small, petty acts against humanity.

There were two quarrelling factions of the Demonhood. One group advocated overtly aggressive acts, good old-fashioned murder and mayhem. The other faction preferred subtler subversive tactics. Of course, murder got more press but quiet malice accomplished more.

Although the tactics employed were small and insignificant, their subversive power accumulated in a riot of chaos, usually noted as a major historical event. These demons always cited the French Revolution and the fall of Rome as their major coups.

Still, the effect was the same. Once a demon had full control of the host, he invariably got bored. Fully possessed hosts acted in a repetitive manner. Deprived of free will, they moved as automatons, which took the sport out of the game. Sometimes, overcome by despair at their senseless actions, the hosts would kill themselves.

Lily didn't pose much of an intellectual challenge but Bubula had been lingering in dark, nether regions for so long that, quite frankly, he was happy to invade anyone. And she was young and healthy, which usually meant that he'd have a nice warm place to stay for at least fifty years. People were living longer so that meant less host-hopping. Other demons of Bubula's acquaintance preyed on vagrant alcoholics and drug addicts. Easy pickings and no challenge, thought Bubula. Skid row demons were a sorry lot, fighting to cram into host after host. There was rapid turnover. One human being could house as many as fifty or sixty demons but Bubula preferred one-to-one relationships.

Drugs are a godsend to demons. So many people were medicated in the twentieth century: drugs to calm one down, drugs to pep one up, drugs for depression, drugs for euphoria. They unlocked people's souls like they were opening all the doors and windows in a house. And of course, television acted as an underground railway to shunt homeless demons into the temporarily evacuated bodies. The initial invasions were not remotely subtle yet, for a while, they escaped human notice. Bubula fondly remembered the children's show *Uncle Stan's Clubhouse*. Children were instructed to chant along with Uncle Stan, "Zero Doctor, Zero Doctor, Hallowed Beelzebub. That's the secret password that we use down at the Club! Oh Zero Doctor, Zero Doctor ...." It was a cheerful little ditty. Very catchy, the sort of tune that stays in one's mind. The body in its passive alpha state, the host chanting to invite the demon in ... well, it was too perfect to last. Some Christian group put a stop to it. The creators of *Uncle Stan's Clubhouse* insisted that the verse was harmless gibberish. It wasn't "Hallowed" but "Hello" and Beelzebub was just a silly name, wasn't it. The Christians countered with "Uncle Stan? Uncle Satan, you mean!" The world at large thought the debate was hilarious, exposing the paranoia of religious factions. The show was discontinued but it had been on the air for enough time to make some inroads.

Eons ago, Bubula had been a human being. In retrospect, he imagined that he must have been invaded by demons himself, because he was a particularly nasty person. When he died, his spirit floated about in some ethereal region. (Bubula didn't have a name for it, having had no religion when he was human.) He could perceive shadowy shapes moving past him. He would reach out to grab one but it would disappear into another dimension. Bubula remembered the frustration of seeing what he should seize and yet not being able to lay his hands on it. He spent a long time in this condition. There were others with him. They couldn't see each other but they could hear each other's thoughts.

"You can get out of here, but you have to give your soul to the Devil."

"I thought I had."

"Your demon pledged for you and that's not allowed."

"There are rules here?!"

"There are always rules."

Bubula figured that his next destination had to be more interesting than this one, so he pledged.

⌒

KAT HOUSE BECAME a solidly built brick oven during the summer heat wave so most of the girls spent the evenings out, just to capture some night breezes. Lily was restless. She needed someone to play with. Jay's door was open. She glanced in. She wasn't there but it looked as though she was around.

Many "artists" had lived in the sorority house over the summers.

Very few of them had talent. Yet, they believed in themselves. Lily had to admire the sheer doggedness of belief. Jay thought she was going to be famous. She didn't actually come right out and say so, but Lily could tell that's what she thought. Lily crept down the basement stairs. Jay, in rapt concentration, was bent over an area of the canvas. It was a painting of a giant foot leaning up against a table. The face of an angry blue-haired woman loomed up from the table's edge and glared down at the foot, though why she would be angry at a foot was anyone's guess.

"Guess what?"

"Agh!" Jay leaped up in fright, dropping her brush to the ground.

"Sorry, didn't mean to scare you."

"Don't sneak up on me like that!"

"I didn't mean it. Guess what?"

"Is this a knock-knock joke?"

"I'm going skydiving!"

"You're what?!"

Lily's eyes glittered maniacally. "Brad and I have signed up for skydiving classes."

"Are you out of your mind?"

"It's not that dangerous."

"Jumping out of a plane isn't dangerous?!"

"We have parachutes."

"I would hope so. You're NUTS!"

"We're on the ground for the first few classes."

"That's nice."

"Don't you think it'd be exciting?"

"I guess so."

"You guess?!"

"I have no desire to do anything like that." Jay stepped back a few feet from the painting and regarded her work grimly. Lily realized the futility in trying to talk to Jay when she was at work. Normally, Jay would have been polite and at least, feigned to be impressed by Lily's daring. But when Jay was at work, politeness went out the window and she said and did exactly as she pleased.

"Do you want to go out?"

"I should work."

Lily realized this was her cue to say something encouraging about the painting. Then Jay could be persuaded to leave. "Oh yeah, the painting looks great."

"Really?"

"Oh yeah. You've done the foot well."

"I've worked on it. I think it's better flesh-toned than it was when it was green. I thought I'd make it more real. If the foot's real, then the blue woman works better. But if the foot's green, then the blue woman looks stupid."

"Yeah. Right." Lily had no idea what Jay was talking about.

Jay contemplated her work. "Mmm, yeah, yeah. It's good. It works. Let's go. I'll just clean up a bit." Jay wiped the excess paint off her brushes, then dipped them in turpentine. "You scared me back then. It's a little weird down here."

"With the foot?"

"No, the ghosts."

"The what?"

"The ghosts. I don't know what else they'd be. I hear people in the house and they're making so much noise that I've gone up to look. But no one's ever there."

"Has this happened a lot?"

"Oh yes, all the time," Jay replied matter-of-factly. "Sometimes, I hear them in the basement. On the stairs."

"And you can work down here?!"

"Oh yeah. It's just ghosts."

chapter eight

STEPPING OUT

ON FRIDAY MORNING, a tall, gangly young man lurched into class and promptly set up his easel right in front of Jay, effectively blocking her view of the model stand.

"Um, excuse me."

"Yeah?" The young man spun around to face Jay. He had very large brown eyes and long brown hair. Jay found it hard to get used to long hair on a man. It seemed effeminate.

"Um, sorry, but you're in my way."

"In your way of what?"

"The model."

"There's no model there."

"Not now, but there will be."

"Are you sure about that?"

"Pardon?"

"The model might not show up."

"Yes, but if she does."

"How do you know it'll be a she?"

"Look, could you please move? If, or when, he or she does show up, you're in my way."

"Not if we're not drawing from a model."

"It says Life Drawing with Snafu Smith."

"Snafu's teaching today?"

"Yes."

"Christ. I thought it was Bowen."

Jay pulled out her date book and turned to the appropriate page."No. It's Snafu Smith today."

"You seem very organized. Would you like to have dinner with me, tonight?"

"Ah —"

"I'll meet you here at five." Before Jay could reply, the strange young man disappeared. His easel remained. As Jay picked it up to move it, a loud voice bellowed at her.

"TOO CLOSE. You'll scare the model."

"Yes, I'm just —"

"STILL TOO CLOSE!"

Jay wondered if it was her fate in life to be singularly misunderstood by those around her. What was she supposed to do about this dinner date? Was this a serious invitation? Jay looked down at her flimsy sundress and dirty feet. She had bought hippie flip-flop sandals in an attempt to be fashionable. Instead of providing the necessary barrier between her feet and the ground, the sandals flipped the dirt onto her feet. She couldn't go out to dinner dressed as she was. She would have to leave class early. While Jay considered these matters, the loud voice barked again in her ear.

"WAKE UP!"

"Huh, sorry."

"Do you want to learn this stuff or are you just gonna stand there gaping?"

Jay regarded Snafu Smith evenly. The instructors at the Artists School were very different from university professors. They were plain-spoken to the point of rudeness. A professor would never bellow at a student. Most of Jay's professors weren't even aware of her existence. Professors dressed in casual business attire: tweed jackets, corduroy pants, sensible shoes. Snafu Smith wore a T-shirt and jeans. Jay glanced down at his feet. Running shoes. Snafu didn't look that much older than the student who'd just asked her out. He wore sunglasses. Jay thought it odd to wear sunglasses inside a building. Most of the artists who taught at the school were eccentric.

Snafu was cantankerous but he was a good teacher. During the class, Snafu paced and smoked and complained and was quite witty. Jay found him attractive, in a jaded, cynical kind of way. He was amusing. At the end of the class, Snafu stopped in front of her drawing, as if suddenly struck by it. She waited, expectantly, for his praise.

"Shit, no wonder it's so dark in here. I left my sunglasses on." He took the glasses off and looked at Jay for a moment. She looked into Snafu's eyes and was surprised to find them faintly familiar. Where had she seen those eyes before? She studied them, searching for clues. Suddenly, she knew everything there was to know about Snafu Smith, knew they would fall in love, saw the whole love affair fly by in an instant, and as quickly, the information was swept away from her and she was left with this strange, sated feeling of knowing, yet not knowing. Jay had fallen desperately in love with Snafu Smith and she had no idea how this happened, save that she looked into his eyes. Snafu, for his part, saw nothing.

"Don't have form," he grunted, "Think three dimensions. Make the leg go in and out of the space. And loosen up. Your drawing's too tight." Jay nodded breathlessly, unable to say a word.

"Who's going for a beer?" Snafu shouted amiably to the class. There was a strange pause. The students regarded him sombrely, then started to put their work away carefully. Brian gave Sheila an inquiring look but she shook her head delicately. Michael remained perched over his drawing, an intense pen and ink study of skulls.

"Sounds great," said Susannah. She smiled seductively at Snafu as she bent over to put away her supplies.

"Yeah," added Jonathan quickly. Jay always was the first to

pack up, so she stood by awkwardly, waiting for the others. She knew she should say something clever to Snafu. She plundered her brain for a smart remark but came up empty. Nothing.

"Meester Smeeth?" murmured a small, quiet voice behind Jay. Consuela looked shyly up at Snafu.

"Call me Snafu."

"Snafuuuu. Ees estrange name."

"War term. Situation Normal All Fucked Up."

"Pardonne?"

"What's your name?"

"Consuela Otero."

"Well, Consuela, are you going to join us?"

"Aaaaahh, I haff obligasiones."

"Can one of them be postponed for half an hour?"

"Perhaps." Consuela rolled her limpid brown eyes.

Jay was surprised to watch this performance. Could the dour Consuela actually be flirting with Snafu Smith?

"Please join us."

"Ah well, when you put it thees way, I reconsider."

"Consuela has to leave early, so we'll go now," Snafu called gaily to Susannah, whose mouth hung open in astonishment. "Head over when you're finished." Jay was too embarrassed to tag along after Snafu and Consuela. Susannah quickly got her gear together and she, Jonathan and Jay headed out.

The Brunswick House was conveniently located right across the street from the art school. They were just crossing the street when a voice called out.

"HEY!"

Jay turned to see the strange young man from the morning.

"I'm a little late but that's no reason to give up on me."

"We were, ah, just going for a beer."

"Beer. Great idea! I'm Rufus, by the way."

"My name's Jay. Jay Wright. Rufus?"

"Starling."

"Are you one of the teachers?" Susannah asked.

"Sort of. I'm a second-year student."

"Let's go. Snafu's waiting for us." Jay hated it when people lingered. Consuela was probably making significant inroads to Snafu's heart. Rufus suddenly grabbed Jay's hand and danced her in the opposite direction.

"You guys better hurry. Don't want to keep Snafu waiting."

"You're not coming?" Susannah called out.

"We made other plans," shouted Rufus, as they were now some distance away. The whole manoeuvre happened so quickly that Jay hardly had time to think.

"But ... but ... Snafu asked me to join him."

"Snafu asks every girl to join him. This time, I beat him to it. So, what do you want to do?"

Jay looked longingly at the Brunswick. Rufus did not pick up the hint, so she said, instead, "Do you mind if I drop my stuff off at home before we head out. I just live around the corner."

"Sure," said Rufus eagerly.

Jay realized, to her horror, that Rufus would now find out she was living in a sorority house. Mamma Sunshine's commune was nearby. Jay considered dropping her supplies off there.

"How'd you manage to find a place in this neighbourhood?"

"Oh, um, it wasn't so hard." The image of Mamma Sunshine's inquisitive face loomed large. Jay reconsidered the plan. She wished she could remember where Nicholas now lived. She led him reluctantly to KAT House.

"You stay here," she said, "I'll just put this in the door."

"Nice house." Rufus walked towards the home.

"NO!" shrieked Jay, "I mean, I'll just throw this in."

"Can't I come in?"

"No."

"Sheesh, all right."

Jay hurriedly opened the door and flung her bag into the hallway.

Eve spun around in surprise. Jay smiled and waved and slammed the door.

"Let's go."

"Aren't you afraid someone will take your stuff?"

"No."

"I see. Your parents live here?"

"No. It's a rooming house."

"And you're not locking your stuff away. Weird."

"I know the people."

"What sort of place is it?"

"You said you'd take me to dinner."

"Oh yeah, dinner. It's a group home, isn't it?"

"Sort of."

Rufus eyed Jay carefully. She seemed too well-behaved to be a delinquent. Perhaps it was a home for mental patients, though she didn't look insane. She might be a nymphomaniac, Rufus mused hopefully to himself.

"So, where should we go?" Jay asked, sensing a dangerous lull in the conversation.

"For what?"

"Dinner."

"Are you hungry?"

"Yes." Jay was ravenous. It might have been nerves. A boy had never taken her out to dinner before. It seemed a very grown-up thing to do.

"Ever been to the Korolla?"

"Uh, yeah ..."

"Let's go there."

Jay was altogether too familiar with the Korolla restaurant. She went there every day for lunch during the first week of school and ordered a small bowl of soup, which, next to coffee and tea, was the least expensive item on the menu. Jay prided herself on discovering the Korolla, though "discovery" is perhaps an exaggeration, since the restaurant was a few doors down from the art school and one would have to be blind not to notice the large sign, placed in the middle of the sidewalk, ostentatiously blocking everyone's path.

Jay thought Hungarian cuisine was very exotic. In Victoria, a bowl of soup in a diner consisted of some canned product, hastily heated up in a saucepan. The Korolla looked like a diner, but the food bore no resemblance to the tasteless fare usually found in such places. The menu said the soup was homemade and, surprise of all surprises, it actually *was* homemade. The roast chicken was genuinely roasted in an oven. And it had dressing. Jay's mother could have cooked such a chicken. The idea of going out and eating a meal better than one you could make yourself was a constant source of amazement to Jay. She told the other students about her "find" and they nursed their respective bowls of soup and cups of tea for the entire lunch hour, much to the annoyance of the owners of the Korolla restaurant, an industrious man and his wife who, understandably, did not appreciate the patronage and groaned loudly when the art students arrived for "lunch."

Mrs. Korolla, a diminutive woman in her forties whose name was not, in fact, Mrs. Korolla, tried to get rid of the art students. She didn't give them bread with their soup. Jay recalled being given bread before and the students noticed that the other diners received bread, so they complained loudly at every meal. To quiet them down, Mrs. Korolla conceded but, knowing that students left to their own devices could devour an entire loaf, put restrictions on the intake: one slice of stale bread for a small bowl of soup, no butter; two slices and butter for a large bowl of soup, no bread with tea and coffee. She thought the students wouldn't notice the bread was a week old but art students are surprisingly attentive to such details. They weren't ashamed to finger the bread and announce that it was stale to the rest of the clientele. Mrs. Korolla instructed the waitresses to be rude to the students. The students left no tips for their meagre meals, blaming it on bad service, repeating that familiar cycle of cause and effect.

Despite the Korollas' ever-increasing hostility, the students still arrived like clockwork, en masse at noon. Finally, Mr. Korolla, whose name was not Mr. Korolla, took action. He went up to the ringleader, Jay, and pleaded with her, "Please, please, you must stop coming here. Lunch hour is our only time for business. You take up all these places and you eat nothing. Either you eat or you leave."

Jay said, "But we do eat. We have soup. It's delicious. Does your wife make it?"

"Please, please, don't come here anymore."

"But I love your soup."

"Please, I know. Technically, you order, so, technically, I can't throw you out. But please stop coming here. In the name of God, go somewhere else."

"But your soup is so delicious."

"Try the Country Kitchen down the street."

"The what?" asked Jay, who hadn't been down the street. She'd never been past the Korolla.

Mr. Korolla hated to inflict this group of mobsters onto his friendly rival, Mr. Szegedy, but he was driven to desperate acts. He lowered his voice. "Their soup is better."

"It can't be better than yours."

"It is. It's just down the street. And try the Transylvanian Castle. It's one block thataway." Mr. Korolla gently eased Jay and her group out of the entranceway and onto the sidewalk.

"But we like it here," Jay persisted.

"Look, try these other places. Go to a different place every day. That way, we share."

"What'll you give us if we do?" demanded Michael, whose father was a lawyer.

Mr. Korolla was dumbfounded. Perhaps his wife's method of systematic abuse would have been more effective.

"How bout two pieces of bread and butter with the soup? Like you gave me the first time," said Jay, pressing the advantage.

"And you only come one day a week?"

"All right. Only one day. But we want fresh bread, like everyone else. Not stale bread."

"But not unlimited supply," said Mr. Korolla sternly.

"Okay."

"Okay. Deal!" Mr. Korolla beamed and shunted the group down the street. "Now, you go to Country Kitchen. But don't tell them I sent you!"

Jay was somewhat chagrined to have been unceremoniously tossed out of a restaurant. She was nervous about reappearing there for dinner. On the other hand, she could finally order a full meal. She had always wanted to try their roast chicken.

Rufus sniffed as he looked at the menu. "Hmph, haven't been here in a while. It's changed."

"The food's delicious," Jay said.

Mrs. Korolla appeared at the table and glared down at them. Jay was about to ask for roast chicken when Rufus waved Mrs. Korolla away. "We haven't decided yet."

"But —"

"Don't even think about ordering an entrée. They raised their prices and I'm flat broke."

"Oh."

"The soup's good here."

"Yes. I know."

"Let's have that." He signalled for Mrs. Korolla to return.

Jay was a little nervous now about how much she was allowed to eat without blowing Rufus's bankroll. "I'll have, um, the small soup of the day. What is it, please?"

"Chicken goulash."

"Yes, a small chicken goulash soup, please."

"Hmph." Mrs. Korolla grunted, then looked scornfully at Rufus.

"I'll have a large soup. And a beer."

Jay's mouth flew open in outrage. The large soup and beer was the same price as the roast chicken dinner. She was about to protest when Rufus leaned playfully into her.

"We'll share the beer."

"Oh. Actually, I don't drink beer."

"Why were you so keen to go to the Brunswick?"

Jay blushed fiercely.

"Right. What is it with you girls? Why are you all crazy about Snafu?"

Jay's face got even redder as she protested. "I'm not crazy about Mr. Smith. I don't even know him. It seemed like a friendly thing to do."

"Yeah, he's friendly all right. You're not his type."

"I'm not?"

"No. He likes big tits."

"Oh."

"Sorry. I didn't mean to imply that yours weren't —"

"It's fine." Jay glanced down at her chest. In her skimpy sundress, her breasts appeared even more negligible than usual.

"I like flat-chested women," added Rufus, helpfully.

"Flat-chested?!"

"Oh, sorry. I guess you —"

Mrs. Korolla plunked the beer in front of Rufus.

"Could we have two glasses, please?"

Mrs. Korolla fixed Rufus with an evil gaze. "You share the beer?"

"It's okay. I don't even like —"

The glass landed with a thud in front of Jay. Rufus filled her glass. They clinked glasses. Jay noticed that Rufus's eyes had very long, dark lashes. He was quite good-looking. She took a large swallow. Beer was as sour and nasty as she remembered. Still, it was gentlemanly of Rufus to insist on sharing it with her. He was a strange combination of chivalry and effrontery.

Mrs. Korolla threw the soup down with such authority that Jay knew this was going to be a short, speedy meal.

"So, I guess this is the first time you've studied art?" Rufus asked.

"No. I've been painting since I was little."

"Really? They said none of the summer students knew anything."

"I don't know why they'd say that. We've only just begun."

"Believe me. They know. You should have come during the year. That's when the serious art happens. Summer students, well, they're just dilettantes. They can't even commit to a full year. Going back to university in the fall?"

"Um, yes."

"See? Hedging your bets. The real artist never hedges his bets." Jay fumed quietly. "I wouldn't say that —"

"Well, I would. A real artist lives for his art...." Rufus went on to expound on the role of the real artist in society. Jay could not get a word in edgewise. Though she agreed with what Rufus was saying, she was furious that he had cavalierly dismissed her as a serious player. When Nicholas spoke down to her, Jay could convince herself that he secretly recognized that she was his intellectual equal. However, she had no such excuse for Rufus's arrogance. He wasn't sufficiently attractive to make her overlook such a blatant flaw. Jay vowed that as soon as this irritating dinner was over, she would go home and paint a masterpiece. Rufus interrupted his discourse to glance at the bill.

"You don't need to pay your half. I'll cover it."

"My what?"

"You can buy the movie."

"The what?"

Rufus grabbed a section of the newspaper from one of the other tables. The diner who was occupying the table glared at Rufus who remained blithely unaware of his offence.

"Let's see. *Last Tango in Paris*. What time is it?"

"Quarter after seven."

"Shit. Just missed it. Missed everything. Oh, hey — if we hurry, we can make *Fritz the Kat*."

"Fritz the who?"

"Let's go." Rufus downed Jay's beer, paid the bill, and hurried her out the door. They walked at breakneck speed down to College Street,

Jay huffing alongside. When they arrived at a shabby little kiosk, Jay barely had time to glance at the series of unpromising cartoons of a vicious-looking cat walking upright before she was asked how many and told how much. Jay paid grudgingly for this cinematic experience. She had never liked cartoons as a child and she was fairly certain that she wouldn't like this one.

It was worse than she imagined. Fritz the Kat mumbled a lot. Jay couldn't make out half of what he was saying. There were big-hipped female cartoon cats. They had large dome-like breasts with long, hard nipples jutting out. Fritz mumbled things under his breath as the female cats walked past. Rufus roared with laughter at Fritz's gibes. Fritz met other cats and they smoked pot together. When Fritz started having sex with one of the female cats, Jay was mortified. If she walked out, then Rufus would follow and want to know why and she would have to explain herself. It was easier to endure the film, then leave and never speak to Rufus again.

As they left the cinema, Rufus assumed that Jay liked the film as much as he had. He rhapsodized at length till Jay could stand it no longer and gave him the large piece of her mind that had been trapped in the cinema for the last two hours.

"It was a porno cartoon! You took me to see a porno cartoon!"

"Porno? There was some sex, I guess, but—"

"It was disgusting!"

"You find sex disgusting?"

"That cartoon was disgusting!"

"But sex is okay with you?"

"That's not the point. That was a really awful movie."

"You found *Fritz the Kat* too sexual?! Jesus, you're really uptight. I could have taken you to see *Last Tango in Paris*."

"I'm uptight?! Just because I don't like a stupid porno cartoon."

"It's pointless. I'll never do this dating routine again."

"Date? You call this a date?! I paid for a movie that I didn't want to see."

"You feminists. You're all alike. You talk about equality but men are supposed to pick up the tab."

"When did I ever talk about equality? When did I ever say a word! You did all the talking! And yes, you invited me so I thought you'd pay. You invite someone for dinner. You give them dinner. You don't take them to a restaurant and tell them they're not allowed to order any food. It'd be pretty lousy if I invited you for dinner and you show up and I say 'You're cooking.'"

"Is that an invitation?"

"What?"

"I'd love to have you cook me dinner. Tomorrow, then. I'll come by at seven." Rufus leaned in, kissed Jay on the lips and quickly sped away before she had a chance to protest.

⌒

WHEN BRAD ARRIVED to pick up Susan, Lily stayed in her room. She told herself that she wasn't hiding, that it was perfectly natural for her to spend time in her room. She decided that she wouldn't bother taking these skydiving classes. Let Brad track her down, if he wanted her to go so badly. She could hear Brad chatting to Eve as he waited for Susan. Lily knew she wasn't eavesdropping. She just needed to open her door a crack so she could hear more clearly. Eve was a notorious flirt. The girls were relieved that she had a fiancé to keep her insatiable libido at bay. She was drawling away to Brad.

"You look very nice, Brad. Where are you and Susan off to, tonight?"

"A movie."

"*Last Tango in Paris*? They've brought it back. It's playing at the Lux."

Brad laughed. "Not really up Susan's alley."

"Up yours?"

"Heh heh, she's later than usual."

"My favourite scene in *Last Tango* is — well, there are so many

— just the idea of it: anonymous sex with a total stranger," Eve sighed.

"It wasn't that anonymous. They made appointments."

"So, you *have* seen it."

"Yes."

"Aren't European films wonderful? They have such a different sensibility. Adult."

"Yes, they do."

"I'm Latvian. Well, my parents are Latvian but I was brought up in that European sensibility."

Just listening to Eve made Lily want to vomit. She was so nauseating, she and her secret sexual code words. "I enjoyed *Last Tango in Paris*" translated into "I'm willing to have uninhibited no-strings attached sex with you, just name a time and a place." Of course, the code was sufficiently vague that one could backtrack and claim one was just talking about the movie. Susan Lipton interrupted the discussion of European sensibilities just before Eve was about to put her hand on Brad's forearm and give it a gentle squeeze. It was an entirely contrived gesture, but boys seemed to go for it. Lily referred to it as Eve's Vulcan Death Grip, the last thing the hapless victim remembered before he lost consciousness and woke up in her grotto. Yes, it was a lucky thing for all of them that Eve was otherwise engaged. Lily waited for Judd the Stud to pick Eve up before venturing out of her room. The last thing she could endure was to be caught by Eve.

Lily! I didn't know you were here. Hiding in your room. Alone, are you? That's too bad. Weren't you going out with ... oh, I guess not. That one bit the dust a long time ago. But didn't you ...? We could have sworn you ... my, I haven't seen you since the barbeque. I just realized that. What have you been doing with yourself?

When Eve and Judd finally left — they always necked a little in the living room before leaving — and when the house was completely emptied of girls and their dates, Lily poked her head out. The coast was clear. Lily had worked herself up into such a high pitch of misery that she was, at last, reconciled to do her long-neglected laundry. She gathered it up and trudged sadly down the street to the laundromat, which was several blocks away.

On Friday and Saturday nights, the laundromat was full of gloomy people watching their clothes spin. One was supposed to sit and guard one's clothes, ever on the alert for the ubiquitous laundry thief. Lily could never understand why anyone would want to steal someone else's clothes, but apparently people did. The laundry thief was welcome to her clothes. It would give her an excuse to start over, buy a new life. Lily wandered down Bloor Street to kill time till the wash cycle was over. She spotted Jay with a lanky, long-haired guy, having dinner in one of the cheap Hungarian restaurants. Even Jay was on a date. The entire world was coupled up, except for Lily and the other disgruntled patrons of the laundromat. Lily returned to retrieve her clothes. The laundry thief had rejected her offerings. She put them in the dryer and, resigning herself to complete misery, sat and watched them turn round and round and round.

Lily was upstairs sorting her clothes when the front door slammed. It was Jay. She was very upset. She made a beeline for Lily's room.

"I'm so glad you're home. It was just awful!"

"Your date?"

"If you can call it that. He thought it was a date. God, it's hot in here. How can you stand it? Let's go out."

"And get some ice cream."

"Yeah, ice cream."

Tonight, Jay didn't bother with the bookstores. They headed straight for the ice cream parlour. Jay gave a blow-by-blow account of the evening while Lily settled back and enjoyed her ice cream cone.

"It was just awful! Awful! I'm waaaay too polite. Now, I've got this arrogant moron coming for dinner. Here, no less!"

"Do you like him at all?"

"I thought he was okay, before he asked me out. When I didn't know him. Now I hate him."

"Just tell him when you see him at class tomorrow that dinner's off." Having sorted out the problem, Lily concentrated on pushing the chocolate ice cream into a smooth line around the cone with her tongue.

"There's no class tomorrow."

Lily looked up. "Phone him."

"I don't have his number. He's probably too cheap to have a phone."

"It's too bad he knows where you live." Lily pondered the situation. "Don't answer the door."

"Someone's bound to let him in."

"Give him a lousy dinner."

"That goes without saying. Actually, the real problem is — I don't know how to say this without seeming rude —"

"What?"

"I don't want anyone to know what sort of place this is."

"What do you mean?"

"I've told everyone I live in a boarding house. He met me outside tonight. God, when he comes in and finds out it's a sorority house, I'm done for."

"What's wrong with the sorority house?"

"No offence and I don't mean you, personally, but you guys are totally out of it."

"Out of it," repeated Lily in the manner of someone drawing something long and poisonous out of a crevice.

"Artists aren't supposed to live in nice places. He'll use it against me. He'll tell everyone else. He'll tell the instructors. I'll feel like even more of a dork than I already am."

Lily started to get annoyed. "It's that bad? Living here? I think we've been very nice to you."

"I didn't mean it that way. It's great. I love it here. It's just that all the other students in the class are — well, they've been around. And I haven't."

"Around?"

"I was in this occult bookstore with Susannah. She's around my age. She's interested in astrology and she's looking up the planets for 1971. So I ask, who do you know born then? She says, without skipping a beat, 'My daughter. I had to give her up for adoption and I want to know what she's like.'"

"Oh." Jay was unusually talkative. Lily wondered if she was drunk. Lily was exhausted. She'd had an unpleasant day. She didn't want to spend the evening consoling a drunk. It was best to head home. She got up to leave and Jay, still talking, followed suit.

"Yeah, oh. And they're all like that. They've all got some awful secret. Even Rufus."

"Rufus?"

"My date."

"His name's really Rufus?"

"He probably made it up so he'd sound more like an abstract expressionist. All our teachers are abstract expressionists so we're all supposed to want to be abstract expressionists. It's completely confusing 'cause when I took classes at university, we were told abstract expressionism was dead and we were all supposed to be conceptualists. One of the teachers made us wear black armbands for a whole day. Another one made us plant zucchini seeds in egg cartons. I mean, I just want to learn how to paint. Think that'll ever happen? Not likely. It's just so —"

"What's Rufus's secret?" asked Lily, steering the conversation to more concrete matters.

"Huh? He hasn't told me, yet. I'm sure it's a doozy."

"Is this guy cute?"

"Are you kidding?"

"One girl's poison is another girl's meat. I need to be distracted."

"He thinks he's cute. I suppose he could be cute, if he weren't such an obnoxious cheapskate."

They walked along Bloor Street, heading back to the house. Lily glanced about for a familiar face to interrupt this tête-à-tête, but she saw no one.

"I never had this problem in Victoria," continued Jay, "I didn't go out a lot but when a boy asked me out to a movie or something, he paid. I never thought about how he got the money. I guess I assumed his parents gave him money. And with Nicholas, well, we'd go out with my best friend and his best friend. They were dating. We'd tag along. We didn't do anything expensive. We'd play tennis or go to someone's house. And at university, well, things just come up. There's a party and we all go. Or we go for coffee after class. I've never been in a situation where I'm broke and the guy's broke and we have to do something expensive together for it to qualify as a date. I am so glad I didn't order an entree. He'd probably expect me to sleep with him if I ordered an entree. What do you do about stuff like that?"

"Don't go out with artists."

"Not even a nice one?"

"Are there nice ones?"

"This dating people you don't know ... It's so weird. I feel like there's a little clock going tick tick tick. Are you going to sleep with him or not? Tick tick tick. When are you going to make up your mind? Tick tick tick. 'Cause I can't do what you girls do. Make out for hours till you're stark naked and then say, 'Home, James.' It's like one of those sucky Doris Day movies where she teases the guy to death. She's too old to do that. I always swore I'd never be like that. I'd like to fall in love but it's not going to be easy."

"Why do you say that?"

"With most guys, I can't get past their table manners. It puts me right off."

"Oh."

"Does Brad have nice table manners?"

Lily laughed. "I haven't noticed. Rufus?"

"Not bad. But the rest of him is so awful."

"Yeah."

"I don't think I'm ever going to fall in love."

"What about Nicholas?"

"That's just me being stupid. I haven't seen him for a month. I think he's got a girlfriend."

"You could still go after him."

"I don't want to play second fiddle. I don't want to be the Other. I don't know why you don't mind Brad going out with Susan."

Lily looked hard at Jay before replying, "Of course I mind, but I know he really loves me, so it's okay."

"Mmmm." Jay was non-committal on this point.

"Well, he's not in love with Susan."

"No."

"And he sees me all the time."

"Then he should ditch Susan and go out with you."

"Life isn't so black and white."

"It is for me."

"You've never been in love."

"I guess not."

And on this melancholy note, the girls arrived at the House. They retired to their rooms. Jay pondered her lack of prospects and Lily wondered whether Brad really loved her or whether she was deluded.

chapter nine

ISOSCELES TRIANGLES

THE DOORBELL RANG at KAT House at six-thirty p.m. Rufus stood on the porch and looked about, ostentatiously, in the manner of a baronial lord surveying his property.

"Oh God, he's here! Plus, he's half an hour early!" wailed Jay.

"Calm down, this'll be fun." Lily answered the door and let him in. "Hello, you must be Rufus. I'm Lily. Oh, you brought beer. Thanks!" she said and took it from him. The baronial lord was momentarily confused. "Come in, dinner awaits."

"What is this place? I noticed the letters above the door."

"KAT House. We're freemasons."

"Shriners?"

"No. Freemasons. Feminist freemasons."

"No shit. I thought you had to be a guy to be a freemason."

"We're an offshoot of the Rosicrucian Society. You're familiar with Madame Blavatsky?"

"No."

"Well, enough said. No point preaching to the ignorant."

"What do you do here."

"Some of us are call girls."

"What?"

Lily looked at her watch. "Suzy'll be down at ten to eight. She's very punctual. Her regular client arrives. He's a little late, today. He's usually punctual as well." Hearing a male presence in the house, Eve headed down the stairs. Lily quickly whispered to Rufus, "She's one, too. Careful now, she's looking for someone to fill in her slot. Had a cancellation. I'll go get Jay. Just wait here for a while."

Eve slinked into the living room and feigned surprise at discovering a strange man sitting on the couch. And he was stranger than most. His baggy black pants were covered in dust and paint stains. His jacket was relatively new and quite smart-looking, so that, on a quick glance from the waist up, he was fairly presentable. He wore a bizarre shirt. It was grey — had it once been white? — with a peculiar cartoon on it.

"Fritz the Kat!" said Rufus, pointing to his chest.

"Oh."

"I noticed you were staring at my chest. Can I take my jacket off? It's fucking hot in here." Without waiting for a response, Rufus tore his jacket off, a cloud of dust billowing out with the motion.

"Oh," said Eve, rendered momentarily speechless by the overpowering odour of a day spent hard at work in the manly enterprise of abstract expressionist painting. "So, who are you here to see?"

"Christ, is the whole house —?"

"Pardon?"

"Ah, nothing. Jay. I'm here to see Jay. Is she one of you guys?"

"No, she's just a boarder."

"Too bad. So, I take it you're available."

"No," giggled Eve, flattered that he'd be so blunt even though she found him faintly repulsive. "No, I'm engaged."

"Oh, they said you were free."

"No, engaged."

"I probably couldn't afford you."

"Pardon?"

"Ever do charity work?" Rufus leaned in and fixed Eve with a dark, lustrous 'I'm dying for you' gaze. Eve couldn't help but notice that this peculiar man had beautiful eyes, deep limpid pools fringed with long dark lashes. As she was admiring his eyes, Rufus leaned in further and kissed her. He was an extremely good kisser. Eve worried about getting her clothes all dirty by the contact but she couldn't quite break away. Not yet.

The doorbell rang and she leaped up to answer it. Judd and Brad had arrived together. There was a flurry of activity. Eventually, Susan Lipton came rushing down the stairs. The girls paired up with their respective dates and dashed out the door.

"Freaky," mused Rufus. "Really freaky." He wandered into the kitchen and found Jay and Lily chopping up vegetables for a salad. His beer was safely on the table so he reached over and was about to share it with the girls, but he noticed that Lily had already helped herself. "Those chicks, they look like that Doublemint gum ad." Rufus broke out into a chorus of *Double your pleasure, double your fun with Doublemint, Doublemint, Doublemint gum.* "Sorry, Guess it's not that funny. Had a joint before I came here."

"Got any left?" asked Lily.

Rufus foraged around in his pockets and eventually dug out a small, withered butt, which he lit and offered to Lily. Jay pulled the roast chicken out of the oven. "It's upside-down," observed Rufus.

"We always cook things upside-down."

"A freemason thing?"

"Exactly."

Lily studied Rufus. She'd have to overlook a hell of a lot before she'd consider him as a suitable distraction from Brad. The art world was a strange one. Lily couldn't understand how a guy who was as good-looking as Rufus could let himself go to seed like that. True, he had a certain shabby charm and oddly enough, he had fastidious table manners. She could see he came from a good family, though he was desperate to obliterate all signs of gentility. Lily thought it strange that a man would deliberately make himself unattractive. Brad was very concerned about his looks, vain almost. Brad had a smooth veneer that took a full evening for Lily to remove. This man had no veneer. He was a rough-hewn block of wood. Lily laughed to herself.

"What's so funny?" Rufus asked defensively.

"The dope. It makes me laugh."

"No. You were laughing at me."

"Well, you are funny."

"Yes, but I didn't say anything funny. You were laughing at me as I am."

"Yes, I was."

"Why?"

"You're different from most people." Lily meant men.

"I should hope so. I try very hard to be different."

"Maybe that's what makes me laugh. You try so hard." There was an uncomfortable silence, as Rufus tried to decide whether he should take offence. "I'm doing my first skydiving class tomorrow," Lily proclaimed.

"Is that where you parachute out of a plane?" asked Rufus.

"Yeah," said Lily, readying herself for a barrage of questions from an awestruck Rufus.

"That's sort of stupid, isn't it?"

"Huh?" Lily's mouth fell open.

"I think so," said Jay.

"I mean, why would anyone want to do that?"

"I don't know. It's weird, isn't it?" agreed Jay.

"Because it's exciting. It's thrilling!" spluttered Lily.

"I guess so. If you're into that sort of dumb action stuff." Rufus finished his beer and reached for another one.

"Dumb action stuff?!" Lily was aghast. Artists had the strangest set of criteria. "You mean you wouldn't want to go skydiving if you had a chance?!"

"You couldn't force me to do it."

"Me, neither!" added Jay.

Rufus looked at Jay in surprise.

"Then, you're both chicken," said Lily.

"Are you calling me a chicken?" Rufus speared his drumstick and held it up to Lily threateningly. "By the way," he said to Jay, "this is delicious!"

"Brawk! BukBuk! Brawk Buk Buk Buk!"

"That is so — oh, wow, man! I can't believe it. She's clucking at me. Ms. Macho."

"Brawkbukbukbuk."

"Yeah. I'm chicken. I'd be scared shitless and I'm proud of it." Rufus set his beer down with authority.

"You admit you'd be scared?!"

"Damn right. Though, I wouldn't call it 'scared.' You'd call it that, 'cause you're this weird macho chick. I'd just call it being smart."

"Macho chick. Is that an insult?"

"Not at all. It just means you're into a lot of male bullshit."

"It is an insult."

"No, honestly. It's not an insult. You got your thing. I got my thing. Your thing's jumping out of planes. My thing's painting. I happen to think my thing's smarter and more interesting than your thing but that's 'cause it's like — it's my thing."

"You're really weird."

"Let's drink to that." Rufus reached for his bottle but it was empty. He groped about for his remaining beer, realized he'd drunk them all and so, looked hopefully at Jay.

"I didn't buy any beer. We just have wine."

"No beer at all?" Rufus opened the refrigerator and scanned its contents. "Aha!" He pulled out a bottle and held it out triumphantly, "It's even got a name. Eve. Oh thou temptress, Eve!" He opened it quickly and leaned over to clink his bottle with Lily and Jay's glasses. "To Being Weird!" Rufus proclaimed.

"To being a thief!" said Lily.

"Replace them tomorrow. No problem."

"Them?" asked Jay nervously.

"We've got a long night ahead of us." Rufus gave Jay an enquiring look. Jay returned it with a blunt gaze.

"I can't drink too much," said Lily, "Gotta be alert for tomorrow."

Rufus took a long, careful swallow. "This is why painting is an infinitely more enjoyable activity than that jock stuff."

"So, you can drink yourself into oblivion?" asked Jay.

Rufus cut off a few more slices of roast chicken before replying, "That's rather harsh. I enjoy life. I work hard and I enjoy my time off."

"So, you don't drink this much all the time?" persisted Jay.

"Don't mind Jay. She's a Puritan."

"I thought she was a freemason."

"That, too," said Lily.

"They weren't call girls, were they?"

Jay and Lily roared with laughter.

"I talked to the first one like she was a call girl."

Jay and Lily screamed, "EVE!" and laughed even harder.

⌣

BRAD WAS HEADING into Sigma Chi when he saw Paul, moving back into his old room. He gave an involuntary start.

"Don't worry, buddy. It's cool."

"I'm not worried."

"I saw the look you gave me. You're safe. How's life with the prom queen? Home early."

"Lipton's been dragging me off to all these bridal showers. Thinks it'll make me pop the question."

"Well, you're a good catch."

"Stop that."

"You didn't say much when you came over. Thought you wanted to talk."

"Your sister was there."

"So, she distracted you?"

"Yes. A lot."

"Well, you can prove your manhood with her. She's a nympho. She's probably done you a hundred times by now."

"Why would you say that? She's your sister."

"It's the truth."

"No one's talked about her in that way."

"Well, she's old news. They've all had her. You seeing her?"

"We're just friends. Doing that course tomorrow."

"The one we were going to take."

"Why not? I still wanted to take it."

"Well, in that case, I'll join you."

"Ah —"

"My sister won't mind. Unless you are —"

"We're just friends."

"So, what's the problem, then?"

"No problem."

"Don't get huffy. Understood, friend. See you tomorrow."

Brad reflected on the days prior to the incident, when he and Paul were best friends. Paul had style. He was smart, athletic, good-looking, witty; everything that Brad longed to be. Paul had his choice of women. He was never in a hurry to bed them. He took his sweet time and eventually, slept with each and every one of them. He would never go after a girl who was taken, just the free ones. And in those days, most of them were free. Going steady was some antiquated ritual from the fifties. Brad kicked himself for getting suckered into this "steady" business.

Susan always got up at the crack of dawn to go to church on Sunday so their dates ended early, leaving him at loose ends for the rest of the evening. He and Paul used to go for a beer at the Brunswick House and watch the Midget who was actually a dwarf, do his Elvis Presley impersonation. Brad didn't like the Midget and he was further baffled as to why people liked Elvis Presley, whom he thought was bloated, fat, old and greasy.

On this particular night, the Midget was in the middle of "Are You Lonesome, Tonight?" and Paul turned and said, "Let's get the hell out of here."

"Where to?"

"You want to do something 'interesting'?"

"Interesting?"

"It's this club. It's sort of a disco bar. The Cock 'n Bull."

"Sounds like an English pub."

"It ain't no pub."

The Cock 'n Bull was in an alley off Charles Street. A tiny brass plate on a fire exit door confirmed the location. They walked through a grey-walled concrete corridor to a door that featured a crude cartoon of two bulls copulating while a rooster crowed on the sidelines. Brad and Paul then entered into a disco version of a casbah — a darkly lit palatial room, drapes of diaphanous cloth floating from the ceiling, mirrors everywhere: on the walls, on the floor, on the ceiling; flashing lights, large mirrored balls refracting the light into a thousand flickering pieces; a maelstrom of activity: disco music pounding away, hundreds of half-naked bodies gyrating rhythmically, en masse. The smell was overpowering. It reminded Brad of the men's locker room, or his frat house on stag nights. Pungent male sweat.

Once his eyes got accustomed to the gloom, he could see that this "club" was full of men. A rope gently dropped from the ceiling. A kid was stark naked and climbing up and down the rope; wrapping his legs around the rope, unwrapping his legs; making a real performance out of it; Paul's voice beside him, "Think of it like a movie. Okay? There's just a lot of stuff to watch."

"Christ! It's a fag bar. Are you a fag, Paul?"

"'Course not. I always wondered what these places were like."

"I thought you'd been here before."

"Nah, heard about it. Anyway, you can't go to a place like this by yourself."

"Christ, no. We're getting a lot of looks, buddy."

Paul put his hand on Brad's arm. "We'll pretend we're a couple."

"Hell no!"

"They won't come on to us. Let's get some martinis. Fags make really great martinis."

"I'm not drinking."

"Aw, come on."

"If I drink, I'll have to piss. And I sure as hell am NOT going into that can."

"Use the alley."

"Yeah, right. The alley'll be real safe. This is fucking weird, Paul. What's interesting about it?"

"I just thought you'd like a little change from Susan. Besides, it's not all men here." Paul indicated some women standing near the bar. They were in their late twenties, early thirties. They had a hard sexy "show girl" look: big bouffant hair, short tight skirts, lean taut legs perched on stiletto heels. Two of them murmured to each other and sashayed over. The sultry blonde went for Paul.

"Hi, boys. You look a little lost. My name's Norma Jean. And this is Rita." Rita had small, glittering eyes framed by a monstrous set of false eyelashes, a crimson slash for a mouth and a mean-spirited expression. Norma Jean leaned in conspiratorially. "A couple of straight boys like you need some help."

"How do you know we're straight?" asked Paul.

"We can tell." Norma Jean's eyes coolly scanned Brad's body.

"Still, they could think we were two gay guys with female friends," persisted Paul.

"Hmm, that is a problem. Well, let's make it clear that you're not gay." Norma Jean leaned over and kissed Paul for a long time.

"Whew, Norma!" Paul gasped, pulling back.

"Norma Jean, sweetie!" She kissed him again and placed Paul's hands on her buttocks. Brad glanced down at Norma Jean's bum. It was lovely; firm and sculptured. Norma Jean murmured something. He grinned and waved to Brad as she gently towed him to a back room.

"I'll be back."

Rita whispered in Brad's ear. "Don't worry, honey. I'll protect you." She then proceeded to lick the inside of his ear, making it tickle. "You're just a little college sweetie, aren't you. I could eat you all up. Do you want me to eat you all up?" Rita put her hand on Brad's cock. Brad would have preferred that it hadn't become firm in an instant because he didn't find Rita remotely attractive. Her face was heavily made-up in an attempt to soften very aggressive features: jutting cheekbones, a square jaw. Brad removed her hand. He couldn't understand what she was doing here. It seemed an odd place for a hooker to ply her trade.

"How much do you charge?"

"Charge? Baby, I'd never 'charge' you."

"You'd just do me?"

"Yeah."

"Why?"

"Questions, questions. I like it. I'm a very sexual person." Rita said this in a hushed movie-star whisper. She ran her tongue up and down the nape of Brad's neck. "And well, you, ah, college boys — you're a very special treat. You smell like — mmmmm, baby powder."

"Fuck this shit!" Brad pulled away in disgust. He caught Rita off-guard. For a split-second, she looked like a frightened boy, and then the eyes hardened and Brad realized he was staring into another man's eyes. Rita winked and walked away. Paul appeared at that moment, looking very pleased with himself.

"Enjoy yourself?"

"Oh yeah, she was great."

"Not like any woman you've ever known?"

"Yeah. You should get Susan to take classes from her. Why'd you get rid of yours?"

"They're guys, you moron!"

"What!"

"They were guys. You just got 'done' by a guy."

"Oh shit. No!"

"Yeah. Christ, let's get out of here. I need a drink."

"Christ! Me, too."

They walked up Yonge Street, past the strip joints and sex parlours and found a bar that was simply a bar; no added entertainment — it was the Midget's dismal singing that had led them into this misadventure. They took solace in their cheap beer.

Paul was clearly agitated. He dropped his mask of cool detachment and asked with a strange earnestness, "Does that mean I'm a homo?"

"Sure does, Paul. You've joined the other side," replied Brad, trying to make light of it.

"I mean, it's weird, eh? If it's a girl doing it, you're straight. If it's a guy, you're a homo."

"You're not a homo, Paul."

"I know. But it's weird that it should be that arbitrary. So, like, if I was to do you, you'd still be straight but I'd be a homo."

"I guess so. I don't know."

"But, having it done doesn't make me a homo."

"No."

"I think what really makes you a homo is the ass thing."

"Probably."

"It's supposed to be really great."

"Yeah?"

"Yeah. Guys who do it never want to go back."

"That good, eh?" Brad was uncomfortable with the direction the conversation was going but could not restrain his curiosity.

"The best. But I think you could do the ass thing and not be a homo."

"Aw, come off it."

"If you were the one doing it. Not the guy it's being done to. 'Cause there wouldn't be that much difference between a guy and a woman."

"I think there's a big difference."

They walked up the street to the house. Brad was exhausted by the evening's events. Paul still wanted to talk about it.

"You know what was really weird?"

"Apart from the obvious?"

"I kept thinking, 'Hey, this broad's really good. She knows all the tricks.'"

"I'm sure a hooker would be the same."

"You think so?"

"Yeah."

"We should try one."

"I don't want to pay. You try one."

"Oh man, I am really loaded."

Brad was about to guide Paul to his room but instead, Paul stumbled into Brad's room, tore off all his clothes and collapsed onto Brad's bed. Brad studied him for a moment, then left to sleep in Paul's room. It was hot and humid. He stripped, lay on top of Paul's bed and fell into a deep sleep. Towards the early morning, he had an erotic dream involving Rita. He found himself aroused and repulsed by him/her. She sucked on his cock, then winked at him, then sucked on his cock some more. He kept trying to prevent the onslaught of pleasure because that would mean he liked her, that he would have to marry her. Rita then changed into Lily. Brad relinquished himself to the orgasm and awoke to see Paul crouched over him.

"Did you just —"

"Some dream you had, eh?"

"Did you —"

From then on, Brad cheerfully, affably, assiduously avoided Paul. Paul moved back home for the summer, claiming the frat house was too hot for him.

⌐⌐

SUSAN LIPTON WENT into the kitchen for her late-night glass of milk. A lone candle, almost down to its wick, spluttered in the holder.

"Fire hazard," thought Susan as she blew it out. The air in the room was heavy with stifled breath. Susan flicked on the overhead light and saw legs protruding from underneath the kitchen table. Lily and Jay's legs. And a man's. "An orgy!" Susan gasped out loud. The room erupted into a chaos of raucous laughter.

"An orgy? That's wild!"

"It's not an orgy, Susan," giggled Jay as she clambered up to show Susan that she still had her clothes on. Lily and Rufus remained, howling with laughter, under the table.

Susan scurried out of the room and up to her bed. Sex was taking over. It was everywhere. And there were some girls like Lily who could use sex to their advantage. They weren't ruined by being promiscuous. Quite the reverse. Their promiscuity gave them a certain power over men. She had allowed Brad to feel her up tonight. Having rendered up this long-sought objective, Susan was surprised that he did not respond with more enthusiasm. He must be having regular sex with Lily. Hence, her offer of a feel would be small potatoes in comparison.

She was losing ground to this carefree slut who, having secured Brad, was now merrily copulating with a grimy stranger under the kitchen table. Susan had all the old rules of sexual conduct worked out. It was very simple. Boys asked and she refused. But women were no longer playing by these rules. They were inventing new ones and men were happily joining in the game. Girls like Lily spoiled it for everyone.

Susan's virginity, once a highly sought-after commodity, was now, suddenly, devalued. She knew that if she capitulated to Brad's sexual demands, then he would simply sit back and do a field comparison of girls he was bedding. Lacking sexual skills, she was earmarked to be an early casualty. Susan wondered what place an old-fashioned vice like jealousy held in the fickle ground of sexual politics. Did promiscuous people get jealous? Would Brad be upset if he knew that Lily was seeking other pleasures? Or would it move Lily to a higher echelon of desire? Amidst the shifting tides of social change,

Susan knew that, ultimately, she could rely on the long-established values of property and possession. Buried deep in unacknowledged atavistic recesses of his mind, Brad believed that women were his property. And he would be very angry indeed if he learned there was a poacher on the premises. Angrier still, if he discovered that the poacher had been invited. And with this incontrovertible proof of Lily's infidelity as her trump card, Susan Lipton settled in to a long, deep sleep.

⌒

EARLY SUNDAY MORNING, Lily hurried over to Sigma Chi House. She was pleased to see Brad standing outside the house waiting for her, but he looked anxious.

"I'm not late, am I?" she asked.

"There's been a change of plans."

"Good! Let's go out for breakfast."

"Paul's joining us."

"Why is he —"

"Paul told me about the course. He and I were supposed to take it. Then he decided not to. But he's changed his mind again." Brad gave Lily a sheepish look. "I'm sorry," he whispered. "We'll go out later." He was about to kiss her when Paul, in exuberantly high spirits, came bounding out of the house.

"Hi, sis," he said, coming between Lily and Brad, putting his arms around their waists. "And how're my sister and my best friend today?" He gave them both a playful squeeze. "What'd you do last night?"

"Pardon?"

"Did you go out with Mike?"

"Um, no."

"You were pretty hot and heavy with Mike. What happened?"

"I haven't gone out with Mike for at least six months."

"Maybe I got the wrong house. Mike from Phi Gamma Delta. Lily likes to do a house at a time."

"Very funny, Paul."

"Oh hey, sis, I got really loaded last night and I'm afraid I'm gonna puke. Do you mind sitting in the back?"

Paul shoved Lily into the back seat of his car. It was more like a ledge than a seat. Paul drove a small Volkswagen Beetle. The Volkswagen's motor was situated where the trunk would normally be, so Lily had the additional discomfort of sitting in what sounded like a great, huge, rumbling behemoth as the car lurched on its way. Something was wrong with the motor and Paul hadn't got round to fixing it. He rolled his window down. Any attempts of Lily's to join in the conversation in the front were foiled by the motor's cacophonous roar and the great gusts of wind whistling through the back, buffeting Lily about.

"Could you roll your window up, please, Paul," Lily shouted.

"Sorry, can't hear you!"

Lily sat and brooded in the back of the car while the boys laughed and joked. She wanted to leap out at the next intersection but she was trapped. When Paul stopped at the lights, Lily shouted, "LET ME OUT! I want to go home!"

"What's wrong, sis?" Paul asked. Lily hated it when he called her "sis."

"I don't want to take these stupid classes." Paul and Brad broke into a chorus of "AWWW, come on. Don't be a poor sport. We're almost there."

"I don't have enough money."

"The first couple of classes don't cost much. They're just tryouts to see if you're interested."

"Anyway, they're not that expensive. We get student rates," added Brad, forgetting that Lily was no longer a student.

Flash, the instructor and jumpmaster, was a relentlessly jolly young man who spoke in a loud voice and called everybody "gang."

"Listen up, gang! Your parachute is the safest piece of equipment known to man. You look surprised when I say that, but it's true. You have your main parachute and if something goes wrong with it, you have your reserve chute. Now, how many of you can say that about your cars. Right, gang? If your car breaks down, you don't have another car to go to. If your brakes suddenly go and you're heading down a steep hill in snow, you've had it. Driving a car is more dangerous than skydiving. Remember that, gang. Of course, there are hazards and you have to be prepared. So, that's my job. To prepare you. Now, we're gonna start with some trust exercises, 'cause trust is all ya got. Get to know each other. Along with the equipment, of course. But ya gotta trust your buddies. It's the buddy system here, gang. So, find yourselves a buddy."

Lily had become separated from Paul and Brad, so she had to pair up with a total stranger, a frail middle-aged woman.

"So, turn around, close your eyes, cross your arms over your chest and fall backwards into your buddy's arms. Don't worry. Your buddy will catch ya!"

The woman smiled wanly at Lily and said, "All right, you go first." Lily obeyed the directive and dutifully hurled herself backwards to the ground just as the woman asked, "What am I supposed to do, again?" Lily landed on her tailbone. "I'm so sorry," said the woman.

Brad saw Lily head for the door and rushed over to her. "You be my partner, okay?"

"Paul's your partner."

"He can find someone else. Come on." Lily grudgingly allowed Brad to pull her back in. Brad jollied Lily out of her sulk very quickly. He had a special way with her. Soon, Lily was just as keen as he, champing at the bit to start skydiving for real.

"Okay, gang, there's falling and there's landing. Today, we're gonna practise landing. PLF, gang. Parachute Landing Fall. Now, how would you guess that you should fall? Go limp like a cat? Anyone for that?" A number of people, including Lily, put up their hands. "Wrong! Break a leg doing that, gang. Nope. Ya gotta absorb the shock. Any of you skiers? Ski the moguls? Really big moguls? Your legs and knees are pressed tight together, but flexible at the same time. Like a big spring. So, when you land from a mogul, you bend into it. Well, it's the same principle. With a few changes, of course. There're no skis and the mogul's four thousand feet high. Haw haw haw. Now, we're gonna be getting on these risers and practise our PLFs. Be thankful, gang, the riser's only four feet high."

Flash told them how to fall to the side and roll. It was more complicated than it looked and it hurt if you didn't do it properly. Flash spent an inordinate amount of time making the "gang" fall from the platforms. Some people got fed up. They were expecting a more glamorous introduction to the sport. Sensing that he was losing his audience, Flash brought out the equipment. They practised handling it and strapping themselves into the gear. Lily couldn't manage the big clamp that went across her body and had to ask for Brad's help to do it up.

"SO, GANG!" Flash bellowed out his closing remarks. "Next week, we'll cover emergency release procedures. AND THE PLFS! Won't get off that easily. You might be a little sore tomorrow but keep practising. Do your counts at home. Do it on a coffee table. If you can't find a table, a bed'll do. Haw haw. Do it till it becomes second nature to you. OKAY? YEAH!"

Lily had an exhilarating day; the only drawback being that Paul was present for every minute of it. She assumed that Paul was still living at home. However, he informed her that he had moved back into Sigma Chi, which was going to put a serious crimp on Lily's rendezvous with Brad. Lily tried to catch Brad's eye, but without success. He was not forthcoming. Paul dropped her off at KAT House and the two boys went on to Sigma Chi.

chapter ten

THE BOHEMIANS

No Handbook
No Tenets

JAY WAS SLOWLY realizing that there was an entire society attached to the art school that had nothing to do with showing up on time for class and doing good drawings. And that to succeed in the art world, one had to be accepted by these people. This latter assumption was erroneous but it led Jay into a series of adventures that changed the course of her life.

The summer students were not aware of this vigorous subterranean life lurking under the aimless facade of classes. They were very poor and single-minded. So, when Mr. Rossco casually mentioned before lunch that he'd see them all at the Brunswick, none of them took him up on the invitation, for Tuesday was Cauliflower Soup Day at the Korolla.

The students had unanimously agreed that it was the best soup of the week. If Mr. Rossco, who was something of an art-world celebrity in a country that didn't believe in celebrities, had known that the pleasure of his illustrious company had been weighed up against a bowl of soup and found wanting, he would have been seriously annoyed. As it was, he was spared this brutal truth. Students from the year before knew he would be at the Brunswick on Tuesday and sought him out, for Mr. Rossco was a marvellous human being and a truly exciting person to be around.

Some people would say that he drank too much and Rossco was quick to point out the difference between a drunk and an alcoholic. A drunk could stop any time he liked. Alcoholics could not stop. William Rossco maintained a well-regulated weekly binge. His drinking began promptly at noon on Tuesday, after he'd taught his morning class and continued unabated until five p.m. Thursday afternoon, when he finished his class at the rival art school. Solicitous students accompanied him to the commuter train and saw him to his seat. He was then whisked away, in a drunken stupor, to the outlying suburb of Mimico. The train stopped and the porter unceremoniously rolled Rossco off the train into the welcoming arms of his wife, Verna.

Verna was an exceptionally beautiful woman; tall, graceful, elegant. She was also extremely kind, which was rare, as the qualities of beauty and kindness are not often found in the same person. Rossco's mistresses, expecting to see a sour-faced frump, were disappointed when they met the radiant Verna, for she was everything Rossco said she was. Rossco adored Verna. She was the light of his life. She was the First Wonder of his World. Mistresses Two through Seven would have to vie for the remaining places.

Rossco lived in Mimico because the city was bad for him. Drink, drugs, loose women lay in wait for Rossco in the city. Creatively, Rossco thrived in the city. Its lurid charms inspired him so he and Verna worked out an arrangement. Like a vampire dividing its time between night and day, Rossco sucked the city dry of its corrupt juices and scuttled safely home to the country to recuperate, or "dry out," as Verna put it. Verna had a slightly different take on the subtle differences between alcoholics and drunks. Rossco swore that he was not an alcoholic because alcoholics got really mean when they were drunk and he got, well, simply drunk. The fact that he was drunk more and more often as of late was a minor inconvenience for Rossco, albeit a major one for Verna.

Rossco's binges had very distinct phases. The first was the amorous stage, during which Rossco had an immense appreciation for female beauty, however unprepossessing such women might appear to the untutored eye. Rossco usually met his future mistresses on the Tuesday that he arrived in town. He was alert and flirtatious then. He could seduce any woman he laid eyes on. This would not be a particularly remarkable skill were William Rossco famous, wealthy or blindingly good-looking but, as William Rossco possessed none of these attributes, it was something of a miracle.

Five years previous, Rossco was the undisputed king of the burgeoning Toronto art scene, which was to say, personally notorious but from the point of view of the average Canadian, not famous at all.

William Rossco believed he was famous and to his own circle of cronies and friends, he was. Some of Rossco's peers went to New York and Paris to seek their fortunes. Rossco disapproved. He saw no point in going to New York when one could establish one's own cultural elite in one's own city. Aspiring artists, jazz musicians and writers clustered around King Rossco and together they turned the scurrilous activity of creating art into a celebratory event. Rossco even allowed that most dreaded species of mankind, the journalist, to be part of the circle so that he or she could report on the brilliant goings-on.

Sadly, William Rossco's body was less than perfect. It fell far short of the rigorous standards required for today's celebrities. In fact, it didn't even match up to the carefree laissez-faire expectations of the 1970s. William Rossco looked like he was made up of a series of rubber tires, laid on their side and stacked in a swaying vertical pile; ranging from a short, thick, deep tire, where his head was and burgeoning out into an assortment of sizes for his chin, chest, stomach and belly. Rossco sometimes lost a tire or gained a tire, depending on Verna's dietary ministrations. Most people did not look at Rossco's legs, their attention being held by his chins and belly. His legs were his best feature. They were strong and solid, two tree trunks planting him firmly into the ground. Curiously, Rossco moved with a strange, feline grace, for his body remembered that it had once been sleek.

William Rossco was thirty-eight years old. In his youth he had been a spectacularly handsome man. Women who had been informed of his previously strapping physique strained to find it, but it was imbedded in mounds of roly-poly flesh; a land that time forgot. No evidence of his former beauty remained, save for his seductive, languorous eyes. They still possessed a wicked twinkle that sent many women to their doom. Snafu Smith, a man who spent an enormous amount of time on his appearance, was astonished at the easy grace by which Rossco could enslave women. Rossco, himself, was not concerned that his beauty had been buried alive. He carried himself with the aplomb of a man used to receiving rave reviews. Clad in a black T-shirt and plain black cotton pants, he conveyed an impression of sartorial elegance; somewhat offset by the large pair of black rubber gumboots on his feet. Rossco liked gumboots. They were cheap and efficient and they kept one's feet dry. His cat instincts recoiled against the wet. Rossco was also pragmatic. He wore black because he knew that in the course of his sojourn in the city, he would fall down a lot, spill beer on himself, get beer thrown at him, dribble mustard on his shirt (Rossco liked hot dogs), sit on a glob of paint, get covered in charcoal, commit any number of nefarious acts and through it all, his humble black T-shirt wouldn't get crinkled and it wouldn't show the dirt. For, buried deep inside William Rossco, was a tidy streak that battled valiantly against the vicissitudes of the weekly binge, its sloppy traces gravitating to Rossco's person, like iron filings to a magnet. Rossco was his own living canvas.

Rossco liked to arrive in Toronto late Monday afternoon, quietly and without fanfare. He spent the night working in his studio. Rossco's studio was a small, cold-water flat above a store on Spadina Avenue. At that time, artists could rent rooms very cheaply in unfashionable semi-industrial areas of town and the owner of the establishment did not concern himself with what went on in the rooms. Though many people now complain of the fumes of turpentine, in comparison with the more noxious substances used by the printmakers and sculptors of the time, the smell of Rossco's turps did not attract undue attention. In another cold-water flat down the street from Rossco, Jack McCrindle was churning out fibreglass sculptures of giant coffee cups. The toxic fumes from the fibreglass were extremely potent and Jack McCrindle was becoming crazier by the day. Few people noticed, however.

Rossco didn't have a phone in his studio. When he was working, he didn't want to be interrupted. When he'd finished his work and wanted to play, he'd leave the studio and go out looking for action or a telephone booth, whichever he happened upon first. On Monday nights and well into the early hours of Tuesday, Rossco painted like a mad fiend. Tuesday was a day for celebration because he had accomplished a lot the night before, so the rest was gravy. Full of vim, he would teach the class on Tuesday morning and thus began Rossco's official arrival in the city.

After class, Rossco, his fellow artists, musicians, writers and past students met to play street hockey on an unused parking lot behind the school. In 1974, no one stopped to wonder why this prime chunk of downtown real estate was left fallow. No one thought to make a paying parking lot out of it. The lot belonged to an Australian social club whose activities began at night. They left the lot empty in case they had to station large vans there to move furniture for catered events. As no one had a rapacious business-oriented mind, the lot remained empty most of the time. The students and teachers of the Artists School took it for granted that there would always be a "street" to play street hockey in.

Since it was too hot to even stagger from one tavern to another and since Rossco believed that one should play hockey in the appropriate season, the hockey games were postponed until the fall. After the class, Rossco went to the Brunswick House where he held court for the afternoon. People wishing to see Rossco dropped in and made suggestions for the evening's entertainment.

And thus, the three-day spree began in earnest: Wednesday and Thursday morning being Rossco's Studio Days, *studio* having a variety of meanings in this context. To Rossco, it was a time to Explore and Investigate. Having done vast amounts of actual work on Monday night, Rossco felt he'd earned the right to be distracted, should the occasion arise. Rossco's mood was hard to gauge on Wednesdays. Sometimes he was anxious to get back to the work he'd started on Monday, so he would cut back on the beer and take a cold, clear look at life. Women who met him on Tuesday were surprised at how serious and introverted he'd become on Wednesday. Other times, there would be so much to amuse and detain him that he'd fritter away his Studio Days in pursuit of ephemeral pleasures.

So, when Rossco arrived in his usual Tuesday morning mood of amorous optimism and glanced around the room at the sad, motley group of lost souls staring mournfully back at him, his spirits sagged. Snafu had warned him that this summer's crop of students were duds. Snafu took his teaching very seriously. Rossco liked teaching because it gave him a chance to visit with old friends and meet the younger artists. For Snafu, teaching was a vocation, second to the priesthood. Rossco was often puzzled at the things that Snafu thought were important. Snafu usually underestimated people but Rossco felt that, in this case, he might be right. With the exception of the tall, strapping guy in the corner, none of these people had an ounce of joie de vivre in them and joie de vivre was essential if one wanted to be an artist. A blowsy young woman in hippie garb stood beside the Strapper. Was that his girlfriend? She acted like she was but Rossco vaguely remembered Snafu talking about making the moves on the Hippie. She'd have to be the one. She had the pleasant doped-out smile of a confirmed pot-smoker.

Rossco looked for the Widow, the other woman Snafu had in his sights. There she was; a small, dark-haired, exotic beauty, huddled at the back of the room. The Widow had never drawn or painted before. She was from Spain originally. She and her husband had moved to Toronto a year ago and he had died in a freak boating accident. She needed to forget and she was hoping that a summer at art school would do that for her. Snafu had invited her to his place for dinner. It was his favourite seduction technique. Snafu claimed that women were suckers for men who could cook. It meant you were sensitive. Snafu's small dining table was adjacent to his large king-sized bed, a location that Rossco found neither sensitive nor subtle, but women seemed to go for it. There was no couch in Snafu's parlour. There were only the uncomfortable triangular teak chairs that fitted neatly into the matching teak table or there was the bed.

Most women, having consumed the vast quantities of earnest Canadian wine that Snafu served, usually tumbled out of their chairs onto his bed. Even in his desperate bachelor days, Rossco preferred to give his women a running head start. Let them have dinner in a restaurant, walk out with him and then decide where they'd like to spend the night. The Widow proved too much of a challenge for Snafu. She fell out of her chair and instead of succumbing to the mood of the evening, said quite coolly, "Why don't you get a proper dining room set? These chairs are ridiculous." While Snafu defended his chairs on aesthetic grounds — they were elegant and Snafu liked elegant things that fit snugly into place — the Widow looked disparagingly at Snafu's dim, cavelike trysting room. "You need a couch," she said, "and a separate bedroom. Dinner was delicious. Thank you." And with those Parthian shots, she stepped neatly into her coat and walked out, leaving Snafu's mouth agape: a prize morsel that wilfully escaped. Snafu swore that he'd never go after a woman his own age again. The Widow was hopelessly bourgeois. A couch. What next!

Even though Rossco knew that none of these people were likely to be artists, he felt the best tack to take was to pretend they were all gifted, aspiring artists anxious to make a big name for themselves. It was a good game and most students liked to play, even though they secretly knew they'd be back to work in their fathers' businesses. Rossco was about to launch into his opening address when he heard the familiar sound of sloshing gumboots. He turned to see a studious young waif attempt to slip into his class unnoticed, an impossible feat when gumboots are involved. She had an imperious manner about her that Rossco felt impelled to deflate.

"You're late, Girl."

Instead of apologizing, she replied smartly, "You're on time."

"Do you have a problem with that?"

"No. It's good. It's good that you're here on time." She smiled encouragingly at him, making Rossco feel like a three-year-old who'd been given a treat. Girls like that always missed sarcasm. Rossco delivered his speech about expression and primal urges and letting go and dark and light and finding order in chaos, ending with, "I'm going to ask the model to move quickly. Remember that thick black charcoal that they asked you to buy at the beginning of term? Well, that's for my class. Don't try and be precise. Just grab what you see. Put it down quickly. Go for the expression."

"Do you want us to draw like de Kooning, too?" the girl chirped.

"What?"

"De Kooning. He's one of the abstract —"

"I know who he is, Girl. Why would I ask you to draw like him?"

"Well, okay, so you're not coming right out and asking. But the other teachers are also abstract expressionists and they say they want this or that and I don't know what they're talking about but I notice if I draw like de Kooning, then they say I'm doing it right."

It took a while for the full weight of the girl's gall to settle on Rossco. He took a deep breath. "In the first place, Girl, there's no way on God's earth that you could draw like de Kooning because the man was a FUCKING GENIUS and you are just a GIRL taking art classes! Where the fuck do you get off saying you can draw like de Kooning?!"

Imperious Girl was entirely unaffected by Rossco's outburst. She replied calmly, "I simply want to know if you want me to TRY and draw like de Kooning," adding, "IN HIS STYLE" as if he, Rossco, were a mental defective.

"In his style," Rossco repeated, then kicked himself for confirming her assumption.

"Yes, in his style. Because I've got my own way of drawing but it's not anything like what you've been describing."

"It isn't."

"No. It's precise and, you'd say, uptight."

"How do you know I'd say 'uptight?'"

"All the other teachers have said that. I'm sure you will, too." Imperious Girl gave him another radiant smile. It was a positive technique with her: insult the bejesus out of someone and then smile at them. She must have gone to university. You could get away with that sort of shit in university.

"Do you remember my little talk? My little preliminary talk?" Rossco enunciated each syllable of "preliminary" with venomous precision.

"Of course."

"Well ... DO THAT."

"Okay. And if it looks like de Kooning, I'm not to worry about it?"

"It's not going to look like de Kooning." Rossco was dumbfounded. Snafu had not mentioned this student. She seemed curiously asexual, which was probably why Snafu hadn't noticed her. She didn't register on his radar. She was thin, angular, and gangly, like a young faun. She wore the most extraordinary dress. All the other students were clad in suitably shabby clothes for aspiring artists. Imperious Girl looked as though she'd just stepped out of a 1950s Technicolor movie, albeit an eccentric one. She wore a bright green-and-white checked gingham sundress — spanking new and gleaming. Everything about Imperious Girl was bright-eyed and bushy-tailed. It was almost nauseating. Her hair redeemed her. It was golden-blond, long and unkempt. If she'd had one of those pert, little, sculpted hair cuts, Rossco would have shot her on sight. She was not the sort of woman who'd normally catch his eye. One couldn't even call her a woman. She had no body, to speak of. No breasts, no hips. Still, she was feminine. Her sundress was short. Very short. And she had very long, white legs, not bony at all. Rossco was obsessed with women's legs these days. He'd been working on a series. Long and lean was what he looked for, though sometimes it was nice to do an old-fashioned curvy leg. Rossco hated muscular calves. A lot of the hippie women had big, thick calves and ankles. That was why they wore those long skirts. Rossco couldn't get a good look at Imperious Girl's calves. They were obscured by the gumboots. It was a very odd outfit though Rossco had to admit that it was eminently practical, in that it was hot outside, thus the brevity of the sundress and it was raining hard, thus the boots.

Rossco glanced at Imperious Girl's drawing. It was bold and surprisingly powerful, coming from that stick-thin body of hers. She even included the hands and feet. Most students couldn't draw hands or feet and tried to cunningly avoid the issue by focusing on the torso. Rossco glanced at the Strapper's drawing. A torsoist.

"She's got feet, you know."

"Yeah. I just wanted to get the flow of it. Grab what I see," the Strapper quoted back at him. Another wiseacre.

"Grab some feet." Rossco then looked at the Hippie's drawing. Lots of wavy lines, no bite to it. The Widow couldn't draw at all and she wasn't likely to learn at this school. Rossco couldn't decide whether that was a good thing or a bad thing. The little, dirty, preppy kid was into angst. "Dark and light, kid. Remember the light."

"Oh yeah," Preppy laughed in a ghoulish manner. The kid's dark black eyes sunk back into his head.

Rossco finally noticed the other couple. He had overlooked them in his initial survey. These two were a serious item, not like the Strapper and the Hippie, who were probably Just Friends Who Slept Together All The Time. Rossco had a hard time getting his head around the new sexual mores. When he was a teenager, the idea of having a woman anytime he felt like it was paradise on earth, yet seeing it enacted and played out, Rossco could not help but be bored by the enterprise. He missed the challenge of seduction, the gentle game of cat and mouse. Snafu called himself a great seducer of women but where was the sport? Snafu's conquests made their desires known, as clearly as if they were booking a dental appointment. Rossco longed for the days when women kept him guessing. Verna could always keep him on his toes. She was the most mysterious woman he'd ever known, and was ever likely to meet, the way things were going. These new women prided themselves on being direct and open, but where was the charm in that? Wide paved empty roads were direct and open but would anyone want to walk down one? Placed beside a curving, shady, winding garden path, who would choose the highway? People in a hurry, Rossco suddenly realized and glimpsed, for an instant, the state of things to come. It was too depressing to contemplate so he drew his attention back to the Serious Couple.

He reflected on the grim spectre of cohabitational love. Art schools were full of serious-minded couples who did everything together. One couldn't move without the other knowing about it. The two of them sitting side by side, their identical sets of wire-rimmed granny glasses perched on the ends of their respective noses, in owlish contemplation of the model, presented a united front, an utterly joyless approach to the lusty art of drawing: she, murmuring little questions like "are you ready for coffee, dear?," he, nodding assent; their joint eyes fixed implacably ahead of them. The art world was simply a stage, upon which their stunted little passion could be played out.

It was all too clear; the bourgeoisie had invaded the art studio. Rossco loathed these art couples who tried to domesticate everything in their path. Usually, the man was the more flamboyant of the pair — the woman content to play little peahen to his peacock. In Serious Couple's case, it was a toss-up as to who was duller. The man was tall, thin and washed-out. He had pleasant but unmemorable features. The woman spoke in high-pitched, appeasing tones. Her face was broad and bland but she had a body that could stop a clock: big

tits, a wasp waist, long legs and a nice, firm ass. Well, that was a surprise. Who would have thought that underneath that veil of mousy
middle-class primness there lay a Playboy Bunny's body? Rossco
gave Wonder Woman a second thought. Her drawing wasn't bad,
but it lacked vitality. She might have some talent if she could get out
from under that stupid boyfriend. His drawing was so dismal that
it managed to be both limp and rigid. Looking at people's work was
unnerving. Rossco learned far more than he wanted to know about
their personal lives.

As soon as the class was over, Rossco called out his usual invitation, 'Liquid Lunch!' and mimed a quaff as he hurried out the door.
A large crowd awaited Rossco at the Brunswick. His close friends,
Harold Bowen and Marco Shiner made a special appearance. As
one approaches middle age, friendships shift and crumble away in
the wake of power struggles between the friends. Rossco, Bowen
and Shiner had all attended art school together. Luckily, their careers
had matched their aspirations, so the friendship remained more
or less intact. Bowen was singled out by the critics as being the best
painter of the trio. Bowen was quiet and introspective. He said
very little so people filled in his silence and decided they liked him
enormously. Shiner's work got the "versatile and innovative" nod
and Rossco's work was "full of vitality." Rossco was satisfied, though
he would have preferred it if the critics had said his work was
"passionate," a word they often used about Bowen. Snafu was
there, as always. He was about five years younger than the Big
Three, a fact of life that he could never put to his advantage. There
was always the sense about Snafu that he had missed out on making
it big in the Toronto art scene because Rossco, Bowen and Shiner
had got there first. There was no room at the top for Snafu Smith.
Still, Snafu kept his jealousy in check and made himself very agree-
able to the Big Three; fully intending to outlive them all and be
heralded as Canada's undiscovered treasure in his old age.

King Rossco was so busy greeting his court and catching up with
the news and gossip of the last month that a full hour passed before

he realized that none of his class had joined his illustrious Oblong Table. Snafu caught Rossco's sudden look of bewilderment. "They won't show," he said, secretly pleased that even Good King Rossco was not able to entice the students into his lair.

"What's the matter with those people? You invite them for a beer and they don't show up?!"

"You can't just ask them. You have to persuade them."

"You're kidding."

"They're weird. I asked one of them to have lunch with me and she said she couldn't 'cause she had to go home and punch her bread down."

"Go on."

"I kid you not. She wasn't ashamed to tell me, either."

"God! Which one was she?"

"The Hippie."

"Oh. Well. Hippies. She was probably coming on to you."

"Huh?"

"Yeah." Rossco loved to tease Snafu.

"You're kidding."

"No. What she meant was — let's not have lunch. Let's go back to my place."

"Well, she did say she'd show me how to make bread."

"Obvious. I don't know how you missed it." Though Rossco had simply tossed out this explanation as a practical joke to play on Snafu, in fact, he was correct. The Hippie was throwing a line out to Snafu, who did not catch it. When there are age gaps between the participants, sexual innuendoes are impossible to interpret.

"Anyway, they're all a bunch of losers," grumbled Snafu into his beer, annoyed to have missed this slender nuance in the language of seduction.

"I disagree," said Fred Bale, the local art critic. "I had them last week and I thought they were great."

Snafu glared at Fred. Fred had given him a bad review four years ago and Snafu had never forgiven him for it. What Snafu found most

annoying about Fred was that he was entirely oblivious to the fact
that Snafu hated him. Fred thought they were friends. "Well, of course
you'd like that group of deadbeats. You're a critic."

"Well, okay, maybe they're not artists. But they're not stupid."

"You think they're bright?!"

"Well, I gave them this assignment. They had to see Sklar Kobek's
sculpture ..."

"What's that asshole done now?" roared Marco Shiner who was
sitting at the other end of the table and thought he'd missed out on
a juicy piece of gossip.

"The usual shit. Blocks of wood lying on their side and they had
to write a review — well, hell, read this!" and before anyone could
stop him, Fred pulled out his briefcase, laid it on the table and began
rummaging through it.

The artists reared back in speechless horror. There were two acts
of social violence that were not tolerated at the Oblong Table. One
was to order food. Fred Bale habitually ordered a tuna fish sandwich
from the barmaid, blandly ignoring the jeers that accompanied this
action, for the gathering at the Oblong Table was not about filling
in the time with lively people while you ate lunch. It was about
drinking, entering the undiscovered void, putting oneself in an altered
state. Food was a banal practicality and the stench of Fred's week-
old tuna fish sandwich (for the Brunswick's regular afternoon patrons
knew better than to order food) brought everyone down to earth in
pretty short order. The other unforgivable action was to talk shop.
Briefcases, paper, pens, any item resembling business were verboten
at the Oblong Table. Fred Bale was crass enough not to adhere to
these simple codes of behaviour.

"This one's vicious!" Fred cried with glee as he flourished a sheaf
of paper under Rossco's nose.

"And if it's vicious, that means it must be good," snarled Snafu,
warming up for his volleys, fully confident that the Big Three would
join him in his assault on Fred.

"Huh?" asked Fred.

"You miserable sonofabitch. You take a bunch of mindless little twits and then you train them to be vicious mindless little twits. Where the fuck do you get off?"

"Pardon?" asked a baffled Fred. There was a strange moment of ceasefire as Snafu realized that he was alone in this endeavour. Though Fred's exposed briefcase was an unwarranted affront to their sensibilities, it was too early in the week for a knock-down-drag-em-out fight. At least, that is what the Big Three told themselves. Fred had given them all very nice reviews in the past so they were naturally hesitant to bite the hand that wrote their praises.

"The world is full of assholes like you," spluttered Snafu, straining to hang on to his meteoric bout of fury.

"What?"

"Take your fucking tuna fish sandwich and GEDDOUDA HERE!!"

"I think I'm missing something here," mused Fred aloud.

"A BRAIN, moron! That's what you're missing! A Brain! Shithead!" Snafu stormed out of the bar, pleased that he had "told it like it was." Snafu was fond of abusing people who couldn't, or in Fred's case, wouldn't help him. It made him feel honest.

"Is he all right?" Fred asked Rossco.

Rossco shrugged. "He's between women."

"Oh."

"Linda left him."

"Christ. No wonder. For a little guy, he's got a nasty temper."

"All little guys have nasty tempers," Rossco replied with the authority of one who was big. "But you know, Fred, we would prefer it, if you ate your lunch before you came in here."

"Well, I gotta save time. I've got deadlines."

"We've all got deadlines, Fred. Do you think I'm not working?"

"Well, you're not. You're sitting here drinking."

"Wrong, Fred. I'm thinking. I'm planning out my next canvas. And the smell of your fucking sandwich intrudes on my process. It intrudes on all our processes." Bowen and Shiner glared menacingly at Fred. "If you must eat," Rossco pronounced "eat" with sad resignation as if it were an indecent act that only the barbaric indulged in, "Eat in the Library."

"Uh, okay," replied a cowed Fred. Eating in the Library was tantamount to banishment. The Library was a small, dank room situated off to the side of the main bar, designed to appeal to the hard-core alcoholic. It was called the Library because it had book wallpaper and its only client, a morose, elderly man, was the spitting image of George Bernard Shaw. No one wanted to drink in the Library. One half-expected Shaw's dissipated incarnation to join one's table and launch into a lengthy speech on vegetarianism and women's rights. The man in question, in fact, sat and drank and said not a word. Still, his aura implied that he had opinions and that was enough to put people off.

"And Fred?"

"Yeah?"

"No papers."

"What?"

"No papers, no briefcases, no work. We don't discuss work at the Table."

"But you guys are always talking about your work."

"Ideas, Fred. We discuss ideas."

Fred was thoroughly chagrined. Rossco's casual admonishment was far more withering than Snafu's rabid attack. He hung his head like a whipped dog. Shiner and Bowen were occupied in a discussion of the relative merits of Shiner's new mistress, a topic that bored Rossco to tears. He felt some pity for Fred, so he glanced at the offending sheet of paper. The first line made him laugh so he read on. Rossco had never liked Sklar's work much and this student was certainly taking the piss out of him. Rossco had always admired writers. He thought it was sad that artists weren't encouraged to be more articulate. Somewhere, in the course of the twentieth century, some moron decided that people should not broaden their scope, but instead specialize in their narrow little field. So, the art schools were full of dumb, inarticulate students who took pride in the fact that they couldn't put a sentence together. Of course, there was the occasional intellectual student who liked to talk. They were interesting enough but they showed no aptitude for the art. The student who wrote this review probably couldn't draw worth beans. Rossco guessed that the author had to be the male half of the Serious Couple, although the review was funny and Serious Husband looked like he had no sense of humour. Perhaps, it was his girlfriend, Wonder Woman.

"Good, isn't it?"

"Yeah. He really hates Sklar Kobel."

"She. That's the beauty of it. She hates Sklar Kobel and she has absolutely no idea of who he is. She doesn't know he started the post-dada-pre-conceptual movement. She just hates his work and goes after him."

"Like a Doberman."

"Exactly. Going for the jugular. No holds barred."

"Do me a favour: don't encourage her. We don't need another ignoramus attacking us."

"What?"

"Not you, Fred. The ignorant turd at the *Globe*."

"Oh yeah. She could learn."

"Don't train her."

There was a melancholy pause as Rossco contemplated the fate of Canadian art. One could spend years befriending and compromising one critic and without warning, a new, stupid, vicious one would rise up to take his place. And then, one wastes more time trying to train the new one. And each time, they get dumber and meaner and more intractable, like mad kings, after centuries of inbreeding, an apotheosis of genetic despair. Canada produced such atrocities by the boatload. It was our cottage industry. Rossco saw that, in twenty years time, Fred Bale would be regarded as an intelligent, genial "friend to the artist" when, in fact, he was a big, slobbering dope, a man who wouldn't know good art if he fell over it but, luckily, allowed himself to be instructed by those who did.

"I offered to train her, but she turned me down."

"Really?"

"Yeah, she said it was beneath her. That any idiot could take potshots at artists."

"She said that to you?"

"Yeah. She didn't even know she was being rude."

"The gall."

"Yeah. She's got gall."

"Oh, wait. I think I know which one wrote this. Dresses strange?"

"Yeah. Clean."

Rossco laughed. "You're right. Clean and new."

"Apparently, some student newspaper offered her a job as a theatre critic. She'd written in to complain because she thought a review was too nice. They said she was so nasty she was a natural. Anyway, she turned them down because she wanted to be an artist. Writing criticism comes too easily to her. She just does it for fun."

"Fun?"

"The girl's tough," Fred sighed.

Rossco reread the review. He admired wit and this girl was certainly witty. She disembowelled Sklar Kobel's entire oeuvre with a few deft slices. She was cruel and disdainful. Though he'd never admit it, Rossco had a masochistic streak, and seeing this girl in the light of possible future cruelties held an enormous appeal for him. Her angular features assumed a clear, merciless beauty. Every Samson longs for his Delilah and Rossco saw his fate looming up in front of him. Imperious Girl would prove his undoing. He hoped. With the enhanced sensitivity of one on the brink of emotional ruin, Rossco saw that Fred Bale had a bit of a thing for Imperious Girl as well.

Further reflections on this melancholy topic were cut short by the boisterous arrival of Rufus, Lynne and Carla, students from the year before. Rufus was a favourite amongst the Big Three. He showed just the right amount of promise. He was talented, yet it was clear that he would never surpass his teachers. Rufus lacked that spark of creative genius that enrages all who come into contact with it, for Rufus was an amiable fellow and his placid good nature extinguished any fires within. The other two, Lynne and Carla, had no illusions about their talents as artists. They were simply out for a good time. Rossco eyed them approvingly. Hot sultry days seemed to inspire women to wear sexy clothes. Rossco's spirits fell when they both asked after Snafu.

Snafu was particularly adept at juggling love affairs and keeping all involved parties on good terms. None of Snafu's women seemed to mind being put on the back burner. The simple secret to Snafu's success was that he never put a woman on the front burner. When the affair began, she was informed of her unimportant place in Snafu's scheme of things. Of course, Snafu would never express such a sentiment so bluntly. He was nothing if not diplomatic. He would say, "Christ, I'm crazy about you but let's keep it simple, okay?" or "You're just so fabulous but I still have this thing with my wife. Oh yeah, we're separated but it's ... well, it's sorta hard to describe ...." Thus, the women put themselves on Snafu's back burner and were quite content to stay there. They even enjoyed meeting the other back-burner lovers, in that the presence of so many others meant they couldn't all be fools. Snafu was honestly deceitful, a winning combination in the sexual politics of the times. Occasionally, Rossco wished that he could lie as adroitly as Snafu, but he felt, ultimately, the lies would show up in his art.

"I hear you're doing legs these days," Lynne said.

"Um, yeah."

"Do you want mine?" Lynne flashed a long, lithe limb out from under the table. She was wearing shorts and the leg was shown off to advantage. Fred Bale peered over to get a better look.

"Um, yeah," replied Rossco, noncommittally. He hated it when women teased him.

"Do you want the heels, too?"

"Heels are very nice."

"You've got me till eight."

"Eight?"

"Yeah, then I have to meet my husband."

"When did you get married?"

"Don't believe her," said Carla. "She's always dragging her husband into things."

"'Cause he's my husband, dummy."

"You got married?" asked Marco, clearly disappointed.

"Yeah," Lynne shrugged. Part of Lynne's charm was that she was an inveterate flirt. She turned all men into ravening dogs. Rufus was bobbing up and down like a deranged puppy. Fred Bale was thinking unthinkable thoughts. Marco Shiner decided that he liked a challenge and reassessed his options. Even Harold Bowen looked up hopefully, before withdrawing into a sad communion with his beer. With the notable exception of Snafu, Lynne rarely slept with the artists she teased. She just liked to pique their interest. However, Snafu's success laid some important groundwork for the future. Rossco decided that an afternoon spent in idle contemplation of Lynne's thighs was not to be sneered at. He might even get some work done.

chapter eleven

DOLDRUMS

LILY LIKED TO get stoned before going to work. She could glide through the day without too much pain. She had expected Brad to call her on Monday. She answered the calls in a very sexy voice till the late afternoon when she realized that she wouldn't be hearing from him. Tuesday dragged on in a similar manner. Lily's casual insouciance attracted the attention of some of the male bosses. They couldn't help but notice this voluptuous red-haired beauty sorting through the office files as though she were picking flowers in a meadow.

For some mysterious reason, Lily found that she intuited secrets about her co-workers. When Mrs. Hinckley dumped a stack of receipts to file on Lily's desk, a thought flashed through Lily's brain: "Her husband's just left her. He's run off with ...," Lily's eyes scanned the room and landed on Miss Rondelle. Lily gasped in surprise and when she saw Mrs. Hinckley stiffen, tuck in her chin and stalk back to her office, she knew it was true. One of the goofier male bosses approached Lily. Lily suddenly knew he had a crush on her and, sure enough, the boss stammered and weaved nervously back and forth as he asked her if she'd mind filing some papers for him. His regular secretary was away.

"It's, ah, in here," he gestured to the filing cabinet, "and here are the files. Ooops!" He was so nervous that he'd dropped the files on the floor. Lily helped him pick them up. Then, this other thought intruded: "Show him a bit of leg. Look him in the eyes. He could go for you." When Lily saw the desire reflected in the man's face, she realized that these thoughts were outside herself. It was the Voice, but it had assumed a new guise. Instead of being separate, it had insinuated itself into her thoughts. The goofy boss had bulging toad eyes. He stared at Lily with such unmitigated lust that she blushed, quickly grabbed the files from him, muttered some lame excuse about doing it later and ran off.

The long day was finally over. The subway was crowded with office workers, all anxious to get home. The air conditioning had broken down. The subway stalled between stops; the rank, muggy, odour of stifled anxiety hung in the air. When it reached St. George Station, Lily and the other passengers were summarily disgorged and replaced by other sweating patrons.

No one was home at KAT House. Lily made a beeline for the kitchen and rummaged through the carefully labelled food in the refrigerator. KAT House had been plagued by a food thief. Usually, summer boarders were held responsible for the casual appropriation of food. However, Jay had been seen cooking meals, so she seemed an unlikely candidate. Lily grabbed Jay's cheddar and some slices of Louise's salami and Kathleen's bread and made a couple of sandwiches. Accompanied by Susan's plums, it would do for dinner.

Lily was determined to hole up in her room for the evening. She started to eat, then realized she wasn't hungry. She shoved the sandwiches to one side. Lily's room had a peculiar odour that Lily assumed to be the stench of failure, but was, in fact, the rotting remains of food that she had shoved under her bed and forgotten about. She was lying in bed, listening to dreary music, settling into a deep funk, when there was a gentle tap at the door. Lily ignored it. It was probably Eve, telling her to turn the music down. Another tap.

"Lily? Are you there?" It was Jay.

"Yeah. I'm here."

"Are you okay?"

"Yeah."

"What's wrong?"

Lily wondered why it was that if you said you were fine, people always asked you what was wrong. "Nothing," she replied somewhat testily.

"Can I come in?"

"I guess so."

Jay entered tentatively. "Aren't you hot?"

"No."

"I am boiling. It's like an oven in here."

"Then, go away."

"I meant the house, though your room is kind of stuffy." Jay sniffed the air cautiously.

"Go away, then."

"What happened? Why are you so upset?"

"Nothing happened, get it? NO-THING happened. That's me. That's my life. Nothing ever happens."

"Did you break up with Brad?"

"Break up? Ha! Am I going out with Brad? Who knows? I sure as hell don't. He doesn't call me."

"Didn't you see him on Sunday? For the class?"

"Yeah," Lily admitted grudgingly.

"Today's Tuesday."

"Yeah."

"That's only two days, Lily."

"He said he'd call me."

"It's only Tuesday."

It was obvious to Lily that Jay had never experienced passion.

How else could she calmly attribute the immense gulf that lay between her and Brad to a mere time span of days?

"Is it your job?"

"I hate it, but that's nothing new."

"You should quit."

"What?"

"Quit your job and go to art school. You could have gone with me this summer. Hardly anyone signed up this year." Jay suddenly became as zealous as a Jesuit missionary in an attempt to convert Lily to art. "Why don't you sign up? They're desperate for students."

"I can't draw."

"Nobody else knows how to draw. It's not fashionable to teach people how to draw, so we're all terrible. Anyway, how do you know till you try?"

"I spent twelve years in public school failing art class. I'm pretty sure I can't draw."

"School!" scoffed Jay. "No one learns how to draw at school! Art is learning how to see. We're taught how to read and write. Some people are better than others but we don't say to the people who aren't immediately good at it, 'you'll never be able to read or write.' Yet, we tell people they'll never be able to draw."

"Mmmhmm," nodded Lily, hoping Jay would be finished soon.

"So, Lily, the arts are where you belong. You must see that."

"Mmmmhmm."

"Take a night class. Start with Beginner's Drawing. There's this great old guy who teaches it. He's really friendly. People love his classes and —"

"Jay ..."

"Yes?"

"Jay, I don't want to be an artist."

"You don't?"

"No."

"Never?"

"No, never."

"Oh." There was a pause as Jay considered this alarming piece of news. "Well, what do you want to do?"

"I don't know. That's the problem."

"What about journalism?"

Lily looked up hopefully. "I strike you as a journalist?

"Well, not necessarily."

"Then, why —"

"It's just that all the people I know who don't know what they want always go into journalism."

"Oh. Well, I did want to be a journalist."

"You should do it, then."

"I'm pretty sure I couldn't get in. I failed English."

"You did?"

"Yeah. I failed most of my courses."

Jay, who always got high marks, could not conceive of such an event. "How did that happen?"

"Stupid, I guess. I guess I'm just stupid!"

"I don't think you're stupid, Lily."

"Thanks, Jay. Everyone else does. My father says I'm stupid. And my mother says not to worry because girls aren't supposed to be smart. In fact, she thinks it's better for them if they're not. Makes it easier for them to get married." Lily laughed. "The only reason most girls go to university is so they'll be able to talk to their husbands. And I can't even get the grades to do that."

"I think you're smart, Lily."

"Not smart enough to make anything of my life."

"Why do you have to decide this summer?"

"'Cause my time is up," Lily replied cryptically.

Jay worried when Lily got into these moods. "You know, Lily, girls don't go to university so they'll have a better chance of getting married. That might have been the case in the fifties, but times have changed."

"Less than you think, Jay."

"I don't like to say this but the sorority house is really old-fashioned. Most people don't think that way now. There's women's liberation ..."

"Do you know what that means? Women's liberation."

"I think it means not having to get married."

"Having a career instead?"

"Yeah," said Jay eagerly, anxious to be making a point of some sort.

"WELL THAT'S MY WHOLE GODDAMN PROBLEM! I DON'T HAVE A CAREER! AND I DON'T WANT TO GET MARRIED! AND I DON'T WANT TO SPEND THE REST OF MY LIFE BEING SINGLE AND WORKING AS A GIRL FRIDAY AT TORONTO HYDRO!"

"I'm really sorry, Lily."

"Let's have a joint."

"You do pot?"

"Occasionally. How 'bout it."

"You go ahead."

"Won't you have some?"

"No. I don't smoke."

"Oh." Lily pulled out, from her pocket, a small, wrinkled miniature cigarette and lit it. "Why not?" she asked, gasping as she inhaled.

Jay could never understand why pot smokers always spoke on the first inhale. Had they seen it in a movie somewhere and that became the proscribed method for smoking pot, like the way women in the 1940s movies held their cigarettes at a jaunty angle from their bodies, with their elbows tucked in by their waists? "It destroys your brain," Jay replied, somewhat sanctimoniously.

"And what's wrong with that? People think too much, anyway," Lily took another long drag and wheezed.

"You didn't do well at school and you smoke pot. I'd say there was a connection."

"Look, you don't know —"

"If I drank a bottle of gin a day, I wouldn't do too well at school, either."

"If you tried it, Jay, you would realize that as far as pot is concerned, your head is completely up your ass. It's just a cigarette, for God's sake!"

"It's not a cigarette! It's dope!"

"You've seen that old movie, haven't you? The one where those people smoke a joint and start murdering each other."

"*Reefer Madness.*"

"God! You *have* seen it. You don't seriously believe —"

"I realize it was a propaganda film. And okay, people don't go berserk. In fact, they get very quiet. And resigned."

"Resigned."

"Yes. They don't try anymore. I don't know, Lily, it's like it destroys your ambition."

"Is that bad?"

"Well, yes, if you want to succeed in life."

"And what's successful? Making lots of money?"

"It doesn't have to be about money."

"Having a position in life? Being at the top of your social ladder? Is that what you mean, Jay?"

"Well, no, not exactly."

"Being famous? Is that what you'd like to be? A famous artist?"

"Ah —"

"Is it just about being famous? Having other people see you as being successful? What about life? Living one's life?

"I don't see what's wrong with wanting to succeed."

"And what's wrong with simply wanting to live? Pot slows me down, helps me enjoy the details."

"It's a drug. And you're just using it to escape from your problems."

"You'll be successful, Jay. But you won't be happy."

"It turns your brain to mush. Makes you passive."

"Impressionable, Jay. Ready to receive."

"Then don't tell me you don't know why you failed your courses."

"That has nothing to do with it!"

"Fine! Receive all you like. Fail. Work at Hydro."

"Girl Friday," Lily giggled. "And they're all fat and old. And where's Robinson Crusoe? I should go in wearing a loincloth." Lily fell into fits of laughter. Seeing Jay's stern face glaring down at her, she said, "I don't think they'd get it, would they? Nah. They wouldn't get it. Like you, Jay. You just don't get it. Where're you going, Jay?"

"Out."

If Lily was the grasshopper, then Jay was the ant. Jay was organized. She made plans. Even her wayward decision to go to art school was encased in a plan. It was an interlude between her years at university. It didn't matter what crazy things she got up to that summer. In the fall, she would resume her studies, get a degree and wind up with a well-paying, reasonably satisfying job.

Lily didn't know where her road led. She had to find a career before the end of the summer, otherwise it would be too late. Lily had a strange sense of urgency within. She didn't know why her life had to be put in order before the summer's end. She was evanescent; a dragonfly, living out its glorious, carefree existence, basking in the heat of the summer sun, before succumbing to the inevitable chill of winter.

⌒

JAY WAS COMING out of the supermarket, laden with her weekly shopping, when a familiar voice chattered in her ear, as if continuing a conversation that had ended only a moment before.

"You shouldn't be shopping there. They're in league with the Establishment."

"Nicholas!" Jay swung round in delight and upon seeing Nicholas in the flesh, was stricken by the change in him. He had strangely diminished in her absence. His beard and moustache were gone. He had lost a lot of weight. He was thin and gangly. His pale white face overrun with freckles, his eyes frantic; he was a small boy clamouring for her attention.

"It's so impersonal. You don't ever see the butcher or the baker, 'cause there isn't supposed to be one."

"How have you been?"

"Fine. The food comes magically out of some unspecified place and it's sealed in plastic with the price tag and you pick it up and buy it. And you don't have to talk to anyone."

"You usually have to talk to the cashier when you pay."

"Yeah, but there're so many cashiers, it's always a different person. It's not like you'd get to know them."

"Where am I supposed to buy my groceries? It's the only place around."

"Kensington Market."

"Kensington Market?! It's a half-hour walk. If you think I'm walking that far in this heat, you're nuts!" Jay was annoyed that Nicholas didn't acknowledge that they hadn't seen each other for over two months. He assumed that she would slide effortlessly into his stream of consciousness. Jay moved away. Nicholas took her grocery bags and walked alongside.

"Well, all right. Not in a heat wave. But you should try it sometime, before it's gone. Before the Establishment has its way. It's through small acts of protest that big things can happen."

"Small, is it, now? What happened to the Revolution?"

"Hand to hand combat, now. Personal." Nicholas's pupils filled his entire iris.

At one time, Jay would have interpreted his luminous gaze as undeclared love, but she knew better now. He was stoned. "Okay, when it cools off, I'll go down to Kensington Market. I agree, supermarkets are impersonal but I don't think some evil conglomerate is deliberately trying to alienate people from each other."

"What about the suburbs?"

"What about them?"

"They are built for alienation."

Jay had never been to a suburb before, so she wasn't entirely sure what Nicholas was talking about, but by this time she was feeling argumentative. "Architecture works that way. Some designer came up with a plan and they built to plan."

"The people who came up with those plans are evil."

"Or stupid."

"Or both."

"But it's not deliberate, Nicholas."

"Then why are the suburbs all across North America exactly the same? And why is it so hard to change the system? Why is there so much resistance to food co-ops? And housing co-ops? Why do people hate hippie communes so much?"

"They're dirty."

"They are not dirty!"

"Hippies do weird things. Like let their kids pee in the living room."

"I knew I shouldn't have taken you to Starhawk's."

"He peed right up against a wall. She thought it was cute. How can you live in that smelly place?"

"Actually, I moved out. I'm living with Irina."

"Oh." Jay's heart sank, more out of habit than passion.

Nicholas glanced up the street. "So, where is this rooming house you're in?" They were steadily walking towards KAT House.

"Huh? Oh. I had to move out of the rooming house. The heroin addicts kept stealing my stuff. So, ah, I'm staying with a friend of my mother's."

"Bet it's nice."

"It has a toilet. Which people use."

"Well, you'd have to live in a nice place. You're a nice girl."

No one strived to be nice in the 1970s. "Nice" was a death sentence to any personal mystique. Everyone wanted to be mean, or at the very least, to be thought of, as mean. "Nice" meant hopelessly banal, dull beyond redemption: stuck in a category with boring aunts and uncles, children's televisions shows, kindergarten teachers, nature films and traffic and safety guidelines. Jay felt the full opprobrium of being "nice" because people often described her as such.

It annoyed Jay that Nicholas would toss such a generic insult at her. "You're nice, too, Nicholas."

"Bullshit!"

"You try not to be, but you are. Deep down, you're very nice. You carried my groceries for me."

"I gotta go." Nicholas handed Jay her groceries and tore off down one of the alleys. Jay knew that reminding Nicholas of his innate decency would send him packing. Jay saw that Nicholas was a young boy playing at life and for a time, the revolutionary's attire fit him better than the other costumes. She wondered if she was really an artist, or if she, too, was play-acting.

⌒

LILY'S MELANCHOLY INDULGENCE the night before had rendered her listless. She no longer expected anything from Brad. She roamed the office in a mournful stupor: her hopes dashed, lying in little leaden piles, waiting to be filed and put away with the rest of her misery. She was grateful for the small mercy that she had not seen hide nor hair of the goofy boss. At the stroke of five, Lily grabbed her purse and raced towards the door. The goofy boss casually leaped out of Mr. Pollard's office cubicle, which was situated near the exit.

"Hey! Didn't see you all day."

"Oh. Hi, Mr. Thall," Lily replied gloomily.

"Call me Dave."

"Oh."

"Well, Lily, do you know what time it is?"

"Time to go home," Lily said and bolted for the door but Dave spryly put his hand on it and replied, jovially, "No, Happy Hour."

"Huh?" Lily was far from happy.

"Drinks are half-price. Care to join me?"

"Uh, no. I, ah, can't. Well, goodbye."

"I'll come out with you." Dave escorted Lily into the elevator. He made no further attempts to make a date. As they were leaving the building, he added, "So, tomorrow, then?" Lily hastily informed him that she was busy.

"Next week, sometime."

"Yes, okay. Sometime."

Lily was furious with herself. Not only was her life a dismal mess, but she had to go out for drinks with the Toad. Dave's determined means of procuring a date had lifted him out of the goofy category. The thought *At least, Brad might get jealous* crossed Lily's mind. Lily looked up and, sure enough, there was Brad, waiting, a short distance away. He was annoyed to see Lily with another man.

"Who was that?"

"Someone from work."

"Has he asked you out?"

"Yes, actually. He has. And I'm going."

"Good," said Brad. "I mean, I guess it's only fair."

"Yes. It's not as if you're chasing me down."

"I'm here now."

"What do you want?"

"You!" Brad gave her a long, lingering kiss.

"Well, you can't have me," said Lily, after she'd enjoyed the kiss.

"Aw, come on. What's wrong?"

"I didn't hear from you all week, and now you just show up and expect me to fall into your arms."

"It's only been a couple of days. What's wrong with you?"

"We were supposed to go out on Sunday night."

"It's a little awkward with your brother around."

"Maybe, we should just tell him."

"I don't want him to know. I want this to be special. Private. Between us. Please have dinner with me."

Lily didn't reply, but she allowed Brad to lead her to his car and take her to a small, romantic restaurant. They spoke little during the meal. Brad kept giving Lily beseeching looks.

"Let's go to our spot," said Brad, gazing at Lily with an intensity that she had never seen before.

"Our spot?"

"Yeah, our spot on the beach."

Desire welled up in Lily. She forgave Brad his casual neglect and, once again, wanted nothing more than to be entwined in his arms. She nodded her assent and they left the restaurant, holding hands in electric anticipation.

Brad drove to a secluded place near where they had been that first evening together. He parked the car so that it faced the lake. After they made love, Lily lay nestled in his arms. She looked like a small child who'd eaten too much candy. Brad bent down gently and kissed her ear. He whispered, "You don't have to do the classes if you don't want to."

"You don't want me there?" Lily murmured.

"I don't want to force you. You seemed pretty nervous."

"I've signed up and I'm going." When Lily had Brad in her grasp, he was firmly held.

LILY AND JAY lay, stretched, flat out, on skimpy white towels on the sunroof of KAT House; Lily, in a bright green bikini, Jay in a modest two-piece. None of the other girls were suntanning. They knew better. The sunroof was comprised of sharp little stones imbedded in a thick black tar. The sun beat down ferociously, heating up the tar and the stones. Jay felt like roast pork being barbequed. She looked down at her body, which refused to accommodate her whims. It would not grow grapefruit-sized breasts and it would not tan. Lily had even fairer skin than Jay, but she bullied it into tawniness every year. "It burns and peels the first few times out. You gotta expect that. But you just keep at it." Jay was about to cry uncle and retreat into the cool recesses of the house when Lily suddenly announced, "You know what I like about you?" She turned her body lazily to face Jay.

"No. What?" Jay tried to be nonchalant but she was desperate to know. The friendship puzzled her.

"You don't have parents."

"Well, actually, I do —"

"But you know what I mean."

"Well —"

"Some people have parents. And it's written all over them. Everywhere they go, you can see their parents."

"Yeah?"

"It's the way they dress. Hoods. People who wear sweatshirts with hoods have parents."

"Oh yeah," replied Jay, getting into the game. "And duffel coats. People who wear duffel coats have parents."

"And proper shoes. People who wear good shoes have parents."

"And cashmere sweaters!"

"Susan Lipton has four sets of parents," Lily proclaimed.

There was a slight pause, then Jay ventured tentatively, "Do you think Brad has parents?"

"I guess so. His clothes are sort of parent-type clothes. He wears runners, though."

"Everyone wears runners in summer."

"Yeah, okay. When he's with Susan, he has parents. When he's with me, he doesn't. All the girls in KAT House have parents. Except for us."

"Except for us."

When one is twenty, one doesn't want to be reminded of one's genetic inheritance: the flabby stomachs, big hips and bald heads, lurking in the future of one's middle-age.

When one is twenty, one is young, free and immortal.

chapter twelve

TRIAL RUN

FLASH DESCRIBED, IN excruciating detail, all the things that could go wrong with a parachute. They had a series of emergency drills. Each student, in turn, climbed up a small ladder and was strapped into a harness. Flash kicked away the ladder, then shouted out the problem and the student performed the actions required to save himself. It was Lily's turn. She dangled uncomfortably while Flash focused on a new problem he hadn't explained before.

"Okay, gang, you should know about this, but you're not supposed to do it. When you're experienced skydivers, you'll be doing this...." While Flash outlined the pros and cons of the breakaway manoeuvre, Lily kept praying that he'd finished soon so she could get down. Her legs ached the way they did when she was little and her sister, Rose, doubled her on her bicycle.

"Sometimes you have to ditch the main parachute and then deploy your reserve." Flash used a pointer to show two buckles on Lily's shoulders. "There are the Capewell Releases. This one here and this one here. You uncap the plates. Underneath are the release rings and you pull down hard. So, we've pulled the releases and we've pulled the reserve ripcord. Gotta get the body position. Now, if your reserve's on your chest, you straighten and spread your legs at a right angle in front of you. Come on, Lily. Pull them straight up in front!" Flash yanked Lily's legs out in front of her. "Okay, keep them out. Bend your back, roll your shoulders and head forward. The rocking-chair position. But if your reserve's on the back, what do ya do, gang?" Lily wished that the "gang" would hurry up and answer but they were being diffident. Flash waited for an agonizing length of time before booming out the answer, "Spread eagle, gang! Okay! Spread eagle. Arch your back, Lily!" That position was a little easier for Lily to manage from the harness. "Okay gang, we're gonna put Lily through her paces. Your reserve's on your back, okay? Ready, Lily?" Flash gave her no time to answer before yelling, "GO!" Lily kept her spread-eagle position and did her count. She got up to "look thousand" when Flash bellowed, "Ya gotta streamer! So, ya CUT-AWAY! GO!" Lily uncapped the plates of the releases. She pulled on one, swung round and spun impotently while she fumbled with the other release ring which, naturally, would not release.

"HURRY! YOU'RE GOING DOWN! PULL IT!"

"I'M TRYING!" Lily shouted back.

"DON'T TALK! USE BOTH HANDS!" Lily yanked ferociously on the ring. Finally, it gave way and she tumbled in a heap to the ground. The class applauded.

"Yeah, oh yeah, great work, 'CEPT SHE'S DEAD. Now, why do you think she'd be dead, gang?"

"Took too long?" volunteered Paul.

"Yeah, partly. But mainly," Flash leaned in to shout in Lily's face, "YOU FORGOT TO PULL YOUR RESERVE RIPCORD! So, let's try this again."

"Please, no!" thought Lily as Flash hoisted her back up.

"Gotta get back in the saddle. You see, gang, that's why they don't want novices doing the cutaway. 'Cause they get so flustered they forget important things like THE POINT OF THE MANOEUVRE!!

You get rid of your malfunctioning main so it won't interfere with your reserve chute. But ya gotta OPEN your reserve chute. Lily got all confused four feet from the ground. Imagine what would happen at four thousand feet. No, don't imagine that, gang. Do your procedures till they're second nature to you. Lily forgot to do the rest of the count. The count for emergencies. LOOK AND REACH! Locate and grab the reserve ripcord. PULL the ripcord. PUNCH the side of the reserve to jar it loose if necessary. Keep doing your count. It'll calm you down. So, we're gonna learn the cutaway but I DON'T WANT YOU TO DO IT. When you've got a malfunction in the main, and you've opened your release, the main might interfere with your reserve. When you're just starting out, it's better to have that happening than no parachute at all. Now, having scared you all, I wanna stress that when you jump, you'll be on a static line. Let's try this again. Ready, Lily? Reserve's on your front this time. GO!" Lily repeated the sequence all over again. She still had difficulty releasing the rings. Flash was concerned. "What's the matter with you, kid? You got no upper body strength. You should do push-ups. Fifty a day. If you can't undo the rings, I can't let you do this."

"I'll work on it. I promise. I was just tired."

"Let's see you do some push-ups."

"Right now?"

"Yeah. I need to make sure you can do them. I'll give you a break, though. You can do them girl-style. Okay, ON YOUR KNEES! 50! RIGHT NOW!" Flash pointed to the ground.

At this point, Lily's tentative dislike for Flash blossomed into a full-fledged hatred. What right did he have to talk to her like that? He had a job where he could talk about his favourite sport and boss people around. It wasn't the same as a real job where you worked at something you detested and other people told you what to do. She did as she was told and grumbled to herself as Paul and Brad went through their paces flawlessly.

‿

ROSSCO ARRIVED IN fine fettle to teach his class and met with the same stoic indifference that he'd encountered the week before. He'd forgotten about his brief passion for Imperious Girl, left it along the wayside of last week's adventures. He sat quietly in the back of the room and watched them draw the model. He had done good work the night before and he wanted to keep the energy to himself, not squander it. Rossco found himself watching Imperious Girl more often than was necessary. She was wearing the gingham sundress again, but without the gumboots. Rossco studied her calves at leisure. She had big feet, which surprised him. After a time, Rossco moved about, offering comments. When he got to Imperious Girl's work, he grunted his approval and moved on.

"Sorry?" she said.

Rossco stopped.

"What did you say?" she asked him.

"S'good."

"Oh. 'S'good.' Well, s'thanks." Imperious Girl smiled at him, looking him full in the face. Her eyes met his and Rossco knew he was a goner. At the end of the class, Rossco casually put himself beside Imperious Girl when he announced his plans to go for a beer. He leaned over and quickly whispered to her, "And I expect you to be there," then waltzed out the door, his business concluded.

Most people would have taken Rossco's muttered entreaty as a direct invitation, but Jay thought that he must have confused her with someone else. She didn't like beer. Besides, she was looking forward to her Tuesday bowl of cauliflower soup, so she, Michael, Brian and Sheila hurried over to the Korolla to claim a booth before the lunch rush. Jonathan stayed in the studio to work on his painting.

A half hour later, they had finished their soup and were deliberating over whether to order another cup of coffee. They had to make up their minds quickly, otherwise the waitress would bring out the reeking, ammonia-soaked cloth, on the slim pretext of wiping the table down. Rufus burst into the restaurant and ran over to Jay. He was agitated.

"Are you nuts?"

"Hi, Rufus."

"You're supposed to be at the Brunswick!"

"Oh, that. I didn't feel like it."

"But he asked you!"

"I don't like beer."

"He asked me to get you. You've had your lunch?"

"Oh yeah."

"Well then, you're coming." And with that, Rufus hauled Jay out of the booth, hastily informing the others that they could join them. Jay giggled as Rufus pushed her down the street.

"What's the matter with you? It's just a beer."

"He wants you."

"He what?" The words had an ominous ring to them. Wanted her? In what sense did Mr. Rossco want her? Before Jay had time to get completely apprehensive, Rufus plonked her down in the empty chair beside Mr. Rossco and retired to the far end of the table, where, to Jay's astonishment, Susannah sat, happily ensconced. Susannah smiled up at Rufus, drew him towards her and whispered something in his ear.

"Girl."

"Oh, hi, Mr. Rossco."

"Mr. Rossco? Oh come now, Girl. You can call me Bill."

"Okay."

"Say it."

"Bill."

"Good. Now, I have a bone to pick with you, Girl."

"Oh."

"I invited you to join me."

"Yes?"

"And you didn't show up."

"I didn't know you were asking me, specifically."

"Girl."

"Yes?"

"Who did you think I was asking? The wall?"

"Um ..."

"But you're here now, so that's good. So, what'll you have?"

"Ah ... tea?"

"Girl." Rossco glared admonishingly at Jay.

"Coffee? No. Well, let's see. I don't really drink much."

"We are in a bar, Girl, and people at the table don't like it when you order SOFT drinks. It makes us look bad. So, what'll it be?"

"Wine?"

"Well, it's alcohol, so you're on the right track, but Girl, you don't want to order wine here. Later, I'll take you to the Pilot. The wine's okay there. Actually, Girl, even though I've asked you what you'll have, as you can see, there's only one drink here."

"Right." The barmaid plunked a small glass of draft beer down in front of Jay.

"Cheers," said Mr. Rossco, and they clinked glasses. Jay took a reluctant sip. "So, Girl, what's your name?"

"Jay."

"Jay. What a ... what a ... um ... What's Jay short for?"

"It's not short for anything. It's just Jay."

"Jay." Rossco sat and savoured the name for a moment. "Jay." He tasted it again and said, "That's a really ugly name, Girl. Your mother didn't call you that."

Jay blushed, "Well, no, actually, she didn't, but I hate my real name."

"I won't ever use it, Girl, but I need to know what it is." Rossco looked at Jay with such urgency that she told him. Janclaire.

"You're beautiful, Girl, and one of these days you'll feel comfortable with that name."

Jay stifled a laugh. "I'm not beautiful."

"Girl, you are the most beautiful woman that I've ever laid eyes on."

Jay was beside herself with embarrassment. Rossco leaned over and quickly drew something on her bare shoulder.

"Don't worry, Girl. It'll come off. It's not indelible." Jay looked down and saw that Rossco had drawn a side profile of a butterfly in flight. The butterfly's head and body were distinct from the wings. It was beautiful. Jay fingered it gently.

"That's what you're gonna be, Girl. It's what you are now, but you don't see it. Now, do me one favour."

"Yes?"

"This is an original William Rossco. You have to leave it on. You can't wash it off. And I'll be checking periodically to make sure it's still there." Rossco caught the look of alarm on Jay's face and laughed. "Just kidding. But leave it on for a couple of days. For me." Rossco looked at Jay in such a penetrating yet gentle manner that she trembled from head to toe. Rossco's warm, brown eyes saw directly into her soul and dallied there for a moment in a strange, mute greeting.

Snafu joined the table and the spell was broken. He sat at the far end but Rossco felt the Girl straighten her back ever so slightly, as if in preparation for an exam.

"Snafu, I want you to meet Jay."

Snafu was flirting with Susannah and grunted a hasty acknowledgement over his shoulder.

"Mr. Smith knows me from class," Jay said apologetically to Rossco, as if to explain Snafu's obvious disinterest. It was odd being madly in love with someone who did not see you. Jay took some comfort in this fact, as it meant that this doomed premonitory love affair was not likely to take on physical dimensions. Jay was not ready to deal with flesh and blood. She watched Susannah trail her hand idly along Snafu's arm, a gesture that implied greater intimacies between them. Jay's blood rose in a quiet, crimson fury.

"No, Girl, he doesn't know you at all. But maybe we should keep it that way." Rossco's gentle, bearlike energy shouldered out Snafu and Susannah. Jay found herself gazing at Mr. Rossco, as if to seek answers to questions that she hadn't yet asked. Jay was puzzled by this mysterious affection springing up between them. Mr. Rossco didn't look like someone she would care for. His face was placid and doughy; his eyes, two small, glinty, brown stones, nestled in gentle folds of flesh and hidden behind the thick, grimy lenses of his glasses. The central meeting place of Rossco's face was not his eyes, but his full, generous mouth. His eyes took in the information but his mouth decided on it. His mouth weighed everything carefully. Rossco resembled a large carp, sitting in state at the bottom of the pond, deliberating on which bait he'll select, patiently waiting for the waterlogged flies to sink down to his depths. Occasionally, an exotic nymph would drift past. Rossco would see the hook and cannily nibble around it. Imperious Girl didn't seem to have a hook. Rossco knew better than to trust appearances. There was always a hook.

Snafu glanced over at Rossco and his latest discovery. Each week it was a new one. She looked vaguely familiar. Snafu tried to remember where he'd seen her. She looked like so many of those mousy, intellectual girls that kept cropping up these days. She wore the ubiquitous wire-rimmed granny glasses, and the accompanying humourless expression. When the hippies brought in the Victorian granny look, they intended irony in the vision of sensual, dissipated youth, sporting the straight-laced trappings of their elders. However, it didn't work if you already looked like somebody's granny to begin with. Rossco's girl was singularly unattractive. She was built like a stick and had a chin like a general: jutting out, determined. Snafu was leery of women with strong chins. It usually meant they were bossy. Snafu's tastes leaned in the other direction. He had a passion for women with overbites, the teeth protruding slightly, gently falling away from the upper mouth, giving a woman a tender, wistful look. Modern dentistry was ruining all that. Snafu noticed it in the new crop of students. The young ones from good families had perfect white teeth set in eerily level jawlines. No vulnerability or hesitation there, just even, blank, expressions. He was wildly excited when he first saw Susannah because he thought, through some miracle, the dentists had overlooked her. He saw, to his dismay, on closer examination, that she simply had a slack jaw. Snafu pursued women with buck teeth and overbites as a connoisseur seeks out rare mushrooms that grow only in uninhabited woodlands.

Snafu slept with most of the girls in the third-year program before proceeding to the girls in the second-year program. The summer students remained untouched for a while. Then, Snafu sighed and thought he might as well sift his way through them. Consuela proved unsatisfactory so he embarked on a little flirtation with Sheila. He might have succeeded in winning her away from the dull Brian but Sheila weighed up the advantages of regular sex with a man she liked against the disadvantages of promiscuous sex with a man she didn't know and voted in favour of routine. After Sheila rebuffed him, Snafu made a play for Susannah and seduced her easily. Jonathan was too caught up with promoting his artistic genius to notice.

While Jay had a fairly high opinion of herself and secretly thought that men should throw themselves at her feet, she never imagined that any man would actually do so. Mr. Rossco's uninhibited admiration made Jay extremely nervous. She couldn't help but wonder what was wrong with this man. He didn't seem drunk. He'd only arrived in town this morning. Did people like him start drinking first thing in the morning?

"What's your number, Girl?"

"Pardon?"

"Your phone number."

"Oh."

"You don't want to give it to me?"

"No, it's not that. I, ah ...," Jay hoped that Mr. Rossco was one of those rare people who would have found it charming that she lived in a sorority house, but she didn't want to risk the derision that usually accompanied such an announcement. She knew that Snafu Smith would make hay with it. "I live in a boarding house."

"That's nothing to be ashamed of."

"You're right. The number's 968-8722." Rossco carefully jotted it down in his black book. "The phone isn't private, but whoever answers it will take messages," and without knowing why she took this stupid leap into the void, Jay added, "And ah, they say a weird thing when they answer but pay no attention."

"What?"

"They say, ah, KAT House."

"Cat house?"

"Yeah. It's just a cute name."

"Girl, are you living in a —"

"Oh no!"

"You're sure about that? 'Cause some of these boarding houses —"

Jay's face flushed with embarrassment as she tried to conceal the outmoded nature of her lodgings. "No, no, it really is just a cute name. The woman who runs the place —"

"Girl ..."

People will happily ignore someone who has something important to say but the moment one has a petty secret one is trying to conceal, then, all eyes and ears are alert. There was a sudden lull in the conversation, as there always is, just before someone is about to say something stupid or incriminating. The entire table heard Jay say, with striking clarity, "She's not a madam. No really, she's got lots of cats. She finds them and then she tries to find homes for them. That's why it's called KAT House."

Rufus instantly jumped in, as he had a few questions of his own regarding his rather peculiar night spent at the house. "What'd you tell me it was, Jay? A house for feminist freemasons." The crowd at the Oblong Table tittered at his witticism. "For call girls, they were very good-looking," Rufus added, with the air of an expert.

"They're supposed to be good-looking, moron. That's why they're on call. Who'd want them if they were ugly?" snarled Snafu. He hated it when students tried to be clever.

Harold Bowen, who'd never been known to talk to anyone other than the Big Three and Snafu, regarded Jay sombrely, "That'd be sort of tough. Living in a place like that." The other students quickly tried to impress Bowen with how awful their rooms were. Jay could see that she was gaining some measure of respect among the crowd at the Oblong Table. Clearly, in Bohemian circles, it was a social advantage to live in a house of ill-repute.

"If you're a feminist, then I can't call you Girl anymore," Rossco sighed. "I'll have to call you Woman."

"I'm not one of them. I'm just a boarder."

"Odd that they would take in a boarder," mused Snafu. "Why would they want to tie up one of the rooms?"

"It was hilarious," said Rufus. "Two of them came down the stairs like that gum ad. Dressed for the prom."

"And their dates?" asked Snafu, intent on pursuing a line of inquiry of his own.

"Clean cut. Super straight."

"How old were they?"

"About twenty."

"No, the guys."

"Same age. How old would you say they were, Jay?"

"Yeah, that's right." Jay nodded nervously.

Snafu Smith looked directly at Jay for the first time since the term started. "And tell me — sorry, what's your name again?"

"Jay."

"So, tell me, Jay, where exactly is this house?"

"It's on Huron Street."

"Huron, eh?"

"Yes."

"And is 'cat' spelled with a 'K?'"

"Um, yes."

"And is the full name 'Kappa Alpha Theta'?"

"Yes," croaked Jay, who could weave elaborate falsehoods but could not lie to a direct question.

With the unrestrained glee of a courtroom lawyer nailing a dissembling witness, Snafu pounced. "She lives in a sorority house!" he roared, thus exposing Jay for what she was: the well-brought-up daughter of upper-middle-class parents. Jay smiled sheepishly.

"Is that true, Girl?" asked Rossco.

"Yes," admitted Jay. "It's cheap rent, and the rooms are clean."

There was a hushed silence as Rossco reflected on Jay's transgression. His lips puckered, then went slack, puckered again to one side in a slight grimace, relaxed, opened slightly as if taking in a bubble of air, then, they stretched into a broad grin. "That's good, Girl." Rossco started to chuckle. "KAT House! Well, she keeps a lot of cats!" King Rossco broke into howls of mirth, so the rest of the Oblong Table, save for Snafu, fell about laughing.

Jay became Rossco's regular companion for Tuesday "lunch" at the Brunswick. The week immediately following her debut was slightly problematic when Jay discovered that no one was allowed to eat at the Oblong Table. She hadn't eaten since early morning and was looking forward to lunch. The beer went straight to her head and almost rendered her unconscious. She managed to procure an ancient egg salad sandwich and ate it on the sly, without anyone being the wiser, but the sandwich caused such gastric havoc that Jay was in pain for most of the afternoon. When she left to go home, Rossco begged her to meet him the next day at his other favourite tavern, the Pilot.

This rendezvous was not a success, as William Rossco on a Wednesday was an entirely different man from William Rossco on a Tuesday. The Wednesday Rossco looked at Jay as though he didn't have the vaguest idea of who she was. The Wednesday Rossco had two other women hanging off him, on either side, both of whom he proclaimed to be incomparably lovely. Different people were at this table: magazine editors, journalists, television and film "personalities"; sharp, glamorous people who talked a lot. After standing awkwardly about, waiting for Rossco to recognize her, Jay finally pulled up an empty chair and squeezed in between two men who were engaged in a fierce debate as to whether television was hot or cold. They took no notice of her. Jay was an invisible woman to everyone but the barmaid who hustled over immediately and demanded to know what Jay would be drinking. Jay didn't want to drink anything. She wasn't even sure if she wanted to stay at the table. If she didn't order anything, she could slip quietly away. However, barmaids have an uncanny ability to suss out uncommitted people like Jay and put them on the spot. Jay was also on a strict budget. Granted, the budget was self-imposed. Her father sent her a generous allowance and she could have asked for twice its sum without causing undue distress, but Jay prided herself on being economical. It made her feel responsible. Sitting in a bar and drinking all afternoon wasn't so great a sin if the alcohol was cheap. For some obscure reason, a glass of wine ordered in a tavern was very expensive. While Jay pondered the economical pros of draft versus the simple fact that she preferred wine, the barmaid plonked two small glasses of draft down and rushed to take another order. The two men each grabbed a glass. Jay was free to leave. As she got up, the Tuesday Rossco emerged from his cocoon.

"My God, Girl! You're here!" Rossco shunted the woman on his left off to one side and motioned for Jay to join him.

"Where've you been, Girl? I was waiting for you."

"I was here."

"Hiding. Don't hide from me, Girl." Mr. Rossco seemed different. He was edgy. On Tuesday, he was in a mellow mood. Now, he seemed critical. It could simply have been that, having been mysteriously and unconditionally adored the day before, Jay didn't know what to do for an encore. Being a king's favourite is a position fraught with complications. Jay felt she should be worthy of Mr. Rossco's admiration, yet any attempts she made to earn it fell flat. When she tried to be witty, he didn't get the joke. If she said something in earnest, he found it hilariously funny. His reaction to what she said was so alarmingly at odds with what she meant that she decided her best way of prolonging the fascination was to be elusive. She had one glass of wine and left before Mr. Rossco could be disenchanted.

chapter thirteen

TALENT NIGHT

IT WAS THEIR last training session before the jump. Lily would never admit it to Brad, but she was frightened. There were so many things that could go wrong. Flash stressed the security of the static line jump and in the same breath, told them a horror story about a static line that got tangled up, so the student wound up unconscious, hanging below the airplane. Lily wasn't sure how the student lost consciousness. She didn't ask, certain that Flash would, with gory relish, reveal it to them.

Paul and Brad enjoyed the horror stories. For them, it added to the thrill. They were defying death. For all Flash's cautionary tales, it didn't occur to either Brad or Paul that anything would actually go wrong, whereas that was all Lily thought about: accidentally opening her chute in the airplane, inadvertently tangling the static line, not being attached to the static line. Lily was not athletic or co-ordinated. She was awkward, ungainly: most of her body lurching forward while other parts were detained, hooked on nearby shrubbery or furniture. During Lily's class exercises, if anything could go wrong, it did. Brad looked on sadly as Lily struggled with the release rings. She could see the disappointment in his eyes as his "wild thing" became a pathetic creature who tagged along behind, vainly striving to keep up.

After the class, Paul drove to KAT House first and quickly leaped out of the car to open up the back seat for Lily. Judging by the alacrity of his movement, Lily was certain that he and Brad were going on to the Brunswick for a beer so she said, "Why don't we all go out and celebrate our second class." There was a guilty silence and Lily's suspicions were confirmed. Brad blurted, "It's a bit late, and don't you have to get up early?"

"It's sweet of you to worry about my work schedule, Brad, but it's really not necessary."

Brad laughed uncomfortably.

"Have a nice time at the Brunswick." Lily slammed the car door and hurried into KAT House, cursing herself for having lost her temper. Tantrums were not going to win her way into Brad's heart.

Kathleen and Louise were in the kitchen, held captive to one of Susan Lipton's monotonous dissertations on the last bridal shower she attended.

"She got a Braun coffee grinder with five settings — one for perc coffee, one for drip, one for Turkish — I don't think many people would use the Turkish setting but it's nice to have one ..."

"Hi, Kathleen, Louise, Susan."

"Hi. Did you steal my salami?" asked Louise.

"... Turkish coffee is very good. It's quite thick. A lot thicker than espresso. Did you know that Turkish ..."

"Of course, I didn't steal your salami!" retorted Lily, doing her best to impersonate innocence.

"... and Greek coffee are the same thing?"

"Well, everyone's got food in the fridge except for you. And all our food is disappearing," countered Louise.

"Someone took two of my plums," added Susan, pleased to be part of an attack on Lily.

"So we figure the food thief has to be someone who doesn't have food and that would have to be you."

"I eat out."

"So you say," Kathleen leapt in, self-righteously. "I don't mind loaning you a few slices of bread from time to time—"

"Loaning? Loaning me bread? Jesus, Kathleen, how cheap can you be?! And how cheap would I be to steal bread?"

"Salami's expensive. It's worth stealing. And it makes a good sandwich with stolen bread," observed Louise.

"I have better things to do with my time than steal your lousy food." At that moment, Susan looked up at Lily, fixing her with blank blue eyes. She looked smug, complacent. Lily hesitated, then launched her missile. "I've been at skydiving classes."

"Skydiving!" Kathleen and Louise squealed.

"Skydiving?" Susan asked casually. Her tiny, manicured fingers gently clawed the table.

"You've jumped out of a plane?! That's nuts!" proclaimed Kathleen.

"Well, I haven't actually jumped, yet. We do that on Sunday."

"We?" The colour drained from Susan's face as her calculations fell into place.

"Ooooh, that's soon." Louise and Kathleen were sufficiently impressed.

Trembling with pent-up rage, Susan left the room as graciously as she could manage. Lily was angling for a confrontation but Susan knew her strength lay in evasion. She now knew why Brad had suddenly taken up skydiving. An unpleasant thought crossed her mind. What if they weren't skydiving? Susan hurried up to the to the second floor bathroom, which was directly over the kitchen. Bending down to the vent, she listened to Lily brag on and on about the classes. Susan breathed a sigh of relief. There were classes. But before or after the class, there would still be time for an assignation. Susan grimly contemplated her next tactic in securing Brad's affection.

"The night's still young, girls. Let's go to the Brunswick!" Lily tried to make the suggestion sound casual.

"I have to work tomorrow. Don't you have to work?"

"Is that how we're going to spend the rest of our lives? Working at jobs we hate?"

"I like my job," declared Kathleen.

"Mine's all right," mused Louise, not having considered it before.

"Aw, come on! Have fun for a change. It's Talent Night!"

"Talent Night!" Kathleen and Louise protested in unison. "That's gross! How could you —"

Jay walked into the kitchen and beamed serenely at them, "What's Talent Night?" she asked innocently.

"Come on! I'll take you." Lily bustled Jay out of the kitchen and practically pushed her up the stairs. "Ya have to wear a T-shirt."

"I don't own a T-shirt," said Jay who took a perverse pride in not following trends.

"Borrow one of mine!" Lily insisted.

Against her better judgment, Jay put on a white T-shirt with KAPPA ALPHA THETA emblazoned across the front.

Jay prayed that she wouldn't run into anyone from the Artists School. She needn't have worried. The Brunswick House was a completely different place in the evenings. During the day, it was quiet and seamy, an easy kingdom for King Rossco to preside over. But at night, the students took over. These weren't art students who had been trained into submissive obedience by the good King Rossco. No, these were rowdy university students — most of them from the non-artistic faculties of business and engineering — and they were out for a big loud time. Thrown into the evening mix was another group that no one ever considered but were, in fact, the main clientele of the Brunswick. They were the locals. The locals were misplaced men and women who had survived World War II, married in the 1950s, watched their marriages collapse in the 1960s, and were planning to spend the 1970s in the alcoholic haze that had attended their other decades. Talent Night was their creation.

Talent Night was resurrected vaudeville. The locals got up and sang songs of their youth, which were lovingly received by the other locals. The management kept a firm hand on the event. The bar's bouncer, the Midget, gave the boot to anyone who wasn't sufficiently respectful.

When Jay and Lily arrived, the tavern was packed with students and fogeys. Lily scanned the room, then headed for a large, crowded table. Brad waved cheerfully at Lily and gestured to some empty seats at the far end.

"He could have found me a seat beside him," grumbled Lily.

"But no one's supposed to know you're seeing each other."

"Susan's not here. What difference would it make?"

"I don't know," replied Jay feebly, unable to enter into the machinations of the unofficial love affair. Brad seemed curiously diminished when surrounded by the other inmates of Sigma Chi. Jay wondered why Lily had singled him out in the first place. He seemed so young and formless. Jay was starting to see the world through the jaded eyes of her art teachers. The boy sitting beside Brad looked more interesting. He was sharp and confident in his movements.

"Who's he?" Jay asked Lily.

"Paul," she muttered, obviously put out.

The screeching whine of a microphone blasted into the room. Talent Night was about to begin.

Jay was expecting a plaintive young girl with long hair parted in the middle to come on stage and play her guitar and sing sad folk songs. The girl's performance would be followed by a homely looking boy who would bring his guitar and sing his sad song. Nicholas used to take Jay to coffee houses and they were subjected to this musical torture as a matter of course.

"Mama Chickie and her lovely bunch of coconuts!!"

The crowd roared with delight. Evidently, Mama Chickie was one of the better acts. A fat woman with great huge swollen legs clambered onto the stage. She wore a brown and white polka-dot polyester dress with a plunging scooped neckline. The polyester stretched across her misshapen lumpy body like a second skin. Her breasts, strangely white and creamy, were crammed into the scant remains of the bodice, like two bowling balls, ready to plop out and cause serious damage. She faced the crowd and took everyone in with her small, beady, brown eyes, while her elderly accompanist arranged the music at the electric piano. Sound of a hurdy gurdy rhythm bellowed forth.

> *Down at the county fair,*
> *One evening I was there ...*

The tune was simple. Mama Chickie sang in a high-pitched quavering soprano.

> *I heard a barker shouting,*
> *underneath the flare ...*

The performance was pleasantly innocuous until Mama Chickie reached the meat of the song. Then, her prim bird-like mouth opened into a smirking lecherous chasm, as she sang and rolled her body in sinuous rhythm, ebbing and flowing like an ocean wave.

> *OOOOOH, I've got a lovely bunch of coconuts,*
> *There they are, standing in a row ...*

Mama Chickie made lascivious reference to her wobbling breasts, which were threatening to spill out of her dress.

> *Big ones, small ones, some as big as your head,*
> *Give 'em a wrist, a flick of the wrist,*
> *That's what the showman said....*

Then Mama Chickie shifted the audience's attention to her hips, which executed an elegant figure eight, a groin foray into the audience, followed by a lumbering slow retreat.

OOOOOHHHH RRRRROOOOOLLL a bowl a ball a
  penny a pitch,
RRRRRRRROLLLLL a bowl a ball a penny a pitch ...

The great mounds of disagreeable flesh that composed Mama
Chickie's midsection roiled in response: large slabs of flesh wobbling
in one direction, giblets of skin jiggling in another. The audience sat
mesmerized, half afraid that, from this ocean of flesh, a rogue wave
would appear and knock them flat.

RRRRolll a bowl a ball
rrrooooollll a bowl a ball
Singing roll a bowl a ball a penny a pitch!

Jay thought she was going to throw up. Watching all that polka-
dot-clad flesh roll and crawl and burble its way through the song
made her nauseous. She looked around at the rest of the table. The
Sigma Chi boys seemed to think Mama Chickee was a grand old
joke. Brad and Paul had some sort of secret amusement, laughing
and nudging each other throughout the song.

Jay was about to excuse herself from the table when, mercifully,
the song ended. Mama Chickie's body wobbled serenely back into
place as she received her accolades.

"My God, that was horrible," said Jay to Lily.

"Yeah, I guess so," mumbled Lily, gloomily.

"I think I'm going to go home, now."

"You can't go home!"

"Well, you seem to be in a bad mood and I don't know anyone
at this table —"

"Sorry. Please stay."

Talent Night proceeded with the elderly trotting out ancient dirges
and wartime comedy acts. Though the students jeered at the acts,
in truth, they were fascinated. The Midget's Elvis Presley impersonation was the highlight of the evening. People were impressed with

the Midget's versatility. He'd be out in the alley doing a drop kick on a drunk's head and then come racing in, grab his white-fringed beaded jacket and be Elvis to the acclaim of a crowd that had witnessed one too many versions of "Danny Boy."

"Can we go now?" pleaded Jay, who had seen enough talent to last her a lifetime.

"Not yet. We have to do the —"

A microphoned voice drowned out Lily's words, bellowing, "THE WET T-SHIRT CONTEST!!"

"The WHAT?!" squealed Jay. The eyes of the Sigmi Chi boys were suddenly upon her and she looked down with horror at her KAT House T-shirt, a clear indication of entry into the contest.

Lily grabbed Jay's hand and danced towards the stage. Jay didn't want to appear to be a bad sport. In the confusion, the word "wet" had flown past her consciousness so she lined up with the large-breasted women and thought to herself, "How bad could it be?" A blast of cold water hit her full in the chest. Jay looked down, past her diminutive breasts, to see a leering man with an empty bucket grinning up at her. The crowd groaned in disappointment. Jay's mortification was quickly passed over as the next contestant was dowsed.

Jay was stunned that she had been tricked into participating in this boorish event. As each contestant paraded her wares, Jay imagined how she would explain this episode to Nicholas.

"Yes, I was making a political statement."

"That your breasts are puny?" In real life, Nicholas wouldn't have been so cruel but in Jay's daydream, he was heartless.

"This is a simple follow up to the Burn the Bra Movement. Our breasts are unfettered. I display them —"

"There's nothing to display —"

"But only for irony. This is my artistic statement."

"You said political."

"I changed my mind. It's artistic."

Jay was losing the imaginary argument. She was in danger of losing complete control and bursting into tears. The spotlight had shifted to the other end of the line, focusing on Lily and another girl with large breasts. The final vote was on. People in the audience clapped heartily for the other girl, but when the emcee's hand hovered over Lily's head for the vote, the Sigma Chi boys stood up on the table and howled — a clear victory for Lily. Jay noticed that Brad remained seated. Paul was whispering something in his ear. Lily's face was flushed with triumph as she stood before the crowd, accepting their roars of admiration.

Then, the house lights came back up, the canned music blasted its cheerful noise and the bar resumed its usual bustle. Jay expected Lily to leave the stage with her. But Lily had forgotten about Jay.

She strode over to the Sigma Chi table. The boys were back in their seats, calmer now. They burst into applause when Lily approached. Lily butted in between Brad and his friend and pulled the wet part of the T-shirt away from her body and yanked it over Brad's head so his face was pinned between her breasts. Brad squirmed to escape but Lily held him fast.

"Why you in such a hurry to leave, Brad?"

The other boys weren't sure what to make of this performance so they made feeble jokes until Lily released Brad and sat in his lap.

"You didn't save me a seat, Brad."

Brad laughed sheepishly. His face was round and pink, bearing the roseate blotches of his imprisonment.

Jay had quietly taken her previous seat at the table. Icy blasts from the air conditioner licked at her body as she tugged at the clammy T-shirt to stop its cling. No one was paying any attention to her. All eyes were on Lily.

"So, this was how women were supposed to be," Jay brooded to herself. Lily was the Conqueror and Brad the Vanquished. Jay wished she could be bold with Snafu Smith but, whenever she was near him, she became tongue-tied and clumsy.

The air conditioning made it impossible for Jay's T-shirt to dry and as she was not like Lily, big-breasted and basking in the warm admiration of the men, there was nothing to distract her from wet, sullen misery. She had been a companion for Lily for as long as she was needed and, having served that purpose, was unceremoniously dumped.

Jay got up and left the table. The Midget stood in the doorway, yelling at one of the old codgers, who was sprawled out on the pavement. Jay tried to squeeze past.

"You do that Dwarf routine one more time and I'm kicking your ass from here to Moose Jaw!"

"Heigh-ho, Heigh-ho, it's off to work we go!"

"That's it, buddy!"

The Midget leaped down and pummelled the old man into submission, while Jay guiltily pushed past and pretended not to see what was going on. She walked down the street quickly. She was at complete loose ends. It was too early to go to bed but it was too late to make other plans. She went into the KAT House kitchen, hoping to find someone to talk to. Susan Lipton was there. Jay's first impulse was to turn and walk right out again but that would have been rude.

"I thought you were out with Lily." Susan had the uncanny ability of knowing one's whereabouts and speaking like one's mother.

"Um, yeah. I was." Jay was horribly tempted to confide in Susan.

"What happened?"

The intrusive, metallic tone of Susan's question put Jay right off. "I left early 'cause I needed to work on my painting. It's due for class," Jay said and dashed into the basement, closing the door behind her to discourage Susan from following.

She sat under the sickly glow of the fluorescent lights and contemplated her painting. It was ugly. Jay was trying the abstract expressionist style. She painted a huge face of a laughing girl. She looked demonic. Jay idly turned the hair into snakelike streams of red.

She replayed the events of the night in her head and her confusion hardened into anger as she realized how Lily had used her.

As if echoing her mood, the ghosts' angry voices rumbled quietly like thunder in the distance, gaining in sound and momentum; the two men resuming their fight over the woman. Jay sat in her little pool of flickering green light, and beyond that light was darkness. However, this night, Jay could see the forms of the men on the stairs with startling clarity. They were young and wearing T-shirts and jeans. One man was on his hands and knees climbing up the stairs. The other man, behind him, was pulling at his pants, dragging them down around his ankles. Their voices, usually muffled, were also clear.

"Hey!"

"You like this? You like this, queer boy?"

The man below was now on top of the other man and had him pinned to the stairs. They formed this dark, rocking entity. Two faces gleamed out, Brad and Paul, and just as quickly vanished into a grey, struggling mass as one man tried to extricate himself from the other. The ghosts returned to their previous state and were now clothed in nineteenth-century garb. Jay blinked and stood up and made noises and did everything she could to make the ghosts go away, but such tactics never worked before and they weren't working now. Jay's only means of escape was running up the stairs, through the ghosts.

Suddenly, the man on the bottom jabbed his elbow into the other man and threw him off. He then grabbed a shovel and hit the man on the head. Repeatedly. In earlier versions of the scene, the man was only hit once. Jay was puzzled by these alterations in the ghosts' routine. This time, the murder wasn't accidental. It was deliberate. The one man smashing the shovel against the other man's skull, over and over again. The air was electric with his rage. Jay could bear it no longer. She wept with the unfairness of it all: that she was forced to bear witness to such things, that she couldn't live a normal life and have a boyfriend like everyone else, that she had small breasts and everyone liked big breasts, that she wanted to be a great artist and her paintings were terrible, that ... that .... She looked up and saw that everything was still. The ghosts had gone. She ran upstairs and went straight to bed, swearing that, from now on, she wasn't going to be a bystander in other people's affairs. She was going to live her own life.

chapter fourteen

MARCO'S PARTY

THE BIG THREE and a couple of visiting artists from New York met to play at Shiner's studio for an all-night jazz session. That was the premise of the evening but, in fact, it usually turned into a huge free-for-all party with at least a hundred people, packed in like sardines, jostling each other to get at the beer and the dope. Shiner had fallen madly in love so the evening provided an unofficial forum for his new mistress to duke it out with his old mistress while he strummed away on his bass guitar, blissfully oblivious to the ensuing catfight. Shiner was too cool to get involved with the ugly business of breaking up. Yoko Ono had set a precedent. It was now up to the women to fight for men's affections.

Rossco asked Rufus to take Jay to the party. Rufus was not entirely happy with his role as Rossco's go-between. He eyed Jay critically when he arrived to pick her up.

"You dressed up."

"He told me to."

"Do you always do what you're told? I think he had something else in mind when he asked you to wear heels."

"Pardon?"

"High heels and a miniskirt. Not that." Rufus gestured disdainfully at Jay's 1920s style dress flowing down around her calves. "You look like ... like ..."

"Daisy in *The Great Gatsby*?"

"No. Blanche Dubois in *A Streetcar Named Desire*."

"I don't!"

"I'm sorry, but you look a little crazy. I mean, who wears stuff like that these days?"

"You're just not up on fashion."

"I don't want you to feel like a freak."

"Fine. I'll change!" Jay flounced up the stairs.

"Don't do it on my account," Rufus called up after her, secretly pleased that he had provoked her. Jay returned a few minutes later, dressed more innocuously, in a knee-length skirt with low-heeled sandals.

"No high heels?"

"Not with a short skirt. They don't go."

"That skirt's not very short. And who says they don't go?"

"This is a nice, safe outfit to wear to a party where I don't know anyone."

"He won't be pleased."

"So, I'm not supposed to do what I'm told."

"It's just that there's an aesthetic to a short skirt and high-heeled shoes."

"Yeah. Tarty."

"I wouldn't say that. It's really a leg thing. Legs in high heels look spectacular. The angle of the —"

"Okay. I'll change into what I had on before."

"No, you look fine. Now, let's go."

RUFUS TOOK JAY into a shabby tavern.

"Why are we going in here?"

"The party's down the street. But it's too soon. It won't be going yet. They'll be setting up."

"Setting up?"

"Equipment, amps."

"Is there a band?"

"They are the band."

"Really? Mr. Rossco plays in a band? What sort of music does he play?"

Rufus laughed for a full five minutes before he could make any attempt to answer her question. "Music? They play. That's all. They just play."

"Well, they must play something."

"They call themselves a jazz band."

"I like jazz."

Rufus howled again and flung himself against his seat, convulsing intermittently.

"I'm glad you find me so amusing."

"Sorry ... ha ... sorry ... I like jazz. I mean, you're really not his type. What do you see in him, anyway? Is it his money?"

Jay was not prepared for the sudden seriousness of Rufus's question. "His money? Mr. Rossco's not rich."

"Well, no, he isn't. But he has more money than me. Is it power?"

"Power?!"

"Why do all you girls go for him?"

"I'm not going for him. He asked me to a party so I'm going."

"Do you like him?"

"Yes, of course I like him."

"Why?"

"I don't know. He's sort of sweet. He has a way of looking at you, like he really knows you and cares about you."

"So, are you planning on sleeping with him?"

"God! Is that ... does he expect ... am I supposed to ... Oh God!" Jay bolted out of her seat, but Rufus held her fast.

"Sorry — hey, stop. It's okay. Nothing'll happen. He's just got a thing for you. He won't do anything about it."

"You're sure?"

"Yeah. I just wondered if you felt the same way about him."

"Oh, I see. Your job is to find out and tell him if the coast is clear."

"That's not why I asked."

"Look, I don't mind. Easier than me telling him."

"That's not why...." To make his point, Rufus took Jay into his arms and kissed her hard. He meant to be gentle and flirtatious but she was so obtuse at times, that some of his frustration found its way into the kiss. To be kissed publicly in a brightly lit, sleazy tavern was not Jay's idea of romance. Before she had a chance to ask Rufus just what the hell he thought he was doing, one of the students from last year waltzed into the tavern.

"Hey Rufus, what're you doing here?"

"Oh, Carla. Hi."

"Aren't you going to Marco's?"

"Yeah, we're just going now." Rufus paid the bill quickly, made hasty introductions and bundled Jay out the door before she could protest.

One could hear the sounds of the party all the way down the street. Marco's studio was on the top floor so some of the party had spilled out onto the roof.

"Jesus, Rufus, you didn't bring any beer," Carla complained as they pushed their way through the crowd.

"There's always lots around."

"He's such a cheapskate. How can you stand him?"

"Hey! Back off, Carla. You didn't bring anything, either."

There was no sign of Marco in the general melee. Jay stupidly expected Marco Shiner and his girlfriend to be at the door greeting people and showing them where to put their jackets and purses. She kicked herself for her bourgeois presumptions. There was a bedroom off to one side, so she tentatively placed her jacket on the bed. Given the general tenor of the crowd, she felt it wise to hang onto her purse. Out of habit, Jay searched for the possible hostess of the evening. Two women seemed to be vying for this position. One was relaxed and happy; the other, anxious and fretful. Both women had long hair and fierce expressions. Rufus went off to forage for beer. Carla was quickly claimed by one of the artists and vanished into the crowd.

Glancing around at the women at the party, Jay felt instantly uneasy. They looked tough. They were heavily made-up so it was hard to tell how old they were. Some of them might have been only a few years older than Jay but their faces were hard with cynicism. They were trying to look as if they were over thirty. Other than her parents, Jay had never known people who actually wanted to be old. She looked at the men and was slightly reassured. They all looked like overgrown boys. Still, they were too old for Jay's tastes. Rufus was the only male her age at this soiree and as he, now, seemed to have designs on her, Jay decided that she would retrieve her jacket and slip quietly out the door, the way she had come. She had to push her way through blockades of people and just as she had a clear line to the bedroom door, the two hostesses decided to fulfill their duty. They each grabbed a hand and spoke in unison.

"Hi, I'm Natasha."

"Hi, I'm Yvonne."

Natasha, the happy one, twirled Jay to face her. "Welcome! I hope you're not leaving!"

Yvonne, the other one, interjected, "Back off, bitch! No sorry, not you, dear. What's your name again?"

"Jay Wright."

"Do I know you?"

"No, you don't, actually —"

"You're a friend of Marco's?"

"Well, no, I'm not —"

"Well, come on in!" urged Natasha.

"I really should be going."

"Nonsense! Not everyone here is so FUCKING unfriendly."

Yvonne leaned in conspiratorially to Jay. "If I'm unfriendly, it's because I live here."

"Not anymore," said Natasha. "Haven't you heard?"

"If I moved out every time he brought back some cheap tart —"

The happy expression left Natasha's face abruptly. She grabbed Yvonne and wheeled her around to face her. "Who the fuck are you calling a cheap tart!"

"You, cuntface."

War was declared. The two women fell upon each other. Yvonne grabbed Natasha's hair and yanked it hard. Natasha gave Yvonne a left hook that sent her reeling into the crowd. Someone caught Yvonne before she hit the ground. The other guests retreated from the room. Yvonne clutched her jaw and stared in bewilderment at Natasha. Marco had brought home some tough tramps before, but she never had to deal with one who could box. Natasha strutted about confidently, daring Yvonne to retaliate. Yvonne called out to Marco to put an end to this nonsense. A nervous little man informed her that Marco had gone out to buy cigarettes. Yvonne drew herself up with as much dignity as she could muster and retreated to the bedroom to pack up her things.

Jay watched with dismay as the sobbing ex-hostess closed the bedroom door quietly behind her. It was going to be difficult to retrieve her jacket. There was no telling when that door would open again. Natasha effusively hailed the puzzled guests who were expecting to see Yvonne as they streamed into the studio. Rufus appeared with several bottles of beer jammed into his pants and jacket.

"Here," he said, handing her one.

"Actually, I don't drink beer."

"Great!" he said, and took it back.

"Is there wine?"

"You gotta be joking!"

"There isn't wine?"

"I wish you'd told me. Christ! Now, I have to go back." Rufus scrutinized the teaming masses. There was a dim possibility that he could bed Jay tonight and a couple of glasses of wine might tip the scales in his favour.

"It's okay. I don't want anything to drink. I think I'm going to head out."

"I'll be back."

"No, really. I don't want any wine." Rufus's head was lost among the bobbing throng.

"Girl." A glass of champagne was thrust into Jay's hand. She turned to see Mr. Rossco grinning back at her.

"Mr. Rossco."

"Bill."

"Sorry. Bill. Thanks!" Jay lifted her glass in a toast.

Rossco's eyes glazed over as he leaned into her. "You are the most beautiful girl." Jay blushed as Snafu Smith appeared at Rossco's side.

"Hey man, when's Marco coming back? Fight's over."

"Isn't she beautiful?"

Snafu saw that Rossco had that same lantern-jawed girl in tow again. She kept turning up like a bad penny. "You guys gonna play or not?"

"Marco's on the fire escape. Isn't she exquisite?"

"Yeah yeah, exquisite," Snafu grunted. "Well, what are you waiting for? Why don't you guys play?"

"We're waiting for Randolph."

"Randolph Stack? That asshole. Jesus, I hate actors!"

The party suddenly took on a new significance for Jay. Randolph Stack was a young Canadian actor who had starred in a Hollywood movie that Jay had seen on television when she was fourteen. She had developed a big crush on Randolph Stack during the course of the movie and might have been encouraged to be a fan of his work, had there been more work forthcoming. But Randolph Stack's career seemed to begin and end with that movie. However, the tenuous prestige was enough for Jay. She was now anticipating the arrival of the Big (Canadian) Star. She felt a strong mystical connection with him when she'd seen the movie. Most people would have called it a schoolgirl crush, but Jay was convinced that it went deeper than that. It was due to a bewildering set of circumstances that she was even at this party tonight. Therefore, it must surely have been destined that they would meet.

Destiny kept everyone on tenterhooks that night. The artists were anxious to play. If they didn't start soon, Marco's mistresses might go for another round. Natasha had won, for the moment, but Yvonne could still challenge her. A low rumble initiated by Snafu Smith reverberated through the crowd: When's that asshole coming? When's that asshole coming? The artists resented postponing the session until some dumb actor showed up. Rossco was often thrusting unsavoury types into their midst and expecting the artists to be nice to them. Rossco's fawning celebration of media folk baffled his friends. As far as they were concerned, actors and journalists occupied the same plateau of depravity. Journalists were annoying because they thought they were bright and talked incessantly. Most journalists were like Fred Bale in that they were singularly unattractive and posed no threat to the seduction and securement of women, which was the real reason for the jam session parties. As in a conservatory, one would throw in a few ubiquitous palms to offset the rare and colourful flora, so journalists were tossed into the mix to make the women realize how lucky they were to have artist lovers. Journalists were therefore tolerated as inoffensive mulch, used to fertilize and protect the more exotic artist plants.

Actors, however, were another matter. An actor could wreak thorough havoc upon the dynamics of a party. They were usually handsome and well-built. They took immaculate care with their appearance and dressed in the latest fashion. Even if the fashion was to look bad, actors managed to wear it and look good. When forced to decide between the fashionably attired, scrubbed, surface charm of the actor and the grotty, in-your-face, squalor of the artist, the women invariably opted for cleanliness and chose the actor. They hovered in a large circle around the actor, content to be part of his harem rather than an individually prized object of an artist's affection. The artists were naturally anxious to put their claims in before the Big (Canadian) Star arrived. On one hand, they were relieved that he was late because it gave them more time. But no claims would be certain until the party had officially begun and it couldn't begin until people got thoroughly drunk, and as one had to be drunk in order to fully enjoy the jazz, the sooner they started playing, the better.

The Big Three and selected friends positioned themselves behind their instruments, about to launch into the marathon jam session. Just at the moment when William Rossco took his first deep breath of the evening and was about to release it into his tenor sax, the Big (Canadian) Star thrust his long, lanky body into Shiner's doorway and stood, silhouetted on the threshold.

A hush fell over the room. All eyes turned to the doorway. Randolph Stack gazed implacably back. He didn't move. He was waiting for the host to greet him. Marco Shiner lacked the social skills to perceive this small nuance. He simply thought, "What's the shithead waiting for? A round of applause?" The band grudgingly put down their instruments as Rossco hurried over to Randolph, who remained dramatically slouched in the doorway.

"Hey man, you made it!"

Randolph nodded grimly and muttered something under his breath. Jay boldly pushed her way through the crowd to get a better look at her secret idol. Randolph Stack looked older and skinnier than he'd been in that movie. His face was gaunt but he'd just flown in from Los Angeles, so that could account for it. His eyes were still as large as ever, though they, too, appeared weary and weather-beaten. Snafu Smith, for some mysterious reason, was being very friendly to the man he deemed an asshole.

"You have Gemini rising, which gives you an affinity with film and TV."

"Really?" Randolph Stack yawned.

"And Neptune in the first house gives you a magnetic presence."

"No kidding. Tell that to the producers. Well, this is all fascinating. Can I get a drink?"

"Oh yeah," Snafu grabbed one of the beers from Rufus's pocket
and handed it to Randolph.

"That was fast. Uh, I don't like to be rude, but do you have any
single malt Scotch?"

"Here, man." Rossco handed Randolph a large tumbler of Scotch
and drew Randolph away from Snafu.

"Thanks for the info, man," Randolph called back, over his
shoulder.

"I've done your chart."

"That's great. Thanks."

"I'll send it to you."

"Great, thanks," and in a low mutter to Rossco, "I thought all
you guys were straight."

"We are."

"Not him."

"Snafu's probably had most of the women in this room."

Randolph glanced around quickly. "I guess it put him off."

In another part of the room, Rufus had Jay pinned against a wall
and was gazing soulfully at her. Jay reflected that Rufus's eyes were
probably just as large as Randolph's and wondered why she could
not entertain similar feelings for him. Perhaps it was because he was
so pragmatic in his conversation, describing, in excruciating detail,
his painting techniques, while his body attempted to seduce her.

"So then, I scumble."

"You scumble?"

"Yeah, you get a thick layer of impasto — make sure it's dry.
Scumbling doesn't work unless it's dry."

"Dry."

"Yeah, usually a light colour. And then you take a thin layer of
a dark colour — one of the glazing colours. And you scrape it across
the impasto."

"Hmm."

Rufus leaned in to kiss her, but Jay neatly ducked under his arm.
"I'll have to try it sometime."

"Your glass is empty."

"Oh."

"I'll get you another." Before she could stop him, Rufus headed
for the bar. Jay could feel herself becoming light-headed. She hadn't
eaten any dinner. She and Rufus were supposed to grab a quick bite
before the party, but then, he took her to a place that didn't serve
food. Naturally, there was no food at Marco's party, eating being
regarded as a crude bourgeois act and Marco being too lazy to buy
anything. Usually, his mistress took care of such sundry details.

In the excitement at seeing his friend, the star, Rossco had forgotten about Jay. After a few Scotches, his enthusiasm renewed itself,
so he led Randolph on a merry prowl through the party to show
him the "most beautiful girl in the world."

"Girl!" Rossco's voice boomed about the hubbub. "Girl! I want
you, Girl!"

"There's some nice-looking women back there. Couldn't we stop
there for a bit?"

"Nah, ya have to meet her." Rossco suddenly spotted Jay. "Aha!
Hiding!" Jay was, in fact, desperately trying to catch Randolph's eye
for the inevitable moment of truth, but the man was too tall. He
kept looking over her head. Rossco grabbed Jay and pushed her in
front of Randolph.

"Isn't she beautiful? Isn't she exquisite?" Rossco crowed with
drunken glee.

The Big (Canadian) Star's luminous eyes snapped to attention and
drank in the spectre of Jay's beauty; scanning her face all too briefly,
casting his glance over her tiny bosom, panning down her skinny,
bony, little, body. The Big (Canadian) Star's full, voluptuous lips
parted into a tender boy-smile as he turned to Rossco and said, "Why
don't you fuck her and get it over with."

Jay was shocked. This crushing remark from someone who had
such large beautiful eyes, this comment from the cute boy-man who'd

stolen her heart when she was fourteen. Jay had always believed that people with large eyes were soulful. Well, Mr. Stack put paid to that theory. She could hardly believe it. Randolph Stack was not the sweet, shy boy that she'd loved in that movie. Randolph Stack was mean.

And worse still, Randolph Stack was not even aware that he'd said anything offensive. His tone was entirely disinterested: a man who'd been asked to assess a house. He inspected the foundations, rolled a few marbles on the floor to check the levels, gave his verdict and moved on. Already he was merrily chatting to a curvaceous blonde while Jay stood frozen in a mild stupor. "Fuck her and get it over with." The words struck a strange terror in Jay's soul. Was it simply because she was a virgin? If she was sexually experienced like the rest of the women in the room, would she find it a great joke? She could feel Mr. Rossco's eyes lingering on her, as if contemplating the pros and cons of Randolph's remark.

"Pay no attention to him, dear." Mr. Rossco put his arms protectively around her. Jay's body seized up in apprehension. She knew she was out of her depth. She couldn't begin to understand these people. While she had eagerly awaited one moment of truth, another had supplanted it. Tonight, she would discover exactly what Mr. Rossco expected of her. When Mr. Rossco hurried off to find more champagne, it was becoming clear to Jay that the hour of reckoning was fast approaching.

Jay fled to the bedroom to grab her jacket. As she rushed into the room, she instantly regretted it. She had forgotten about Marco's mistress who, having indulged for a full hour in a high pitch of solitary misery, was now anxious for sympathetic companionship. Yvonne fell, sobbing, into Jay's arms.

"What should I do? The fucking bastard!"

"I ... ah ... don't know."

"What's he doing now?"

"Um ... I ... ah ... think he's playing with the band."

"They've started?"

"I think they're about to start."

"It's all over, then." Yvonne burst into a loud wail and clutched on to Jay. Jay looked over Yvonne's shoulder to the place where she'd left the jacket, but it was gone. She rocked Yvonne in her arms so she could rotate around and check the rest of the room.

"What are you doing?"

"Uh, nothing."

Yvonne suddenly pulled away from Jay and looked at her suspiciously.

"I don't know you."

"No, you don't."

"Well, why the fuck were you holding me just then?"

"I just came in to get my jacket. Have you seen it? It's peach coloured."

"Oh, fuck. It was yours?" Yvonne reached over to a dim corner of the room and pulled up a rumpled ball of material which she handed to Jay. "Sorry, it's a little messed up."

"The sleeve is missing."

"Oh." Yvonne looked around the floor and finally retrieved a scrunched-up piece of matching material. "I thought it was Natasha's. I'll pay for it." She staggered to the bureau and rummaged through one of the drawers.

"It's okay. I think I can fix it." Jay noted that the sleeve was still in one piece, so it was possible to sew it back into the armhole.

Yvonne looked at Jay fiercely. "Who are you?"

"You don't know me."

"Duh huh, figured that out. What's your name? Why are you here?"

"Um ... Jay Wright. Mr. Rossco asked me."

"What do you do?"

Jay was often struck by the fact that everyone in Mr. Rossco's circle of friends always asked people what they did. They never asked the conventional, "How are you?" The state of a person's well-being was either too personal or of no interest to the inquirer, whereas what one did for a living was of paramount importance. It defined one. For now, Jay could safely answer that she was a student but she dreaded the time when she would be finished with school and had a job that would put her in a specific category.

"I'm one of Mr. Rossco's students."

"Yeah, right. Rossco's okay. You could do worse. Marco's an evil prick."

"Why are you with him, then?"

"Because I love the bastard! Are you stupid or something?"

"Why do you love him if he's so awful."

"You think I have a choice?"

"Don't you?"

"No. Course not. No one has a choice. It's Cupid's goddamn arrow. You get hit and that's it."

"Oh."

"Obviously, you've never been hit."

"I guess not."

"He's such a bastard."

"Um, I should really get going."

"Found it. This'll replace the jacket. I'm really sorry." Yvonne thrust a hundred dollar bill into Jay's hand.

"Oh no. That's way too much."

"I didn't want to insult your taste."

"But that's way too much."

"I don't have change."

"I can fix it. You just sew the sleeve back into —"

"Take it and get outta here! Stupid bitch!"

Yvonne lurched menacingly towards her. As Jay left, she heard Yvonne mutter, "Anyway, it's not my money. It's Marco's."

Jay glanced over at Marco and decided that he would not take kindly to being robbed at his own party. Marco Shiner was not a man to cross. He was large and burly. His black hairy eyebrow crossed his entire face in an angry V-shape, continuing unabated in the area between the eyes, giving him the look of a man in perpetual wrath.

The eyebrow, coupled with Marco's florid red face and snarling yawn of a mouth left no doubt as to his choleric disposition. A cheerful Marco Shiner was a terrifying enough prospect, let alone an angry Marco Shiner. Jay couldn't understand why so many women fell for Marco, unless he intimidated them into it. Jay slipped the bill back under the door and fled the premises.

She almost fell over Snafu Smith, who was sitting alone on the stairwell, smoking a joint. Normally, Jay would have relished a tête-à-tête with Snafu Smith but her senses were overloaded. She simply wanted to make a clean escape.

"Want some?" he proffered a small, sputtering butt. Jay shook her head and went to pass him. "My joint's not good enough for you?" Snafu laughed to himself.

"Your joint's fine."

"Damn right it's fine! Have some!"

"No thanks. I, ah, don't smoke pot."

"Why not?"

"It's bad for you."

"That's nonsense. They don't want people to see the truth. And dope slows you down so you see it."

"Is that what it does? I thought it made you stupid."

"I've been smoking since I was twenty. Do you think I'm stupid?"

"No."

"There you are."

Jay's logical mind could not resist asserting itself. "But you're probably not as smart as you would have been if you hadn't smoked pot."

"Come again?" Snafu's mouth twitched in annoyance.

Jay noticed that Snafu's mouth was his worst feature. He could look really spiteful, at times. "I guess what I'm saying is that I have no way of knowing how smart you were when you were twenty. And yes, you seem fairly smart now —"

"Thank you very much."

"But you might have been a genius when you were twenty."

"So, you're saying I'm no genius."

"Um ..."

"How the fuck would you know what a genius is!"

Jay thought of Nicholas. "Well, ah, I have a friend who's a genius."

"You're sure about that."

"Well, ah, it's just a feeling you get. And well, there are IQ tests."

"IQ tests. What bullshit!"

"No, not really."

"I guess you scored high on those tests."

"Actually, yes, I did. The top four percentile in North America."

"That is extraordinary."

"Well, yes, they did say it was unusual."

"That is really extraordinary. 'Cause you are the DUMBEST fucking broad that I've ever come across!"

"I often appear that way. I lack social skills."

"Lack? LACK?! You are BEREFT! Do you hear me? BEREFT of social skills!"

"I think I'll go now."

"What about Rossco?"

"He's very nice. Say goodbye to him for me."

"You should tell him yourself." Snafu leaned into the room and bellowed, "HEY, ROSSCO! YOUR GIRLFRIEND'S LEAVING!"

Jay abandoned all attempts at sophistication. "NO, DON'T!" she shrieked and ran quickly down the stairs and out the door, as if the Devil himself were after her.

chapter fifteen

FIRST JUMP

LILY'S FINGERS TREMBLED as she strapped on her gear. When she was finally outfitted, she felt like a child in a snowsuit. She was so encumbered that she could no longer feel her own body, save for her heart, which was pounding furiously, as if it would leap out. By the time they were airborne, all of Lily's body was shaking, quaking and pounding. Lily couldn't attribute these raging sensations to a fear of flying. Usually, she felt safe and protected inside the belly of those giant airborne buses, great white whales that flew in the sky.

The plane that the skydivers used was not large and safe and comforting. It was a real airplane that rattled and roared, doggedly straining to stay aloft, its innards quivering as it battled its enemy, the air. The roar of the engines was deafening. The interior of the plane had been stripped to reduce the chances of snagging one's gear on such unnecessary elements as seats. Lily found it hard to sit upright, weighted down, her parachute drawing her backwards. She wanted to lie back, try to relax. However, she risked snagging her bottom pin or break cord tie on something, which would cause the main parachute to open.

Lily had always been accident-prone. Even simple tasks were fraught with risk. Last week, she walked into the laundromat and her purse strap caught on the gumball dispenser. Lily tugged to release it, but instead knocked over the dispenser, which wasn't bolted to the ground, though it should have been. The round glass orb containing the gumballs smashed into smithereens and hundreds of brightly coloured gumballs rolled and scattered to Kingdom Come. Lily tried to help pick up the gumballs, and knocked over the adjacent jawbreaker dispenser. The laundromat owner didn't even get angry. It was as though he knew Lily was a walking minefield and the best thing to do was to get her off the premises as quickly as possible. Causing mild havoc had been so much a regular part of Lily's life that she had not considered that it could actually be dangerous. But now, she was in a perilous situation, which required co-ordination and control and Lily had to admit that she had neither.

She sat up straight, as instructed, clutching onto her static line with one hand and holding the rip cord handle of the reserve chute firmly in place with the other. She didn't like holding the rip cord. That was tempting fate. If the plane gave a sudden lurch, she'd pull it and the reserve parachute would burst open, like an inflatable raft in a closet. She was a time bomb. Pull the wrong pin and she'd explode. She started to tremble uncontrollably. Brad looked at her with concern. Lily smiled back, trying to keep her teeth from chattering.

The plane had reached its proper altitude and was flying over a huge open field. Flash had dropped the wind indicator and was studying it. The principle danger in skydiving was not the actual jump and descent, but the landing. If a person wasn't vigilant, a wind current could suddenly grab the chute and send the person careening into a tree or a power line. Power lines were particularly dangerous. A person could get killed in an instant. Flash didn't want to scare people by dwelling on all the potential hazards, but sometimes he felt that they weren't aware of the serious nature of this undertaking.

Flash motioned to Brad to come forward. Brad gave Lily and Paul a cheerful "thumbs up." Flash unlatched the door. Wind roared into the plane and Lily caught a sudden scent of machinery. She knew she was going to die. Her accident-prone life was simply a rehearsal for this moment, the ultimate accident, the static line, a lethal purse strap. It would invariably get tangled up with the plane. Flash had mentioned this possibility in the class. Lily tried to remember what Flash said one should do. Brad was now sitting on the door. The plane slowed down and he climbed onto the step, his head disappearing from view. Lily was next. She thought if she were sandwiched between Brad and Paul, she wouldn't lose her nerve. Now, she realized she'd signed her death warrant. If she'd gone last, she could have chickened out with impunity. She glanced over at Paul. He didn't seem to be at all nervous. Flash reached out the side of the plane, shouted a command and Brad was gone. Flash watched his descent. He seemed to be satisfied with it. He reeled in the static line. The plane circled around for the next run. Flash motioned for Lily to come forward. Lily nervously edged her way to the front. She could hardly bring herself to look at Flash. He was uncharacteristically solicitous.

"Hey kid, don't panic. Take your time and I'll do the rest. When you're set and have a good grip, look at me. I'll slap you and yell 'Go!' and I want to see a hard arch. Look up. Keep your eyes on me. Count loudly, 'cause we want to hear you. And don't forget, you always have the reserve. Don't be afraid to use it. Okay?" The plane had reached the target site. It was time for orders. "SIT IN THE DOOR." Lily obeyed, certain that she would be sucked out of the plane. "CUT!" The plane slowed down. "GET ON THE STEP." Lily climbed out carefully, one hand, one foot at a time. Clutching on for dear life, she silently implored Flash not to make her jump. "GO!" he shouted, and he slapped her hard across the thigh. Flash had instructed them to step off the side like they were getting off a bus. Some bus. She was going to throw up. She knew it, but no, instead she stepped out, hurtling through the air in a spread-eagle position, shouting the count that she'd practised so diligently on the KAT House coffee table.

"ARCH-THOUSAND. LOOK-THOUSAND." She looked at the rip cord handle. "REACH-THOUSAND." Still maintaining her arch, she grabbed the handle. "PULL-THOUSAND." She had the timing right. She felt a sudden lurch as her parachute opened. "LOOK-THOUSAND." She looked up to make sure there was nothing wrong with the chute. The canopy billowed out. Her body righted itself. Lily looked down.

The pattern of the ground below was frozen in a mosaic. She started falling gently towards the earth. She turned her canopy into the wind and gently guided it towards the drop zone. It was glorious. She was mesmerized as she watched the ground. It was as though she were entering the world of a miniature train set, with its mock hills and valleys, little houses interspersed with tiny roads and toy cars. Lily felt a surge of happiness. Many years ago, she had a vivid dream, in which she was a particle of air and she had this over-whelming feeling of happiness, the joy of being part of something huge and immense. She felt loved. All the other air particles loved her. They were travelling somewhere, going off to join other air particles in the universe. The dream came back to her in an instant. Lily was revelling in her joy when the Voice spoke, casting a shadow over her heart.

"Thanks for doing this. This is fun."

Thanks? As if she were a gracious hostess and it were a guest in her home.

"Yeah. I like this. We're gonna do this next week, right? And the week after. And the week after that. WHEEEEEE!!" And suddenly, Lily got a glimpse of this gargoyle-like bird-man fly out of her chest, then come skittering back in. "Oooops! Almost lost you, there! To be free, to be free! That's what I want. To be free!!" Lily put her hand on her chest to feel for the hole from which the creature had escaped. Was she losing her mind? Or, did she, in fact, just see a demon?

Bubula cursed himself for his indiscretion. All his well-laid plans undone by his foolish instinct. A demon must always leave the host before he or she dies. If the host's spirit leaves first, then the demon is trapped inside and must die with the body: buried alive in human flesh. When Lily jumped out of the airplane, Bubula instinctively flew out of her body. Bubula was terrified of the Big Void, which was what the demons called it since none of them knew what happens to trapped demons after the body decomposes. Demons are caught between two extremes: a complete addiction to pleasures of the flesh coupled with an immense craving to return to their spirit state. Lily was necessary for Bubula's survival, yet he longed to be free of her body's clammy walls. The air whispered its siren call to Bubula, daring him to reunite with his natural element. Then, Bubula looked down and saw the ground rushing up to interrupt his reverie. "Wake up, you idiot!" he shrieked.

Lily saw the small toy trees change in an instant into large pines with giant boughs. She was no longer a miniaturized observer, drifting along. She had plunged into the world of rock-hard surfaces. She had to land soon and she had better land well. She prepared her legs so they'd act like a spring when they first touched the ground. She was ready: legs pressed together, knees slightly bent, elbows together in front, hands clutching on the riser. She tried to look at the ground as Flash had instructed — 45 degree angle, not directly at it. She touched the ground. Her legs bent to absorb the shock and she fell to one side, trying to distribute the force along her body; ankle, calf, thigh, bum, then into a roll. Land! She made it, safe and sound, body intact. She was on fire with the relief of it all. Every capillary and vein, throbbing, her body — pushed into panic mode — had prepared itself for sudden death and now that the crisis was over, relief streamed out of her, through every pore. Her face was bright red, her hands hot and sweaty. Lily was dizzy with relief. She stood up and waved triumphantly at Brad. Brad, staggering, some distance away, returned the wave and lurched over to her. Lily couldn't unbuckle herself from the chute. Brad undid the clasps, drew her up and the two of them hugged each other and danced clumsily about, astronauts cavorting on the moon's surface, for earth was no longer earth, now that they'd been airborne. Paul ran over and joined them. He was calmer, less giddy.

THEY WENT TO the Brunswick to celebrate. Lily drank quickly and said nothing. She kept turning over the events of the jump in her mind. Did it really happen? If there was a demon, it wasn't talking to her, now. When Paul left the table to go to the men's room, Brad took her hand.

"You haven't said much."

"Don't need to. Paul's here."

"Don't be like that. Be happy. You made it."

"Yeah. I made it."

"I thought you liked it."

"I did. It was great."

"Well then, what's wrong? You had a good day."

"I, ah, when I left the plane ... I, ah, saw something."

"A bird?" sneered Paul, who had taken care of his bodily functions with swift precision and had now materialized behind Lily.

"Very funny. Yeah, a bird. I saw a Canada goose."

"What did you see?" asked Brad.

"It's not important."

"No, I want to know."

"You'll think it's silly."

"Lily, what did you see?"

"Well, I ... I ... saw this creature."

"Creature."

"Yeah, like one of those gargoyles in those old churches." Lily could see Paul leaning in to make a snarky comment but Brad glared at him fiercely, so he withdrew.

"When you were up in the air?"

"Yeah," Lily couldn't bring herself to say that she saw the demon come out of her body.

"On the plane?"

"Well —"

"You know, pilots see gremlins."

"What?"

"Yeah, when they're flying. There're all those stories about pilots seeing gremlins sitting on the wings."

"Now you're making fun of me."

"No, I'm serious." Brad was excited.

Paul was beside himself with derision. He could contain it no longer. "It's pile of bull! It's like sailors seeing mermaids. Does anyone see mermaids now? No. Of course, Lily does. When's she's driving Dad's boat on Lake Ontario, she sees mermaids all the time. Don'tcha, sis?"

"Forget it."

"No, Lil, this is fascinating," persisted Brad. "It's probably fear, right? When people were frightened of the sea, they saw mermaids. Air travel is new. The pilots who first flew planes were frightened. Of course, they wouldn't admit it to themselves so they saw gremlins. The modern equivalent to mermaids."

"Mermaids were beautiful women and gremlins are ugly little men so what does that say about us now, Brad? That we're afraid of men?" asked Paul.

"What are you talking about?"

"Well, there's an attraction repulsion thing happening with mermaids. Beautiful women — very sexual."

"Except the bottom half's a fish."

"Exactly my point, sis. Sailors want to have sex with a mermaid but can't. Presumably then, pilots want to have sex with the gremlin."

"That's ridiculous," laughed Lily. "Gremlins aren't sexual."

"Because they're male, sis? And men can't be sexually attracted to men?"

"Gremlins aren't men, Paul. They're animals," said Brad.

"And mermaids are fish. Yet mermaids are female and gremlins are male."

"What's the point here, Paul?"

"Simply that I find it very interesting that pilots see threatening male creatures instead of threatening female ones."

"Jesus, it took you a long time to get round to that! Big deal."

"I think it is a big deal, Brad. I think men have now been identified as the mysterious other. Before, it was always women. You should be happy, sis. It means these days, men don't see women as a threat."

"Or that they don't see women at all. We aren't part of the picture. We don't count."

"Are you going to go off on your women-don't-get-a-fair-deal routine again? You want to be treated equally, but you want to be respected, too. Men aren't nice to each other, sis. They don't treat each other equally. Why should they treat women as equals?"

"If a woman's doing the same job as a man, she should get the same pay. That's what we mean by equality."

"Uh oh, the 'we' word. Now we're in for it, Brad. Women's liberation. They just don't get it. A man's got a wife and family to support. He should get paid more. Plus, you spend a lot of time training a woman for a job. She works at it for a little while, then she goes off and has a baby. You train a guy and he's there for you."

"What do you think, Brad?" asked Lily.

"Well, it is different for men."

"Brad's an old-fashioned guy. He's gonna marry Susan, have babies and spend the rest of his life supporting them, aren't ya, Brad?"

"Sounds like fun," said Lily. "Don't you ever wonder why it's taken for granted that you have to be the one to earn the money?"

"It's a fair division of labour. I go out and work. She stays home and looks after the house and kids."

"You could pay someone to do that. They're called housekeepers."

"You couldn't pay someone to have your children."

"No, ain't that a shame," said Lily.

"Brad's in love with Susan so he doesn't think of it in such ruthless terms. My sister's a very cold-hearted woman."

"And Susan's so warm."

"How did we get onto this topic?"

"Nervous, Brad?"

"Yeah, nervous? Anyway, sis," resumed Paul, "I don't know why you're so fired up on this women's liberation shit. It's not like you're gonna be a big-time female executive. You can barely hold down a crappy girl-Friday job." Paul leaned in towards Brad confidentially. "She failed all her courses, so she can't go to university anymore."

"I didn't fail them all."

"Your best bet would be to do the old-fashioned girl routine and find a guy like Brad to support you. It's too bad Brad's taken."

There was an uncomfortable pause as Brad and Lily looked at each other, Brad suddenly realizing that Lily didn't have many options in life and that perhaps she was a desperate, needy woman; Lily, having a horrible inkling that despite her ardent desire to be an active member of the women's movement, she might not be fit for anything in life, other than to be a man's wife and have his children. It was a sobering thought. Lily withdrew from the conversation. Paul delighted in making her look foolish. He was a past master at it.

"Lily's thinking about her gremlin," joked Paul.

"Yeah, right," Lily pretended to laugh but the laugh caught in her throat as the Voice inside her hissed, "You tell anyone else about me and you're dead meat. Get it? Dead meat!"

It had never threatened her before.

chapter sixteen

INTERLUDE

SUSANNAH HAD ASKED Jay to meet her in the "Library" of the Brunswick after classes. She wanted Jay to help her with her painting. Jay had been seeing a lot of Susannah lately. She wanted to learn more about Snafu. Susannah constantly talked about him and Jay quietly listened and made mental notes.

It was late afternoon. Susannah hadn't arrived yet. George Bernard Shaw was propped up in his usual position, quietly nursing his Scotch. Apart from him, the only other person in the room was one of the regulars from the Oblong Table. Jay tried to remember his name, then shrugged, realizing that he wouldn't know hers, either. She liked him. He made her feel at ease. He usually sat across the table from her. He was very witty. She flirted with him, eyes only. She was too shy to talk to him. The Oblong table, for all its emphasis on wit and repartee, did not encourage actual conversation. People were too preoccupied with appearing clever to talk to each other. Susannah leaned over and whispered in Jay's ear, "See that guy across the table? We're seeing each other," she giggled. "Don't tell Snafu. It might bug him."

"What about Jonathan?"

"Jonathan? Oh, we're just friends."

Jay was quietly appalled. Susannah took a number of liberties with Jonathan's person that a friend, by Jay's reckoning, wouldn't dream of doing. Not that Jay wanted Jonathan. However, she had respected what she thought was a love affair between the two and thought of Jonathan as "taken." But Susannah, now, seemed to be laying claim to every available man in the school. Every time Jay turned around, Susannah had "taken" another one. Since Jay was a virgin, she couldn't compete with Susannah, but even if she could, she found it distasteful. She didn't want some woman's castoffs. Potential lovers were far less alluring when Jay found out that Susannah had a go at them. It was like buying a utility turkey. A missing wing doesn't ruin the taste, but it spoils the appearance, and thus checks one's appetite. Jay mentally crossed the man off her list and didn't think any more of him.

Jay was sure the man wouldn't remember her, but he did. He was waiting for Susannah as well. He asked Jay to join him. She thought it would be rude to refuse, so they started talking.

He was bright but conceited. He talked about what a good draughtsman he was and how he could have gone to art school, but it was too easy. Jay didn't like his attitude. She didn't know why he was so anxious to impress her. She was getting tired of it and engaged him in a little sparring match. Whenever he spoke to Jay as if she were stupid, she carefully one-upped his statement so that he'd realize that she knew just as much, if not more, about that particular topic. His interests were primarily in the arts, so she was on secure ground. He skated from subject to subject, trying to catch her out. When he got onto the World Wars, as men invariably did, Jay thanked God that her father and grandfather fought in both World Wars and never stopped talking about them. Jay knew she was being

244 • Sally Clark

obnoxious and that she was carrying this contest to an extreme but she couldn't help herself.

"They were fighting German paratroopers in Ortona. It was house to house fighting — guerrilla warfare, just like Viet Nam," she corrected him.

"How the hell do you know that?"

"I read about it. Don't you know any girls who read?"

"You think you're pretty smart."

"Yes. Is there a law against two people being smart? Or is the problem that one of us is female?"

"All right, you win. Can we stop this, now?"

"Sure."

"Can I say something without you adding to it?"

"As long as you're not being patronizing, yes."

"Most of the girls in this bar are pretty stupid."

"You should get out of the bar, then."

"Good point. I was just trying to impress you, but you're impossible."

"I was impressed."

"You hide it well. Besides," he added, "I don't think all women are stupid."

"That's encouraging."

"My fiancée's smart."

"Your who?!"

"My fiancée. You don't think anyone would want to marry me?"

"You can't marry her," blurted out Jay, surprised at the ferocity of her feelings.

"Pardon?"

"You don't love her." The words were coming out of her mouth and she seemed to have no control over them.

"Look, I don't mind your correcting me on military battles, but my personal life is my own business."

"I'm sorry. It slipped out."

"You have very uptight bourgeois attitudes."

"I just don't know how you can be in love with one person and, ah, see Susannah."

"Susannah and I are just having a fling."

"I know."

"Oh, she told you."

"It's as you said, you're one of many."

"Many? That's what she said?"

"You shouldn't care. It's just a fling. But you still shouldn't marry your fiancée," Jay mumbled into her ginger ale.

"What did you say?"

"Nothing."

He looked at her for a moment before speaking. "My fiancée is beautiful. She's kind. She's a good person."

"I'm sure she's a great person. She doesn't seem to be part of your life."

"You've never met her, that's all. She doesn't come to the bar. It's not her type of place. She feels uncomfortable. And yes, it is like I've got a separate life here." He drank his beer and savoured it. "I like this life. I'm alive here. But you can't keep living like this. The booze, drugs, et cetera," he said, looking at Jay pointedly. "So, I gotta stop this eventually. Better sooner than later. She's my straight and narrow. She's an angel."

"I don't think that's a good reason to marry someone."

"You'd rather hook up with a devil?" He looked at Jay with mischievous inquiry. She blushed and entertained the notion of what it would be like to be in love with this man.

"I'm your man. Nah. I don't even want to think about what would happen if I didn't get married."

"Why? What are you afraid of?" Jay asked.

"Getting lost." He smiled and took another drink, "You never drink, do you?"

"No. I don't like it."

"Good girl. You're a good girl."

"Don't say that."

"Why not? That's what you are."

"It's insulting."

"Oh God, I didn't mean it that way. I mean, you really are a good person. If I wasn't marrying Louise, I'd marry you."

"I wouldn't let you marry me."

"Why not?"

"I've got better things to do than to keep you on the straight and narrow."

"Sharp tongue." He fingered her pencils. She had left them on the table. "Sharp pencils, too. Too sharp. You can be more subtle when you're not so sharp." He looked at her with a clear gaze that sent a shiver through her. Then, he pulled a pencil out and read the label. "Mitsubishi. They're into everything."

"They are?" Jay didn't know why he was paying so much attention to a label.

"Well, yeah. Stereo systems, cameras, electronics —"

"Really?"

"And birth control." He gave her another searching look. "You didn't know that?"

"I don't pay much attention to labels."

"I've embarrassed you."

"Oh, no."

"You really are a good girl."

"I'm not good. I just don't read labels, that's all." Jay rose to leave but he took her hand and looked up at her.

"I've been way too personal. I'm sorry."

"Um —"

"You be careful. Okay? You don't want to wind up like me."

"There's nothing wrong with you," said Jay, and she meant it.

"Not yet. But I can see where I'm going. I'm starting to really like the booze and that scares me. And I like the other stuff, too. And I like women."

"If you like women, then what in God's name do you see in Susannah?"

"Wow! Where did that come from?"

"Sorry."

"I bring it out in you?" He gave Jay a flirtatious smile.

"I should go." Jay rose to leave.

"Stay." He took her hand and looked at her. "Please stay."

Jay was wracked with indecision. "You have enough on your plate," she said, staring down at him.

"You're right," he agreed and let her go.

Susannah breezed into the bar. She was about to swoop down and give the man a kiss when she saw Jay and stopped in her tracks. "Jay? What are you doing here?"

"You asked me to meet you."

Susannnah looked genuinely puzzled. "I did?"

"Yes. You wanted to ask me about painting. You said it was important."

Susannah wracked her brain for this elusive, important thing. Then she smiled. "Oh yeah. Oh yeah, right. It's okay now," she said brightly, pleasantly indicating that Jay should take off.

"You don't need to talk to me anymore?"

"No, but thanks for coming." Susannah quickly positioned herself beside the man, so they sat tightly together, as a couple.

"You're welcome," replied Jay and left.

The summer was almost over and Jay realized that she had not done any of the things she had planned to do. She had not fallen in love. Or rather, she had fallen in love but nothing had come of it, so it amounted to the same thing in her mind. She had not become a great artist. She had fallen into the trap of competing with Jonathan. His work now covered the entire top floor of the Artists School. Everywhere you looked there was a painting of Jonathan's and they were all appalling. At least, Jay thought so. In his painting of a reclining male nude, the man possessed large leprous claws. Jay surmised they were Jonathan's crude attempt at rendering hands. She waited for Marco or Bowen to criticize them, but they seemed to approve of the painting. Snafu walked in one day and stopped in his tracks. Jonathan, ever on the alert for praise, hurried over to him.

"Well? What do you think?" he asked with that oblivious confidence, which Jay now despised.

"Frightening. I wouldn't let that hand anywhere near my cock."

Jay's estimation of Snafu rose even higher. She went home that day and hauled her work out of the KAT House basement. She would bring her paintings to the Artists School so they would be revealed in all their glory. The world would see that Jonathan was a fraud. She was the real artist. Snafu would recognize that she was an undiscovered master. Her work would turn his head and he would fall madly in love with her genius. She arranged the paintings in a row against the back garden fence of KAT House and studied them. The sun blazed down on them.

The paintings were awful. Jay was shocked at how bad they were. In the basement, they possessed a certain potency but in daylight, she could see the subject matter was maudlin and the colours were harsh. Her parents had always maintained that her painting had gotten steadily worse as she attended the various art schools. Jay cringed at the thought of how they would react when they saw these paintings. Her father would say, "Looks like he's got a bad case of the DT's." The first basement painting was the best of the lot. It had some of her original intent in it. The others were dreadful. Jay couldn't even cite the distraction of a torrid love affair as an excuse.

She had felt in her bones that something pleasantly momentous was going to happen and yet, she remained, unchanged and still solitary. She thought of ditching her virginity, just to be rid of it. Rufus was the obvious choice. He had taken her to his studio to show her his work. He planned to seduce her but he was easily distracted. Jay only needed to ask him about one of his paintings and he quickly abandoned his amorous agenda to point out a particularly brilliant section.

Over the summer, Jay watched as Snafu Smith made a play for each and every girl in the school except her. There could be no better way of demonstrating his consummate lack of interest and yet, why, she asked herself, did she keep believing that they were destined to become lovers? If he went after her now, it would only be because she was the only girl left. Jay was fastidious by nature and something of a snob. She was appalled by Snafu's democratic excess. He slept with pretty girls and ugly girls and smart girls and dumb girls and seemed to find something to admire about all of them. Jay's mouth flapped open every time he made a new conquest. How could someone who was attracted to Consuela possibly be interested in Sheila? And if he liked Sheila, as Snafu seemed to, then what could he possibly see in Susannah? And most important, why wasn't he interested in Jay herself, who was smarter and prettier and more talented than all of those girls put together? Jay's sense of self-importance was taking a severe buffeting in the face of Snafu Smith's potent indifference.

⌇

"GEEZ, SKYDIVING! THAT'S really something!" The goofy boss beamed encouragingly at Lily. Lily wished she were anywhere else but this perky little singles bar where, as it turned out, happy hour extended well into the evening and was, in fact, a big long chunk of time to spend with someone you didn't know and didn't care to know. Lily had only agreed to go out with Dave because he'd cornered her into it. She reasoned, unwisely, that if she went out on this date, she would have fulfilled her obligation and need not have anything more to do with Dave. For his part, Dave saw Lily's acquiescence as a nod of encouragement for him to proceed further.

"Weren't you scared?"

"Ah, yeah, I was." Having brought up the topic, Lily was now reluctant to talk about it. What had she seen that day? The Voice that burbled up inside her, giving advice, issuing commands and more recently, threats; was it still hovering over her thoughts? She hadn't heard or seen anything since the jump, but she was alert for its presence. Bubula was wisely maintaining a low profile. As in any love affair, one makes one's move and then one beats a hasty retreat, allowing time for the object of one's desire to reflect on it. Time spent apart is as important as time spent together. Lily's thoughts spun a cocoon around the incident, thus binding her further.

"So, I guess you like living dangerously?" persisted Dave.

"Huh?" said Lily, absorbed in her thoughts. "Yeah, I guess so."

"So, you wanna come back to my place?"

Lily stared at him blankly.

"Yeah, it's not like leaping out of a plane but it'll do in a pinch. Hahaha. I guess not. A joke. I was just making a joke." Dave took a quick gulp of his half-priced margarita, then winced. "Shouldn't have ordered this. It's way too sweet."

"It's a lady's drink," Lily replied, with a shrug, as if to indicate that if Dave didn't know a man's drink from a lady's drink, then he was a bigger fool than she thought he was.

"It's a what?!" Dave slammed it down and glared at it suspiciously.

"So, Dave, tell me about yourself."

"Me? Ah. Not much to tell, really. Waitress! A beer, please."

"Are you from Toronto?"

"No, I'm from Moncton, originally. You probably don't know where that is. New Brunswick ..."

Having launched Dave into an oral examination of his past, Lily was free to attend to her own thoughts. She couldn't remember to the day when she first heard her Voice but she placed it around the time she was eleven. She'd been following this creature's advice for more than half her life. It seemed absurd. Lily wondered if she might be crazy. She had to talk to someone and the only person Lily knew who could handle the information was her sister, Rose. Rose was five years older than Lily and Paul. She had gone into nursing and was used to dealing with extraordinary situations.

"And then I came here," proclaimed Dave, whose dissertation was shorter than Lily expected.

"Oh my," Lily said with appropriate awe.

"So, it's been a bit of a struggle."

"Mmm, yes," Lily hoped that she wasn't agreeing to anything in particular. Getting a man to talk about himself is a time-honoured technique among women who have their own lines of thought to pursue. The major flaw in it is that the man, having unburdened himself, is convinced that the female receptacle for this bountiful information is the most fascinating woman he has ever encountered. Lily did not want Dave to fall in love with her, but had she studied up on the subject, she could not have stumbled upon a better way. Oh, if only she could apply this skill to her relations with Brad, but no, Lily wanted to impress Brad so she unwisely told him all about herself: all her anxieties, her secret thoughts — enough to put Brad off thoroughly. And what little stream of passion remained between them, after Lily had revealed all, her brother, Paul, took a tourniquet to, and put the squeeze on further flow.

⌒

ROSE WAS EVERYTHING Lily wanted to be: beautiful, wise and practical. Briefly, Lily considered following in Rose's footsteps and becoming a nurse as well. But that was like expecting an orange to become an apple. Lily liked the idea of wearing white starched uniforms and marching efficiently down white hospital corridors but sick people gave her the creeps. She was even leery of visiting people in hospitals, afraid that she'd go in and never come out. Unfortunately, Lily made the mistake of telling her parents about her interest in nursing. Mr. MacFarlane was delighted and asked one of his friends to hire Lily as a receptionist for the Young People's Paraplegic Ward. The idea of dealing with people her own age who had lost the use of their limbs was too much for Lily to bear. She refused the job. Mr. MacFarlane was furious. He railed at Lily, saying she was too self-centred and that she needed to witness real suffering. Mrs. MacFarlane wasn't entirely convinced of Lily's aptitude for nursing, but she did agree that Lily was selfish. Family lines of combat were drawn up in preparation for a long siege. Unexpectedly, it was Rose who rescued Lily from the oncoming opprobrium.

"You know, Mother, not everyone can be a nurse. I know most girls are told they should go into it, but it's a calling, like anything else. And Lily simply isn't cut out for that sort of thing. She's too sensitive." *Sensitive* was Rose's polite way of saying that Lily would be a walking disaster. Rose could see it all too clearly. Lily would drop the sterile instruments and replace them without telling anyone they'd fallen on the floor. She would frighten the patients by blurting out their true medical condition. Just anticipating the trouble Lily would get up to by simply trying to do a good job made Rose cringe. Rose took pride in her work and resented the fact that her parents thought that someone as flighty and undisciplined as Lily could do it. Lily looked upon Rose as her great defender, little realizing that Rose was simply stating the truth as Rose saw it. Lily idolized Rose. And Rose accepted Lily's admiration as her due.

In the last six years, Lily hadn't seen much of her sister. Rose worked long, irregular shifts. She married a doctor three years ago, so between her job and her marriage, Rose had little time to spare. Even getting in touch by telephone was difficult because neither Rose nor her husband were home often. Lily left a message for Rose at the hospital, asking if she could meet with her on her lunch break. Rose confirmed a time for the next day.

"Are you pregnant?" Rose liked to get to the point.

"No."

"Thank God for that. Well, what's the problem?"

"Does there have to be a problem?"

"Yes, or else why are we meeting?"

"To have a sisterly chat?"

"Drugs. Is that the problem?"

"What?"

"Are you taking drugs?"

"Um —"

"You are, aren't you?"

"Well, a little. I smoke pot from time to time but that isn't the —"

"Oh Lily, stay off drugs."

"Pot is harmless. Anyway, that's not —"

"You start with pot. It leads to stronger stuff. So many people get in trouble over drugs."

"But that's not why —"

"No wonder you failed your courses."

"Look. I know lots of people who do drugs and they get honours."

"Yes, well, they're a lot smarter than you to begin with. You can't afford to do drugs."

"I am SO SICK of people telling me I'm stupid!"

"Smart people don't do drugs. If you saw what happens to these kids who do magic mushrooms —"

"You're working with drug addicts, I take it."

"Yes. And it's fascinating work."

"Let me know when you get transferred and I'll talk to you then."

"I'm serious, Lily. Don't do drugs."

"I know, Rose. You're very serious."

"I'm sorry to jump all over you, Lil. Tell me what's bothering you. Please."

"I can't."

"Now, don't get like that."

"It's not me. It's ... my friend. I think she's going crazy. She lives at KAT House. She's an artist, and lately she keeps talking about hearing voices."

"Many voices or one?"

"One. I think."

"Mmmm. And what does the voice say?"

"It tells her stuff. Some of the things are true. At least, Jay says they're true. Jay says they tell her things that are going to happen and then the things happen. Small things like phone messages, or people trying to get in touch. Not big things."

"Does the voice tell Jay that people are conspiring against her?"

"No ... I mean, I don't think so."

"Does the voice tell Jay that people are talking about her, saying bad things?"

"No."

"Or that she needs to defend herself from these people?"

"No."

"Has she accused you of doing anything against her?"

"No. Why?"

"I'm just trying to figure it out. Does she see colours around things?"

"Like an aura?"

"A bit like what you'd see on an LSD trip. You've never done LSD, have you, Lily?"

"No."

"Good. Stay away from it. Does Jay do drugs?"

"No. I mean, yes, she smokes pot a lot."

"Tell her to stop."

"What do you think's wrong with her?"

"I don't know. She should see a psychiatrist."

"Why did you ask me all those questions?"

"I thought she could be a schizophrenic. They hear voices but from what you've told me, it doesn't match up."

"Is a schizophrenic like Dr. Jekyll and Mr. Hyde? Will she suddenly start killing people?"

"It's not like that. But a schizophrenic could potentially be dangerous. Get her to see a doctor."

"Can they fix it so she doesn't hear the voice anymore?"

"They'll put her on medication, which may or may not help. They're experimenting with drugs all the time."

"So, it's incurable."

"Yes."

"And you wind up in the nuthouse."

"Now, don't call it that. Psychiatric hospital. And she wouldn't necessarily stay there. If the drug works for her, she would only need to check in once in a while. To monitor the behaviour. You should get your friend to a doctor right away."

"Monitor the behaviour." The phrase threw a chill into Lily. She saw herself spending the rest of her life in a drugged-out stupor; joining the ranks of the outpatients of 999 Queen, the local mental hospital; Flying Dutchmen in search of their meds; not daring to live further than a few blocks away from the hospital; a lifetime of being tethered to a medication that knocked you flat. Lily thought, "Maybe I imagined the whole thing. Like those pilots. I'll wait and see what happens. Right now, it's mainly a voice. I can handle it. Maybe it will go away."

Lily absent-mindedly wandered down the hospital steps and straight into traffic. A car screeched to a halt, almost knocking her down.

"What's with you?! Are you crazy?!" the driver shouted.

"Sorry," said Lily. "Sorry."

"I warned you," said the Demon. "Dead meat. And it can happen in the wink of an eye. Or perhaps you'd like to join the Young People's Paraplegic Ward."

"I just wanted to find out if I'm crazy."

"You're crazy, all right. Dead crazy."

"I didn't tell her."

"And make sure you don't!"

"Am I a schizophrenic?"

"Whatever makes you happy, baby."

chapter seventeen

FREE ENTERPRISE

BRAD ARRIVED TO pick Susan up for their Friday date. He hoped he wouldn't run into Lily. He hadn't called her all week. What Paul had said about her being needy and desperate had stayed with him.

Brad had never considered his future with any degree of earnestness. He was at university, taking all the right courses to get himself a well-paying job that he hoped he'd enjoy. Somewhere along the line, he would fall in love, marry and have children. However, it appeared to the world-at-large that the first two steps had already been taken care of.

Susan never talked about her future. It was "their" future from the moment he met her. "We are going to do this, Brad" and "We are going to do that." How easily he had fallen into her plans. Her sweet, old-fashioned innocence had beguiled him, but no longer. Over dinner, he tested her.

"Susan ... um ... I ... ah, how do I put this ..."

"Yes, Brad?" Susan beamed up at him.

"Um ... what exactly are you studying at university?"

Susan looked puzzled and answered tersely. "A BA, of course."

"Yes, but what are you studying?"

"Are you all right, Bradley?"

"I'm fine. I just want to know what courses you're taking."

Susan regarded Brad with suspicion. "Why?"

"I'm interested."

"You never cared before."

"Well, I do now! What are you taking?"

"Don't be silly, Bradley. It's summer. I'm not taking any courses now."

"In the fall, then."

"Well, I haven't decided."

"What did you take last year?"

"Are you okay?"

"I want to know."

"Oh, the usual. English ... Biology — 'cause they make you. The usual things."

"What did you study, though? What really grabbed you?"

"I don't know. I took an art history course. That was nice."

"Do you plan to be an art historian?"

"Of course not!"

"Why'd you take it?"

"Out of interest. To broaden my mind."

"What do you plan to do?"

"Do?"

"As in occupation. As in 'earning a living.'"

Susan could see the conversation was taking a dangerous turn. She couldn't very well say "I don't plan on doing anything. I plan on marrying you and you'll do something" so she covered her tracks by saying, "I haven't decided, yet. That's what a BA is for — so you can study all sorts of things and make up your mind." Brad didn't appear satisfied with that response, so Susan hastily added, "Teaching. I'd love to teach. I love working with children." In actual fact, Susan couldn't think of anything she'd hate more than trying to deal with forty screaming hellions, day after day, but it was a clever evasion. It always shut people up if you said you wanted to work with children.

"Shouldn't you be applying for the bachelor of education degree?"

"Um ... later. You do it after your BA. At least, that's what I was told. I'll have to look into it." Susan feigned an air of righteous indignation, thus assuring Brad that she would correct this situation.

Though Susan's answers had allayed Brad's fears, there was a hardness at the centre of her that he could dimly sense. He couldn't say what it was. He simply felt its presence. On their last date, they were sitting in the car saying their goodbyes and suddenly she unbuttoned her blouse and expected him to fondle her breast. He squeezed it a bit. She writhed around in such a state of ecstasy that he felt like a mere useful prop to this misadventure, a helpful sexual aid. Brad's desire for her fled in that instant. He didn't want to continue the charade so he begged off, using the early morning jump as his excuse.

Everyone around him was acting a little crazy. Paul had become a sex addict. He would go out to the Brunswick, come back with some girl, and they'd be at it all night. He'd done this almost every night since he moved back in. Brad's room was right next to Paul's and he could hear everything. It made him very horny. And the worst of it was he couldn't conjure up images of Lily. Placed in its context, it was too incestuous. Susan didn't spring to mind easily, so he wound up thinking about Paul.

Paul's favourite rutting site was the wall between his and Brad's room. Brad's bed lay against that wall and, more precisely, Brad's head lay against the spot. Brad tried going to bed early so that he'd be asleep when Paul came home. And at times he was asleep but some other part of his brain was ever-alert for the suppressed giggles, the drunken lurch against the door, its quiet click shut. There'd be a brief flurry of activity in another corner of Paul's room, then the familiar thump as they landed against the wall. He could feel Paul's lithe body pressing against her, his taut arms holding her tight, rhythmically pounding at that one spot against the wall, driving himself into Brad's head. Brad tried moving his bed to the other wall, but that made it worse. Being at a distance from the event made him more of a spectator. He could now visualize the action, see Paul's erect body slamming into that formless, flabby, female mass. The woman was incidental.

If Brad did imagine a woman, he thought of this grubby flower child and her friend that he and Paul had picked up one night. Unlike the fresh-scrubbed girls of the sorority house, these girls delighted in their own natural smells. And smell they did. They reeked of over-ripe female secretions: cat piss and anchovies. And he had to kiss them and lick them to show he wasn't a prude but, really, it made him want to throw up. Whenever he got a whiff of that particular odour, he would freeze. With Lily, it was all right. She didn't have that smell. Susan Lipton had it, though, lurking under the baby powder like unopened Limburger cheese. He caught scent of it when she proffered up her breast for fondling.

And coming on to him again, like some mechanized Barbie doll, Brad had to admit that he found Susan repulsive. Perhaps because she was so organized and bossy about it all. This time, she was offering more than her breast. "Touch me here. No. Lower. Yes, there. Perfect!" A few moments of female purring, then, "I shouldn't let you do this, you know. This is wrong." Brad withdrew his hand, sat up and started the car.

"What are you doing?"

"What do you think? You told me to stop so I've stopped."

"I didn't tell you to stop."

"It sounded like that to me."

"Brad?" Susan reached over and turned the car off. Now, her scent was cloying: runny, stinky cheese cloaked with baby powder. A big female baby and he was stuck with her. "Come back, Brad."

"No, really, Susan. It's all right."

"Are you mad at your SooSoo?" She put on a little baby voice. SooSoo had been his pet name for her. She was so cute that SooSoo seemed appropriate. It was still appropriate except now it was Big Stupid Baby SooSoo.

"No. I'm not mad, Susan."

"Why are you calling me Susan, then?"

"Because it's time you grew up."

"I'll grow up, Brad. I'll do it right here for you." She tried to drag him back over to her.

"Just stop, okay?"

"But Lily's got the advantage. She's sleeping with you."

"She's not sleeping with me. We're taking classes together. With her brother, for Godsake."

"You've slept with her, though, haven't you?"

"You knew that, Susan. When I tried to break up with you."

"Oh, now it's my fault. You're sleeping with someone else and I'm to blame." Susan started to cry.

"I'm not sleeping with her anymore." Brad hated himself for lying but it was partly true. It depended on how you defined *anymore*. *Anymore*, for Brad, meant the period since the last time he slept with Lily. And in Brad's view, it had been a while.

"Promise?"

"Promise what?"

"Promise you'll never sleep with her again."

"I just told you —"

"I know what you told me. Promise?"

"It seems sort of pointless to promise not to do something I'm not doing anyway."

"Promise?"

Susan's persistence irritated Brad. "Or else what?" he thought, and suddenly he had a revelation. Or else nothing. Susan was behaving as though she had some sort of hold over him, but now that he no longer wanted to be her boyfriend, he didn't even desire her. She could hardly call the shots. He could do as he pleased.

"Bradley?"

"I can't promise you that, Susan."

"Don't you love me?" Susan's eyes welled with tears.

"No," said Brad, rather brutally. "No, I don't."

"But you'll learn to —"

"No. No I won't. I'll take you home now." He started up the car and was careful not to look her way, lest he be frozen in her regard like some mythical hero.

"She's sleeping with that guy," Susan said in a quiet, bitter voice.

"What guy?"

"An artist guy. They had an orgy a couple of weeks ago. I caught them."

"An orgy?"

"She's a nympho. She sleeps with anyone who's around. But I guess you knew that." Susan could see that Brad was upset by this piece of news. His jaw clenched slightly and he stared at the road with ridiculous concentration. He didn't say another word to her till they arrived at KAT House.

"Goodnight, Susan."

"Why don't you come in? Go up to her room and catch her at it."

"GOODBYE, Susan."

"Find out what it feels like to WATCH!" Susan's eyes gleamed with a mad fury. For the first time since he'd known her, Brad glimpsed some passion in her. "Go on. I dare you!" she hissed at him, Medusa ready to strike.

Brad knew that if he lingered with Susan, accepting dares from her and suchlike, he'd become her eternal bridegroom, so he leaned over, opened the car door on her side, pushed Susan out quickly, closed the door and sped away like a blur. He allowed himself the luxury of glancing in the rear-view mirror to catch a glimpse of her picking herself up, dusting off her frills and stalking into the house.

Nervous sweat poured out of Brad and he shook with relief. He couldn't believe he was actually free of Susan Lipton. No more dutiful dates, no more bridal showers, no more weddings of people he didn't know, smiling pleasantly as the women looked meaning-fully at Susan, enduring the relentless jibe, "So, when are you two going to tie the knot?" Hangman's noose, more likely. He was free of all that. And it was so easy. And unexpected. He was so ecstatic over his lucky escape that the news about Lily sleeping around barely impinged on his consciousness. From that night forward, he was free of all women. Women were a nuisance, an encumbrance to life's natural pleasures.

Brad danced up the stairs of Sigma Chi. He felt like going out and celebrating. He had to find Paul. The house was empty. Brad remembered that there was a party at Phi Gamma Delta so he strolled over there. He could hear it a block away: raucous laughter, catcalls, shouts augmented by cries of angry neighbours threatening to call the police. It was a hot, sultry night so the male half of the party was on the front porch and the mixed half, men and women, were on the back porch, spilling out into the backyard.

The front porch guys were engaged in suitable male activities: chugalugging beer on one side of the porch, spewing it out and over the railing on the other side. Sitting on the stoop were the Greeters, who commented on people unfortunate enough to be walking past the house. Attractive women who passed by were invited to join the party. Neighbours and elderly people were routinely jeered at with remarks like, "Hey Gonzo!" or "That you, Igor?" The Greeters spotted Brad half a block away and erupted into a cacophony of congratulatory roars. News had already reached Phi Gamma Delta that Brad had given Susan Lipton the heave-ho.

"Hey, Bradley Boy! Way to go!"

"How did you —"

"News, buddy. Travels fast."

"But I just —"

"Eve and Judd were there. Saw everything."

"Way to go, Brad!" crowed Judd from the back porch, his cry accompanied by Eve's giggling aside, "That's not nice, Judd." Brad decided that he would ignore the hypocrisy of the back porch kitchen party and hang out with his buddies on the front porch. Tonight, women were off limits.

"We heard you threw her out of the car."

"Um ..."

"Fantastic! You really did that?"

"Um ... yeah."

"Hey!" They rammed their beer bottles together in a toast.

A couple of good-looking girls gingerly picked their way up the stairs. Brad stepped over the bodies of passed-out frat rats, ignoring the leers of the Greeters, and headed straight for the kitchen. Couples and single women hung out in the kitchen, which was the civilized room at the party. It was unlikely that Paul was there but Brad went to see. He was not expecting the room to be filled with the entire population of KAT House (minus Susan Lipton) and their dates. A hush fell over the room. Lily was standing right in front of him, looking expectant.

Her anxious upturned face imprinted itself, burning a hole in his memory. He was struck by the glow in Lily's eyes — pure love announcing itself to him, launching itself across the room and into his heart. "Now, Brad? Are we together now?" And the heavy steel grate of his heart's gate closing.

Brad did what any red-blooded young man would do when faced with the prospect of another promise, another declaration. He fled.

It was a beautiful evening. He couldn't see the stars — one could never see the stars in Toronto — but it was a good, clear night so he knew they were there; a good night to start the rest of his life. Paul would probably be in the Brunswick so Brad headed over there.

⌇

"YOU GOTTA LOVE hippie chicks. As long as you say you love lentils and worship Buddha, you can do whatever you like with them."

Brad took a long swallow of his beer and followed Paul's gaze to the hippie chick in question. Brad didn't find her remotely attractive: mock-peasant clothes, hairy legs, thick-soled clumpy sandals, a string of rocklike beads about her neck, and lank, dirty hair. "God, not again. Can't you find a clean one? I don't get it. What do you see in chicks like that?'

"Easy sex."

"No women tonight, okay? I'm celebrating ... oh shit, she's coming over here."

The girl glided over to Paul and stood smiling vacantly at him for a full minute before she spoke.

"Hi. I felt these vibes. I wondered if you felt them too."

"No," said Brad.

"Not your vibes. Yours." She smiled down at Paul.

"Vibes?" Paul asked, his eyes wide with innocence.

"Vibrations. It's like a wave. Like surfing. And you're on the wave together."

"Do you surf?" asked Brad in an attempt to shatter the spell. The girl regarded Brad with scorn. The pragmatism of his questions was clearly offensive to her.

"Like a wavelength?" Paul asked and she zeroed back in on him.

"Yeah, wavelength. Do you wanna dance for a bit? I need to feel your energy." Paul got up and carefully mimicked the girl's gestures. They stood together, swaying in one spot.

"My name's Etherea."

"Paul. Can my friend dance with us?"

"I guess so. You like threesomes?"

"Three is a holy number," said Paul, motioning for Brad to join them. The three of them swayed together for a while till the Midget told them to stop.

"This isn't a discotheque. No dancing allowed."

"Hey man, we're just vibing."

"Well, vibe somewhere else."

"We could do that." The girl looked slyly at Paul. He nodded in agreement.

She took them back to her hippie palace: a squalid little room in a boarding house, cheaply and inventively decorated to look like a sultan's tent; large Indian scarves tacked across the ceiling in billowing loops, smaller scarves draped on lamps so that drug-addled eyes were not subjected to the indiscriminate glare of the sixty-watt bulb. There were no chairs. A large mattress lay on the floor, surrounded by an array of soiled cushions. Cats prowled the room, seeking food, or perhaps, simply, a quick exit from the drapes and makeshift canopies. The pungent smells of marijuana, patchouli oil and cat piss assailed the boys as they gingerly stepped across the threshold. They were fastidious by nature and considered beating a hasty retreat.

"Do you want some mushrooms?" Etherea gaily called out from a murky corner of the room.

"I'm not hungry, thanks," said Brad, anxiously peering into the gloom.

"Not mushrooms!" Etherea giggled. "MUSHROOMS!" She was humped over her desk, sorting out her dope paraphernalia; in rapt concentration, a scientist at work to launch her new experiment. "It's organic," Etherea said and offered some to Paul. Brad tried some, too, and the three of them got very stoned very quickly. Etherea lit some incense and made them all say a Buddhist prayer. Paul knew they were in for a Big Time when she did the prayer. It was a specialty with hippies. The more pious they acted, the more down and dirty they were going to get. They all took their clothes off and mumbled more incantations.

Paul and Brad were well-brought-up and paid due attention to their hostess. Initially, she was the pivot point of the triangle. Then, it shifted. They had to take turns. Paul could see Brad hesitate but he knew he didn't want to be seen as being uptight. He and Etherea worked on Paul, Brad being careful to just relate to the chick. And Etherea and Paul focused on Brad. And it went round for a while.

Then, a friend of hers came in. Another strung-out girl who performed the requisite voodoo ritual, quickly stripped and joined them. Etherea intoned that four was a balancing number and it was good for grounding. Brad and Paul nodded in agreement and were about to take a girl apiece when Etherea's friend announced that the male and female energies should fortify themselves before unification. Which basically meant that the two women went at it. So Brad and Paul followed their example and went at it with each other and couldn't ... wouldn't stop.

The hippie chicks had not intended the male fortification ceremony to be so prolonged. They got fed up with the boys and booted them out; nicely, of course, with lots of banal platitudes. Brad and Paul, coming down from the high, walked home in silence.

chapter eighteen

POOLSIDE CHAT

LILY WAS ENTIRELY unprepared for Brad's abrupt appearance at the Phi Gamma Delta party. She was so used to meeting him secretly that when their social lives converged in a public manner, it was an affront, a brutal reminder that, in fact, she had no relationship with Brad whatsoever. The love affair was a delicately constructed house of cards, situated in the realm of Lily's imagination. When Brad stared at her blankly, her illusions about his true affection for her were laid bare. The girls from KAT House were watching Lily closely to gauge her reaction. Lily maintained her composure. She proved to be a consummate actress in that regard. Even Jay was puzzled by Lily's cool demeanour. She expected to spend at least half the night consoling her but Lily simply went quietly to her room.

"Poolside chat tomorrow. Okay?"

"What?" asked Jay.

"Poolside chat."

The next morning, Lily summoned Jay and the two of them took the subway to the end of the line.

"So, who do you know who has a pool?" asked Jay, anxious to make some sort of conversation, for Lily was curiously silent.

"You'll see."

Lily led Jay out of the dim surrounds of the subway into blazing sunlight and the intersection of two highways. Once they turned off the main roads, the neighbourhood changed abruptly from a sea of whizzing traffic into labyrinthian enclaves of suburban seclusion. It was both barren and verdant. There were no trees to speak of. Newly planted saplings trembled in the wind, striving to maintain their sovereignty. The lawns, however, were a brilliant green; perfectly trimmed and surrounded by dark grey asphalt roads that curved in luxurious arcs around the houses.

Lily and Jay walked for what seemed an interminably long time to cover what turned out to be a short distance. Suburban streets did not follow the logical plans of straight lines intersecting with other straight lines. Instead, they were a series of confusing arcs, semi-circles and cul-de-sacs, winding around each other, establishing a decorative chic but entirely useless as navigable terrain. There were no sidewalks. Lily and Jay wandered along the meandering road, the sun beating down on them.

They approached a sprawling low-slung house, almost identical to the houses preceding it. Lily walked to one side, opened the garden gate and headed straight for the back of the house. A large turquoise blue swimming pool glimmered seductively. Lily had her bathing suit on underneath so she threw off her shorts and top and dove straight in.

"Where are we?" inquired a puzzled Jay who had not dressed to undress and carried her bathing suit in a rolled-up towel, but Lily remained luxuriating in the cool depths at the bottom of the pool.

An angry middle-aged woman flung open a screen door and shouted at Jay, "What the dickens do you think you're doing!"

Jay considered making a run for it but a tall wooden fence surrounded the backyard so there was no easy means of escape. "I'm with her," Jay said and pointed to the deep end of the pool where Lily still lay prone. The woman approached cautiously.

"You've got a lot of gall coming in here."

"I assumed Lily knew the people who had the pool."

The woman glanced into the deep end. "'The people who had the pool.' That's how she described us?"

"Well, not exactly. So, you know Lily?"

"Yes. I'm her mother."

"Oh. I'm so embarrassed."

"I think that was the point of the exercise. LILY!" Mrs. MacFarlane shouted into the pool. "LILY! Come out of there! NOW! She turned to Jay. "Some neighbourhood teenagers have been doing this odd thing —"

Lily bobbed to the surface and gasped cheerfully, "Surprise you, Ma?"

"Please don't call me *Ma*, dear. It's vulgar. And you mustn't play jokes on your friends. I don't even know your name, dear."

"Jay Wright."

"Nice to meet you, Jay. Do you call your mother, *Ma*, Jay?"

"Um, no, Mrs. MacFarlane."

"Where did you meet Lily?"

"I told you, Ma. KAT House."

"I was asking Jay."

"Yes, we met at KAT House."

"So, you're a Kappa Alpha Theta as well. How nice. Anyway, these teenagers come into the gardens, dive into the pools, swim across, hop the fence and then go on to the next person's pool. It's harmless, but I like to know who's on my property. And lately, I admit, I've found it rather annoying."

"You wanted to go after them with a BB gun."

"I would never use a BB gun — not after all the trouble we had with the Willis boy. It was very naughty of you, dear. Did you want me to shoot your friend with a BB gun?"

"No. I just wanted you to get mad."

"Well, now, you've had your little joke and we've all had a good laugh." Jay couldn't help but think that Mrs. Macfarlane having a good laugh wasn't that much different from Mrs. MacFarlane being greatly annoyed. Mrs. MacFarlane had cold, grey, appraising eyes. "Jay, you must be dying of heat. Why don't you change into your swimsuit? The cabana's there. The girls' room has a 'G' on the door."

"Thanks." As Jay walked away, she heard Mrs. MacFarlane whisper urgently to Lily, "You might have told me you were bringing someone."

"I didn't think you'd mind."

"I don't. But it means I have to make more sandwiches."

"Jay can have my sandwiches."

"That won't do. You'll have to go out and get some more bread. Fairly soon, if you want to eat."

"Yeah, yeah, Ma," Lily grumbled.

Louise MacFarlane strode grimly back into the house. She didn't know why this schism existed between herself and her youngest daughter. She never had any trouble with Rose. Her husband, Jack, always claimed that Lily wasn't as smart as Rose and that was why she was a problem. But Louise knew better. She knew the difficult girls were the smart ones and the easy ones lacked the imagination or the brains to be otherwise.

Jack was determined to tame Lily. Louise wondered if there was any point to it. He'd started her on the job at Hydro, hoping that she might pick up the skills and interest to pursue a managerial position, but Lily viewed the enterprise as some silly summer job. Left to her own devices, Lily would have fallen in love, got pregnant, married and settled down and Mrs. MacFarlane would have two cherubic grandchildren frolicking in the pool instead of one overgrown adult child.

It was always clear to Mrs. MacFarlane that Lily was a girl born to love and be loved. She anticipated a shotgun wedding to a nice boy. Mrs. MacFarlane had been careful to keep Lily in a social circle where she would only meet nice boys. But, in the short space of time between Rose's adolescence and Lily's, the social climate shifted dramatically. Suddenly, it was unfashionable to get married and have babies. And with the Pill, girls could take matters into their own hands. Mrs. MacFarlane hoped Lily wasn't taking the Pill.

Girls were also now expected to be self-sufficient. Mrs. MacFarlane worried that she and her husband may have put too much pressure on Lily to find a career. She noticed a certain desperation about Lily — a need to cling to her adolescence. Either Lily did not want to grow up or she had lost the will to do so. But how does one force one's children to grow up? Mrs. MacFarlane's generation had the War. Lily's generation didn't even have Society to point the way. They were set adrift in a sea of unlimited choices. Mrs. MacFarlane reminded herself that Lily probably never gave a second thought to her future. This generation lived firmly in the present. Perhaps it was she who was the fool for worrying. The future would take care of itself. It always did.

Lily loved to lie at the bottom of the swimming pool. The water gently weighing down on her gave her comfort. Lily could just make out the rippled form of Jay walking along the side of the pool, towards the stairs. She swam up to meet her.

"Sorry I played that joke on you."

"It was a pretty weird thing to do. Why'd you do it?"

"I don't know," Lily laughed.

"I don't think your mother likes me."

"Sure, she likes you. Come on. Dive in. What are you waiting for?"

"I like to go in slowly."

"Cautious. Not like me." Lily pulled herself up to sit beside Jay at the pool's edge. The two of them dangled their legs in the water.

"No. Not like you."

Lily took Jay's observation as an invitation. She described, uninterrupted and at length, her blighted romance with Brad, ending with the resolution that she should give him one more chance.

Jay contemplated telling Lily about what she'd seen that night in the basement, but in the context of their lives, she could not make sense of it. Drama, passion, violent acts were things of the past. People like Lily and Jay grew up in safe, new, sterilized environments; clean slates for the world to write on. Jay replied in the parlance of her times, "Dump the moron," and idly glided her leg back and forth in the sparkling turquoise water, admiring the effect.

Lily was a bit taken aback by Jay's casual dismissal. "It's too late. It's over. I didn't even get officially dumped."

"You'd want to be thrown out of a moving car?"

"I'm sure Eve's exaggerating."

"You're too good for him. He's just a frat boy."

"So, what's wrong with frat boys?"

"There's nothing to them. They're cute."

"What's wrong with cute?" asked Lily cautiously. Jay was not supposed to be the expert on sexual relationships. She had taken a condescending tone towards Lily of late. Lily had the uneasy feeling that Jay was doing some exploring on her own, that perhaps she was no longer content to be Lily's acolyte.

"Lightweight," Jay said. "He doesn't know what he wants."

"He wanted me."

"And Susan Lipton."

"Yeah, well, now he doesn't want either of us."

"Maybe that's for the best."

"Do you know something? Is he seeing someone else?"

"How would I know?" Jay flushed, recalling her vision.

"You sounded like you ... Eve! Is it Eve?"

"Of course not. Brad isn't right for you, Lily. You need someone who's real. Like Rufus. Rufus is real."

"Yeah, real dirty, real smelly, real rude."

"I thought you liked him."

"If he's such a catch, why aren't you going for him?"

"He's not my type."

"Yeah, right. Not good enough for you, but good enough for me."

"No, I didn't mean that."

"Well, who's your type, then? That Nicholas guy?"

"He's got a girlfriend now. Anyway, he's just a kid." Jay shocked herself as she realized that she meant what she said. Her infatuation with Nicholas had vanished. "I'm sort of interested in someone else. An artist."

"A friend of Rufus?"

"No, not a student. One of the teachers."

"Uh oh."

"It's not like that, Lily. He's pretty young. I mean, yeah, he's older than me but I don't know, he must be about twenty-nine. Yes. I bet he's twenty-nine."

"I bet he's forty."

"Aw, come on, he can't be forty. He wears jeans and sneakers. He must be twenty-nine. So, that's not too old."

"Ten years."

"Well, he might be thirty." Jay assessed the age with great deliberation. Current wisdom maintained that people over thirty were traitors to the Revolution. They were greedy, grasping pawns of the Establishment. Anxious to feather their own nests, they would stop at nothing in their quest for money and power. Now, Jay was not aware of the exact reasoning of this particular zeitgeist; possibly because it was entirely irrational, but it did leave her with an uneasy feeling about people over the age of thirty. "No, I'm sure he's twenty-nine," she reassured herself. "Oh, and I think he had a hard life. He looks so sad."

"Mmm," Lily nodded in frustration. Usually, Jay had no love interest of her own to report on.

"He seems to be a really mean guy but I know he's just pretending. It's just a front." Jay's generation had been indoctrinated with a fallacious principle of psychology that declared that people were the opposite of what they appeared to be. If someone seemed mean-spirited and nasty, they were really generous and tender-hearted. "He must have had a very unhappy childhood," Jay added. Unhappy childhoods were the other favourite psychological excuse for bad behaviour. People exploited it fully. The blame for all the trouble in the world lay squarely where it belonged: on the parents, who coincidentally, were also the Establishment.

"Brad had an unhappy childhood, too," said Lily, anxious to turn the topic back to more urgent matters. "His parents were cold and distant."

"Well, I don't know about Snafu's parents, per se, but I'm sure they mistreated him."

"Snafu?"

"Yes."

"His parents named him that? For sure he had a bad childhood!"

"His real name's John but no one's allowed to call him that 'cause his last name's Smith."

"Oh. Well, has he asked you out?"

"Oh no! He'd never ask me out. He hates me."

"Then why are you talking about him?" Sometimes Lily could not figure Jay out at all.

"We're meant for each other. It's just something I know."

"And this small barrier of him hating you —"

"Well, I guess he doesn't hate me — he doesn't like me, though."

"I don't like to be rude, Jay, but I'd say you don't have a hope in hell of getting this guy."

"That's not what it's about. It's about love. I love him. I can help him."

"Well, if he asks you out, let me know and we'll have something to discuss." Lily slowly slid into the pool. "So, do you think I should just show up tomorrow?"

"For what?"

"The next jump." Lily floated on her back and glided past Jay.

"Oh yeah. I still can't believe you did it." Jay entered the water and did a gentle breaststroke alongside Lily.

"It's perfectly safe."

"And you weren't scared?"

"I was terrified."

"Good. I'm glad you've got some sense. But if it scares you, why do you do it?"

"It's amazing, Jay. It's ... well, I can't describe it, but I love it. I just keep wanting to do it again."

"Then I guess it doesn't matter whether you or Brad are still an item."

"Huh?"

"'Cause you're just going for the jump."

"I guess that's right." Lily had never considered that she might actually enjoy skydiving more than a love affair with Brad. That was the way men thought, wasn't it? She was excited to think that she might be a liberated woman after all.

At that moment, a scantily clad young man streaked out of the house, dove headfirst into the pool, and smashed up and down the length of it in a boisterous Australian crawl. Jay did not have a chance to get a clear look at his face, but something about him was very familiar. He did not stop to catch his breath, nor did he acknowledge the two girls.

"Who's that?" Jay asked, somewhat discomfited.

"Paul. Damn! Why'd he show up today?"

"Was he in the Brunswick?"

"Yeah, he ruined that as well. He's not supposed to come. We do alternate weekends."

"Is he a friend of the family?"

"No. He's my twin."

"You have a twin brother?" Jay was astonished that Lily had never mentioned that she had a brother, let alone a twin.

"Yeah. Shit! It's not fair. He was here last week."

Jay's head was spinning in her attempts to reconcile this Paul with the vision that she saw in the basement. She decided she would focus on concrete matters, instead. "He doesn't seem very friendly," Jay observed as Paul roared past, kicking furiously.

"He's not."

Because Jay came from a happy home where the family members liked each other, she assumed that Lily and her twin brother had a mild dispute that could be easily resolved through a friendly hello. Jay planted herself at the end of one of Paul's lengths. Jay thought Paul would see her as he approached, but he didn't. He rammed right into her.

"What the fuck!"

"Hi," Jay gasped, having some of the wind knocked out of her.

"Do you always stand in people's way when they're swimming lengths?"

"I'm Jay Wright, a friend of Lily's. I thought I should introduce myself."

"Don't bother," said Paul as he spun around and resumed his strokes.

Jay was genuinely puzzled. She had met the brothers of her friends in Victoria. Some of them were shy, but they would still reply in a friendly manner if asked a direct question. She turned to Lily. "Is he mad at you?"

"He's a pig. He's always been that way."

"Oh."

"Sometimes he can be nice. Usually when he wants something. God, I wish he hadn't come today. It won't be any fun with him here."

Jay had to agree. Having Paul around was like trying to organize a picnic with a thundercloud lurking on the horizon. His presence was rancorous enough to cast a pall on the party but not sufficient to call it quits and go inside.

Paul had finished his lengths and was striding over to claim one of the chaise longues when Mrs. MacFarlane called out cheerfully, "Paul, dear. How wonderful you've stopped by. You've met Lily's friend?" Paul grunted an assent and dragged the chaise longue to a secluded area.

"No," countered Lily. "He swam into her but he didn't want to meet her."

"Now, Lily, don't be difficult. We're all going to get along today. Your father should be back any minute. Rose and her husband will be here soon. And we'll all have a nice lunch."

"Rose?" gasped Lily in alarm. Jay would be furious if she found out what Lily had told Rose about her.

"Yes. Isn't that nice? You hardly ever see her."

"Great." It was unlikely that Rose would give anything away. She was very discreet, though she could be frighteningly persistent in "sorting things out."

"Who's Rose?" asked Jay

"She's my sister."

"You have a sister, too?"

"Yeah. She's a nurse."

Further inquiries on Jay's part were cut short by Mrs. MacFarlane calling again for Lily. "Oh Lily, now that you've cooled yourself off, would you be a dear and just pick up a few things for me from the grocery? And that reminds me. Paul! Is your friend coming over?"

"Which friend?"

"That nice one from your house."

"Brad?" asked Lily. "Do you mean Brad, Ma?"

"Yes, that's the one. Is he coming?"

"No," said Paul tersely.

"Why don't you call him up and invite him, dear?"

Paul threw down his towel in disgust. "Look, I just want to be alone! I came here to be alone. I didn't come here to meet Lily's stupid friends. And I didn't come here for any family party!"

"Oh." Mrs. MacFarlane debated as to how she should react to Paul's sudden outburst and decided that discretion was the better part of valour. "You'll feel better after you've had some lunch, dear. I've made some devilled eggs. Would you like one now?"

"No!" Paul said sharply, then added, "Thank you, Mother."

"Your father's hypoglycemic. And an egg always settles him down."

"I don't need an egg. Thank you, Mother." Paul then turned his attention to arranging his body for the perfect tan. He poured out a sweet pungent oil and slathered it all over his body. Jay knew it was rude to stare but she couldn't take her eyes off Paul. She'd never seen a bathing suit that small or that tight before. Most of the boys she knew wore boxer-style suits or Bermuda shorts. Paul wore small, tight, bright blue bikini briefs. He was proud of his body and showed not the slightest hesitation in displaying it. Jay had to admit that Paul was extremely good-looking. His body was too muscular for her taste but his face fascinated her. He had large blue eyes, a small nose and a perfectly formed mouth. He could have appeared prissy but a wanton turn to his mouth suggested danger.

Having administered his unguent, Paul glistened like a basted bird in mid-roast. He clapped two small plastic discs over his eyes and stretched out on the chaise longue; dead to the world, a sacrificial offering to the Sun God.

"Come with me to the store?"

"What? Oh, great idea." Jay leaped up. She did not want to be left alone with Paul or Mrs. MacFarlane so she eagerly accompanied Lily to the car. Lily threw on a large shapeless towel-dress, so she wouldn't have to change out of her suit. She tossed one to Jay to put on. It was a savage shade of orange with a large yellow daisy emblazoned on the front. Jay felt odd going out in public wearing such an outfit.

Going to the corner in Lily's parents' neighbourhood was not the simple five-minute stroll that she and Lily routinely did in the city. There were no corners here. Even by car, the winding roads were a nuisance. Jay marvelled at the stupidity in creating this environment. Presumably, the cul-de-sacs and horseshoe-pattern roads were supposed to hearken back to more elegant times, but since no one walked down these aimless byways to enjoy their seclusion, what was the point? Any pretensions to elegance the suburbs might have claimed were shattered when Lily and Jay approached the mall. It was a hideous structure: a large parking lot with a cluster of concrete blocks in the centre. The parking lot was jammed with hot, sweating drivers trolling around slowly, waiting for someone to leave his parking space. Lily found a spot on the outer fringes. Few people parked there. Jay could understand why. It was a long walk across baking hot asphalt. The fumes of car exhaust mingled with the hot clammy air of a Toronto summer.

"Do you like malls?" Jay asked Lily tentatively.

"I did when I was a kid. It meant you got to go shopping and look at stuff."

"Did you ever go downtown?"

"Oh yeah, but only for special stuff. It was a long way to go."

"Doesn't it seem crazy, though? It's going to take us at least an hour to get one loaf of bread."

"I thought you wanted to come."

"I did. But if we were at KAT House we'd walk to the corner and be back in ten minutes."

"Yeah, well, this isn't downtown."

"Doesn't it strike you as odd?"

"Look, I'm tired of people taking potshots at the suburbs. I grew up here. It's my home."

"I didn't mean —"

"Sure you did. Everyone does. It's a target these days."

"Really, I didn't. I've never really been to malls before."

"Oh, give me a break."

"We lived quite close to the city."

"The Victoria equivalent of Rosedale, I presume."

"Um, no." Jay hesitated. Her home neighbourhood of Fairfield was very similar to Rosedale but Jay sensed that she'd lose Lily's friendship if she told the truth. "Not at all. I guess we had more corner stores in Victoria."

They walked into the largest supermarket that Jay had ever seen and were immediately assaulted by blasts of frigid air that made Jay's flesh tremble and go goosepimply. Her wet bathing suit went crisp and cold against her skin.

"Great, eh?" proclaimed Lily.

"Oooh," nodded Jay, certain that at any moment her teeth would start chattering. Though Lily only needed a few items, they were situated a long way from each other. Lily grabbed a couple of loaves of sandwich bread from the shelf. Ice cream was next on Lily's list. The frozen food department was even colder than the rest of the store. Lily deliberated for so long on what type of ice cream to buy that finally Jay couldn't stand it any longer and ran outside to warm up.

She watched people walk into the mall and was struck by how they seemed to change upon entering. Outside the mall, people moved with a sense of purpose. It was blisteringly hot and their motions were languid but they possessed an individual energy. They went inside and suddenly were transformed into sleepwalkers. Jay noticed that some people took longer to succumb, but eventually everyone moved in a slow, sedate walk: a slight waddle from side to side rather than a forward motion. There was something sinister about the way people adapted to the mall's somnambulant rhythm.

"Oh God, it's so hot! How can you stand it!" Lily handed Jay a grocery bag. "The ice cream's gonna melt before we get home."

"What type of ice cream did you get?"

"Double chocolate fudge, of course."

"Yum."

"Paul and Rose like vanilla so I had to get that, too."

"They actually like vanilla ice cream?"

"Yup."

"That's perverse."

"So, you see, there are advantages to going to the store to pick up a few things."

"Real chocolate ice cream."

"You got it, Pontiac."

Lily's sister, Rose was at the house when they got back. She was replacing a screw in one of the patio chairs. Satisfied that she'd fixed it, she turned her attention to Lily.

"Hi, Lil. I might have been a bit short with you the other day. It's been a tough week."

Rose smiled at Jay. "Hi. I'm Rose." She took Jay's hand and pumped it up and down a few times.

Jay was struck by how austerely beautiful Rose was. She had Paul's colouring — dark, black hair, pale white skin combined with her mother's penetrating grey eyes. Her forthright manner brooked no interference. It was clear that Rose's beauty would not be employed in such frivolous activities as flirting. Jay thought it was rather sad when naturally beautiful women dressed in plain clothes and looked stern, but Rose was evidently one of those women.

"Your name's Jay?" A steely look crossed Rose's face. "The artist?"

Lily sighed inwardly. Rose had a mind like a steel trap. She forgot nothing.

"Yes. Lily told you?" Jay was most surprised that Lily had told Rose about her paintings. She'd never seemed particularly impressed by them.

"Just a little," Rose replied hastily. "Not much. Nothing to worry about."

"Pardon?"

"Here. Have a glass of lemonade and sit down. Lily has to help Mum make sandwiches." Rose put a friendly hand on Lily's back and shoved her in the direction of the kitchen. Lily could do nothing but obey. She reflected that, perhaps, it was best that she was out of the way. Lily recalled, from Rose's interviews with her prom dates, that once Rose was on the trail, she was a bloodhound. Nothing would deter her from sniffing out the traces. It was excruciating to watch, so she might as well escape to the kitchen and hope for the best.

"So," said Rose, arranging her dragnet as she pulled a chair out for Jay. "How are you enjoying Toronto?"

"It took a while to get used to it, but now I love it."

"I guess it was stressful."

"Stressful? No, I wouldn't say that. Homesick — I was homesick for a while."

"But you're not homesick anymore?"

"No."

"I deal with a lot of stress-related factors in my work."

"Yes. Lily said you were a nurse."

"I'm working in drug rehab right now. Most of them get hooked on drugs during times of stress." Rose looked meaningfully at Jay. "Drugs don't help, you know."

Jay wondered if Rose knew about Lily's drug habit. "Yes, I know. I mean, I haven't tried pot but I can see the effect it has on people."

"You can?"

"Yes, it makes them listless. They lose their ambition. Of course," Jay cast a quick glance to the kitchen, "some people think ambition is wrong."

"Some people?" asked Rose. "Which people?"

Jay felt she'd dropped enough hints. Did she have to spell it out for her? "Oh, I don't know. People I meet. Do you think ambition is wrong?"

"No. It's good to be ambitious. Is that what we're talking about? I thought we were discussing drugs."

"Oh ... No. Well, we could talk about drugs if you like."

Rose was so thoroughly bewildered by the turn the conversation was taking that she artlessly blurted out, "They're working on a cure for schizophrenia."

"Are they?"

"Yes. That's my actual field of study." Rose blushed. She always blushed when she told a lie. "They think van Gogh was a schizophrenic."

"Really?" asked Jay, straining to be polite, because she knew her art history and had never heard of such a thing. "I thought he was crazy. I didn't know he had a split personality."

"No, no — that's schizoid. They have split personalities. The names are similar — there's the confusion. And of course, the movies don't help. All that misinformation. I hope all this talk about schizophrenics isn't alarming you." Rose looked intently at Jay. "Making you paranoid."

"No. Should it?"

"Of course not. Anyway, it's nice to know there's a cure."

"There is a cure? I thought you said they were working on it."

"Oh, well, yes. They have one now. But they're working on a better one. The hardest thing is for a schizophrenic to admit they're sick — to step forward and seek treatment. They don't like doing that."

"Oh."

"It must be fascinating being an artist."

"Oh. Well —"

"You must see things differently from most people."

"I guess so."

"See beyond the surface reality. The objects in van Gogh's paintings have that funny aura around them. Is that what you see, too?"

"Aura? In van Gogh's paintings?"

"The landscapes. All the swirls."

"Oh. I thought it was just texture."

"Yes, texture. Do you see texture?"

"No, my paintings aren't anything like van Gogh's."

"Oh."

"I actually don't like van Gogh's work."

"You don't."

"No. I think he's overrated."

"Oh."

The conversation came to a dead halt, but Rose rallied on. "I guess the reason I keep bringing up van Gogh is because he's the only artist I'm familiar with. And it seems that he has his own little world. And I wonder if it's that way for you. When you paint, do you have a different sense of reality?"

"How do you mean?"

"Oh, I don't know. See things, hear things that other people can't see."

Jay could not make out what Rose was getting at, till she remembered telling Lily about the ghosts in the basement. She wondered why Rose didn't come right out and ask her about them but people were strange when it came to ghosts. "Oh! I get it! Lily told you."

"What? NO! She never told me anything!"

"I don't mind talking about them."

"Them?"

"The ghosts."

"Is that what you call them?"

"I don't know what else to call them. Do you know their names?"

"Why would I know their names?"

"Well, you lived in KAT House, didn't you? I thought you'd know its history. Didn't anyone talk about the people who had the house before?"

"What are you talking about?"

"The ghosts. They have to be people who lived in the house. Was there ever a murder in KAT House?"

"Murder?"

"Yes. Suicide, murder, that sort of thing."

"Is that what the ghosts talk to you about?"

"Oh no, they don't talk to me. I just hear them arguing."

"Arguing about murder? Suicide?"

"Well, they used to just run up and down the stairs and shout. But the other night, one of the ghosts beat the other ghost's head in with a shovel."

Rose's mouth dropped open and snapped shut again. Jay mistook her reaction for the wide-eyed amazement people usually displayed when hearing about ghosts. She continued blithely, "I can't really make it out. Their voices sound as if they're a couple of floors up but the running sounds like it's right beside me in the basement."

"You live in the basement?"

"No, I've got a room upstairs. It's a horrible green colour. I thought of painting it, but then I thought they wouldn't want me to. I'm only a boarder."

"They?"

"I chose the room because it was really big and it had a really pretty Tiffany lamp."

"But you spend most of your time in the basement."

"Well, yes. My art."

"Your art."

"You see, the lamp is green stained glass, so it gives off a sickly green light. And the walls are lime green and well, green's a really weird colour to live with. It does things to you."

"Paint the room."

"It's too late, now. Summer's almost over."

"Paint the room immediately. Paint it white." Very few things in life unnerved Rose, but she had to admit that Jay scared the living daylights out of her. "Excuse me, I'm just going to check on things in the kitchen." She dashed out to the kitchen, found Lily and, abandoning all pretence to medical propriety, whispered, "She's gonna blow!"

"What?"

"Your friend. Any day now, she's gonna flip her lid."

"Jay?"

"She's on the verge. You don't want to be the one to push her over."

"Jay's fine."

"I admit she doesn't have all the symptoms, but she's dangerous."

"Dangerous?" asked Mrs. MacFarlane, catching wind of the conversation.

"Nothing, Mum," Lily and Rose answered in unison.

"That pleasant little girl dangerous? What nonsense!"

At that moment, Jay poked her head in the door. "Is there anything I can do to help?

"No!" said Rose abruptly.

"It's all right, dear. We're fine. You go out and talk to Paul."

Jay reluctantly walked back to the patio. Paul still lay stretched out on his chaise longue. Jay thought she would leave him where he was and have a swim instead. She had just got herself thoroughly wet when Mrs. MacFarlane suddenly announced that lunch was ready: Mr. MacFarlane and his son-in-law had arrived.

Jack MacFarlane was a large, exuberant man whose forceful personality set everyone in motion, usually out of his path. Rose's husband, Rick, having spent the better part of the day with Mr. MacFarlane, fled to the kitchen for some respite. He had put in his dues for the family occasion and looked considerably the worse for wear.

"Paul!" Mr. MacFarlane bellowed. "What are you doing! Lying there like a girl. Say hello to your old dad."

"Hi, Dad," Paul replied meekly, for his father intimidated him thoroughly.

"Weeza! Weeza! Where are ya!" Mr. MacFarlane remained on the patio, crying out like a blind man.

"I'm right here, dear." Mrs. MacFarlane stepped out, carrying a plate of sandwiches.

Mr. MacFarlane grabbed and ate one as she walked by. "It's too early for lunch. The sun's just past the yardarm. What'll you have to drink? G and T?"

"A G and T would be lovely. I'll just set the lunch out."

"Put the sammies back in the fridge. Let's set up the bar. Drinks first, lunch later."

"But it's rather late and I think the children —"

"My God, Weeza. They're adults now. You'll have a beer, won't you, Paul?"

"Sure," said Paul who remained comfortably basking in the sun.

Rose, on the other hand, had urgent business to discuss with her husband. Seeing that everyone was miraculously out of the kitchen, she seized her opportunity.

"Rickie!" she whispered in an undertone and motioned for him to join her in the pantry. Rick mistook her intentions and followed eagerly. He loved making love to Rose in her parents' house.

"No no, not that. Not now."

"There's got to be some advantage to being here."

"I have to talk to you."

"Talk away."

"Mom could come in any minute."

"That's what makes it so great. Danger."

"My mother might turn your crank, but she doesn't do it for me. Now, cut it out! I have to talk to you."

"Do we have to spend all our free days with your parents?"

"We hardly ever come here."

"Doesn't feel like it."

"We're here because of Lily."

"What's wrong with her now?"

"Her friend."

"What friend? Where is Lily, anyway?"

"She went to her room, I guess. Her friend's out by the pool."

"Oh yeah." Rick gazed out the window.

"She's about to have a psychotic break."

"She is? She looks like she's doing the crawl, honey. Oh! Now it's the backstroke."

"This is serious."

"Okay, what is it?"

Rose informed Rick of her alarming encounter with Jay. While Rick was a general practitioner and not an expert in such matters, he was secretly pleased that Rose consulted him.

"Well, honey, I think —"

"What'll you have to drink, Rose? Rick, my boy!" Jack MacFarlane roared as he strode into the kitchen, and the conversation between Rick and Rose ended there.

Mr. MacFarlane's boisterous arrival had thrown Jay into a panic. There wasn't enough time to change out of her suit. She didn't want Mrs. MacFarlane to know that she'd gone for a swim instead of talking to Paul. She dried herself off quickly and threw the towel dress back on, but water collected at the bottom of her bathing suit and dripped into conspicuous puddles on the patio. The pools of water did not escape Mrs. MacFarlane's notice.

"Did you and Paul have a nice chat?"

"Ah, he was asleep so I didn't want to disturb him."

"I see." Mrs. MacFarlane's attention was suddenly claimed by Mr. MacFarlane, who wanted to know where she kept the tonic water.

"It's where it always is! Oh, honestly!" She hurried into the kitchen where Mr. MacFarlane could be heard, rummaging noisily through the cupboards, as a bear at the town dump pawing through bags of garbage.

The sandwiches lay undisturbed on a small glass table. They looked deliciously insubstantial. The crusts were cut off and they'd been sectioned neatly into small triangles. Jay had not eaten since early morning. Lunch had occupied her thoughts well before she and Lily made the trip to the grocery store. The swim had piqued her appetite even more. Jay knew it was rude but no one was looking so she quickly grabbed an egg salad triangle and stuffed it into her mouth.

Mr. MacFarlane reappeared from the kitchen, laden with his bar apparatus. Catching sight of Jay, he boomed out, "And who's this?!" The bread held Jay's jaw fast in a thick, gluey clamp. Unable to speak or to swallow, she could only nod and bob her head like a demented mime, ferociously and surreptitiously chewing, before finally gasping out, "Mmmph ... Jay!"

"Who?"

Jay swallowed carefully. "Jay Wright. I'm a friend of Lily's."

"Couldn't wait for lunch, eh? Where is that girl!"

Jay wondered, too. Lily seemed to have been swallowed up whole by her family. Jay was overwhelmed by their radically varying dispositions. She thought Mrs. MacFarlane was difficult until she met Paul. But compared to the inquisitorial Rose, Paul was easy. And just as she thought she had the situation somewhat in hand, along came the capper: Mr. MacFarlane, who, as far as Jay could surmise, was capable of just about anything.

"WHERE'S LIL?!" he shouted again.

"She went upstairs, Dad," Rose replied, coolly, giving the nod to her husband that he should help out with the drinks.

"Why isn't she here? She's got a GUEST! She should look after her."

"I'm ... ah ... fine."

"You don't have a drink."

"Oh. No, I don't."

"What'll you have, Jay Wright? A G and T?"

"Sure, that sounds nice."

"Are you sure you want a drink?" Rose asked with concern.

"Um —"

"Don't be a bully, Rose. Jay's having a drink."

Jay actually wanted another sandwich but Mrs. MacFarlane had taken the plate away. Mr. MacFarlane measured out two large jiggerfuls of gin into a small glass, threw in a couple of ice cubes and a slice of lemon and topped it off with a soupcon of tonic water. It was an excellent drink for someone who liked gin. Jay, however, preferred more tonic water, but was too embarrassed to ask for an adjustment in the proportions. She sipped her drink and over the course of the afternoon, got quietly and thoroughly swacked.

"Well, isn't this nice. A little family get-together," said Mrs. MacFarlane, then seeing that half the family was not actually present, shouted, "PAUL! Are you going to lie out there forever?" and upon receiving no reply, consoled herself with, "Well, he'll be here when the food's out. Jay, have you met Rose's husband, Rick? Rick, this is Lily's friend, Jay —"

Lily emerged from her hiding place in the bowels of the house. She slouched onto the patio, looking somewhat annoyed that Jay was still present.

"Lil!" her father proclaimed. "Ah, there she is!"

"Hi, Daddy."

"What'll you have, baby?"

"A Coke, please."

"Just a Coke?"

"Yeah."

"Your friend's having a G and T."

"She's what?!"

Jay smiled sheepishly, wishing desperately that she were somewhere else.

"Tell me, Jay," continued Mrs. MacFarlane. "Is it your first year in Kappa Alpha Theta? How do you like it? Did they do dreadful things to you for initiation? I really think some of that is getting quite out of hand. I had such a wonderful time when I was a sister. Mind you, we didn't have that lovely house that you have. We rented this funny little place underneath a Greek Orthodox Church. It was such fun. Are you having fun at all the parties?"

"Jay's a boarder," said Lily.

"A what?"

"A boarder."

"Is that true, Jay?"

"Um ... yes."

"You're not a Kappa Alpha Theta?" Mrs. MacFarlane looked stricken.

"Well ... I ... ah ... you misunderstood."

"I what?!"

"I was an A O Pi. Briefly."

"So, you're not even a member of a sorority?"

"No."

"And, being a boarder, I suppose you're not from Toronto, either."

"No." Jay saw that she'd now committed a cardinal offence. While Jay didn't think it was a particular advantage in life to be born and live in Toronto, Torontonians evidently did. Jay now lost any vestige of respect she might have commanded from the MacFarlanes. She was now branded as one of the ignorant multitude who lived outside Toronto. The next question a Torontonian needed to know was which direction outside of Toronto, as that information had a bearing on the intelligence of the person in question. East Coast people were viewed as being shrewd, though their personal hygiene left a lot to be desired. As one progressed towards Toronto, the bad hygiene retreated from the dangling body parts and concentrated itself in the teeth, so the individual was viewed more favourably. (Not taking into account the entire province of Quebec, which was summarily dismissed by the good Torontonian.) By those stringent definitions, Ottawa was a very good place to be from, though not as good as Toronto. West was a problematic direction. Historically, people who were unpleasant headed west. If one's querulous ancestors went north, that implied a certain vivacity. But west was the direction for shiftless, lazy, ne'er-do wells. The further west one went, the worse it got, until one arrived at the West Coast where the lack of industry culminated into full-blown inertia. West Coasters blamed it on the effects of living at sea-level in a moderate climate. Easterners knew better, called it Sloth, and dubbed the entire area Lotusland.

"Well," said Mrs. MacFarlane grimly. "Whereabouts are you from?" *Whereabouts* was her polite way of putting it, when, in fact, Mrs. MacFarlane wanted to know precisely where.

Jay was vaguely aware of the slurs on her homeland but she didn't believe that anyone took it seriously, so she answered quite cheerfully, "Victoria."

Mrs. MacFarlane's face fell. It was worse than she thought. This girl was not going to be a suitable friend for Lily. Lily had a knack for picking up odd-bobs. The girl was pleasant enough. A nice, sweet good-natured simpleton. No good could come from the liaison but Mrs. MacFarlane consoled herself with the thought that no harm could come from having a fool for a friend. "Victoria," she repeated, in an effort to appear gracious. "My, that's a long way away. You must get homesick."

"Do you have any relatives here in Toronto?" asked Rose, with peculiar concern.

"No. They're all out west."

"Really," said Mrs. MacFarlane. "How nice."

"None at all?" Rose persisted.

"Well, actually, I do have some relatives in Guelph. I've never met them. My grandfather's family. He was the youngest and he went west."

"Oh. And they're still in Guelph?"

"Far as I know. A big clan."

"You should look them up."

"Yes, yes. I guess so."

"It's very important to know your family." Rose emphasized *know*. "You should go out and meet them. It's not far."

Jay found Rose rather bossy. "It's not far if you have a car, but it is far if you don't."

"Take the bus."

"Yes, well, when I feel like seeing them, I will take the bus," Jay replied testily, emboldened by the gin and tonic.

"The girl doesn't want to see any more family, Rosie," declared Mr. MacFarlane, rising to Jay's defence. "Geez! That should be apparent. She came across hell's half acre just to get away from them."

"You can learn a lot from meeting your relatives, certain illnesses that run in families. Rick's big on genealogies, aren't you, dear?"

"Huh? Oh yeah."

"Rick found out that one of his aunts had gone mad and we were both a little worried. We want to have children, of course."

"What?!" exclaimed Rick and Mr. MacFarlane in unison, but for different reasons. Mr. MacFarlane turned to Rick. "You have crazy relatives?"

"But it turned out the madness went through the female side of the family," continued Rose before her father could get out of hand.

"I didn't know that," said Lily, "Which aunt was it? Did I meet her?"

"No you didn't, Lily. Nobody ever met her. She was locked up, wasn't she, dear?"

"Yeah, sure, whatever," replied Rick, inured to the casual insults hurled upon his family.

"I met her," said Paul, his voice slightly muffled. His face was embedded in cushions as he presented his back to the sun. "She was tall and skinny with a weird laugh. Phyllis. Yeah. I think her name was Phyllis. She was at the wedding."

"That was my mother," said Rick.

"Oh yeah?"

"Must we talk about this?" said Mrs. MacFarlane with some exasperation. It was turning out to be an unpleasant lunch and lunch hadn't even been served yet.

"Who's for another drink? Yours is low." Mr. MacFarlane grabbed Jay's glass and replenished it before she could blink. In her nervousness, Jay hadn't been aware that she'd downed the entire drink. Initially, she took little sips just to be polite. She was amazed at how quickly it went. She wasn't even hungry anymore.

"I think we should have lunch," declared Mrs. MacFarlane, looking suspiciously at Jay. The girl was an alcoholic.

Jay mistook Mrs. MacFarlane's scrutiny for a bid for help. "I'll help you," she said and tumbled out of her chair.

"It's quite all right, dear. Lily and Rose will carry things in." And Mrs. MacFarlane scurried off to the kitchen, content that Lily and Rose would form a blockade against Jay's unwanted assistance. However, Lily and Rose were in close consultation, and either didn't hear or paid no attention to their mother, so Jay followed Mrs. MacFarlane into the kitchen and watched as she took an enormous platter of devilled eggs out of the refrigerator and laid it on the table.

During the morning, Mrs. MacFarlane had painstakingly boiled one dozen eggs, waited for them to cool, cut them carefully in half, put the hard-boiled yolks in a separate bowl, wrapped the whites up in saran wrap and chilled them so they wouldn't dry out. Then she mashed up the yolks, adding mayonnaise, salt, pepper, a dash of curry and a smidgen of Worcestershire sauce. Mrs. MacFarlane liked to beat the mixture with an electric beater so the egg goo became really luscious and creamy. When it was just the way Mr. MacFarlane liked it, she would stuff the gloppy mass into a cake icing bag, arrange the twenty-four half-shelled whites on the platter and squeeze a decorative gloopful of yolk into each.

The bag had little metal caps that could be attached to give a variety of squeeze lines. Some produced a high, thin ridge; others, a short, squat ridge or a jagged ridge. Of course, there was the simple, small-holed cap that rendered a thin line to write "Happy Birthday" on a cake. Mr. MacFarlane liked his devilled eggs to have high, thin ridges. If Mrs. MacFarlane had used the cap with the large jagged hole, she could have accomplished the work in half the time but she deferred to Mr. MacFarlane's wishes and selected the cap with the small, rippled hole.

She spent at least an hour fiddling with the goop. The heat made it impossible to get a proper purchase on it. She tried to do all twenty-four at once but the humidity in the air was against her. The ridges in the completed eggs wilted and sank while she struggled with the other eggs. So, Mrs. MacFarlane cleverly performed the task as a relay race, doing only three at a time, putting them quickly in the fridge and then selecting the next three. The eggs were perfect an hour ago, chilled to just the right texture, smooth and cold. But Jack had insisted on his yardarm hour, so now the eggs had a nasty little crust. Mrs. MacFarlane had just put the last parsley sprig around the eggs and was deliberating as to what she could do to mitigate the crust when a pair of eager hands reached in and took the platter off the table.

"Don't!" cried out Mrs. MacFarlane as Jay marched out to the patio with the platter. For unbeknownst to Jay, devilled eggs that have sat in the refrigerator for any length of time will emit small drops of water when exposed to hot summer air. The surface of the platter then becomes a slippery rink upon which all twenty-four devilled eggs, if not carefully attended to, will skate off in unison. The velocity at which Jay headed out the door equalled the force of propulsion, so the eggs were held in abeyance for a few moments by a crude law of physics. However, when Jay heard Mrs. MacFarlane say "Don't!," she came to an abrupt halt and all the eggs flew off at once, a volley of curried yellow yolks heading straight for Mr. MacFarlane's brand-new white sports pants.

"What the hell!" he roared as he leaped up to escape the yellow missiles but he succeeded only in meeting them halfway, most of them landing, downside, in his lap. All twenty-four found a home on Mr. MacFarlane's person. A few clung to his turquoise blue sports shirt. One landed on his head. Mr. MacFarlane, who up to this point had been predisposed to like Jay, now decided that he loathed the sight of her and, as he was not a man to hide his feelings, the afternoon for Jay went downhill rather rapidly.

"Oh God! I'm so sorry," cried Jay, who immediately rushed over and tried to remove the offending eggs from his person.

"GET AWAY FROM ME!" Mr. MacFarlane reared back. Several whites plopped to the ground at this sudden motion, but the yellow yolks clung to their target.

"I'm so sorry," said Jay again, not very convincingly as she was fighting a drunken instinct to laugh. Lily, Rose, Rick and Paul remained wisely silent. Mrs. MacFarlane was simply horror-struck.

"DAMN RIGHT YOU BETTER BE SORRY!" shouted Mr. MacFarlane, who had been looking forward to his eggs all afternoon. Dignity forbade him from pulling one off himself and eating it.

Jay foolishly approached Mr. MacFarlane again. "Let me help."

"Help?!" Mr. MacFarlane roared. "HELP?!" At this juncture, he was ready to lay hands on Jay, but Mrs. MacFarlane quickly interceded.

"We'll just take them off, dear. Calm down. It won't take a minute." She set to work with her paper towels and spatula. The spatula is an extremely useful item for getting remaining batter out of a bowl. However, the rubber edge applied to the white cloth only succeeded in smearing the curried yolk deeper into the fabric. Luckily, Mrs. MacFarlane brought a knife and she scraped the creamy yellow goo off Mr. MacFarlane. After a few minutes, she sensed that this action, however useful, was annoying the hell out of her

husband so she thought it best to take him out of the vicinity altogether. "Come along, dear. We'll get you some nice clean clothes."

There was a hideous silence as Jay looked to the remaining
members of the MacFarlane family for reassurance. They stared
gloomily back at her. Lily closed ranks with her family. Jay, who up
to that moment had not seen any family resemblance, now perceived
a certain glacial countenance that held them all in good stead. Even
Rick, the in-law, managed a good glare.

"I feel terrible about this. I don't know what I can do to make it
better."

"You could go home."

"Paul! That's rude," exclaimed Rose, unconvincingly.

"You know what Dad's like when he's mad," Paul added darkly.

"Excuse me, but I think I'll change out of my suit." Jay retreated
to the girl's cabana. She hoped that Lily would follow her. However,
Lily remained in conference with her family. Jay had never seen that
side of Lily. It was as though she disappeared for a while and became
someone else, someone that Jay neither knew, nor understood. Jay
considered slipping out the back way, but decided that was cowardly.
A guest should always say goodbye to the host, even under such
adverse circumstances as these. Besides, she wasn't sure she could
find her way out of this suburban maze. Armed in her clothes (Jay
felt much better now that her bottom wasn't perpetually damp), she
returned to the patio with the firm resolve to say thank you and
leave. Mrs. MacFarlane came out with a platterful of sandwiches.
She held onto it tightly.

"Who's for lunch?"

"Goodbye and thank you, Mrs. MacFarlane. I'm sorry I spilled
the eggs."

"It could happen to anyone."

"Well, goodbye and thanks again."

"You're not leaving?"

"Well, yes."

"No, I insist. You must stay and have lunch."

"Where's Dad?" asked Paul.

"He's upstairs getting changed."

"I feel really badly."

"Look, have some sandwiches." She thrust the plate at Jay who took one gingerly. "More than that — take a couple. Now, sit down and eat your lunch." Jay did as she was told. To her great relief, the family carried on as if she weren't there. Most of the conversation revolved around Rose and Rick's hectic schedule and Paul's plans for next year, Paul's opinion of the people he was working with, Rose's opinion of the people she was working with (Rick wasn't allowed to discuss his patients) and amusing nursing stories from Rose. Jay noticed that Lily said very little. Sitting on the other side of the patio, she, too, seemed to be outside of this family circle. When Mr. MacFarlane finally returned, in a complete change of clothes, he was quite subdued. He ate his lunch and occasionally glared thoughtfully at Jay.

Later, when Lily and Jay were clearing plates — Jay had been reinstated, in that she could be trusted with one empty plate at a time — Lily muttered to Jay, "I'll show you my room." Lily's offer to show Jay her childhood bedroom put the friendship on a new level of intimacy and was, at the very least, a silent apology from Lily for withdrawing her support during the devilled-egg incident.

Lily's room looked like a miniature version of a bedroom at the Palace of Versailles. Its decor showed the firm, tasteful hand of Lily's mother: off-white mock Louis XIV furniture trimmed with gold, the centrepiece being the tall, delicate, four-poster bed, covered with a floral chintz counterpane, its dainty design evocative of Limoges china. The bed was quite high. One had to hoist oneself onto it. There were copious layers of unnecessary bedding: a skirt ruff for the bottom of the bed, ruffles on the quilted counterpane, ruffles on the pillowcases, various pillows — ones to put one's head on and ones that were simply decorative, and a bolster with its attendant ruffles. There was so much bedding that there was barely room for a body to lie in the bed. A child could get tangled in the bedclothes and suffocate. The entire room felt padded. The carpet was thick and luxurious, made of long, soft, off-white, furry material that Jay had never seen before. The windows were adorned by Limoges fabric, curtains that couldn't be drawn easily, but had to be hauled back and tied into place. There was a vanity table, also à la Versailles, with a matching curving mirror. There were two elegant chairs so Lily could entertain visitors. It was a beautiful room but it bore little or no relation to the Lily Jay knew.

In Lily's room at KAT House, the double bed, jammed against the wall, took up most of the available space; the rest given over to a broken-down armchair that Lily had covered with a black and beige, batik-style, cotton bedspread. The remaining floor was bare. Recently, Lily tacked a couple of Picasso blue period posters on the wall and painted her bedside light bulb blue, so the room had a strange blue glow. The dusky ambience of her room at KAT House was so different from this crisp, floral clutter that Jay wondered where the real Lily resided.

"Your room's very pretty." Jay didn't know what else to say.

"Thanks," said Lily, listlessly.

"I'm sorry I made such a mess."

"I should have warned my mother you were clumsy." Lily saw a reflection of herself in Jay and hated her for it.

"I think I'll go now."

Lily grabbed Jay's arm. "Look. Don't use me to get to Paul. Talk to him yourself if you're so crazy about him."

"What are you talking about?"

"I saw the way you looked at him. Couldn't take your eyes off him."

"Is that why you disappeared?"

"All my friends fall in love with Paul. Sometimes he asks them out and sleeps with them. Mostly he ignores them. It doesn't matter. They always get hung up on him and they always want me to explain Paul to them. So, don't lie, okay? If you're interested in him, say so."

"Lily, your brother is awful. Truly awful."

"Yeah. They all say that to begin with. They like a guy who's hard to get."

"I was staring at him because —"

"Yeah?"

"I saw him in the basement. He was one of the ghosts. Or else it was a vision. I don't know."

"What?"

"After that night at the Brunswick ...," *when you deserted me*, Jay wanted to add but restrained herself, "... I went back to KAT House and painted and I saw the ghosts but for a split second, they weren't ghosts. They were Paul and Brad."

"That doesn't make any sense."

"I know."

"What were they doing?"

"That's not important." Jay realized that describing what she saw would involve an awkward explanation, so she decided to be discreet rather than valorous. "I just think you should stop seeing Brad."

"Why?"

"He's not for you."

Lily found Jay's evasiveness extremely annoying. "Why not?" she demanded.

"Well, the ghosts —"

"They're ghosts of people who aren't dead."

"Yeah."

"Well then, they're not ghosts. They're hallucinations."

"Meaning?"

"You saw them. You made them up. I see things, too."

"You do?"

"Yeah. I see a little demon who tells me what to do. But he's not real. He's something I made up." Lily waited for the Demon's voice to intrude, but it was silent. She wondered if getting rid of a demon was as simple as declaring that it wasn't real.

Jay hated it when people made fun of her. It had been a long, trying afternoon. She was glad that she hadn't told Lily everything.

It would have simply given her something else to tease her about. As Jay turned to go, her attention was caught by a beautiful antique shawl draped over one of the chairs. It was a delicate shade of pink silk, with pale embroidered flowers all over it. She swooped it up and put it on. "Where did you get this?" she asked excitedly.

"It's my grandmother's."

Jay gasped, "My grandmother has a shawl just like this!" Lily and Jay paused to reflect on the significance of such a coincidence.

"Wow," Lily said softly.

"Yeah. Hers was white ... Well, it was more like a yellow. It was old and sort of dirty. It had a long fringe just like this one. We didn't know how to clean it without wrecking the fringe. Yours is beautiful. It's pink. I love pink! You must wear it all the time."

"Not really. 'Cause of my hair." Pink was a colour that girls with red hair were warned never to wear. Jay was pleased that her hair wasn't red.

"I went to a costume party where you dressed up as somebody famous. I went as Isadora Duncan," said Jay with some satisfaction. "Do you remember the movie?"

"Oh yeah!"

"Well, that's how I found out about her but I found a reprint of one of her old dance books so I learned the dances. I'll show you." Jay danced around the room, performing a few postures. "Your shawl is just perfect. My grandmother's shawl is too large." She put the scarf back onto the chair and gazed at it longingly.

"Would you like it?" Lily asked.

Jay's heart raced with excitement. "But it's your grandmother's."

"Not anymore. She's dead."

"Still, it's an antique. It's precious."

"Not to me," said Lily.

"Maybe we could trade. I could give you my grandmother's shawl. It's the right colour for you, so you could wear it." Even as Jay made this feeble promise, she knew it was an unlikely event. Though elderly and unlikely to dance à la Isadora Duncan, her grandmother was still

alive and would object strenuously to her shawl being given away
to a total stranger. There would be no slipping a shawl of such mag-
nitude past her. Jay's grandmother was normally very gracious, but
in the matter of family treasures, she was ferocious.

"You take it." Lily thrust the shawl into Jay's hands.

Jay knew she was taking advantage of Lily's guilt over being so
cold to her earlier. She should have refused the gift, but she couldn't.
She grasped the shawl closely to her and hugged Lily in the raptures
of ecstasy that girls that age are prone to. "Oh, Lily, thank you,
thank you so much. It's so beautiful! Thank you!"

"You'll have to wear it to a party and dance in it."

"Oh yes, I will!" she said, excitedly, though she doubted that she
would wear it to any art school parties, as they were not suitable
places to take precious items like antique shawls, but she would wear
it soon.

Jay and Lily tacitly agreed that Lily's generous gift should be kept
secret from Mrs. MacFarlane and Rose. Had Lily openly discussed
the details for smuggling the shawl out of the house, Jay might have
felt some remorse and given it back. But Lily quietly rolled it into a
ball and stuffed it into a plastic bag so that it looked for all the world
like Jay's wet bathing suit. "You should go now," Lily said.

"Aren't you coming too?" Lily's moments of ecstatic delight
were far too swift for Jay.

"No. I have to stay here for a while. I'll drive you to the subway."

Jay made her goodbyes, feeling only vaguely guilty about the
additional round sack dangling from her arm. Under the harsh
fluorescent light of the subway, Jay stole little peeks inside the bag,
the shawl safely nestled there like a large silken egg. If the shawl had
been in Jay's pocket, the shame of the transaction would have burned
a hole through the lining, but as it was encased in plastic, Jay felt
nothing but glee at having procured such a treasure so easily.

chapter nineteen

THE CONTRACT

BRAD WAS LOADING the car in preparation for the jump. He almost leaped out of his skin when he saw Lily. She was so far removed from his thoughts that he'd forgotten about her. Yet here she was, a boomerang that just kept coming back, placing itself in his hand, ready for the next toss.

Lily leaned against Brad's Volkswagen and desperately tried to smile nonchalantly. "Surprised to see me?"

"Ah, no ... well, yes. Look, I'm sorry. I just need some time to myself for a while."

"It's okay, Brad. I know it's over." Brad glanced nervously at Paul, who was hurrying towards the car. Paul saw Lily but this time, he didn't look angry about her being there. "But it's too late to get my money back and I'd like to finish the course."

"Oh ... Yeah."

"Besides, I like it."

"You do?"

"Yes. I love it. How many more jumps do we have?"

"Till the end of the summer."

"How appropriate. My summer jumps."

"You're joining us, sis?"

"Yes, Paul, rumours of my death have been greatly exaggerated. I believe it's your turn to sit in the back."

"With pleasure, dear sister. I like being behind."

Brad snorted out loud. Lily looked at Paul suspiciously. "What's got into you? You're being nice."

"Aren't I always nice?"

"You were mean to my friend."

"She was an idiot. Brad and I are celebrating. Aren't we, Brad?" Brad blushed a deep crimson and he started to choke. "We're celebrating the end of an era," continued Paul. "The Susan Lipton regime is now over. Brad finally got rid of that bloodsucking bimbo."

"Last week you said that Brad should marry her."

"I said he would. I didn't say he should."

"Didn't you like Susan?" Lily was surprised that she and Paul might actually have agreed on something.

"Couldn't stand her."

"You didn't know her, Paul. You liked her, didn't you, Lily?"

"No, but that's because I knew her."

The highway swallowed up any further attempts at conversation.

LILY TRIED TO stop the uncontrollable shaking that had overtaken her as she stepped up for the jump. Brad and Paul had already gone. She was glad they weren't there to witness her weakness. She approached the open door of the plane and was preparing to exit when Flash grabbed her harshly and pulled her back. "Your static line!" he shouted. She looked down and saw that, in her preoccupation, she had allowed the line's slack to fall out of her hand. The plane made another round while Flash checked it. Satisfied that everything was in its place, Flash guided Lily to the door. At the "go" signal, she jumped, arched her back, looked up at Flash and shouted the count for the descent. She pulled the rip cord and checked the canopy, making certain that it had opened correctly.

Once again, Lily fell into a gentle embrace with the sky. She surrendered to a pure moment of joy and lost it in an instant when the snide familiar voice broke in. "It's a bit of a rush, isn't it?" Lily looked quickly about to catch a glimpse of it. "Concentrate, you idiot! Concentrate on what you're doing."

Lily gasped.

"Relax. The air is good here. Thoughts carry well."

"Go away!"

"Can't do that. Besides, you don't want me to leave. I make you feel good. Like now. You feel good now, don't you?"

Lily said nothing.

"You should trust me more. I could get Brad for you. You want him, don't you?" Bubula knew that if he got Lily to ask for his help, then he would have a secure foothold. As long as she was an unwilling host, his powers were severely curtailed. "I'll help you get Brad," Bubula said with as much earnestness as he could muster.

"How will you do that?"

"I could tell you what he's thinking. Wouldn't you like to know?"

"Yes," said Lily, reluctantly.

"Do you want my help, then?"

"Yes," said Lily.

"Sometimes, though, it's not a good idea to know what people are thinking. Sometimes it messes you up," Bubula felt he should warn her. That way, she wouldn't blame him and have him exorcised. Exorcisms were very rare but Bubula liked to cover himself. "Do you think you can handle it?"

"Yes."

"So, you want him?"

"Yes."

The third and final "yes" constituted a contract. Bubula was beside himself with delight, until he happened to glance down. "HOLY SHIT! WE'RE LAAAAANDING!"

Luckily, Lily had been keeping careful track of her whereabouts. The worst had happened. The creature had not only reappeared but had spoken to her. What was once an anonymous inner voice was now a confirmed external entity. She was losing her mind. There was nothing she could do about it so she concentrated on the task at hand. Her heart and mind were racing in tandem, waves of panic rising up and ebbing away as she calmly located the drop zone, the windsock, worked out the air currents and guided herself down.

⌐

AFTER THE JUMP, when Lily went out for drinks with the boys, she tested the Demon out.

"What's Brad thinking about now?" she asked him.

"Sex," Bubula replied.

"So, he still wants me."

Bubula was silent.

"He doesn't want me?" Lily persisted. "If he doesn't want me, why is he thinking about sex?"

"He's not thinking about sex anymore. Now he's thinking about his hamburger. He thinks they overcooked it."

"When he was thinking about sex, was he thinking about me?"

"You might not be aware of this but young men think of sex every eight seconds."

"Really?"

"Yes. It's a scientific fact."

"Does Brad wish we were together?"

"Stop pestering me. If he thinks something interesting, I'll tell you."

"You lied to me."

"Here's the truth, then. It's all over between you and Brad. He doesn't want you anymore. Cut your losses. He's not worth the trouble."

"Are you all right, Lily?" Brad looked at her intently.

"S-sorry." Lily stammered and turned pale.

And Bubula was free of her questions and could daydream for a little while.

chapter twenty

THE MOMENT OF TRUTH

JAY WAITED UP for Lily on Sunday night. The skydiving class was over hours ago but Lily hadn't returned. Jay couldn't shake the feeling that Lily was angry with her. She had hidden the shawl in her cupboard because she didn't want the other girls to see it, but now she reached in and took it out. It was so beautiful. She stroked it and rubbed it against her cheek. Just at that moment, Lily hurried past her door. Their eyes met briefly. Jay blushed, feeling she'd been caught in some obscene act. She was about to run after Lily when Kathleen stopped her.

"Wow! Where'd you get that?!"

Jay looked down at the shawl in embarrassment. "Oh, um, Lily gave it to me."

"Lily gave this to you?!" Kathleen fingered one of its embroidered roses.

"Yes."

"I see. On loan."

"No. To keep."

Kathleen looked at Jay in frank disbelief: a remarkable impersonation of Mrs. MacFarlane's icy gaze, which prompted Jay to wonder
if there was a series of Kappa Alpha Theta facial expressions that
they all learned. And she realized that she was being judged by Kathleen — that she had been being judged all along. She had been so
busy judging the sorority sisters by Nicholas's lofty socialist standards
that it had never occurred to her that they had judged her, in turn.

"You can ask Lily if you don't believe me. I'm tired now and I'd
like to go to sleep." Jay spread the shawl flagrantly across her bed.
Kathleen withdrew. Jay closed the door firmly behind her.

She didn't see Lily for the rest of the week but she was too preoccupied to worry about it. Art classes were finishing. The term ended
in early August to give the instructors time to recuperate before they
faced the serious fall-term students. Jay was ashamed of her paintings.
She thought it would be easy to paint like an abstract expressionist
and was surprised to discover that it wasn't easy at all. She couldn't
convey any joy in the freedom of expression. She was puzzled by this
because she didn't think of herself as an unhappy person. Her paintings were usually serene and somewhat austere, but this summer,
even her realistic work was bad. It was strange to be robbed of her
talent. Jay wondered if the ghosts had affected her work.

She waited fretfully for the inevitable announcement that the
instructors would be looking at the students' work. The days passed.
The week was over and it never came. The instructors simply assumed
that no one other than Jonathan had paintings to show them. They
weren't particularly interested in examining students' work, anyway. They saw no point in it. The chances were one in a hundred
that any one of them would actually be an artist. And the one
who was an artist didn't need them to encourage him. So, Jay was
mercifully spared this final indignity.

There was an artists' get-together and quasi end-of-term party that
Friday night. There weren't enough students to call for a full-fledged
celebration but the artist instructors liked to party, so they decided
to throw a jam session in the Coffin Factory. It was an old ware-

house in an obscure part of town where the art students had cheap studios. It had no actual street address. The area was so unprepos-sessing that no one had bothered to name the streets.

Jay decided that it was too much trouble to take the subway and bus out to this remote area of town. She had just settled in for a quiet evening at KAT House when the phone rang. As this was a Friday, all the girls had gone out on dates and answering machines had not yet been invented, so it was with ill humour that Jay took herself out of her comfortable perch in the big easy chair in KAT House's sitting room, walked the length of the corridor to the kitchen and answered the phone.

"Girl? Is that you?" A familiar voice bellowed within a cacophony of shouts and music.

"Mr. Rossco?!" Jay was astonished. Mr. Rossco never called her himself. He usually appointed some emissary.

"There's a party happening, Girl, and I don't see you here."

"I'm not really feeling well."

"Girl —"

"Yes, Mr. Rossco?"

"Call me Bill and don't lie to me, Girl. I hate it when people lie to me."

"Oh."

"Here's what I want you to do. Put on your prettiest dress. One that you like. Pay no attention to what Rufus tells you to wear. He has no taste. Put on your favourite dress. And Girl, here's the important part: high heels. Wear your high heels. And don't say you don't have any, Girl, 'cause I know you do."

"Mr. ... um ... Bill, where exactly is this Coffin Factory?"

There was a long pause, followed by a sigh. "Oooh. Shit. It's in some godforsaken shithole. 'Scuse my French, Girl, but what's the world coming to when an artist can't find a decent studio anymore? Greed and real estate, Girl. They're going to destroy this city. It'll be as bad as New York. Just you wait. 'Scuse me for a sec. HEY MAN! YEAH! YOU!" Jay heard Mr. Rossco's bellow fade into the noise of the party. There was a slight scuffle as someone else tried to use the phone on Mr. Rossco's end. "You still there, Girl?"

"Yes."

"Rufus will escort you there personally. He'll be there in fifteen."

"Fifteen minutes," Jay gasped, looking critically down at her tatty dressing gown and fluffy bunny slippers. The phone clicked off and Mr. Rossco was gone.

Jay ran upstairs. Selecting a dress usually took fifteen minutes in itself but Jay had no time for indecision. The antique shawl lay draped across her chair, prize booty awaiting display. She threw on her 1920s dress that Rufus had mocked, her high-heeled shoes, tossed the shawl over her shoulder and looked, she thought, very elegant; too good for this sort of party but the dress made her feel special. When Rufus arrived to fetch her, Jay fixed him with a steely look so he would not comment on her outfit. Instead, he looked worried and strangely shy.

"Wow. You look really beautiful."

"Thanks."

Rufus and Jay got into the back of the cab and they rode off in silence.

"Thanks for coming and picking me up. Sorry you had to leave the party."

"It's okay. Just call me Igor."

"Igor?"

"Jah. I fetch the bodies." Jay looked at him blankly. "Frankenstein."

"Pardon?"

"I guess you never saw those movies."

"No."

"The allusion is lost on you, then." Rufus laughed bitterly. "Well, you did what you were told so far. How obedient do you plan to be tonight?"

"Is there a crime in getting dressed up and looking nice?"

"No. No crime in that. Look, I like Rossco. He's a great guy but he's not for you."

"You're sure about that?'

"Yes, I am. And if I showed at a gallery and made enough money to take cabs everywhere, then I think you'd be a lot more interested in me."

Jay flushed in annoyance at the truth of Rufus's statement. "I admire Mr. Rossco. I admire anyone who's smart and funny and ambitious and makes a life for himself." In actual fact, Jay liked Mr. Rossco because he was kind but she didn't think Rufus would believe her.

"And he flatters you senseless."

"It's true. Mr. Rossco is very attentive."

"Attentive?! Makes me wanna puke. All that mushy stuff he bilges out about you. He's gassed out of his mind half the time and you call that attentive!"

"Drunken flattery is a lot more warming than sober abuse."

"Whoa! What book have you been reading!" Rufus tossed his head from side to side and spoke in a high-pitched parody of Jay's voice. "'Drunken flattery' is a lot more warming than 'sober abuse'! What time period do you live in, with your old clothes and your freaky little homilies? That's what's so irritating about you. You're so out of it!"

"You're mean and you're a cheapskate. And I wouldn't go out with you if you were the most famous artist in the world and had gobs and gobs of money. 'Cause you know what? Even with all that money, you'd still be mean and you'd still be a cheapskate!"

The cab arrived spectacularly on cue, so Jay could get out and slam the door in his face. Her cheeks were flushed with the perfection of the moment. She rarely got angry but she had to admit that when she blew her top, nothing was more satisfying. Jay had a slight moment's pause when she looked up at the gigantic warehouse and realized that she did not have a clue where the party was, but finding it should be a fairly simple matter of listening for the noise and heading for it.

Rufus paid the driver and gazed after Jay with a burgeoning sense of awe. Like most men who are unable to sweet talk a woman, Rufus had a strong masochistic streak. His barbs were designed to provoke a reaction and when Jay finally responded in kind, his passion rose. Rufus had always sensed she had a cruel tongue lurking underneath that placid countenance. He ran after her to capitalize on what he hoped would be a hate-love-argument-in-the-rain moment, for Rufus lived too much in the world of cinema. He should have realized that if Jay didn't get his Frankenstein reference, she would hardly pick up her cues for the next sequence.

It wasn't raining, but Rufus plunged ahead. He grabbed Jay by the hand and spun her around. He drew her to him and kissed her hard on the lips. Jay was supposed to pull away, look at him with pure hatred, say, "Bastard!" or "Damn you!" and then kiss him back with total abandon. She was supposed to thrill Rufus with the ferocity of her passion. Jay played along up to a point. She drew away and looked at him with disgust, but instead of abandoning herself to the moment, she kicked him hard in the ankle and fled.

It was a rude awakening to a cinematic fantasy. And it hurt. Rufus hopped up and down, contorted in pain, amazed that something so simple should hurt so much. Her high heel delivered the blow with canny accuracy. He stumbled after her and saw that she was going in the wrong door. He could still salvage the situation, at least appear to have brought Jay there, unmolested. He hobbled off directly to the party and lurked by the door, waiting for her. She gave a small gasp when she saw him. She tried to brush past, but he stopped her.

"Don't you dare touch me!" she hissed with a quiet fury.

"I'm sorry. I won't do it again, I promise." Rufus couldn't stop himself from adding, "I thought you wanted it."

"Wanted it? I just told you off!"

"I thought it was foreplay."

Jay froze in her tracks at the word *foreplay*. She had no idea that it was so easy to completely misunderstand someone.

"Please, let me take you in. We'll pretend none of this happened. I'll do what I'm supposed to do and you'll do what you're supposed to do."

"And what is that, exactly?" asked Jay, concerned that she might be heading into another monumental misunderstanding.

"Isn't it obvious? The sultan needs another woman for his harem," said Rufus, as he guided her through the door with his hand.

"You said something like that the last time and it's just non-sense," stammered Jay, somewhat shaken.

"You ran away the last time. And he was too drunk to catch you. He's not too drunk, now."

Jay caught sight of Mr. Rossco's expectant face as he looked up from fiddling with his saxophone — the serene, smug face of a tom-cat who was getting his cream delivered to him.

"She's all yours now," Rufus said as he deposited Jay in front of Rossco.

Rossco saw the frank look of alarm cross Jay's face. "Hi, Girl," he said, casually, "Glad you could make it."

"Um ... yes." Jay looked nervously away in an affectation of shy-ness. She was actually trying to see who else was at the party — in particular, Snafu Smith. She knew it was hopeless but habit prevailed on her to look. He was in the corner, talking to an older woman. He didn't appear to be flirting with her but they were far away so Jay couldn't tell for sure.

"And thanks for dressing up." The Girl's strange apparel told him more than he wanted to know. Though her dress wasn't exactly a costume, it gave off an aura of the 1920s, but a slightly bookish one, as though the sensibility had been refined down to one book, *The Great Gatsby*, and one heroine, Daisy Buchanan. The Girl's face took on the delicacy of the era and she moved with a peculiar grace. Most of the young women Rossco knew, if they decided to wear clothes from another era, usually wore something old, tired and dirty, as if the outfit were a spoof on the era and themselves. Rossco's last mistress, Lena, once wore a 1950s prom dress with bright pink ankle-high sneakers. It was a fetching outfit, though Rossco yearned for high heels. Jay's dress was, like herself, clean and spanking new. Rossco realized that she was a girl who took certain things in life very seriously. A beautiful old shawl was draped around her shoulders. There was serious intent in that shawl, as well. She was dressed for an occasion yet there was a glumness about her that made Rossco feel she was attired for some distasteful but inevitable task.

Sacrificial virgin — the words leapt into his head. Rossco immediately fell into a panic. He cursed himself for not having seen it before. Her shyness, her diffidence — it all added up. That wicked look she got in her eye from time to time completely blinded him to this obvious liability. It had been a long time since Rossco had encountered a virgin. Very few virgins made it through the doors of the Artists School. Most girls who wanted to be artists had the virginity knocked out of them a long time ago. Occasionally, nice, polite, virginal, middle-class girls enrolled in the Artists School but they always dropped out after the first week. Marco Shiner's frequent use of expletives, applied to simple transactions, ("Would someone get me a fucking coffee?") usually sent them packing. They quickly scurried off to the nearest art college or university, where they could get a diploma saying that they'd done something, and failing that, they could meet a nice boy who'd provide for them. The Artists School gave out no diplomas or certificates. It was strictly for people who wanted to be artists. Imperious Girl didn't seem to mind the bad language or the rough trade. Her composure had fooled Rossco.

With virgins, presentation was everything. Rossco accepted the fact that young women weren't likely to be physically attracted to him — not as they were, in the old days when he had a physique — but he was amazed at how far he could get on charm. Seasoned girls were more than willing to take Rossco on because he was interesting and wanted to please them. So, they could overlook his physical shortcomings. But virgins were another matter. A virgin had to be able to look at you and want what she saw. Rossco knew that Imperious Girl did not desire him.

Rossco remembered Anne, the virgin who'd surprised Shiner. That was an ugly story. The girl looked and acted like a hippie so Shiner was totally astonished when he got down to the deed and she screamed blue murder. She had been brought up in a devout Christian household where men married the girls they deflowered. Having surrendered her virginity, the girl assumed that she and Shiner were betrothed. Shiner, of course, knew nothing of her background and her beliefs. The girl was stunningly beautiful and he was smitten and so, naturally, he asked her to move in with him. She mentioned marriage and Marco said sure, in his casual way, thinking she was making a joke. She had enormous doe eyes. Marco swore he'd never get tired of gazing into them. She wasn't the brightest of creatures but Shiner thought he could live without wit. Sharp-tongued women inevitably focused their critical attention on his defects and that got to be tiresome. Anne adored him. Rossco thought that there was something sinister about her undivided attention. She seemed too focused on Shiner. Up to that point, Marco Shiner had never considered that there could be anything wrong with having a lovely nymph attending to his every whim. He spent six pleasant months basking in her adoration.

Then the boom fell. It all happened at once. For about two weeks, a feisty girl, one of the new students, started arguing with him every lunch hour at the Brunswick. She wasn't particularly good-looking, but her mind was sharp. Shiner didn't realize how much he missed intelligent conversation. It made him feel sexy again. He had been feeling rather too contented lately. There was something deliciously provocative about the way that wiry little girl made her points. Anne usually avoided the Oblong Table discussions, but she must have gotten wind of something. She knew that Marco's roving body would eventually follow his roving brain so she turned up unexpectedly, one afternoon, when Marco and the feisty girl were engaged in one of their heated discussions. Anne announced in a loud voice that Shiner was to cease his discussion and go home with her right that minute. Well, no girl ordered Shiner about. He was bored with Anne anyway, and was looking for an out, so, not only did he continue his argument with the feisty girl but they took it out the door and back to her place. Shiner was confident that his flagrant infidelity would drive Anne away. She would pack up her stuff, slink mercifully out of his life and he would come home to a blissfully empty studio. Instead, she went stark raving mad, which was a complete surprise for Shiner.

Anne followed Shiner and the feisty girl back to her place. She lurked outside and peeped through the windows. The feisty girl's bedroom was once the dining room of an old house. It was on the main floor and had French doors leading out to a small patio. Anne made a quick trip to the hardware store, purchased a long, sharp knife and hurried back to the feisty girl's house. She positioned herself on the patio, tested the French door — it opened, so she didn't have to break the panes — and waited for the appropriate moment when Shiner was stark naked and about to put it to the feisty girl. Anne crashed through the doors, fully intending to plunge the knife into Shiner's back. But the feisty girl had terrific reflexes, and in the split second that she saw Anne, she shoved Shiner off to one side and rolled away. Anne fell, sobbing, onto the bed, stabbing at it savagely. Shiner grabbed the knife and threw it across the room. He pulled Anne's arms behind her back. The feisty girl found a scarf and they tied her arms together. Anne was kicking and screaming to beat the band. When she tried to kick him in the balls, Shiner grabbed her foot and tipped her over. He tied her feet together and secured her to a chair, so she couldn't get at them. A torrent of obscenities poured out of Anne's mouth and she spat at him and the feisty girl.

Shiner was horrified to witness Anne's transformation from docile lamb to screaming polecat but what really astonished him was that, in the midst of all this activity, he still retained his erection. He saw the feisty girl eyeing it and smiling to herself. Marco felt he might as well finish what he started. Anne's shrieks of outrage acted as an aphrodisiac. Marco was angry, too. The girl had just tried to kill him. He saw no need to spare her feelings. He and the feisty girl acted as if she weren't there and continued about their business. When they were spent, they called the police and told them what happened, more or less. Anne lay crumpled in a ball in the corner. Her obscenities had long since subsided into strange droning whimpers. She was a pitiful sight but the police saw the knife and the slashes in the mattress so they took her away, first to the police station and later, to the nuthouse.

Marco maintained that he never felt the slightest remorse about the incident. Once, the girl escaped from the nuthouse. She turned up one evening when the school had night courses. She wore a long, white nightgown. She slipped past reception. Rossco found her dancing like a mad ballerina up and down the length of the room where Shiner taught. Rossco watched her for a long time. She finally became aware of him and stopped her dance.

"Anne."

"It's my parent's fault," she said. "If I was brought up to expect that sort of thing, I'd be fine now."

"Maybe you should go back home. See your parents."

"I guess I should go back to the hospital," Anne replied in a sad, wispy voice. I'm getting those bad thoughts again."

She allowed Rossco to lead her down the stairs and she waited meekly in the reception area while he called the hospital.

Imperious Girl didn't have doe eyes and she didn't speak in a wispy voice, but that dress was giving him the heebee-jeebies. What if she turned out to be mentally unstable? Virgins were bad enough but crazy virgins were the worst. Rossco decided to release this girl into the wilderness of the party. Let her fend for herself. If she got caught in a trap, it wasn't his responsibility.

"You look great, Girl. Really great!"

"Thanks!" She blushed with pleasure. Her timid uncertainty changed into a confident air and she suddenly looked quite different. Radiant. Rossco felt some regret as he said, "Girl, I've gotta play

tonight so I can't socialize with you but you know most of the people here. There's Rufus, of course." A frown crossed the Girl's face.
The Girl and Rufus must have had a fight. Rufus would normally
have been hovering about but Rossco saw he was at the far end of
the room, flirting with the Hippie Chick. "Ah, and there's people
from your class and the other classes. Some of the artists who teach
in the fall are here." Rossco was at a loss as to the best means of
disposing of the Girl. He'd gone to all this trouble to bring her here.
It seemed strange to suddenly drop her. The big problem was in
determining who might rush in to take up the slack. Shiner had kept
his distance, knowing that Rossco had a prior claim. If he backed
off, Shiner might move in and he'd be right back to feeling morally
responsible.

Then, Rossco saw the solution to this dilemma, wandering past
in the personage of Charles Cafferty, or Chuckles, as he was affec-
tionately known for his hallucinogenic giggle. At one point, Charles
had experimented fairly heavily with mescaline and LSD. He came
out of it with a slightly crazed look in his eye and an infectious
gurgling laugh that accompanied everything he said. The world
suddenly seemed very amusing to Chuckles and remained so for
the rest of his life. Rossco wondered how his wife could stand it.
Much to his own chagrin, Chuckles was a faithful husband. He
wanted to be like Snafu and Shiner but didn't have the nerve, so he
usually wandered around, looking agog, like a kid in a candy store
who wants to buy all the different coloured gumballs but only has
a penny. Shiner couldn't stand Chuckles, so if Imperious Girl hung
around him, Shiner would keep his distance. All in all, it was a perfect
solution, a nice, safe berth to put the Girl in.

"Hey Chuckles!"

Chuckles spun his head around, delighted that he was in demand.

"I'd like you to meet someone." Upon seeing the Girl, Chuckles
hurried over. For a horrible moment, Rossco couldn't remember the
Girl's name. He stabbed at his brain for clues. It was an initial —

like *The Story of O* — and it stood for ... J. "J, this is Charles
Cafferty. He's one of the artists here. He's teaching in the fall."

"Well, hi there, Jay!" Charles's face broke out into a huge grin.
Jay liked him immediately. He was warm and friendly. He didn't have
the cynical stand-offish attitude that the other artists had. Mr. Rossco
asked Mr. Cafferty to take her to the bar and get her something to
drink. Jay was so comfortable with Mr. Cafferty that she could even
tell him that she didn't like beer.

"That's okay, Jay. You don't have to drink beer."

"Usually, that's all they have. Anyway, I don't drink."

"Nothing at all?"

"No." Mr. Cafferty looked so disappointed that Jay relented.
"Well, I like wine."

"White wine, I bet."

"Yes. That would be nice."

Mr. Cafferty brought her back a large tumblerful of white wine and
they had a nice, long chat. Mr. Cafferty was extremely animated,
almost uncomfortably so. He waved his arms about and did peculiar things with his fingers to illustrate his points. He also had the
bizarre laugh that accompanied everything he said, sounding like
the cartoon mouse Speedy Gonzales. With his poncho, heavy sandals
and scruffy jeans, his grizzled beard and gnarled, sun-baked face, Jay
could picture Mr. Cafferty wandering around some Mexican desert.
She asked him if he'd ever been to Mexico and that opened up a
floodgate of enthusiasm in Mr. Cafferty.

"Mexico! Oh yeah. You bet I've been to Mexico. Did mescal and
peyote." He described his drug-taking as if it were a cultural event
like seeing the pyramids — or rather, as if drugs were all that were
worth seeing in Mexico. "I mean, Mexico! It's crazy. They're crazy.
You drink a bottle of tequila and you're gone. *Under the Volcano*. You
read that? Gotta read it. Mexico is so crazy that Luis Buñuel thinks
it's crazy? Mr. Cafferty broke out into a round of unsuppressed
giggling. His eyes popped out of his head and his arms flapped up

and down. "Luis Buñuel!" Jay tried to laugh enthusiastically but Mr. Cafferty was sensitive enough to see that she didn't have a clue what he was talking about.

"Luis Buñuel was one of the world's great surrealists. He was a friend of Dali's."

"Salvador Dali!" Jay replied in delight, "I love Dali!"

"Dali's crap, but that's not the point. Buñuel's a genius."

"He's a painter?" Jay was puzzled that she hadn't heard of him.

"Filmmaker. Le Chien d'andelou."

"Oh. I saw that film. The one where the eyeball gets sliced."

"Yeah."

"It was really weird."

"Yeah. He's done weirder. Anyway, the world's el primo surrealist goes to Mexico and he can't handle it 'cause it's too crazy for him."

"Wow, that's something." Jay waited for Mr. Cafferty to stop giggling before asking, "In what way was it crazy?"

"Huh?"

"Why did Buñuel think they were crazy?"

Mr. Cafferty looked discomfited. Jay noticed that people always seemed to dislike it when you got down to specifics. "Oh, well," he said, "it was mainly the newspapers that freaked him out."

"Newspapers?"

"Yeah. Local stories and how they were reported. Okay, here's one. Buñuel read this in the paper. A guy is trying to find his ... Actually, I can't remember who he's trying to find.... Someone. He goes to the last address that the person gave him, an apartment building, knocks on the door. This guy answers. It's not his friend. So, he asks the guy if he knows where his friend is. The guy says 'Sorry, don't know. Try next door.' It's an apartment complex. It's got two sides. So, he goes next door and the woman who answers says 'Oh yeah, I know your friend. He lives at ...,' and she gives him the address of the apartment he'd just been to. So, he goes back to that place and he knocks on the door and says, 'Hey, the woman next door says my friend does live in this building, in fact, in this apartment. Are you sure he didn't live here before you moved in? He might have left a forwarding address.' The man who lives in the apartment stares at the guy, then he smiles and says, 'Excuse me.' He pulls out a gun and shoots the guy dead."

"Oh my!"

"That's not the odd part. The headline read, TOO MANY QUESTIONS! The newspaper took the side of the killer. It was an article all about how infuriating nosy people can be and the guy deserved to die because he asked so many questions."

"Surely the court didn't —"

"Court?!" Mr. Cafferty roared with laughter. "It never went to court. The guy wasn't even charged with anything. I never read the papers when I was in Mexico."

"I guess not." ·

"I spent most of my time in the desert. Chewing peyote buttons. Man, the visions you get on peyote. I'd come to these extraordinary realizations about myself. And that's all it was — stuff about myself. I couldn't put it into practice."

"It?"

"The stuff I found out. But I couldn't stop. It was the best time of my life. Then Martha came and got me."

"Martha?"

"My wife. She's a great lady. She had a dream that I was about to lose my mind so she hightailed it out there and dragged me away. I was really mad at her at the time, but she was right." Mr. Cafferty locked his face into a sober, serious expression, as if willing it to stay still, as if it was his only means of indicating to Jay that he meant what he said. Jay could see it was a strain for him.

"So, she fixed me up till I was good as new." Then, the laughter gushed out, geyser-like, and Mr. Cafferty surrendered to another bout of giggling. His sad eyes looked out at Jay as his mouth chortled merrily away.

Jay smiled politely and scanned the room. Snafu was talking to

Susannah now. Susannah had a coterie of men around her: Rufus, Snafu and the man from the Brunswick's Library.

"Is that one of your friends?" asked Mr. Cafferty suddenly. Jay realized with some embarrassment that she must have been staring at Susannah and the man for some time.

"Um ... she's in my class." The man from the Library turned and looked at her.

"You know the guy she's with?"

"Not very well." As Jay said this, the man excused himself from Susannah and walked towards Jay.

"He seems to know you," burbled Mr. Cafferty. "Oooh, here comes trouble."

"Why is he trouble?" Jay turned to ask Mr. Cafferty, but he had disappeared into the crowd.

"Jay Wright," the man said.

Jay blushed, because she did not remember the man's name.

"I'm a little drunk, which is why I can do this."

"Do what?"

"I've fallen in love with you. There! I've said it. Now I'll leave you alone." He made a move as if to go, but Jay could see he had no intention of leaving.

She hated to break the spell but the practical side of her prevailed. "You're in love with a lot of people."

He looked puzzled.

"Me and Susannah and your fiancée."

"Susannah? I was never in love with Susannah."

"But you are —"

"Not now. We're just friends. I ended it a long time ago. That afternoon, actually." He looked at Jay with a seriousness of purpose that was irresistible. "I think if I were to be around you more, I could become the sort of person I want to be."

Jay felt her heart turn over, a delightful flutter mingled with apprehension. "And your fiancée?" she forced herself to ask.

"I've known her for years. We have all this history between us."

"Is that good?"

"Oh yeah. It binds you. But it makes it hard to decide."

"Maybe you shouldn't decide."

"Maybe I shouldn't. I'd only mess you up. And I would hate to do that." He leaned over and gently pushed Jay's hair away from her face. "You're really lovely. Stay that way, all right?" He leaned in to kiss her, but suddenly thought better of it. "A drink — a glass of wine?"

Jay was feeling light-headed. She wasn't sure whether it was all this sudden attention or the large beaker of wine that Mr. Cafferty had brought her. "I ... ah ... probably shouldn't," she tried to say but the man nodded, as if in agreement.

"Back in a flash," he said and quickly left her. Jay's heart and mind were in turmoil. On one hand, she felt as if she were falling in love with this man; on the other, she wanted to exercise her new-found allure and flirt with every man in the room. She felt like Cinderella at the ball. She only had a short time before her mysterious powers would turn to ashes. She wondered if Lily's shawl had magical properties. She was attracting men to her like a magnet. She had never experienced anything like this before in her life. Mr. Cafferty and Rufus were standing a short distance away. She caught them glancing over at her. Rufus shuffled over, closely followed by Mr. Cafferty.

"We're here to protect you," laughed Mr. Cafferty.

Rufus whispered in Jay's ear. "I'm sorry about being so rude about that dress. You look stunning."

"Well, thank you. It's about time you said something nice."

"Yeah. You know, you're kind of intimidating in it. Even Rossco's laid off. Did you shut him down?"

"No, he just seems to be busy, which is fine by me."

"I bet it's fine by you. You've got enough guys after you."

"Really?

"Don't be such a bullshitter. You better watch out — Robert's tricky."

"Robert? That's his name?"

"You looked like you were going to run off with him and you don't even know his name!" cried Rufus in disgust.

"If he doesn't tell me his name, how am I going to know it?"

"Christ, I don't believe women sometimes."

"He's interesting."

"Interesting. Yeah, right. He's back."

Robert handed Jay another large glass of wine and whispered sweet flatteries in the ear that was not occupied by Rufus.

⌒

IT WAS THE witching hour, the time of the night when Snafu surveyed the party's available women and decided who he'd take home. He had to pick the right time because if he went in too early, he'd run out of steam and the chick would move on to fresher pastures. But if he waited too long, then it was pretty obvious why he was there and the chick got offended. It had to appear as if they had just discovered each other at the exact, perfect time, an hour before the party wound down. Jam sessions went on indefinitely so that left lots of room for error. Snafu noticed that the more attractive women arrived an hour or two after the party started. The really skanky chicks showed up after midnight. One had to be desperate to settle for one of those. He'd taken one home once and got a bad case of crabs for his trouble.

Snafu gave a small sigh of satisfaction. "End of term and a full month of vacation before the next one starts." Snafu loved the tail end of summer. It was his favourite time of year, particularly if it was an Indian summer, hot days, with just a slight chill to keep one alert. He needed this vacation. This summer's group weren't as bad as he thought they'd be. He scanned the party for the Widow, but she was a no-show. He had unfinished business with her. She had stopped going to classes around mid-July. Duncan Schneider's "Painting in the Wilds" week-long camping trip must have done her in. Most students fled screaming from those camping trips.

Snafu reflected that he'd been remarkably restrained this summer. Susannah had kept him pretty occupied and there had been no point in pursuing Sheila. He'd tried to pry her away from that boring turd of a boyfriend, given it his best shot, but it was hopeless. That left the weird skinny girl but she was Rossco's. Not that he wanted her. She was attracting a lot of attention, which surprised him. Until Rossco got all inflamed about her, Snafu never even noticed her but since she ran screaming down Marco's stairs, he couldn't stop thinking about her.

She irritated him. He couldn't put his finger on it. Everything about her was irritating. He didn't like her ghostly, white skin or her jutting jaw or her skinny body (no tits) or her large, serious eyes. And just when he was ready to dismiss her as a featureless nobody, she would square up those broad shoulders, thrust her chin out at him and give him such a look that he didn't know what hit him. Most of the time, she was excessively polite. It was so fake, all that nicey nicey stuff. Snafu watched her pretending to be polite and accommodating but he noticed that she always got what she wanted and just the way she wanted it. Brahmin WASPs had a way about them. They assumed that everyone in the world was at their disposal, ready and willing to help them. It was simply a matter of asking politely. It was a school so yes, he was supposed to help her but he could see that answering her dumb questions was not enough. This girl wanted praise, and not only that but high praise. She wanted to be told she was a genius. He wouldn't even tell her she was good. She had a very high opinion of herself. He wasn't going to feed that inflated ego.

She had a little datebook that she would haul out when anyone asked her to do anything. He caught sight of it once and she had things marked down by the hour. "See so and so at two-thirty, so and so at three-thirty." Her life was jammed full of useless trivial appointments. How could they be other than trivial? She was too young to know any interesting people and make appointments with them. And she had the gall to think she was an artist. And what was she doing that was so important? She was only a kid. Whereas he — at the ripe age of thirty-three, a successful artist and teacher with two bad marriages under his belt, and a shitload of women willing to fuck him at any time — he didn't use a date book. The calendar on the inside of his Players package was good enough for him. When the cigarettes were smoked, he'd be on to the next set of plans. He wasn't so self-important that he needed things laid out by the hour. Where did that girl get off thinking she was so damned important?

Now, Susannah had a tough life. She ran away from home when she was thirteen, lived on the street for a couple of years, got knocked up when she was fifteen, and had to give the kid up for adoption. She quit the streets and joined a wacko religious cult. Then she ran away from them and lived on a hippie commune. Then she met Jonathan and decided to go to art school and be an artist. She had done a lot of living and the awful thing was that Snafu didn't find any of it interesting. Or rather, he didn't find Susannah very interesting. So, that was a bit of a mystery to him: with a life like that, why was she so boring? Susannah was nice enough, very accommodating in that, once the ice was broken between them, she was always ready and willing for a roll in the hay; happy, casual sex, just the way Snafu liked it. But he could take her and leave her and most of the time, he preferred to leave her.

Jay was thoroughly enjoying herself. School was over. She was never going to see these people again, so she could relax and say whatever silly thing came into her head. She'd had a fair amount to drink, so that loosened her tongue. She'd had a splendid time talking to Chuckles. Mr. Rossco had let her alone. So, she didn't even need to worry about a possible altercation with him. She and Rufus had made up. Robert kept circling around her. All in all, it was a perfect night. Right at the moment when Jay was congratulating herself on finally being a success at one of these soirees, Snafu Smith joined Jay's enchanted circle and glared at her as though he were really mad about something he couldn't put his finger on. Now that the term was over, she could admit it. He disliked her. His aloofness, his reticence, his lack of pursuit, were based on nothing more complicated than pure, simple dislike. Her bizarre premonition that they would have a love affair was simply a trick of the mind. Jay saw that clearly. Since there was to be no future with Snafu Smith, she didn't have to walk on eggshells, careful not to offend him. She could be rude right back. Jay could tell by the grim set of his mouth that Snafu was about to say something unsettling and sure enough, he did.

"Why aren't you with Rossco?" he snarled.

"Why should I be with Rossco?"

"He asked you here."

"It's my class. I've already been invited."

"He brought you here."

"Yes. That's true. He wanted me to show up. And I have. That's the beginning and end of the bargain."

Snafu glanced over at Rossco who was pleasantly occupied with a buxom beauty. "Hmmmph," Snafu muttered, then launched into a rant about economics, focusing his ire on the rich pigs who control Canada and their spoiled offspring.

Jay was fed up with socialists, communists, the entire left wing. She had listened to Nicholas too many times to be impressed. A month ago she would have pretended to be fascinated. She would have politely agreed with everything Snafu said. Tonight, she simply found him tedious. She was having such a nice time flirting with all these men and he had to come along and spoil it.

Snafu did have a fresh approach to the subject — at least, Jay had never encountered it before. When Nicholas went on a tirade, he always talked about the poor as some generalized mass of humanity. Snafu was more specific. He didn't refer to the poor. He called them the working class.

"And I'm working class. And proud of it. We say there's no class system here. That we're not like Britain. Well, that's bullshit. There's a class system — we just don't acknowledge it. If you're working class, you can't hobnob with the rich. You're in your place and you have to stay there."

"I don't think that's true," said Jay.

"Huh?"

"I think if you want something badly enough, you can go get it. There's nothing stopping you from socializing with the rich, if that's what you want to do."

Chuckles roared with laughter. "Hey, Snafu, is that what you always wanted to do? Join the Boulevard Club? Is that why you're so angry all the time? 'Cause you don't have a yacht?"

"Or a cottage," added Rufus.

"I don't want to fucking socialize with the rich!"

"Sorry," said Jay. "It sounded like you did."

"I worked hard for what I got in this life."

"And if you'd worked harder, you would have gotten more."

"Huh?"

"Well, I don't know. Who are the working class, anyway?"

"Oh, no one, really. Simply all those suckers who work their asses off so you can live the way you do."

"It's people who work, I take it."

"Yeah," Snafu sneered. "It's people who work."

"Well then, my father's working class."

"Bullshit your father's working class!"

"He fits your definition. He's one of those suckers who works his ass off so you can live the way you do."

"Huh?"

"Look at it this way. You're an artist. You live a pretty leisurely life. How many actual hours of work do you put in a day?"

"I put in my eight."

"Say I believe you — which I don't — but say I believe you. My father works all day. He comes home at six. He has dinner with us and then he goes upstairs and works some more. Till eleven or twelve. Every night. Sometimes, he works on the weekends, too. So, if it's about work, then my father's working class."

"What does he do?"

"He's a lawyer."

Howls of derision greeted this announcement.

"A lawyer?! Your father's the enemy."

"Back off, Snafu. Her father might work for Legal Aid," put in Chuckles gallantly.

"I'll lay bets he doesn't work for Legal Aid. Does he?" snarled Snafu.

The image of her father, who dressed meticulously in hand-tailored three-piece suits, English gabardine raincoats and formidably expensive shoes, looking like a scruffy Legal Aid lawyer almost made Jay burst out laughing. "He's a corporation lawyer," she stated boldly and added, putting the knife in, "and he specializes in tax law."

No one said anything in response. They sat and mulled it over for a time. Finally, Snafu broke the silence. "He must earn a bundle."

Jay took exception to Snafu's tone and said huffily, "I really wouldn't know."

It was the opening Snafu was looking for all night. "Wouldn't know, eh? You mean, you have no idea how much money your father earns a year?"

Jay realized that she'd made a huge tactical error. Judging by the looks of astonishment on Rufus, Chuckles and Robert's faces, it was clear that while it was a partial misdemeanour to not be working class, it was an unforgivable sin to not know, to the dime, how much one's father earned in a year.

"Spoiled little rich kid doesn't even know how much her father makes. And you, my dear, are a perfect illustration of what I'm talking about. The class system in this country. You can bet that a working-class kid knows how much his dad makes. He needs to know. Money means something to him. But to people like you, money means —"

Jay drew herself up haughtily and she used her "special" voice. This was a voice she used on her dog, Lucky. It was slightly louder than her usual voice, low and very clear. She said, "I know EXACTLY how much my father earns in a year and it is NONE OF YOUR BUSINESS."

Whenever Lucky heard this voice, he froze in his tracks. It had the exact same effect on Snafu. The actual words were simple and ineffectual, and an outright lie, but the tone held him spellbound. It struck a chord in him. He gazed at the girl in a puzzled stupor.

When Snafu set about to draw something, he could spend hours looking at the object. At a certain point in his meditation, the object would suddenly reveal itself to him. For the first hour, Snafu would be gazing at a tree as Snafu saw the tree. Then, suddenly, there'd be a shift and Snafu saw the tree as the tree sees itself. Snafu would become the tree, the building, the landscape, whatever it was he happened to be drawing. He wasn't always able to leave the boundaries of his own perceptions but transcendence was what he strived for. He wanted to lose himself. Jay's voice sent him tumbling from his protective ego perch and he fell and rolled into Jay's thoughts, surrendering himself to a strange communion of spirit. For the first time, he saw Jay as she was.

"Let's get out of here," Snafu said, looking intently at Jay and holding his hand out to her, across this small circle of gaping bystanders clustered round.

"All right," said Jay and she put her hand in his and they walked out. Jay vaguely remembered Robert's astonishment and Chuckles' laughing admonition to "Be careful," but it was as though she were in a waking dream and the dream took over.

As they walked outside in the cool night air, Jay felt herself sobering up. "What next?" she thought, with some apprehension. Jay lived in her imagination for most of her life. She had extravagant romantic fantasies that took place in the safe confines of her head. They left the party together in grand fashion, but to be suddenly deposited on the grey, drab streets of Toronto seemed an incongruous letdown. Jay liked to flirt. She loved the idea of a man being smitten with her, but she didn't necessarily want to get caught.

"Let's walk for a while," she suggested. The walk would give her time to collect her thoughts. She and Snafu could have a nice leisurely chat as they strolled the rather long distance to their respective houses.

Snafu must have read her mind, for he nodded as if in perfect agreement, then hailed the first cab that came along. "Don't you want to walk?" Jay asked in response.

"Of course. Walking's great. Get in," and Snafu ushered Jay into the cab and gave the driver his address before she knew what hit her. Jay thought that she could always get the cab to take her to KAT House, but she was desperately curious to see Snafu's home. She was on this adventure and she should see it through. Her longing for Snafu all summer had finally coalesced into this fork-in-the-road. Jay didn't make many momentous decisions but she could recognize one when it was upon her.

She knew as she entered Snafu's home that she was not going to be allowed to neck with him on the couch for an hour and then say "I'm going home now."

Snafu was nervous, though he hid it well. He was so practised at seducing women that the motions were second-nature to him. His body simply had to follow through on the course of action, but his mind ran amok. He had a towering headache that would not go away. He was sweating and his mouth was dry. He had no idea what prompted him to suddenly hold his hand out to the girl and take her away. And what was even more astonishing, she agreed to go, casually and effortlessly, as if she'd been in preparation for the event. She was having second thoughts now, but Snafu could see she was intrigued by his home.

Snafu was proud of his place. It was a work of art. He'd put time and energy into it. It was a perfect reflection of himself. He had no respect for those morons who live in squalor, waiting for a woman to tidy the place up and rescue them from themselves. The women Snafu knew weren't likely to rescue any man. Snafu wondered if women had fundamentally changed since he was a boy. His mother was a wonderful cook and she kept a beautiful home. His father was this evil asshole who beat them up and did everything in his power to turn her comfy little haven into a living hell. What was it about his life that kept attracting opposition? He loved his mother deeply and secretly hoped to find a woman like her but he kept falling for slovenly, bullheaded women. They gloried in the fact that they couldn't cook. They brandished the burnt pot roast with a vengeance, plunked it down on the table and expected him to eat it. Snafu tried to have a proper marriage, be a good husband, but clearly he wasn't cut out for it.

So now he had his own home. He could feel his mother's ghost within him, giving him small points of advice on decorating and cooking; encouraging him to buy more books, expand his learning, improve himself. Snafu had satisfied his mother's ambitions and fulfilled some of his own. He had grown from a scrawny kid who knew nothing into an educated, cultured man-of-the-world. He hadn't gone to university but he knew more and read more than those snot-nosed kids would in their entire lives.

Snafu offered the girl a drink. She asked for wine. He didn't have any, so he gave her a glass of sherry instead. Drinks were a formality, anyway. He took another beer and felt instantly queasy as he took his first swallow. The headache still wouldn't leave him. The girl sat in his big, leather swivel chair. She looked relieved, as if she'd found a nice, safe place to station herself, as if she could ignore the palpable aura of sex that filled the room. Snafu sat on his bed and lay against the headboard. The bed was quite a distance away from the chair, enough of a distance to make a person sitting in the chair feel foolish for choosing to be so far away. The girl tried to make small talk with him. He waited for her to flounder around for a while, then he smiled at her and patted the place beside him. She rose reluctantly and joined him. He was at a loss to understand her reticence. She had seemed quite cocky at the party. He kissed her. She responded shyly. They kissed for a time. He took his shirt off. She looked alarmed. He kissed her again. Then he undid her dress.

Snafu loved to look at women's bodies. When he was drawing from a model, it was different. It was a job. He had to examine the general structure, see how the pieces fit. He viewed the body as a problem that he had to solve. But when he was on his own time, about to make love to a woman, all the formulas went right out the window. He could surrender to the sheer bliss of gazing at the female form. Making love to a woman for the first time was like unwrapping a present. Snafu lost himself in it.

He peeled Jay's clothes off slowly, nuzzling every undulation in her skin as he slid them away. The girl had very soft, white skin. He stroked her body, feeling ripples of tension running through it. She was trembling. He slid her childish white cotton underwear off and licked his way around her thighs before darting his tongue into her. She shot up in surprise. She was quite new at this game. Those college boys, thought Snafu, they have no finesse.

"Don't worry," he said to her. "You'll enjoy this."

"Really?" she asked.

"Yeah," he said and resumed his attentions.

She propped herself up and watched him as though he were part of a scientific experiment.

"Lie back down," Snafu said. "You're not going to enjoy it if you keep looking at me like that."

"It's such a strange thing to do. Don't you mind?"

"No. Honest, I don't mind. Lie back and close your eyes. And don't think about anything, okay? Don't think."

"Okay."

He took the rest of his clothes off. He was glad the girl had her eyes closed so she wouldn't notice that he wasn't hard. He continued and made some progress with her, though she said unnerving things like "oh, that's quite nice," as though she were having a cup of tea in a garden. Snafu was determined to get a proper reaction out of her and persisted until she gasped in surprise and pushed his face away. He slid his face along her body, sucked on her small, pink nipples while she gazed at him with large, bewildered eyes. He drew himself up, kissed her and was about to enter her.

"Um," she stammered awkwardly.

"You're on the Pill, aren't you?"

"Um ... no."

Snafu was surprised. All the girls he knew were on the Pill. He ran over to his chest of drawers and fumbled around for a condom. He hated using them. It was about five in the morning — the sun would be rising soon. He closed the curtain and lit a candle so she wouldn't see daylight and decide to go home. He glanced over at her. She looked much better without clothes on. He caressed her leg and ran his hand over her body. Her cool, appraising eyes still unnerved him. He couldn't figure her out. She seemed so passive. When he attempted to enter her again, she gave him such a strange look that he stopped.

"What's wrong?" he asked.

"Oh, nothing much. But I guess you should know: I'm a virgin."

The word stung Snafu like a wasp. The throbbing headache that had been quietly assaulting Snafu's brain all night now erupted into a huge, thudding roar. His putative erection left him. Snafu staggered under the weight of this disastrous information. He hadn't encountered a virgin in years.

"Oh Christ, you're kidding."

"No."

"Oh Christ, well, I've had it. That's enough for me."

"I'm sorry."

"I can't do it. I just can't do that. I mean, it's a job. Christ, that's work. A fuck of a lot of work." She gave him such a beseeching look that Snafu relented. "Okay, okay, I'll have a shot at it." He tried to put himself in the appropriate frame of mind. He pressed against her for a while, hoping that he might become aroused. It was futile. His body broke out into a cold sweat and he felt dizzy. "Excuse me," Snafu mumbled as he raced to the bathroom. His head was spinning and he just made it in time. He threw up the entire contents of the evening — his dinner, the copious beers, the sickly brown avocado dip that Susannah brought to the party, the stale potato chips that accompanied the dip, the single malt from Rossco's secret stock — all of it, into the toilet bowl. He gasped and waited for the dizziness to subside. Then he staggered to his back porch for a breath of fresh air. He collapsed on the stairs. Either he had the flu or food poisoning or he'd drunk too much. It couldn't possibly be the booze, although he didn't like Scotch much. It was a snob drink, not to his taste. His stomach gave another lurching heave and he almost fell over with the force of it. He clutched the railing and considered passing out. Then he felt a hand timidly touch his shoulder. He looked up and saw the girl. It was awful but he realized that he didn't remember her name.

"Are you all right?" she asked.

"Ah, yeah."

She took his hand and held it companionably. "I'm really sorry," she said. "I guess I should have warned you."

"Well, you just don't meet many virgins these days."

"It was great. Thank you very much. I had a lovely time. And it didn't hurt a bit."

Snafu didn't know how to tell her that nothing had been accomplished, so he said, instead, "Yeah. I was real gentle."

"You were, you know. It surprised me. I didn't think you'd be gentle."

"Why not? What sort of boor do you take me for?"

"I'm sorry. I didn't mean it that way. It's just that you're so ferocious in class."

"Yeah, well, that's in class. School's over now, so come to bed."

"Oh. I was going to go home. It's morning now."

"You can't go home. We've just begun."

"There's more?"

"There's a lot more."

If one is going to do a job, one must do it well, Snafu decided with grim determination. Having emptied his stomach of its contents, Snafu felt much better. He was ready for action. "Lovely time," she'd called it, in her silly tea-party language. He was going to give her a time she'd never forget. It was a challenge but Snafu was up for it.

He spent three days with her. The curtains were drawn the entire time. Snafu wanted her to be so bowlegged with desire that she wouldn't know what day it was. He instructed her in every position and technique that he knew. She was a quick study. He had lots of leftover food from a dinner party he'd had a few days ago, so they snacked on that, drank some wine he found in the back of the fridge and discussed philosophy, history, art, literature, whatever topic entered their heads. The important thing was that, except for occasional forays into the kitchen and bathroom, they never left the bed. He would make a sensualist out of this clear-headed girl yet.

She was smarter than he thought and she wasn't afraid to argue with him. She held very cynical views of the world. This cynicism seemed at odds with a childlike innocence that she contained in her body. Her body was malleable, anxious to learn and ready to conform to anything that he might teach her but her mind was fixed and determined. The dichotomy between her intellectual acuity and her sexual innocence was a source of fascination to Snafu. She was so different from her earlier incarnation — that of a nervous stammering girl who was so anxious to please him that she couldn't look him in the face. This new persona — Snafu supposed it was probably only new to him — was bold and saucy and not remotely shy. She spoke to him as if she'd known him all her life. He hated to admit it, but he was having the time of his life.

Since his wife left him, Snafu had felt a certain detachment in his relations with women. Even though he made love to hundreds of different women, the encounters were all different, some radically so; there was a certain predictability to them. He played his part and the women played theirs. But with the girl, it was all different. The days blended together in a blur of time, entirely out of his control. He didn't know what was going to happen next. There was no pattern to it. One thing flowed into another. Instead of leading, he was following — though she was following as well. What they were following was anyone's guess. The days passed slowly and mysteriously, contained in a bubble of time that he would, later, at his leisure, revisit.

Deep inside him, amidst the dead ashes of his past loves, something fluttered and came to life. Snafu felt his heart open up.

chapter twenty-one

SECRETS

IT WAS ABOUT four o'clock on Monday afternoon when Jay left Snafu's house. She was giddy with joy; the sheer exhilaration of the past three days sated her senses. She wasn't even sure why she left. She felt this urge to get away and examine the experience, to maintain some sort of control over the emotions that were overwhelming her. She was in love with Snafu Smith. That was clear. She had fallen in love with him the moment she saw him and now she knew why. They were soulmates. She understood him. He projected a tough, cynical exterior, but inside he was warm and kind. Jay appeared to be soft and gentle, but deep inside she knew she was tough as nails. They were two halves of the same person and when they came together, it was alchemy. The days flew by. It was as if Snafu's bed were a life raft and the two of them clung to each other, knowing that eventually the world would come and rescue them, torn between a desire to be saved and an urge to remain adrift.

Jay crept into KAT House, certain that she would be besieged by cries of "Where were you? We were looking for you! We thought something awful had happened to you!" She planned to meet the ensuing hysteria with an enigmatic smile. Jay now knew the source of those pleased smiles.

But the house was eerily quiet. All of the girls were still at work.

Lily should be back soon — Jay was desperate to talk to her. She hoped Lily would be happy for her when she told her about Snafu. Girls only seemed to be pleased to hear about another's love life when theirs was going smoothly.

Jay drew a bath. She didn't need one. She and Snafu had taken many baths together. She had been shocked when the door opened and he entered, naked, and climbed into the tub with her. Sharing a bath seemed far more intimate than any of the things they got up to, sexually.

Jay lay in the chalky, excessively scoured KAT House bathtub and dreamed of Snafu. She imagined him opposite her, taking up the big seaweed sponge and squeezing warm bathwater down her back as he kissed her. Jay smiled and luxuriated in the memory. Two small, nagging questions lay nesting at the back of her brain. What day was it? What was she supposed to be doing this week? Jay tried to chase these thoughts away but they persisted. Classes were over but there was some important thing she had to do. Monday night, Monday night, kept insinuating itself into her daydream. Jay rose with a start. She was booked to go home for a visit and the flight left that night. She tore out of the tub, ran to her room, grabbed the clock and stared at it, as if willing it to go backwards and give her more leeway. Five p.m. Jay rummaged in her drawer for the ticket. The plane left at seven. She had to be at the airport by six. She hastily checked her wallet to make sure she had enough money to pay for a taxi, ordered one and ran about in a blind panic; throwing her clothes into the suitcase, taking them out, throwing them back in again. She charged down the stairs, narrowly missing a head-on collision with Kathleen, who was trudging up after a long day's work.

"Whoa!"

"Sorry, Kathleen. I gotta go to Victoria!"

"Where were —"

"Cab's here. Can't talk. I'll be back in two weeks."

"Is everything all right?"

"Yeah, just forgot, that's all. Bye! Tell Lily, okay? Thanks!"

Kathleen was worried about Lily but there was nothing she could do for her. She'd seen her face when Brad walked into the kitchen party. She knew then that Lily had been seeing Brad behind Susan's back. Stealing another girl's boyfriend was an unforgivable offence. A girl could get kicked out for doing that. But Lily didn't seem to care anymore. She'd set herself on this strange destructive course and Kathleen was powerless to stop her. Instead of confiding in her, Lily had put her trust in an aimless wanderer, a West Coast flake who would not be there for her. Kathleen did not pass on Jay's message and she felt entirely justified.

⌒

BRAD LOVED SECRETS. He wondered if his attraction for Lily was simply based on the fact that it had been a secret. The trouble with women was that they were always being hurt. Secrets hurt them, sex could hurt them, the truth could hurt them. He always felt guilty with Lily, as if he were deriving too much pleasure from the sex and that, by enjoying her, he was doing her a disservice. He felt no guilt with Paul. Brad had no intention of becoming a homosexual. He simply liked the sex. He could be ruthless with it. Paul liked it when he was rough. Brad could taste the smooth, velvet texture of his skin just by looking at him. Paul would glance at him from under his dark lashes and Brad would melt. He experienced a sensuality that was so potent it overwhelmed him.

Outwardly, nothing had changed. To the world, it appeared that Brad and Paul had become friends again. They hid their passion behind a hearty jocularity and no one suspected a thing. Paul's parent's house was the best place for an assignation. Brad and Paul developed an inordinate fondness for swimming. They could fuck themselves silly in the cabana and when they were done, Mrs. MacFarlane would bring lemonade and cookies for the "growing boys." Sometimes she'd ask slyly if they'd prefer a beer and she'd leave a couple of cold ones with the lemonade.

⌇

THERE ARE MANY ways for a demon to manage a host. Usually, a demon will focus on his own particular shortcomings and infuse the host with its pure essence — an aroma-malady of the spirit. Bubula was a fairly lustful demon and that particular tincture found a home in Lily. Lily wasn't driven mad by lust, which Bubula found rather disappointing, but she was seriously distracted by it. However, lust was a secondary vice to Bubula's overwhelming sense of pride. A casual rule of thumb: when listing the Seven Deadly Sins, the one you leave out is the one you possess. In the latter half of the twentieth century, most people could not even name them. Bubula possessed Pride in abundance, so the notion of posing as Lily's subordinate by offering to help her win Brad went entirely against his grain. He preferred to bully his hosts. Of course, Bubula was not aware that he was proud or even that Lily had absorbed his deadly sin into her psyche. Pride and Self-Loathing go hand-in-hand and her oscillation between these two states was more extreme. In short, Lily was getting out of control and Bubula hadn't even begun.

⌇

LILY DROPPED OVER to her parents' for dinner one night and discovered that Paul and Brad had spent the entire day at the house.

"Brad's here quite often, isn't he?" Lily asked her mother.

"Yes, dear, isn't it nice? Paul and he have become friends again. It's like old times — when they used to swim in the pool all day."

"Is that what they do? Swim all day?"

"They might as well act like kids now, while they still can." Mrs. MacFarlane giggled. "Look at them. They could be twelve years old."

Lily watched the boys. Paul was engaged in his usual horseplay with Brad. He was pulling at him, tousling his hair, yanking his bathing suit down as a joke — was it a joke? — flipping him in the bum with his towel. As if echoing her thoughts, the Demon's voice murmured, "See what I'm trying to tell you?" Lily watched as the scene unfolded. They were in the shallow end. Paul had splashed Brad. Brad retaliated. Paul grabbed him from behind and pulled him further into the water. And there, his hand went down in front of Brad and lingered there. And Brad pushed himself against Paul. And the two of them were locked in an embrace. Spoons. Lily liked to hold Brad that way, too. And although they were wrestling, Lily could see in that instant that it was a pretend struggle. They were pressing against each other, enjoying the frisson.

Lily watched, spellbound. Brad suddenly broke free and ran playfully out of the pool, into the cabana. Paul followed. Lily had left her sunglasses in the cabana. She knew she should leave them there but the Demon goaded her, "Go on, go get your sunglasses. What's the matter? Afraid of what you'll see?" The room was full of steam. Underneath the steady pelting sound of the shower, Lily heard Brad's quiet moans. She grabbed her glasses and hurried away. The Demon chortled in glee, "See! Told you! They're in love. Boys in love. You were so busy trying to be a New Woman that you didn't notice what's been going on in the boys' room. They don't need women. There's no place for you in this world. Nobody wants you."

"Shut up! Shut up! SHUT UP!" Lily screamed back at him.

"Lily? Is something wrong?" Lily's mother called out to her from the kitchen.

The front door slammed. Mrs. MacFarlane rushed to the door. Lily had taken her car and was tearing out of the driveway like a bat out of hell. Mrs. MacFarlane saw with horror the other car heading straight for Lily. Too late, a shriek of brakes, the hideous crunch of colliding steel and tinkling glass, the horrible reckoning. Her heart prepared her in an instant.

"YOUR SISTER'S BEEN in a car accident." reported Mr. MacFarlane to his son, slightly puzzled by the peremptory manner in which the event had occurred.

"What? When?"

"Half an hour ago. Just outside the house."

"Is she all right?"

"We don't know. Your mother's at the hospital. I'm going to drive over now and see what's up."

"Look at Ma's car. It's totalled!"

"You two boys didn't hear anything?"

"No."

"Are you both deaf?"

"We were taking a shower."

"Both of you?"

"Course not. Brad was in the changing room. I was in the shower. The water makes a lot of noise."

"I didn't hear the crash, but I did hear the ambulance," volunteered Brad. "I just didn't think it had anything to do with anyone here."

"'Course not. Well, I'll see how she's doing. You might as well help yourself to dinner. I'll call as soon as I know anything."

"Thanks, Dad."

"Don't tell Rose just yet. We'll wait till we have news."

"Okay."

"Ah, Mr. MacFarlane?"

"Yes, Brad?"

"Send Lily my best."

"Sure thing, kid."

As soon as Mr. MacFarlane was out of the house, Brad went berserk. "Oh God, this is punishment," he wailed.

"Don't be so fucking melodramatic. It's not our fault she can't drive."

"She must have seen us."

"She was in the house."

"But the timing. Doesn't it seem weird —"

"It had nothing to do with us. Why are you so hysterical?"

"Isn't it obvious?"

"What's obvious is you just want to feel guilty. Go ahead. Flagellate yourself. Next time I can bring a whip."

"Shut up."

"I don't know what you're so uptight about. It's just sex. Unless —"

"Unless what?"

"You were sleeping with her, weren't you? That's it, isn't it? Bradley, you are a very confused boy. You like doing it with her and you like doing it with me. But admit it, you prefer doing it with me."

Brad gave Paul a quick hook to the chin and knocked him flat. He drove to the hospital, inquired after Lily, lied and said he was her brother so they'd give him the information. He bought a small bouquet of flowers at the hospital gift shop, accompanied with a little note, "Thank God you're alive — Brad." He knew he should write "Love Brad" or "I love you — Brad" or something like that but he felt that would be too hypocritical. She was going to be all right, a slight concussion. It was a miracle. She was alive. When Mr. MacFarlane announced that Lily had been in an accident, it awakened a strange sense of déjà vu in Brad.

Brad asked the gift shop to deliver the flowers and slipped out again, without being seen by the MacFarlanes.

～

ONCE THE MACFARLANES were assured that Lily was going to be all right, they concentrated on the terrible things that could have happened.

You could have severed your spinal cord.

You could have broken your neck.

You could have been killed.

Lily lay in her hospital bed, listening to her parents' pronouncements. She desperately wanted to sleep but the nurses said she had to stay awake. Her mother pushed a tacky bouquet of flowers into her range of vision and murmured something about how nice Brad was. Lily fingered the note. He cared enough to send flowers. Perhaps ... Lily turned her head away and closed her eyes, as if willing the spectre of his passion out of her mind.

"Don't close your eyes, dear. You have to stay awake." Lily wondered why she was surprised to hear her mother's voice, then realized that, for once, the voice was unaccompanied by Demon commentary. Could it be gone? Had the shock of the collision jolted it out of her body? She hardly dared to hope.

"Call Jay," Lily whispered to her mother.

"You don't want to talk to her now, dear."

"Call Jay."

⌐⌐

FINALLY, LILY WAS given permission to sleep. She had a strange, complicated dream involving Brad and Paul. The two of them locked in a carnal embrace kept replaying itself in her mind. Lily kept trying to change the dream but it held fast to that image. The Demon offered to make Brad fall in love with her. Lily knew she should refuse this time and she did. "No," she tried to cry out but the words wouldn't come out of her mouth. They froze into hard chunks of letters and they remained there, cramming up her mouth, making her choke. Then Lily saw the dark, hooded young man from the dream she had when she was little. She recognized him by his mercurial, glistening eyes. He moved in to kiss her.

Lily tried to run away, but now her body was frozen in slow motion. It took all her strength to lift just one foot off the ground. It was like moving through glue. The man could move like the wind. Clumsy and ineffectual as her efforts were, she knew she must resist. She managed to turn away from the hooded man and there, in front of her, was Brad, as he appeared that first night they made love in his room. His eyes blazed with passion. Lily, now able to observe objectively, could see that Brad had been in love with her. It was obvious. Why hadn't she seen it before? And if he was in love with her then, he could fall in love with her again.

Brad held his arms out to her. Lily walked into them. He kissed her. In the middle of the kiss, Brad's tongue grew longer and longer and turned into a twisting serpent that grabbed Lily's tongue and held it fast. Lily pulled away but the serpent's tongue simply stretched to accommodate the distance. The hooded man's yellow eyes gleamed out from Brad's face. "Gotcha!" a voice said. Lily knew who the voice belonged to. And that she was caught.

chapter twenty-two

RETURN

AS SOON AS Jay returned to KAT House, she ran up to Lily's room. The door was slightly ajar. She flung open the door and bounced in, crying out, "Surprise!" A small, dark-haired girl sat up stiffly on the bed and peered at Jay as if she were an insect.

"Who are you?" she inquired coldly.

Jay was dumbfounded. "I'm sorry. Where's Lily?"

"She's not here. This is my room. And I'm getting a little tired of people barging in when I'm studying."

"Sorry. But do you know where Lily is?"

"No, I don't."

"No one told you?"

"No one's told me anything. If they had, I would never have rented the room. This place is crazy. Constant interference."

Jay dialled the number for Lily's mother to ask her where Lily was and, surprisingly, Lily answered.

"Lily?"

"Yeah."

"What are you doing at your parents' place?"

"I live here. Who is this?"

"Jay. What do you mean, 'Who is this?'"

"It's been a while."

"I just went to Victoria for a couple of weeks. What's the matter with you?"

"I had a car accident. Almost died."

"What?!"

"Oh, it's nothing. Concussion, bruises — I just thought you might have come to the hospital to see how I was." Reproach was in every word Lily uttered.

"I didn't know about it."

"Nobody told you?"

"I wasn't here. I was in Victoria."

"Oh, right. Victoria." Lily repeated, as though Victoria were a clever device that Jay had made up. "What's in Victoria?"

"My parents."

"Your parents." There was a sullen pause.

"Kathleen didn't tell you where I'd gone?" Jay asked.

"No. Are you going back to university?"

"Yes."

"Looking forward to it?" Lily's tone got a little warmer.

"Yes, of course." This was, in fact, a lie, as Jay wasn't sure that she did want to go back. She now viewed university with the contempt of an aspiring Bohemian.

"Are you gonna stay in KAT House?"

"No, I'll go back to the residence."

"Do you want to share an apartment instead?"

"What? When?"

"In September."

"That's, like, next week!"

"Week and a half. There's enough time, if we start right away."

"When did you think of this?" Jay was not very good at quick decisions, particularly ones she had never considered making.

"Just now. Come on, do it with me."

"Oh. I don't know."

"You'd rather live in some dorm than have your own place downtown?"

Downtown. The centre of the action. Jay thought immediately of Snafu. She still had this premonition about him and she didn't know where to place it. Conventional wisdom of the time said to enjoy what came your way and move on. Jay knew she should live in the moment, but something in her wanted to linger. "Apartments are expensive, aren't they?" Jay asked, trying to come up with a reason why she shouldn't jump at the opportunity.

"Come on. It can't be much more than the dorm."

"Well ..."

"Come on, say you'll do it."

"Okay! I'll do it."

"Fantastic! Oh great! This is great! With three of us, it'll be a lot cheaper."

"Three?"

"Oh yeah. Franny and I had talked about it. She's at home and I'm at home so there was no hurry. But now we can rent a place right away."

"Who's Franny?"

"Oh, she's great. You'll like her."

"Do you know Franny well?"

"Yeah. Why?"

"It's just odd you never mentioned her."

"Tomorrow's Saturday. Let's meet then and start looking. But buy a paper and make some calls tonight."

In a matter of minutes, Lily changed Jay's life. Jay called the university residence and cancelled her room in the dorm. She lost her down payment. She dropped her favourite subjects and replaced them with ones that didn't interest her so she only had to be at the university two days a week. Jay turned her life around for a girl who appeared and disappeared like a rabbit in a conjuror's hat.

And what was more, Jay didn't think twice about it. It seemed perfectly natural to her to suddenly decide to share an apartment with a girl she'd only known a couple of months and one she'd never met.

⌒

MRS. MACFARLANE GLARED sullenly at Jay. "I suppose this was your idea?"

"No, actually ..."

"Jay was looking for a place and I was looking so we thought we'd combine forces —" burst in Lily.

"And tell me, Jay, who is this Franny? What does she do? Where did you meet her?" demanded Mrs. MacFarlane.

"Um ...." Jay wondered why she was suddenly held accountable for the person and whereabouts of Franny.

"Franny and Jay went to art school together."

"Art school?!"

"Sorry — math classes at the university. Isn't that right, Jay?"

"Yes." Jay thought it odd that Lily routinely lied to her mother, but then, Mrs. MacFarlane was pretty intense and perhaps lies were needed to keep her at bay. Jay didn't stay for dinner and no invitation was proffered.

As she left, she tried to confirm a time with Lily to meet again. "Tomorrow at KAT House?"

"Oh. I can't look tomorrow. I'm jumping."

"You're still skydiving?"

"Yeah."

"Even after your near-fatal accident?"

"It wasn't that fatal."

"You made it sound that way."

"I was just hurt that you didn't visit me in the hospital. But it's okay — I'm over it now."

"Lily, I wasn't even here. I was in Victoria."

"Yeah." Lily did not look entirely convinced. "Anyway, we'll look Monday night."

"You can't really tell what a place is like at night."

"Well, I work during the day."

"Why don't Franny and I look during the day? What's her number? I should meet her."

"Ah ... Franny's out of town."

"For the weekend?"

"No. For the summer. She's in the bush — got a job in a lumber camp. But she'll be back soon."

"When?"

"After the Labour Day weekend."

"How are we going to find a place?"

Lily gave Jay a look of mute gratitude.

"I see," said Jay. "I'm supposed to find the place."

"Well, you don't have a job. I'll help you. After work," said Lily, but Jay knew she was now responsible for the entire enterprise.

chapter twenty-three

GHOST

THE LANDLADY BANGED on a door and shouted, "Pipples to see apartment! Hokay?" She waited a few minutes, then drew out her keys and unlocked the door. There was the sound of many feet scurrying. Urgent, rustling noises. They entered a dim gloom. Jay had never seen so many foreign children and old people gathered in one place before. Old people stood behind the children and held them in place. They nodded solemnly at Jay as she tried to pick her way past to see the apartment.

The landlady barked at one of the old, wizened faces, "What's wrong with you pipples? No light! Got to have light!" She stormed around the apartment, cranking open the venetian blinds and cursing as she tripped over dormitory cots and mattresses. Light streamed into the rooms. Jay could see the apartment more clearly. It was enormous, ungainly. Although the apartment was below ground, the living room had a bank of windows in the upper third portion of the wall, facing west. Now that the landlady had opened the blinds, the room was bathed in warm late afternoon light.

Beside the kitchen and adjoining the living room was a dining room. At least, Jay supposed that was its original function. It was now used as a dormitory.

Jay followed a long, narrow corridor that ran the length of the building. She opened a door, thinking it would be a bedroom, and was thrilled to discover that it was a back entrance. Jay loved the idea of living in a place that was so large that it required two entrances. As Jay re-entered, she glanced up and saw that someone had nailed a horseshoe over the sill. The horseshoe was nailed in upside-down. At least, Jay thought it was upside-down, or was the luck supposed to flow down and out into the lives of the inhabitants of the basement apartment? Jay suspected this was not the case. The horseshoe should be upright like a cup to hold all the good luck in its happy arc. Jay made a mental note to turn the shoe around.

Jay continued down the hall as though she knew instinctively where to go. She glanced at a small, dark room — the "other" bedroom. She knew where she was headed: the room at the end of the hall, the back bedroom. Bolder now and with a growing sense of possession, Jay pushed past the makeshift encampments and drew up the blinds. Again, there was a sudden transformation as light streamed into the room. The marvellous sense of performing magic persuaded Jay that this apartment was a hidden treasure, a rare gem waiting to be discovered. Jay looked past the mattresses, the huddled masses, the uninviting view of the derelict backyard and saw her very own room, private, at the back of the building, her sanctuary. And in that instant, Jay knew the apartment would be hers.

She would take the large, sunny bedroom. She found the place — that entitled her to something. She would pay a little extra towards the rent to make it a fairer division. Lily could have the small bedroom. Franny could have the dining room. A room divider placed appropriately could insure some privacy, but not much. Franny would probably not be thrilled with the arrangement. "I'd expect my own bedroom," a small voice in Jay said, but Jay quickly silenced it.

"I'll take it," said Jay, then quickly added, "but I need to bring my friend to look at it, first."

"You come tonight."

Jay beamed, grabbed the landlady's hand and shook it vigorously. She waved merrily to the milling horde, then danced up the stairs and out the door.

⌒

WHEN LILY FIRST entered the basement apartment, the walls closed in on her and she had a shuddering glimpse of the future. The place wrapped itself around her like a shroud. She knew it inside out, or rather, outside in, for that was the vantage point from which she saw it: outside, in the rain, peering in through the basement window at the life within. Though her body was physically present in the apartment — going through the motions of looking it over — the other Lily, the real Lily, remained outside.

As Jay ran excitedly through the place, talking a mile a minute, Lily silently prayed for Jay to change her mind. Lily wanted to refuse the place but its familiarity held her in thrall. She knew it. It was part of her. It was too late to turn away. Her future was unfolding and she was powerless to change it.

⌒

IT WAS THE beginning of the Labour Day weekend — their first night together in the new apartment. Lily moved dejectedly about the place, as if it were her last night on earth. She had refused to take the small bedroom, claiming to prefer the dining room. Now, she wasn't happy with the arrangement. There was no privacy, she complained. Jay was a bit fed up that Lily hadn't voiced these objections earlier. She had done nothing to improve the place. Her room looked like a way station. A thin, foam mattress lay askew in a corner on the floor. She hadn't even unpacked her suitcases. One lay open, clothes casually tossed inside.

"I thought you were going to put up a curtain. For privacy."

"It doesn't matter."

"Oh, Lily, you have to make it look like a bedroom."

"Why? So you'll feel better?"

"Why don't you take Franny's room?"

"I couldn't do that to her. It wouldn't be fair."

"Well, you try finding a place that's dirt-cheap and all three bedrooms are nice!"

"Only one bedroom is nice in this place."

"You and Franny should have looked, then. Found a place together and left me out of it. I was supposed to room at the university. I'd booked it."

"I'm sorry, Jay."

"What's wrong with you? Why won't you move in? You won't even put up a poster. I've got lots of art posters —"

"Draw me," said Lily urgently. "Do my portrait."

"What? Now?" Jay didn't feel like sitting down and drawing.

"Yes, now." Lily found Jay's sketchbook, thrust it at her and sat opposite, expectant.

Jay reluctantly pulled out a piece of paper and reached for a pencil. "Can we do this later? I don't really feel —"

"Please. I want you to draw me. It's important."

Jay looked at Lily and started to draw. Lily's features were hard to pin down. They kept shifting. There was something very odd about Lily's mouth. Her mouth and chin were quite delicate but in Jay's drawing, they were thick and blunted. Jay threw the paper away to start a fresh drawing.

"Show me," said Lily.

"Later," said Jay. "It's awful. It doesn't look like you." She looked again at Lily and fell into her artist's trance. Yes, she had the eyes, now. Jay liked starting with the eyes. Jay blinked and looked again at Lily. They weren't Lily's eyes. Someone else was staring out at her. For a split second, she saw an evil dog-like face superimposed on Lily's features. It smiled back at her with ancient cunning.

"Do you see it?" Lily whispered, choking to get the words out.

"Yes. What is it?"

Lily did not answer.

"Lily? Are you all right?

"I have to go freefall tomorrow," said Lily, bleakly.

"You don't have to go. Stay home," said Jay.

"No. I have to go."

Jay couldn't understand why Lily was being so obstinate. "No, you don't! Tell the teacher you're not ready."

Lily repeated, tonelessly, "I have to go."

Jay knew then that she couldn't stop Lily. It was as if she were under a spell. "How did you jump before freefall?"

"We had a static line that opened the chute."

"Well, use the line. Promise me you'll use the line."

"All right, I promise." Lily leaned across to look at the drawings.

"You don't look like that," said Jay hastily.

"I do now."

"It's as though there's something on you."

"Don't say any more, Jay."

"It's your face, Lily, but something else is there. What is it?"

"I can't tell you and I can't stop it."

"But you can keep yourself safe."

"Safe?"

"You must keep your promise."

"Yes, I will."

"You don't have to do what it says. You have free will."

"Do I?" replied Lily. "Do any of us have free will?"

⌒

LILY CONTINUED TO mope about the apartment, gloomily shifting her foam mattress from one wall to another, a desert nomad refusing to set camp. Jay finally gave up trying to jolly Lily out of her funk. She was also feeling uneasy about the apartment and wished that she had stayed at the university residence where life was relatively carefree. If someone was moody, you could avoid them. She was nervous in her new bedroom. She felt at any moment something would reach out and strike her. Her fear focused on Lily and turned into anger. She fumed to herself as she fell asleep and her anger fortified itself that night in her dreams.

Jay was awakened by a loud pounding on the apartment door at six in the morning. She threw back the covers, stomped out to the kitchen and opened the door. Lily stood, shivering in the doorway, cowering under Jay's glare.

"I locked myself out." Lily's eyes pleaded with Jay. "Tell me not to go, tell me not to go, don't let me go."

Brad and Paul were supposed to pick Lily up in a few minutes. Why did she have to wake Jay out of a sound sleep, drag her out of bed, just to let her back in? It was stupid. The whole thing was stupid. And now this can't-say-it-won't-say-it game, as if something was preventing her from speaking. Lily walked into the kitchen sheepishly. She looked at Jay once again, as if she wanted to say something but couldn't.

Something snapped in Jay. She was tired of being at Lily's beck and call, living in the shadow of her melodrama. She had her own life now. Her own drama. There was no room for Lily.

"Look, go or don't go. Jump or don't jump. Live or die! Make a decision. I'm sick of hearing about it! On and on and on! You're ridiculous!"

"I'm — wh-what?" Lily stuttered.

"Ridiculous! Do something about it!"

"But I can't! You saw it!"

"I saw nothing! Do you hear me? NOTHING!" And Jay stormed off and went back to bed.

Later, she wondered, "Why was I so angry?" It seemed to have come out of nowhere and yet it had been building; that night, that weekend, that summer. A quiet frustration with Lily's frailties suddenly erupted into a ruthless, full-blown rage.

AT FIRST, IT didn't look as if they would jump that day. The winds were wrong. Lily felt a giddy sense of reprieve. They were heading back to the car when Flash called out, "Wind's changed. There's just enough time. You three!" Lily's heart froze. Paul and Brad hurried over, taking her in tow. Flash noticed her tremble even more than usual. Lily remembered her promise to Jay and Flash anticipated her request. "I don't want you going freefall, kid. You're not ready for it." Lily nodded with relief. It was going to be all right, after all.

They were in the plane. Paul's hand slipped into Brad's and gave it a gentle squeeze of complicity. Lily caught the gesture. Brad looked nervously at Paul, but Lily could see desire in his eyes. The scene in the shower burst into her mind again with startling clarity. They thought they had fooled her. They thought she was a fool. Rage welled up in Lily and she was about to scream at them, but before she could do it, Paul walked over to the hatch for his jump. Instead, she glared at Brad, willing the words into his head: *You don't fool me.* Brad looked at her in puzzlement, like a dog who desperately wants to understand his master but cannot. She didn't break the gaze till he left to do his jump.

She was no longer nervous. She executed her jump with a strange precision. The parachute opened in a comforting cupola over her head. Her rage dispersed into the air. She was enjoying the fall, feeling at peace with herself. And then the Demon started in, with its incessant natter; on and on and on about Brad and Paul and how Lily wasn't good enough and how she was doomed to be stupid and unhappy and hopeless at life, how she was a fool, a ridiculous fool. And Lily thought, quite simply, *Fuck you! FUCK YOU ALL!* and with a superhuman strength that she did not know she possessed, she pulled at the buckles that held her in place, uncapped the plates and yanked down hard on the release rings. She cut herself away from the main chute and fell.

"Pull the reserve! Pull the reserve!" Bubula shrieked. He knew he had gone too far. How could he have known his host would be so rash? He had infected her with the smallest amount of pride and she had seized on it as though it were her only means of survival. He had planned on a longer sojourn in this fine body. She wasn't supposed to do herself in. Interior-decorating human souls was a delicate job. One had to be so very careful. Bubula adds what he thinks is a small drop of green to the human beaker and it immediately turns a hideous shade of chartreuse when all Bubula was after was a pale, avocado green.

Lily smiled and calmly watched the colours of the ground crush up towards her, as if in a kaleidoscope and she were the object being split asunder.

‍‍‍‍‍‍‍‍‍‍‍‍‍‍‍‍‍‍‍‍‍

THAT SUNDAY NIGHT, Lily's face appeared in the window of the basement apartment. It was an anguished face. The hair was wild and unkempt and the eyes blazed with a frightening intensity. Thin, gaunt hands pressed against the pane, barely containing the yearning of a restless spirit that looked for all the world as though it wanted to get in. Jay saw it every night from then on. It frightened her so much that she left the apartment for a month and stayed with relatives. Franny also stayed with family for the first month after the "accident." Eventually, they both sheepishly returned to the apartment. Neither mentioned the ghost.

‍‍‍‍‍‍‍‍‍‍‍‍‍‍‍‍‍‍‍‍‍

WHERE HAVE ALL the revolutionaries gone? Did they die in their beds, embittered old souls, or were they murdered in dark Bolivian jungles, betrayed by their comrades; sacrificial lambs to the pragmatism of their peers? Or did they just grow up and become too old to care anymore?

There are casualties in every revolution; needless deaths that profit no one. The survivors must continue and in order to do so, we pretend that certain things never happened.

Jay moved upstairs. It was a suitable place for her, suitably solitary and confined. At times, Jay felt the apartment building had cast some sort of spell over her — locked her in it, forever, like Rapunzel; a postwar low-rise building instead of a tower, but just as effective. Over the years, the subterranean murmurs of her dead friend gradually subsided.

And every Sunday night on the Labour Day weekend, the tenant below would telephone Jay and cry out hysterically that someone was trying to get in through the window. And Jay would go downstairs and see Lily's face pressed against the pane.

"There! Look! She's trying to get in!"

"No, I don't see anything. It's fine." And Jay would walk up to Lily's face, put her hands against the pane, touch her cheek through the glass and say, "See? There's no one there."

And while we wait for the Revolution, an elephant dances in the room of our desires. It is not acknowledged. It is not seen. We learn to live with ghosts.

Thank you to Karl Siegler, Hrant Alianak, Chapelle Jaffe, Colleen Subasic and David Stephens for their editorial expertise and encouragement.

I would like to thank Wayne Grady, Peter Hochochka and Janice Kulyck Keefer for their generosity and support.

Many thanks also to: Joan Clark, Maureen Phillips, Eric Ladelpha, Mehernaz Lentin, Aaron Bushkowsky, Michael Petrasek, Val Brandt, Susan Gimbel, Judy Chorney, Jacob Unger and Yvonne Prinz.

And a big thank you to my friends and family for their ongoing support.

ACKNOWLEDGEMENTS

I WOULD LIKE to thank Marc Côté for his remarkable insight. He understood exactly what I was trying to achieve in my early manuscript and set me on the path. I would also like to thank Barry Jowett for his fine work on the editing. I extend my appreciation to the rest of the Cormorant team.

Thanks to my agent, Angela Rebeiro, who recommended me to Marc in the first place.

I wrote most of the novel during a summer residency at Berton House in Dawson City and subsequent stays in Whitehorse and Dawson. My thanks to my Yukon hosts: Kim Adams, Steve Robertson, Pierre Berton and the members of the Berton House Committee, Suzanne Saito, Joyce Sward, Carol and David Harwood and Gloria Baldwin-Schultz.

Thanks also to Carol Holmes and the Leighton Artists Colony at the Banff Centre.

I would like to thank Bill Gilliam for being brave enough to be the first person to read the first draft of this novel.